THE GHOST OF LILY PAINTER

Caitlin Davies

THE GHOST OF LILY PAINTER

HUTCHINSON
LONDON

Published by Hutchinson 2011

2 4 6 8 10 9 7 5 3 1

First published in Great Britain in 2011 by
Hutchinson
Random House, 20 Vauxhall Bridge Road,
London SW1V 2SA

www.rbooks.co.uk

Addresses for companies within The Random House Group Limited can be found at:
www.randomhouse.co.uk/offices.htm

The Random House Group Limited Reg. No. 954009

A CIP catalogue record for this book
is available from the British Library

ISBN 9780091937034

The Random House Group Limited supports The Forest Stewardship
Council (FSC), the leading international forest certification organisation. All our
titles that are printed on Greenpeace approved FSC certified paper carry the FSC logo.
Our paper procurement policy can be found at www.rbooks.co.uk/environment

Typeset in Fournier MT by Palimpsest Book Production Limited,
Falkirk, Stirlingshire

Printed and bound in Great Britain by
Clays Ltd, St Ives plc

To four devoted cousins:
Ruby, Amelia, Amarisse and Sienna

PROLOGUE

It is a bitter winter's evening and the little girl is in her bedroom standing confidently before her mirror. The mirror is affixed to the wall at such a height that she has to tiptoe herself up to see her body entirely, but then, how dramatically she tilts her head! How regally she nods at her reflection as she pulls at the wispy black feathers of the wrap that hangs loosely around her shoulders. I fancy she is pleased with herself as she adjusts her white shirt with the fussy embroidered collar, tugs at the elasticised waist of her thin pink skirt, and she smiles, a wide smile that shows two gaps where teeth used to be. How beautiful this child is, how innocent she looks when she smiles like this and her pale brown cheeks, so full and unblemished, rise up and push against her dark, deep-set eyes. There is lightness, a pleasing symmetry about her face, framed as it is with an abundance of curly black hair as soft as cashmere.

But it is cold in the little girl's room. The single window overlooks the small garden of forlorn winter trees, their branches as brittle as stripped bone. Inside the room the walls have been papered and painted many times and still there are signs of the past at the base of the cracked white skirting board, at the edge of the square, finger-smudged light switch, at the cream inlaid cornice of the ceiling. The walls now are white, but once they were pink, once they were beige, and long ago they were wallpapered with orange flowers on deep-brown stalks.

Along one wall is a thick wooden shelf and on this the little girl has arranged her books. It took her some time to do this, for she is a fastidious child and she ordered her books according to whether they were big or small and then, more ambitiously, whether they were fact or fiction. In front of the books, perched on the edge of the shelf, is a row of small toys: a little brown bear; a fairy seated on a mushroom; and the little girl's favourite, a green rubber lizard that she sometimes cups in her hand and talks to about her day.

Above the shelf are pictures, school certificates and photographs of family members. In the centre of the wall is a framed cross stitch of yellow and gold that spells out the little girl's name: Molly. Her grandmother made this, and the little girl brought it with her from Edinburgh the day they moved in. Below the shelf there is nothing at all but a small open grate through which the winter air blows. And I want it to blow, I want it to invade this house and shake its inhabitants from their comfortable life, to pervade their days and disturb their dreams. I want them to know I am here.

The room is cold because the heating has broken, and there have been several telephone calls about this already today. But I fancy the little girl has an internal heating system of her own, for her skin glows as she surveys herself in the mirror.

Now see as she turns her body around, away from her reflection in the glass, how she closes her gap-toothed smile, tightens the black-feathered wrap and looks back over her shoulder at the mirror. She is frowning now, a terrible frown, and her face is grave. What is she saying? Her lips are moving, but the words remain unheard. Perhaps she does not want to disturb her mother in the next-door room, or perhaps she wants to savour the words like this, keeping them within her lips, because they mesmerise her so. Every day at just this time she comes to her room and performs in front of the mirror because two weeks from now she has an audition and she has a dream this girl, just seven

2

years old, a dream of being an actress. She has her whole life before her and she has no sense of what might have happened here or of what is yet to come.

She stops now, examines her face in the mirror once more, and then flings off the wrap and marches to the shelf that runs along her bedroom wall. It is the gait of a child who is used to getting things done. She is about to take a book from the shelf when a sound outside startles her and she darts at once across the room, forgetting the persona she adopted in the mirror, the regal figure with the frown. She is a little girl again and she lifts herself on to tiptoe once more and opens the window. The wind begins rustling in the grate on the wall and she shivers. It has begun to snow outside; specks of white like broken moth wings float in the air. Down below, the garden bench is coated with fine new snow but the slate tiles on the ground remain grey and wet. The girl closes the window and her face is wistful; she is looking for something but whatever she is looking for is not there. Look, I tell her, just look and see what you might find, listen and see what you might hear.

'Well, you can't fucking have it,' the mother hisses into the telephone, 'because I'm the one who wanted it, aren't I? Aren't I, Ben? Wasn't I the one who *found* this house?' The mother is on her bed, seated on the very edge so that her feet lie flat upon the floor. She holds the telephone in her right hand and looks at it while she speaks, her body hunched. Hers is a womanish body, full and plump. Her skin is darker than her daughter's, and her short, uncombed hair is lifted from her forehead with a band as black as night. Her face is smooth and only a little lined, but her expression is tired. 'Ben,' she says, shifting slightly on the bed, trying to change the pitch of her voice, 'be *reasonable*.'

3

She waits, listening to the man on the other end of the telephone, and as she does she plays with the bedcover, tugging fitfully on the blue tasselled fringe. Then suddenly she cries out, 'How can you do this to me! You *know* I don't have that sort of money! Well, I can't! I'm not going to sell the house just so you can . . .' The mother looks at the telephone in disbelief and then throws it across the bedroom floor. It lands next to a notebook, a newspaper, and a book she bought yesterday on Edwardian architecture that she was so eager to show her husband, calling out, 'Ben! Look what I found!' when she arrived home, until she remembered he was no longer there. And she cursed herself and she cursed her former husband and she kicked at the wall in the hallway with the tip of her brown leather boot.

I wondered then, maybe this mother is the one. Maybe after all these years, this mother is the one I have been waiting for, because there is an anger and a grief about her that matches my own. She did not sense me when she first moved in, she was happy with the house she had found and she was hopeful then. But she is vulnerable now, her husband has gone and her family is fractured.

The mother's room is a little warmer than her daughter's, but outside the snow is falling hard and steady on Stanley Road. The lights in the houses opposite are dim behind their curtains; in the twilight the bins on the roadway are covered in a bright confetti of ice. People hurry down the short terraced road towards the light and bustle of Holloway Road, where they will catch a bus or the overground into the City of London, or stop a while at the Crown to take a drink and warm themselves. Beneath one of the cars on Stanley Road a white cat crouches, its eyes an eerie green in the light of a passing cab.

Inside the mother's room the light that hangs from the centre of the ceiling is weak, and beneath it everything looks as frayed

4

as the bedcover. Two suitcases poke out from underneath the bed, their blue handles covered with airline labels of trips returned from long ago. There are other things that do not fit under the bed either: a tennis racquet, a large canvas heavy with thick hardened paint, a blue suit still on its metal hanger and wrapped in cellophane. This is the suit she bought for her husband the summer they moved in.

'Mum!'

The mother sits up on the bed. 'Yes?'

'Jojo is acting strangely!' shouts the little girl.

The mother steps out of her room and on to the landing. She stands for a moment on the blue carpet, indented with the marks of household objects that once stood here and whose history she will never know: the four legs of a hard-edged chair, the long rectangular base of a packing case, a three-footed hatstand with a broken hook. She looks up at the door of the attic, a place she is yet to explore properly, and then across the landing to a skylight that frames a single chimney pot. The mother grips the bannister for a moment and then she walks downstairs.

'Oh, Jojo,' she sighs as she comes into her office. 'What is it now?'

Jojo is a nervous dog, as large as a hound, with a shiny brown coat and a heavy square jaw concealing an array of fearsome white teeth. It is a rescue dog, a Staffordshire mongrel, brought home by the mother two weeks past, and she has explained to her friends on the telephone that she hopes the dog will comfort her daughter now that her husband has left. But Jojo is not a happy dog. She whines pitifully when left alone, she has gnawed at the wooden legs of the kitchen table, scratched at the walls, pulled belongings from cupboards, urinated and defecated on the floor. The mother does not know what to do. She has looked on her computer for ways to solve the problem and failed. And now the dog has started barking, loudly, insistently, in this same room, in this same spot, every evening, because she senses something here. She alone feels my presence and the sorrow within these walls.

The dog's tail twitches at the sound of the mother's voice. But she does not turn as the mother enters the office, she simply stares at the bare white wall, barking. 'Stop it!' says the mother, but the dog doesn't stop. 'What on earth is she barking at?' she asks her daughter. 'There's nothing there.'

'Maybe there's something outside,' says the little girl, eager to offer a suggestion, and she places her hands on the windowsill and looks outside. The dog stops barking, then she starts again. She comes no closer to the wall, but remains in her one precisely chosen spot, body trembling.

'Oh please!' says the mother, and puts her fingers to her temples. 'Jojo! What the hell are you barking at?'

'Maybe she's scared,' says the little girl. 'Mum? Maybe Jojo's scared of something.'

'Don't be silly,' says the mother, and she grabs the dog by the collar and pulls her out of the room. She is upset and impatient and as she leads the dog quickly down the stairs I am here watching her and I am thinking, *At least you have your child*.

I

Annie Sweet

Stanley Road, Upper Holloway, London
Winter 2008

The moment I saw this house it *spoke* to me. I know that
sounds ridiculous, but it did. I never thought a house would
speak to me, let alone that I'd be in a position to buy it if it did,
but it did and I was. I'd gone out of my way to contact the
estate agent and set up a viewing of the house on Stanley Road
the moment I'd seen it on the firm's website, so neat and modest,
a two-storey house as tidy as a child's drawing. Places were
selling quickly then and there was no open viewing, I was told;
instead all viewings had to be made on a single Saturday
morning, in time slots of twenty minutes. If we wanted to make
an offer it was to be in a sealed envelope by the end of the day.
The owner of the house had moved to France, all offers would
be forwarded to him, and there was no doubt, said the estate
agent, that they would all be over the asking price. That was
how it was in the summer of 2007.

We had already been to see three other houses, all in the
Holloway area, all within easy reach of Ben's north London
firm. One was on Mercers Road, not far from the Holloway
Odeon, an impressively large old cinema that still has an air of
grandeur about it. From the outside, the house on Mercers Road
was pleasant enough, but inside everything seemed to be set out
the wrong way round, especially the master bedroom, which

was below street level and without any natural light, and as we stood there I could smell the heavily sweating estate agent beside me. The second house was a building site, a shell of a building hidden behind a quite normal-looking front door. The third I don't remember now.

But Stanley Road, that was different. I'd arranged for Ben to meet me at the Odeon because I wanted to walk, to get more of a feel of the area, which, despite seeing three other houses, we still didn't know that well. We'd only been in London three weeks, but we'd found Molly a place at primary school, and now I wanted to find somewhere to live. 'You always want instant results,' Ben had said, laughing, 'you think we can just move down here and find something just like that!'

Well, I did.

Holloway Road, a London street if ever there was one, a litter-blown artery into the City, a road clogged with trucks and buses where every tenth vehicle is a police car or an ambulance. The pavements are always covered with chewing gum, half-empty takeaway cartons and kebab sticks, and on the benches people sit with blurred eyes and cans of cider. Ben turned up ten minutes late and I rushed across the road to meet him, dodging through a long line of people queuing to use the NatWest ATM machine. In the bank's doorway a man was dozing, a green sleeping bag wrapped around his body like a big fat caterpillar.

We set off down the Holloway Road, past a huddle of men standing by a yellow police crime board asking for witnesses to an early morning stabbing two weeks earlier. They were selling cartons of cigarettes from beneath heavy, pocketed jackets. It was a Saturday morning and the pavements were busy with shoppers and workers: men in low-slung jeans, in overalls, in uniforms, in kaftans; women with nearly every body part exposed – a stomach, a cleavage, a thigh – or with every body part covered in black but for the eyes. Ben and I parted as an elderly woman shuffled between us and she stopped to shout back at three dogs tied together with a long piece of knotted rope, each trying to lead the others, each dog being pulled back by the neck. Molly would have found it cruel, I remember thinking, the way none of the dogs could go in the direction it wanted.

As we walked on I could feel the sun on my face, and when I closed my eyes for a moment it almost seemed that I was somewhere else, somewhere it was always sunny, and that the traffic wasn't traffic at all but the sound of waves at the shore. Then a truck hurtled past, spraying exhaust fumes into the air.

But when we turned off Holloway Road, all at once the noise dipped and the light seemed soft and clean. We entered Stanley Terrace and we could see, in the distance ahead of us, the beginning of Stanley Road. We walked past the Crown pub, a crooked corner building with stained-glass windows that looked like it had been here for centuries. A small group of people were sitting outside on a wooden picnic bench drinking wine, the bottle kept on the table in a bucket of ice the day was already so warm. We passed a small children's park with one slide, one roundabout and a bed of flowers as colourful as if they had just been bought in full bloom from a shop and planted ten minutes before. And then we came into Stanley Road, and I could see that some were painted; one was the pale blue of an early morning sea, another was the milky purple of drying heather. Something made me cross the road then – I knew at once that number 43 would be on the right-hand side, even though I hadn't taken in any of the numbers yet. I already liked the fact it was number 43, the same age as me.

The house was white on the outside and quite perfect, like a marzipan house; you wanted to shake the hand of the person who designed it, who built it, who created it like this, so square and handsome on this neat little road. 'Edwardian,' said Ben, 'probably built at the turn of the century.' I didn't answer; there was no point arguing with an architect.

In front of the house was a low stone wall and behind this, in a small front garden, a bush bursting with smooth orange rose hips. I lifted the latch on the black wrought-iron gate and walked down the gravel path. Oddly the ground level dropped slightly at the front door, so that Ben was already bending his head, ready to duck when the door was opened. I rang the bell and waited. When no one answered I rang again. Then I knocked.

Ben sighed and moved over to the downstairs front window. The sill was worn and cracked, and in the middle was a brown pot of white geraniums. Ben knelt down and inspected the wall nearest the door. 'They've had some damp work done out here.'

'Have they?' I asked, annoyed that he seemed to want to find fault with the house.

'Have you got the right time?' Ben stood up, brushed his hands down his jeans.

'Yes. Eleven a.m.'

Ben shrugged and set off back down the path to the *For Sale* sign nailed to the front wall.

'Wait!' I cried, because now I could hear the sounds of people inside. Then the door opened and there was our estate agent, recently shaved and wearing a grey shiny suit, standing just behind a young couple, the man with a baby in a carrier around his neck.

'Sorry,' I said, stepping to one side. 'Are we early?'

'No,' said the estate agent, chewing impatiently on some gum, 'you're late,' and he smiled over my shoulder at Ben, a smile that said, Women, eh?

'I thought we arranged eleven?'

'Not a problem,' said the estate agent, as if he was doing me a favour. He ushered us in through the front door and into the hallway, and I just knew that this was it. It was like walking into my very own home, it was as if I knew this hallway already – even its smell was familiar, a smell of fresh coffee and wet shoes and something else, something Christmassy like tangerines or pine needles. I didn't even have to see the rest of the house; I already knew it was ours. I put down my bag of shopping and I could see in a strange flash of something like déjà vu that I'd either done this before, or would be doing it exactly this way in the future.

The estate agent had already led Ben through a door on the left, and I followed them into a reasonably sized wooden-floored room. It was peaceful and silent inside, and there was a thick, hazy sort of light that sent specks of dust dancing in the air. I looked around. It seemed as if the owner hadn't been here for some time, and that someone was keeping the place ready for viewing. There was a glossy magazine on a small wooden table in the centre of the room, arranged in such a way that it was there for effect, not because anyone had read or was going to read it. There was a bowl of flowers on the table too, a little wilted in the vase. I moved over to the window, where heavy white wooden shutters were folded neatly into sunken alcoves on either side, and I looked out on to Stanley Road and wondered what our neighbours would be like.

When I turned around, Ben was standing by the fireplace, his elbow flat against the mantelpiece, and that was when I saw there were two rooms, the one we were standing in and one just in front of me. They were almost identical, divided by two wooden doors that now were open but could be pulled to and closed. Ben winked at me. Eagerly I took his hand and we followed the estate agent through the second room, stopping at the double glass doors on the threshold of a kitchen extension.

It was warm in the kitchen, as warm as a greenhouse because of the sun pouring in through two large panes of glass above. Through the back door I could see a small garden with a wooden lattice around the boundaries, heavy with honeysuckle and jasmine.

'Beautiful,' I said. Ben dropped my hand and put his finger to his lips; I wasn't supposed to say I liked the house, he'd told me that whatever happened we were to act as if we were unimpressed. I looked up then. I could hear people coming down the stairs above; hear the creak of the stair boards, footsteps heading down the hallway, the front door opening and closing with a bang. I hope whoever is just leaving doesn't like it, I thought, I hope they hate this house. Then there was a sharp knock at the door and I could hear new voices, a man and a woman, hear them as they came in, chatting away to their estate agent, and I waited for the moment they would join us in the kitchen. 'Shall we?' asked our estate agent, and he led us out of the kitchen through another door and along the hallway. The wall here was covered with odd wallpaper, great swirls of flowers that were soft, almost velvety, to the touch.

Ben stopped by a small wooden door. 'Is there a basement?' he asked.

'No,' said the estate agent, 'that's just a cupboard.' He took us upstairs where the carpet was a worn dark blue, but in my mind I was already replacing it with something warm and cosy and red. 'This is the smallest bedroom,' he said, stopping on a half landing. Although from the outside the house looked two-storey, now I could see there were two more rooms at the back.

The estate agent flattened himself unnecessarily against the wall as I went into the room. It was small and bare inside, with a slightly dipped ceiling like an attic. The air was oddly cold, like stepping out of sunshine into shade. From the centre of the ceiling hung a single strand of spider's web. 'Why's it so freezing in here?' I asked, but neither Ben nor the estate agent replied. I looked around. There wasn't much to see: a single bed, an empty wire shelving unit, an old Arsenal poster on the wall. On the back of the door was a dartboard, the wood pitted with tiny jagged holes. I imagined a teenage boy throwing darts in adolescent fury; I could almost feel his frustration as the darts hit the board. I felt the boy hadn't liked being in this room; there was something unloved about it. But it would have to be changed, that was all. Once we had moved in then we would get rid of the bed, take down the poster and the dartboard, paint the walls cream, set a table by the window so I could look out into the garden as I did whatever it was I thought I could do if I had a space of my own.

I walked to the window to see what the view was like, and as I did I felt strangely off keel, as if something was pulling me, with a force as strong as gravity, down to the wall on the left. I put my hands flat against the radiator under the window. I couldn't understand why, on a day like this, it was so cold in the room. I looked out, but the view was partly blocked by an overgrown bush, and I saw a movement then, heard the dull swarm of wasps or bees, saw a group of five or six leap out of the bush and fly away.

'The floor slopes,' said Ben, joining me at the window.

'Oh, old houses!' said the estate agent from the doorway, as if this were to be expected. 'Shall we?'

I hesitated. I wanted to stay in the room a while longer; there was something more I needed to see, something I had missed, and I couldn't think what it was. But we could hear the sound of voices from below – the couple were coming out of the kitchen just as we had done, and would be right behind us soon; there wasn't much time left. Quickly I came out of the room, looked into the small, basic bathroom next door, and then hurried up another short flight of stairs to a larger landing. There were another two bedrooms up here, and I knew at once which would be Molly's and which would be ours. Hers would be the one on the right, the one that overlooked the garden of jasmine and honeysuckle; ours would be the one before us that looked out on to Stanley Road. I stepped into the room, surprised at how large and airy it was inside, with a big double bed set against a boarded-up fireplace. There was a calmness in the room, but also an emptiness, as if no one had slept here for a very long time. I stopped myself from saying anything, but I took Ben's hand again and gave it a squeeze. He had his inheritance from his uncle and I had mine from Granny Martha, and I so wanted to buy this house.

That afternoon we put the offer in a sealed envelope and I walked round to the estate agents. 'Can you tell him we really, really want it?' I asked the estate agent, and he smiled in a way that suggested everyone else wanted it as well. I handed over the envelope, the form inside filled in as carefully as possible – even the blank space at the bottom that was headed 'Additional comments' and in which I had written in a fit of desire, 'Please, please, please, sell me your home!'

2

When the phone rang I knew who it was, because I'd been willing it to ring all morning. I felt ridiculous not being able to leave the flat we'd rented in case the estate agent called. But I just couldn't. Even though he had my mobile number, I couldn't bring myself to move more than a metre from the phone.

'Hello?' I said, picking up the receiver on the second ring.

'Mr Sweet?' asked the estate agent.

'No,' I said, because it was obviously me and not Ben; he was assuming we shared the same surname, and why did he want to speak with Ben anyway? It was me who'd arranged the viewing and hurried round with the offer on Saturday. And Ben had gone to a meeting this morning, something about settling in at the firm.

'Is this Mrs Sweet?' asked the estate agent.

'Yes,' I said, and I couldn't tell from his voice if it was good news or bad. But if it was good then wouldn't he have said so already? 'What did he say then? Did he accept our offer?'

'Well, Mrs Sweet . . .' the estate agent said, drawing things out infuriatingly. 'As a matter of fact I might just have some good news . . .'

'You mean he said yes? Did he, has he, has he said yes?'

'Well, Mrs Sweet, there were seven offers . . .'

'Seven?'

'All over the asking price. But following strong representation from myself . . .' the estate agent waited, as if for applause,

'I'm pleased to tell you, Mrs Sweet, that they've accepted your offer.'

Ten minutes later Ben came back. 'We've got it!' I told him. 'The estate agent rang just this minute! There were seven offers! Seven! And they took ours.' Ben held out his arms and hugged me tight. 'I'm going to ring Molly and tell her now,' I said excitedly.

'Hello, Mum,' said Molly in her grown-up telephone voice. 'Are you having a nice time in London?'

'Guess what?'

'Actually, Mum, I've been feeling a bit sick and Granny Rose said, "Only three sweeties, pet," and I said, "Well, Granny Rose, if I have only three sweeties then . . ."'

'Molly! We've found a house!'

'Hurrah!' Molly shouted, so loud that I had to move the phone away from my ear. 'Granny!' she yelled. 'Mum's got a house!'

'Have you, Annie?' Mum came on the phone. She sounded a little worried, but then Mum always sounded a little worried. 'Molly's saying you've found a house.'

'Oh Mum, you won't believe it, it's brilliant. Is Dad there?'

'Your father's gone out. He wants his head examined, going out in this heat.'

'Oh well, you can tell him later. We saw it on Saturday but I didn't want to tell you then in case they didn't take our offer, because you wouldn't *believe* how many people saw it. Anyway, it's number 43 Stanley Road.' I slowed down then, speaking carefully as if Mum was going to write this down. 'It's just off the Holloway Road, which means it's really near Ben's firm.'

'Holloway Road?' Mum said a little doubtfully.

'Yes, it's brilliant,' I said, rushing on in my enthusiasm. 'It's two-storey. Edwardian, Ben says. Three bedrooms – well, two really, the third is tiny, but . . .'

'You could always get a lodger.'

'Mum! We don't want a lodger!' And I laughed because Mum is a great believer in lodgers, because her childhood was spent in Granny Martha's Edinburgh boarding house with people endlessly arriving and then leaving again. 'I thought the third room could be my office. Anyway, it's in a little terraced road, very quiet, but near the Tube, the hospital and everything. And right near Molly's school!'

'Holloway Road, though.'

'Holloway Road though, what?'

'Don't do that . . .' Mum said to Molly, and I waited to hear what mischief she was up to and whether she was now doing as she was told. There was something that made me think Mum was deliberately derailing this conversation, but then she is pathologically unable to conduct a phone conversation without interrupting herself. I have seen her put the kettle on, make a phone call and then say she has to run because the kettle's boiling.

'How has Molly been?'

'Oh, she's no trouble at all.'

'Good,' I said, although I felt a bit defensive because Mum was always saying what a pleasure Molly was, with the unsaid reminder that I had been a difficult child. Perhaps it was because she had been so young when she had me, but she hadn't found it easy to cope. I had colic as a baby, I had tantrums as a toddler and I had been a handful at school. So even now, although it was no fault of mine, I felt I had to make up for this somehow.

'Molly wants to speak with her father now,' said Mum, and she said 'father' like she always did, like Ben was some authoritative figure to whom we all needed to pay more attention.

Mum felt I didn't defer enough to Ben, or at least I didn't pretend to defer to him the way she did with Dad.

'Oh God,' I said to Ben when he'd spoken to Molly and put down the phone. 'There's so much to do! How are we going to get everything down here?'

'The firm can help,' said Ben. 'I'll ask the secretary, Carrie. She'll know.'

The day we moved in, three months later, was still and hot and the sky was heavy with thick, white, end-of-summer clouds. By midday the estate agent had handed over the keys and we were at the house, waiting for the removal van. Ben was upstairs; I was standing by the front window, my arms holding on to the wooden shutters, looking out on to Stanley Road the way I'd done the day we first saw the house. The van pulled into the road and I stood there watching it, waiting for it to park. I saw a woman on the other side of the road, walking slowly as if she wasn't familiar with where she was. She stopped, looked carefully both ways along the road and then crossed. Her lips were moving as if she was singing to herself. She went up to our removal van and I thought perhaps she was asking for directions. But then she opened our squeaking black gate and walked down our path and I went quickly to the front door, happy to have a visitor.

'Hi, you must be Annie,' she said. 'I'm Carrie. I'm *so* glad the van got here on time. Oh,' she said, taking a step into the hallway, 'I do love your house.' Then she put out her hand and her grasp was firm and I thought how nice it would be to have a friend when I knew no one in London at all.

By Christmas that year we were fully settled at 43 Stanley Road. It was just as it was supposed to be: small enough that wherever anyone was all they had to do was call out and they would be heard, but large enough that if we wanted we could all retreat to our own little worlds – Molly reading in her room, Ben at the computer in the downstairs back room, and me in my office. This was the only room that still wasn't quite right. I'd put a desk by the window as I'd planned, but I wasn't prepared for just how severe the sloping floor was, how if I laid a pen on the top of the desk it would start to roll down to the other end.

'Do you feel this?' I asked Ben one evening. 'When you sit in the chair, here, like this, do you feel how your body slopes? It's like I'm on a boat, like I'm being pulled down to one side.'

'Annie,' Ben laughed, 'we knew that when we bought the place. The joists are probably rotten. You're going to need a whole new floor in this room.'

I didn't answer, I just folded up a piece of cardboard until it was a tight hard wad and stuffed it under one side of the desk so the surface was level and pens no longer rolled. I didn't like the idea that there was something rotten about the joists, and I didn't like the way Ben had said, *You're going to need a whole new floor*, and not, *We're going to need a whole new floor*. It was as if I had made a bad choice and it was up to me to fix it.

On Christmas Eve I went to Tottenham Court Road to buy Molly a rug for her room, a hairy, soft sort of rug in vivid orange. I carried it back on the bus, thinking about where I would hide it when I got home, and whether it should be a present from Ben and me or from Father Christmas. It was cold and raining and the bus was crowded with people speaking loudly on their mobile phones, and the more I tried to ignore them, the more I couldn't. I felt old all of a sudden and too easily irritated by other people. Behind me a young woman was moaning about her diet to an invisible friend: 'Well, I didn't have anything at lunch, only an apple, which is OK, but then after work I was fucking starving, you know? So yeah, I broke it a little bit, just one piece of chocolate, yeah, but then I walked home so that's nearly a hundred calories and for dinner I made soup, yeah well, I heated it, I didn't make it, but then after that . . .' In the aisle next to me a young man was saying 'exactly' over and over again. 'Yeah bro, so how's it going? Is it? Ha ha ha. Zactly, Zactly. So have you done your assignment? Yeah, yeah bro. Zactly. What time did you get home? Six thirty! Ha ha ha. What she puked every-where? I bet you still kissed her though, bro! Yeah, zactly, zactly . . .'

Suddenly I couldn't stand it any longer and when the bus stopped I jumped off, and even with the rug to carry I walked home quickly, slowing only when I came to the beginning of Stanley Road. Every time I came home, I slowed down at this point. I liked seeing the terraced road before me, and I liked playing a game with myself: *Which house would you like, Annie? If you could live in this street, if you could choose any house here at all, which one would you fancy?*

I could see the lights were on in the front room of number 43, the walls glowing warmly against the gloom of the rain outside and the fairy lights on the Christmas tree making smudges of green and red and purple against the glass. I looked in through the window. Ben and Molly had put up more decorations: sparkly silver stars hung from the picture rail, and one large red stocking with a white furry trim had been nailed above the fireplace.

I opened the front door, hid the rug in the hallway for a moment and put my head around the living-room door. The room looked perfect: everything was ready for Christmas – the tree, the lights, the decorations; there was even mistletoe hanging from the ceiling. But it was empty. 'Ben!' I called.

'In here.' He was sitting in the back room, hunched up in front of his computer.

'Why are you sitting in the dark?' I laughed, switching on the light, my fingers already so familiar with the feel of the switch that I didn't have to look to see what I was doing. 'Where's Molly?'

Ben closed down a screen on his computer and leant back in his chair. 'Upstairs.'

But why aren't you together? I wanted to say. It's Christmas, shouldn't we all be together? I wanted Christmas Eve to be the way it had been when I was a child, when Mum and Dad and me would sit in our front room with Granny Martha. Mum would decorate the tree and sip from her glass of Baileys; me and Granny Martha would sing carols and lick paper chains until our tongues were sticky and blue.

'Is something wrong?' I asked.

'No.'

'Are you sure?'

'Oh honestly, Annie,' Ben sighed, switching off the computer, and he went into the kitchen.

That evening Ben put Molly to bed. 'Remember,' I heard him say from the landing outside her room, 'Father Christmas isn't going to come until you're sound asleep.'

'Dad!' she shouted as he started coming back down the stairs.

'Molly . . .'

'But Dad!'

'What?'

'Why is Father Christmas always white?'

'What?' Ben asked in that bewildered way he used when responding to any question about colour or race, as if he'd never considered why Father Christmas was white. But Molly had begun asking questions about colour. She was developing a desire to identify people.

'Granny Rose is mixed race, isn't she?' she'd asked me the night before.

'Yes.'

'So are you?'

'Well, everyone is a mix of something, aren't they, Molly? But yes, I am, because my dad is white and my mum is mixed. Her mum was white and her dad was black.'

'But you never met him.'

'No.'

'Because he died before you were born.'

'That's right, Molly, we've had this conversation lots of times. I never knew my grandfather. But you have a granddad, don't you? And you're lucky because you can speak to him whenever you want.'

I couldn't hear what Ben said in reply to Molly's question about Father Christmas, but a little later he came into the front room looking pleased with himself.

'Do you think she still believes in Father Christmas?'

'Of course she does!' Ben took the stocking down from the fireplace and picked up the mince pie Molly had left out for Father Christmas on the mantelpiece, eating it in two quick bites. Then he picked up the little tumbler of whisky she had put beside it and drank that as well.

'Don't do that now! What if she comes down and the mince pie and the whisky have gone?'

'Come on, Annie,' Ben laughed, 'don't make it into a drama.'

Oh God. Jojo's barking again. What *is* it with this dog? She does this every single evening, takes up position in the same spot in my office and stands there barking. There is nothing there, not on the walls or hanging from the ceiling or outside the window, but still she stands there with her tail rigid, barking dementedly at a completely blank wall.

I've been sitting on my bed most of this evening, and Molly's been in her room too, preparing for her audition. I don't even know if I want her to go for an audition, but she's so pleased with herself, going to her drama class with her new London friends on Wednesdays after school, then getting asked to try out for the agency, and ten days from now, her very first real audition. 'If you like drama,' I told her, 'can't you just do drama?' She didn't have any interest in acting until we moved to London, and when she joined the drama class I thought it was just a way for her to make friends. But having been chosen for the class and then chosen for the agency she now has a steeliness about her, a determination to do an audition and to win a part.

'Mum!' Molly shouts. 'Jojo's going really crazy!'

I go down to my office with an awful sinking feeling that's been getting worse over the past few days because maybe I made a mistake, maybe I should never have got a dog at all. I didn't really know what I was doing when I went to Battersea; I wasn't prepared for all the dogs in their small stone rooms behind bars, or for the sense of abandonment and distress. None of the dogs could live with a child under eight, I was told, except one, a Staffy mongrel called Jojo, and that's why we took her. I thought perhaps if we had a dog, like the dog we'd had when I was a child, a silly brown spaniel that slept on my bed, then it would be company for Molly. And Ben had never wanted a dog. 'They're a lot of responsibility, Annie,' he always said. And I'd thought, *Life is a lot of responsibility, Ben.*

But Molly does love Jojo, she cuddles her big soft flank and she strokes her silky ears and she whispers to her and sings her songs. She thinks Jojo can understand her, she thinks the dog would speak to her if only she felt like it.

'I think Jojo's seen a ghost, Mum,' says Molly as I come into my office, and she looks at the dog almost admiringly. 'I think that's what she's scared about.'

'Oh please!' I say, and I put out my hand to take Jojo's collar. But the movement startles her and her tail drops down suddenly between her legs and she looks at me with the whites of her eyes. For a second, I'm afraid. How well do we know this dog? We don't know anything about her or why she ended up in Battersea, because they don't tell you that. 'It's OK, Jojo,' I say, but I take back my hand and I stand there a little uneasily. Molly kneels down to pat the dog and Jojo relaxes and allows her body to be stroked, and when Molly looks up there's a strange hint of satisfaction in her eyes as if she's won an argument I wasn't even aware we were having.

3
Inspector William George

Stanley Road, Upper Holloway, London
Winter 1901

Monday, 28 January 1901

A cool, damp day. My dear wife Fanny has bought me a journal for Christmas and I have resolved, at last, to write some few lines a day. It is a way to record day-to-day events, in what I trust will be a manner much interesting for posterity, especially considering the sorrowful occurrences of the past few days. Now how an empire mourns, how a deep gloom pervades the country, how wherever one walks it is the same sight: men, women and children all dressed forlornly in black as if life stood still and could never continue without the Queen.

The keeping of a journal will also, I trust, provide an opportunity to note down observations relating to my work, although I have no intention of producing anything resembling the sort of police memoir so popular these days. I find such publications devoid of personal interest, containing as they do a series of anecdotes written for no other purpose than that of self-aggrandisement. What is missing, one feels, is the reflections of an ordinary police inspector doing an extraordinary job. For the role of the police officer today is no longer confined to the prevention of crime, rather we are expected to fulfil the role of social inspector. Be there bonfire or smoke, traffic accidents or tardy dust contractors, abandoned children or missing dogs, then a person's first port of call is a police officer. Divisions differ of course: an inspector at Kensington is likely to be inundated with elderly ladies reporting the loss of a cat or a purse, while an inspector at Tottenham Court Road will find himself in a veritable hot bed of crime. When it comes to Upper Holloway, barely a day passes without one sergeant or another bringing in a drunk or a thief. And then there are the children, particularly around the Seven Sisters Road, who quite deliberately get themselves 'lost' and report as much to the beat constable in the hope of being taken to the station for a slice of bread and jam. Divisional Superintendent Dyball has let it be known that this practice is to cease forthwith. Instead, any stray children with homes to go to are to be given a good clip round the ear and told to make their way whence they came.

There is the door. Our new lodgers have arrived for interview. I shall study them with a keen eye, for our last lodgers proved to have a very unsettling effect upon the household and indeed through their fecklessness lasted only four months before driving dear Fanny to distraction. We moved here not long ago and it is a largely respectable area where small houses in particular are in great demand. There are a number of clerks and police sergeants, and to the west, where the district improves towards the Holloway Road, quite a few doctors and dentists. My original decision to purchase the house was not taken lightly, but the fact it is a ten-minute walk from the police station was a deciding factor.

The purpose of our new lodgers is twofold: the first is financial, for an inspector's salary leaves plenty of room for additional income; the second is that Fanny is a sociable creature, as women tend to be, and has much need for company during the day. Since our sons Albert and Arthur left home, and since Violet married this very summer and moved with her husband to Clerkenwell, Fanny says the house is too quiet. Without family, my wife is quite bereft, and I have no doubt this is owing to her own sorrowful childhood spent within the grim walls of the workhouse.

Fanny much appreciates our proximity to the Holloway Road and all the gaiety and attractions to be found therein. She is a frequent visitor to the coffee houses and department stores, in particular Jones Bros, which she commends for its courteous service, and where she purchases all manner of fabrics and bits and bobs of fussy prettiness. But Holloway Road remains too busy for my liking, providing an illustration, if ever one was needed, of the speeding up of daily life. A prime example is the crossing sweepers, whose job it seems is never done, forever darting between the hansom cabs and trams, the latter driving at high speed in fierce competition for passengers. A week before Christmas one of my constables was seriously injured by just such a tram, while vainly attempting to assist in an arrest, and he is not expected to be able to resume his duties for some time.

But my dear wife is a city girl at heart, born and bred on the busy streets of Islington, whereas I, despite my many years in London, like nothing better than the tranquillity of the countryside. I am much comforted therefore by the relative proximity of Hampstead Heath, truly a stretch of real country as yet unspoiled by improvement, although it is not a place I care to visit on a summer Saturday or Sunday when it is quite overrun with people and donkeys.

Fanny, however, is a seeker not of fresh air but of entertainment, as eager to attend an agricultural fair as she is to watch a gun-juggling wonder on the stage. Just this morning she implored me to arrange another visit to the Holloway Empire, once the mourning period is over, where she assures me I will be delighted by the antics of Cinquevalli, the Polish fellow who has set London all agog. He is able to do incomprehensible and inexplicable things with cigar holders and cigars, all sorts and sizes of hats, basins, slippers, lighted candles, daggers, bottles and barrels, and the remarkable thing is that there is no deception about the fellow, all is done through cleverness.

There is the door again. Will Fanny not open it?

I have returned. What struck me firstly was this: when I opened the door our new lodgers stood neither too close nor too far away, neither leaning forward as if eager to enter, nor standing back as if reluctant to proceed. This, I feel, is indicative of character. Frederick Painter, currently employed as an omnibus driver, appears an amiable fellow and not as excitable as his kind tend to be. He is a tall, stocky man, dressed in a coal-black jacket, with boots well polished and in good repair. I detected a subtle, though distinct, Dublin accent. His wife, Elizabeth Painter, a neat, matronly woman, is a dressmaker. They have two daughters, Ellen, eighteen, and Lily, seventeen, and it is clear that Mr Painter dotes on both. It is Lily who draws the eye, a youthful flush on her face, a profusion of curls and most becoming clothes – which Fanny commented on at once, saying Mrs Painter is clearly a skilful dressmaker to make garments such as these. Mr Painter asserts when we are alone that his younger daughter Lily has theatrical ambitions and has more than once sung upon the stage, beginning at the tender age of six with her uncle, a comedian apparently well known in the Irish music halls. She is soon to make her debut as a chorus girl at the Holloway Empire. Fanny is beside herself with happiness over our new lodgers. We resolve the rent of 6s for two unfurnished rooms, the larger on the top floor for Mr and

Mrs Painter and the smaller on the landing for the two girls. They will move in tomorrow.

Our new lodgers have settled in nicely. Mrs Painter rises early of a morning and hums to herself from a popular song before setting to work on her sewing machine. This morning it was a rather annoying ditty and one of Fanny's favourites. 'Has anybody seen our cat? Oh! Has anybody seen our cat?' I was forced to listen to this several times until I was tempted to reply, *Yes! I have seen your cat!*

But Mrs Painter strikes me as an industrious and somewhat pious person, despite her love of music-hall songs. She previously worked in the East End, Fanny tells me, where for many years the poor woman subsisted on a daily herring and a cup of tea. It was only after her marriage to Mr Painter, who arrived in England with his two daughters after his first wife passed away, that she was able to set up as a little dressmaker and work from home. She is ably assisted in this by Lily, who is clearly a hard-working girl and willing to take on the more arduous tasks around the home. Her sister Ellen, on the other hand, appears rather weak both in body and mind, with a voracious appetite for popular novels. Ellen is about to take up a position as a feather curler, which her mother approves of but which the girl is evidently not keen on, saying the feathers will tickle her nose and make her sneeze.

Fanny and Mrs Painter are to be firm friends. This evening she invited both mother and daughters into the back parlour to admire the new pianoforte, which we have just recently hired, and it was not long before she began to implore Lily to sing, which she did and in a most pleasing and sonorous voice.

'Lily, my dear, you could be a Gaiety Girl,' said Fanny with much admiration. 'Quick,' she cried to Mrs Painter, 'fetch my largest hat from the hall stand. And here, Lily, take my white gloves.'

Mrs Painter did as she was bid, although with some reluctance, for there is a certain coldness between Mrs Painter and the girls. There was much fussing then as Fanny dressed Lily, but at last, once she had draped a pretty piece of lace around her neck and tied a white sash at her waist, her work was done.

'A Gaiety Girl, indeed,' said Fanny.

'They're nothing but a bunch of show-offs,' muttered Ellen.

'And the ones that aren't careful,' said Mrs Painter, 'get a very sorry reputation.'

'Careful?' said Lily with a sudden burst of annoyance, 'What do you mean, careful?' And she began to remove the hat and the gloves and the sash and the lace with such furious concentration that not one of us could quite tear our eyes away.

Friday, 1 February 1901

A most miserable day of rain and cloud. I resolve that once the weather improves we shall visit my dear brother Henry in Southend-on-Sea and enjoy a few days in the sea air. He writes, just last week, that it is about time we ventured down to see the pier, but warns against visiting on a bank holiday when the entire East End of London descends upon the town. I have not seen my brother for some time, owing to the pressures of work. And while I believe he is now very well settled with his seafood business, it saddens me still that he and his dear wife Mary Ann have been unable to have a child and now, I fear, they never will.

I slept but fitfully last night and Fanny is concerned I may have caught an infection. This evening she implored me to take a warm bath, to endure the resulting perspiration and then to rub myself most earnestly from top to toe. She then made mutton for tea, but begged me to accompany it with a very hot cup of milk, which she assures me is more nourishing than the beef tea to which I am more partial. I shall retire early, for tomorrow the entire force will be on the streets for the melancholy drama of the funeral procession.

Saturday, 2 February 1901
Today has been a most sombre day, although the list of accidents, as noted by this morning's *Times*, is not so long as it would have been had the route not been so well kept by the military and police. One constable from D division was detained in hospital owing to a kick from a troop horse at the Marble Arch, where the pressure of the crowd was especially severe; several women were treated for faintness or fits; and a score of men were injured through falling from trees. Now, however, the solemn ceremony is over, the last gun-salute silent, and all that is mortal of our Queen rests in the chapel ready to be taken to the mausoleum. At least, says Fanny, Her Majesty will soon be reunited with her dear Albert.

4

Monday, 4 February 1901

This morning I am much startled to receive, upon the doormat in the first post, an anonymous letter. It is written in what I detect to be a woman's hand, somewhat childish and over eager and with a great deal of ink caught in the heavy crossing of the letter 't'. It reads as follows:

> To Inspector George
>
> Sir, I am writing to tell you that things are not as they should be at 12 Arthur Terrace, East Finchley. There have been as many as 6 infants enter the house in a single month and on Satday there were 3 never to be seen again. She the 'midwife' is not doing right by the mothers nor those children as she is very hartless and we dont know who is fetching them.
>
> Yours obedintly
> Anon

To my annoyance, Fanny discovered me with the letter and set about, in her womanly way, to avail herself of the contents. When I remarked that it appeared to be a police matter, she simply stood there in the hallway, her neat, pretty hands folded before her, waiting. 'It's a complaint about a baby farmer,' I said with a sigh, for I knew then that I faced a lengthy cross-examination on a matter that is ever close to my dear wife's heart. Fanny is much taken with the plight of unmarried mothers who are driven through circumstances, as she tells it, to find a home for their offspring. 'What else can a poor woman do,' she asks, 'with a child born out of wedlock?' This is a topic we have discussed before, and indeed it is little wonder that some women are forced to turn to the services of a baby farmer. And while there are a great many honest baby farmers, who simply require an income to support their family, there are also those fuelled by greed and who, in some instances, dispose of the child without any regard for the consequences.

While such cases are extremely rare, they do occur, and who can forget the Williams girl hanged at Newgate last March? That was quite an unusual case, firstly as Williams at the age of twenty-four was remarkably young to be a baby farmer, and secondly because, having read reports about an infant's murder, she took the rather astounding step of writing to the police to deny that she was involved, thus neatly assisting in her own arrest. However, if the body of the infant had not subsequently been washed up at Battersea, there would have most likely been no case. The deciding factor proved to be the distinctive manner in which the infant had been wrapped, using a fisherman's bend, for parcels were found at Williams's home done up in the exact same manner.

'What do you mean?' cried Fanny, still standing before me in the hallway. 'A complaint about a baby farmer? Why, what has she done?'

'My dear, it is simply an allegation. Infants have been seen coming into the house and . . .'

'And? And what, William? And not coming out again?'

'So it seems.'

'And what's her name?'

'No name is given, only an address.' I folded up the letter rather quickly, for while anonymous tip-offs are common in my line of work, I have not received such a letter at home before and in truth was a little uncertain what to do with it.

'So what is the address?'

'Arthur Terrace, East Finchley.'

'Oh!' Fanny declared, for she still has a number of friends in that suburb since my days at S division. 'Arthur Terrace? And what does the letter say? Are the children not being cared for properly?'

'I have no idea,' I said thoughtfully, 'why the letter has been sent to me.'

'Because you are a kind man. Everyone knows that, William! Will you investigate?' She asked this with such faith in her lovely blue eyes that I was forced to say I would try my best and, comforted somewhat by my assurances, she set off at last for the church service for our late beloved Queen.

Wednesday, 6 February 1901

I return from work to find Fanny busy making a set of baby garments for a neighbour's child. My dear wife is quite unable to hear of an expectant mother without at once setting forth to make some item or another. I suspect her strong mothering tendencies to be a result of her experiences with her own poor mother. Fanny was but a young girl when her father so cruelly deserted the family, and while her mother tried to eke out a living for a number of years she was at last driven to the workhouse, unmarried and heavy again with child. I do believe that every day spent in that place burnt in some way upon my dear wife's soul. Her mother died a year later, followed by both her sister and the newborn baby, and so Fanny only briefly enjoyed the sort of mother to whom she could fly with open arms. It is as a result of this that she is ever ready to be just such a mother to each and every infant she might meet. As for our own daughter

Violet, who is nearing the end of her confinement and from whom we expect an addition to the family within the month, Fanny has made so many items of infant clothing that I am surprised there is any more room in my daughter's modest Clerkenwell home. Fanny bent her head to her sewing and we sat a while, silent but for the spitting of the lamp. 'And what of the letter?' she asked at last.

'What letter?'

'Oh, William!' Fanny laid her sewing in her lap. 'The letter you received the other day. Just think, those poor little infants without a proper mother's care. William, what is to become of all the unwanted children coming into this world? Their mothers can't care for them and their fathers – well, their fathers won't even claim them!'

There was little I could say to this; instead I sat a while and watched my dear wife at her work and thought how remarkable life can be, how but for a single stroke of coincidence those whom we are destined to meet may never even cross our path. I was but a young man when I first met Fanny, I had only recently come to London and, after a brief spell in a cab yard, had applied to join the force. It was a year later that I met Fanny and still I feel it is remarkable that if I had not been on duty that evening, if I had not been required to take two abandoned children to the workhouse, then what would have happened? I remember well my approach that day and the sound of the bell echoing about the entrance hall. It was a March day, a few days before Easter, and the receiving officer took the poor infants from my charge and gave them each a bun. And then he called Fanny and said she was a girl with a loving heart who often helped with the little ones in the nursery and had, on occasion, received a few shillings for her work from the guardians. And something struck me about her then, something other than her torn, ill-fitting gingham gown, her arms as thin as a sparrow's legs, her crudely shorn hair, for there was a pride about her that quite tore at my heart. And if Fanny had not been sent into service at the Crossleys' house, if they had not been burgled six months later, if I had not been first on the scene when the whistle was called, why then I never would have met her again! And that, I believe, is the nature of life: things have a tendency to fall into place when we least expect them.

Saturday, 9 February 1901

Weather fair but rather dirty looking. What is taking Fanny so long? This afternoon she set off to pay a visit to her good friend Mrs Edith Hacker of Danbury Street, Islington. Her husband, Constable Hacker, is a former colleague of mine, a cheerful, hard-working fellow who has long been frustrated in his efforts for promotion. He knows as well as I that promotion is often a matter of filling a dead man's shoes, and if there be no shoes to fill there is very little to be done. We have often found ourselves at the same police picnics and dinners and so forth, for there is something about being in the force, and this has struck me before, that makes it strangely difficult to mix with other people. But if a man seeks a stable job and not a roving life, then the force is for him.

Fanny and Edith are as close as sisters, as women can be, and while it is quite a journey to Danbury Street and back, I assume they are so deep in idle conversation that she has quite lost track of time.

Friday, 8 March 1901

I have been highly distracted over the past weeks and unable to write in my journal as I would wish. Suffice to note, the King has opened Parliament and a gayness, albeit muted, has returned to the streets of London. While we were visited by a gale of unusual violence during the night, it had cleared by morning and there were momentary gleams of brilliant sunshine today on the London streets.

I spent a most frustrating morning with Divisional Superintendent Dyball, attempting to discuss the anonymous letter regarding the East Finchley baby farmer. While Superintendent Dyball is a very fine individual to look at, with a pair of broad shoulders fit to carry a side of beef, he is rather abrupt if not to say brutal in his manner.

'Yes?' he barked when I knocked upon the door.

'Sir –'

I took but one step into the room before he barked at me once more.

'What?'

'Sir,' I tried again, approaching his desk with caution. I decided then to let the letter speak for itself, and placed it before him. He took but a moment to peruse its contents before casting it impatiently to one side.

'Well, Inspector, it's not your division, so what do you want me to do about it?'

'Perhaps,' I ventured, 'the matter could be discussed with the relevant inspector at S division? It may then be possible to observe if there are indeed any suspicious goings-on at Arthur Terrace and whether children are entering that establishment never to be seen again . . .'

'Perhaps,' barked Superintendent Dyball, 'but babies die every day, Inspector, and God knows we have our own problems with that,' and he gestured that I retrieve the letter and leave.

I returned home to relay the gist of this exchange to Fanny, but my beloved wife will not leave the matter alone. 'But couldn't you just pay a visit to this baby farm and have a look? Something is going on, otherwise why the letter?'

'And when,' I asked rather sharply, 'would I have the time to do that?'

'Oh William, it's only East Finchley, you could just go there and pretend to be a gentleman enquiring about the care of an infant.'

'My dear,' I said, 'if you're expecting me to go undercover . . .'

'I'm only saying,' and here Fanny lowered her voice in that beguiling way she has, 'find it in your heart to at least visit the place.'

After much heated debate on the matter and in order to keep the peace in our household, I agreed to visit Arthur Terrace as soon as time will allow. Tonight, however, all thoughts of work shall be set aside, for our lodgers' daughter Lily makes her debut as a chorus girl and Fanny begs me not to delay my dressing any longer.

5
Lily Painter

That night I first appeared at the Holloway Empire, what a fuss there was among the chorus girls! There was barely room for all of us in the makeshift dressing room beneath the platform, awash with dresses and baskets, feathers and sequins, blouses and hats. I had had my time by the mirror, affixed to the wall so low that all but the shortest performer was forced to stoop to see their face, and now I was pushed up against the washstand as the lady baritone had her turn. Such a bill there was that night: after the acrobats and the lady baritone would come a coster singer, then Violet May and Frankie Monk, and then the chorus girls.

'Chop chop, everyone,' called Mr Vernon H. Ryde, the ever-energetic Empire manager, as he appeared suddenly at the doorway. Mr Vernon H. Ryde liked at all times to be called by his full name, he had a moustache and beard so lovingly grown and preserved that it was no longer possible to see his lips, and like so many people in the world of music hall he was allowed to be both larger and louder than life. 'Can't keep the punters waiting in this popular palace of varieties!' he cried at the top of his lungs. When no one answered, he strode further into the room. 'Ah, what a comely lot in here!' he said lustily, and he wiped his brow and declared as if mightily forlorn, 'Ah, what is man? Wherefore does he why?'

'Oh, he drives me mad,' muttered Daisy Morris, a girl from Kentish Town who had become, so quickly, a friend of mine.

She was just sixteen, with a face as cheeky as Marie Lloyd's and a tongue that could hit a man between the eyes. And although younger than me, she had already taken me under her wing, for Daisy Morris was a Londoner and she knew the ways of the world. 'What is man?' she mimicked as Mr Ryde left the room. 'I'll tell you what man is, mister, not a lot if you ask me! Come here, Lily; don't look so shy, you still have powder on your nose. Excited?'

'Not really,' I said, although my whole body was trembling because this was where I wanted to be and this was only the beginning; it was the way I would make a life for myself. I picked up my parasol and swung it nervously in my hands; I only wanted to be upon that stage and to forget about everything else.

The girls went quiet as Violet May stood at the doorway to be admired. She looked as fine as Vesta Tilley that night, in top hat and tails, her hair greased flat with Vaseline, both hands in her trouser pockets, a cigar held rakishly between her lips. 'Good luck, everyone,' she said with a smile, but I saw how tense her shoulders were, for Violet May was going solo that night.

'Good luck, ducky,' said the lady baritone, her large pinched face staring wistfully at the mirror, her jaws sucking on a peppermint lozenge. She turned and saw that Daisy had lifted herself up on to a shelf where she was kicking her ankles and humming a song. 'Close your legs!' she shouted.

'Why?' Daisy asked cheekily.

'Don't let the world see your drawers!'

'And why not, when they're silk!' and Daisy leapt down from the shelf and hitched up her skirts as high as her garter and began to sing. 'Oh, I'm a modern actress, and I play all the up-to-datey parts today . . .'

'Ten minutes to curtain!' shouted the callboy, and in a flurry of excitement we ran backstage and, as we took our places in the semi-darkness, I could hear the mumble of the audience growing louder like the hum of bees around a honey pot. I stood there amid the props and the instrument cases and, as I looked around, I fancied I was inside the belly of a whale; the musty wooden rafters above were its rib bones and the stained pitted floorboards its stomach.

As I peeped out from the comforting blackness of the wings, I could see the acrobats in their final turn, see the lady acrobat in her ruffled skirt stretch her leg up high upon a pole, her other leg balanced on the foot of the acrobat below. The audience roared their approval and then how quickly the lights dimmed, how suddenly the acrobats cleared the stage. Beside me the lady baritone crunched upon her lozenge, pulled roughly at her skirts and, with a surprisingly lightness of step, tripped briskly on to the stage. From where I stood I could just see the audience as they jostled expectantly at their tables, the girls with their sweethearts, the flushed young clerks, the matrons with their kindly faces.

'Filled to capacity!' hissed Mr Ryde, appearing suddenly beside me as he so often did. 'There's a thousand of them here tonight!'

Still I peeped out from the wings. There in the circle I knew Father sat, our stepmother next to him in her new red shawl. There too sat our landlord, Inspector George, a little stiff, a little disapproving, and beside him his sweet wife Fanny, who found me as comely as a Gaiety Girl. But my sister Ellen was not there that night. She had pleaded faintness, and now she was lying alone in our little room in the house on Stanley Road.

I wondered if they had taken their refreshment yet, Father his ham sandwich, Mother her glass of port. I knew they would have enjoyed the acrobats as they somersaulted across the stage, and soon they would be waiting for me.

The lady baritone took her spot upon the stage and the lights dimmed once more. Her figure, caught in a single spotlight, was sharp and bright against the curtain, and as she began to sing she held her arms out wide as if to fly.

'Face like a slapped arse,' whispered Daisy.

'Sshh,' I giggled, although the audience was making such a din that I wondered they could even hear her words. It was a melancholy song, and they had been expecting something different, something bawdy perhaps, or a rousing song of empire.

'Chuck it off your chest!' a man in the pit cried, exasperated.

The lady baritone came unhappily off the stage, her face pink, sweat upon her brow, pushing angrily between us. And then waiting beside me in the wings was the coster singer, a man I had never seen before. There was nothing remarkable about him, nothing about his manner or his countenance or his dress to suggest anything out of the ordinary. Instead, he seemed so very awkward and so very tall, his arms overlong, his shoulders stooped. I watched as he went on to the stage, shuffling somewhat in his suit and shiny shoes, pushing his barrow before him. The audience did not know of him, and nor did I, for he had been hired for just this night, and they chattered restlessly as he blinked in the spotlight. He looked as if he might at any moment turn and shuffle off, but then he seemed to draw upon something deep within himself.

'Ladies,' he said at last, with a bow that was as fluid as a butterfly in flight, and from the gods I heard a titter of female appreciation. Then how his body changed, such a transformation there was! He moved with confidence now, holding one hand to his ear and making an exaggerated step to the right, listening to the sound of the most beautiful bird call in the world. It took me a moment to realise there was no bird hiding somewhere in the wings, that the man himself was making this call, and I laughed in delight at his skill. And then he began to sing, not the coster's song the audience were expecting but a sweet, soft lovers' tune in the finest tenor I had ever heard. I felt the hairs on my arms quiver and my eyes became fixed upon him; I could not let him go. I listened and I thought, Who does he have in his mind when he sings like this?

'Who is he?' I whispered to Daisy.

'Oh, that's Gus Chevalier,' she said. 'Take your fancy, does he?'

And then he came off the stage, and the transformation was over; he returned to the figure I had seen in the wings, an awkward young man with overlong arms.

'Watch it, boy!' growled Frankie Monk, who was waiting for his cue. I saw him tug fiercely on his chequered tie and then breathe deeply, several times, before running on to the stage. At once the audience applauded; this was a turn they had come to see. 'I've had three wives,' he began in a sing-song voice.

'Oooh!' the audience replied.

'And I lost them all.' Frankie Monk shook his head sadly and rocked back on his heels.

'Aaah,' said the audience in sympathy.

'One died from poisoning. She ate some poisonous mushrooms . . .'

'Oooh!'

'The second died from poisoning, she ate some poisonous mushrooms . . .'

'Oooh!'

'The third died from a blow to the skull. She'd refused to eat the mushrooms . . .'

Frankie Monk pulled on the end of his nose, the audience roared and I felt a shiver about my body, for there was a violence in the laughter that night and I wondered what they would make of us, the chorus girls.

At last the orchestra began to play our song and as we lined up I thought, If my uncle could see me now, his little Lily on the London stage! I had wanted this for so many years, anticipated it from the very beginning when my uncle had first brought me into his act. There had been nothing fancy about those Dublin halls, no dressing room, however makeshift, no backdrop, no proper stage, instead we walked through a threadbare curtain and straight into the auditorium. 'Come on, Lily,' my uncle would say, 'after the first plunge you'll feel better.'

And if they didn't like you, how they would let you know, throwing anything that came to hand, eggs and fruit and chicken bones, once even a cooking pot and the body of a strangled cat. But my uncle was a clever man and he knew how to work an audience and to keep them on his side. He was tall and thin, with soft grey hair and little round glasses, and for his act he always wore the same red waistcoat embroidered with a fine gold thread. He had a way about him so that when he began his turn it seemed that he would not be able to juggle at all. And this, somehow, brought the audience on to his side, so that very soon they were urging him on. And all the time he kept up his chatter, his voice low, never shouting, but making sure everyone heard him at the back of the hall. He would throw out one joke after another as he opened up a card table and balanced one leg upon his nose, as he juggled seven shiny balls in one hand, as he swung two plates on a rope of string. And the audience grew to be amazed, dazzled by his juggling skills. And there was I, little Lily his helper, curtsying at the beginning and the end, handing him a prop, catching the deliberately dropped ball. And then one night a chairman came from a larger hall and he offered my uncle a contract there and then. So from the age of six I worked the halls with my uncle, until Mother died and Father, alone with two girls, announced he was going to try his luck in London. And how grim a place London seemed to me then, how alone we felt, my sister Ellen and me, how downcast we were when Father met his dressmaker and said we should call her 'mother', for we didn't want a mother and she did not want us girls at all.

The stage seemed so vast that night at the Holloway Empire. I stepped out in time with the others and, as we turned on our well-rehearsed spot, the audience began to whistle. Then there it was, that terrifying, electrifying moment when everything could be forgotten, when the words, the steps, the tune, could disappear. But my uncle had taught me well. It was like walking along the road, he told me as a child: if you walk upon a road and come to an obstacle, Lily, why, you find another way around it. And if a performer forgot her words, her steps, she had but to take a deep breath and find another way in.

I looked up then – at the balconies as polished as gold sovereigns, at the deep shadows of the plaster cherubs carved upon the ceiling – and I felt like a princess in a music box. And I knew one day I would be standing there alone, a leading lady on a magnificent West End stage in front of a curtain made of crimson damask, beneath a sparkling chandelier, before an audience of finely dressed ladies drinking fizz. Then Father would retire and I would buy him a public house in the country and I would have a house like Marie Lloyd's, with a stable for my horses and a private carriage. Perhaps I would even buy a houseboat or two.

'Lily!' Daisy hissed, for she could see I was in danger of

losing my concentration. And so we began our song and dance, and all the time I wondered if the man I had seen, the coster singer Gus Chevalier, whose voice had sent shivers down my arm, was watching me now.

And then it was over, finished and done. Both the seven o'clock and the nine o'clock show had ended, the stage was swept, the performers gone, and there was I, as reluctant to leave the Empire as the audience had been reluctant to allow us to leave the stage. Such applause that night! If any turn were well received it was the chorus girls, and I wondered what the newspaper would make of us the next day, if they would single us out for review and what Father would say if they did. I thought how my sweet landlord's wife would say I could have my pick of the Stage Door Johnnies now, and how my stepmother would frown and warn me to be careful. Careful! I didn't want a Stage Door Johnnie; I didn't want any such thing. I didn't want to marry; I didn't want to end up as a wife. I wanted to be a star, in a drama or opera, in a show grand or comic, I didn't care. I would not be a chorus girl of yesteryear left at home rocking the cradle, living only with my memories of what I had wanted to be. I would not marry and turn to port and quarrel with my husband and make my children's life a misery.

How cruel it felt when the final curtain fell. I wanted the excitement to last; I wanted to be whirled now in a carriage to the West End for a restaurant supper; I wanted the night to go on. But at last there I was, tightly laced, standing by the stage door, preparing to step outside. All too soon I would be home where Mother and Father would be waiting, arguing fiercely as they had begun again to do. I opened the stage door, smelt at once the vinegar of the hawkers' pigs' feet and the warm, musty monkey nuts. And as the door opened a crowd of faultlessly

46

attired young men rushed forward. I cast my eyes downward and then glanced up, looking again to see if he was there, if Gus Chevalier should choose this moment to leave the theatre as well. But I could not see him and I drew my cloak around me, looked up momentarily at the moon and the sky bright with stars, and then at last stepped through the throng.

'Ah!' a gentleman exclaimed and he went as far as to tap me on the shoulder proprietarily with his gold-topped stick. 'I wondered if . . . ?'

'I wish,' I said to him, still with my eyes to the ground, 'that you wouldn't bother me.' I heard a peal of laughter behind me and turned to find Daisy upon her bike.

'How do you like me, boys?' she shouted, ringing her bell, waving to the gentlemen at the stage door. Daisy wobbled for a second. 'Come on, Lily, I'll ride with you.'

So we left the Empire and headed home and Daisy said goodbye on the corner of Stanley Road and rode off towards Kentish Town. It was cold and silent then, but for the wheels of a solitary dustcart upon the road, and I hurried home thinking of the man I had seen sing upon the stage and that moment he had so magically come to life.

6
Annie Sweet

Winter 2008

'Mum! Can we *go*?' Molly is yelling from downstairs and she must have been yelling for a while because she sounds very worked up. I come out of my bedroom, look down the stairs from the landing and there she is. I don't know whether to laugh or cry. She's standing in the hallway, fully and completely dressed when on school mornings it can take half an hour to get her out the door. But now here she is in black boots, neon-yellow leg warmers over black leggings, a pink-and-white stripy long-sleeved top, a thick purple waterproof jacket, a soft black cap on her head that is actually mine and white gloves that have a sparkle woven into the wool.

'Oh,' I say, smiling, 'so you're ready then?'

'Mum! I've been standing here for *hours*!'

'OK, OK.' Ever since Ben moved out I have moments like this when I think Molly has grown up and I've regressed, like she's the adult now and I'm the child and she has to remind me what I'm supposed to be doing. 'Wait while I get the email and everything,' I tell her. I come down the stairs just as the dog bursts out of the kitchen and runs along the hallway, tail wagging, trying to squeeze herself between Molly and the front door, anxious that we might be leaving home without her.

'Do you really want to do this?' I ask Molly, taking the dog by the collar, pulling her back down the hallway. 'What if you don't get the part? Wouldn't that just upset you?' *And it's nearly Christmas*, I think, *I don't want another reason for disappointment this first Christmas without her father.*

Molly doesn't answer, she just narrows her eyes at me as I take my bag off the hook in the hall and rifle around for the email from the agency. 'Let's see,' she says.

'There,' I tell her, and we both look at the email in my hand:

Hi Annie!
Molly has been asked to audition for a feature film called *The New Day*. This is shooting from 5th January for five weeks on location. Role: Leah. Time: 10–11.30. This will be an hour-and-a-half workshop. Come casual and be natural. RP accent.

I'd had to ring the agency to ask what on earth "RP accent" was, and was told it meant Received Pronunciation. I fold the email up and put it back in my bag. How will Molly be able to go filming on location for five weeks if she does get the part? Will they let her off school for that? And surely I'll have to go with her. But how will I be able to get a job *and* go with her? It's been six months since Ben left, and although he gives me a monthly amount to look after Molly I can't go on like this much longer. I have to get a job.

We're in a studio room on the top floor of an old warehouse building in Camden Town and it's swarming with children with RP accents. Molly's been quiet, strangely so, ever since we got off the bus, and instead of asking questions she's let me lead the way entirely, through a courtyard, up an echoey stairway, past hand-drawn arrows pinned on the wall, and then finally into this studio room. There's a feeling of suppressed excitement.

Every table is full of seated parents, with big paper cups of coffee and freshly bought copies of today's newspapers. I feel people watching us as we come in; guess they're checking out the competition.

'Mum!' Molly hisses as I walk right into the room, looking for somewhere to sit, and she pulls me back to where a young man waits at the doorway.

'Hello there!' says the man cheerily. He's wearing a T-shirt and low-slung jeans, so low I can see the elastic waist of his Calvin Klein underpants. He seems a bit hyper; maybe he's an actor. 'And what's your name?' He picks up a clipboard and I see a list of names, most of which have been ticked off.

'Molly Sweet,' says my daughter, and as the man finds her name and ticks it off I feel really glad I kept my surname and that Molly has it too. It wasn't what Ben wanted; when we got married he wanted me to change my name to his and to become Mrs Dimmer. 'I want us to have the same name, Annie,' he'd said. 'It's a new beginning, it just feels right.' But I hadn't wanted to. It wasn't just that I didn't like his surname; it was that I liked my own. I wanted to keep it and Ben had got annoyed. 'It's not like it's even your name, Annie,' he'd said, 'it's your father's.' And for a man who wasn't that concerned by family, who barely kept in touch with his own father, I couldn't understand why he wanted me to take *his* father's name. I liked my name and I wanted to keep it, and that was one of the few arguments I ever won.

'Right you are.' The audition man picks up an instamatic camera and gestures to where Molly should stand. Her face breaks into an instant beam – Molly always beams when anyone takes her picture, she can't see a camera pointing at her and not smile. It's a trigger for her, a sign that she must at once assume a role. Where on earth does she get this from?

We wait while the audition man takes out a measuring tape. He holds one end at the top of my daughter's head, reads off the number and writes it down. Then he writes her name on a sticker and sticks it firmly on her chest. 'Take a seat,' he says generously, although I still can't see a spare chair. But then a group of children come rushing noisily into the studio room and at once the seated parents get up, abandoning their coffee cups and newspapers, reclaiming their sons and daughters. I take the opportunity, pull out a free chair and expect Molly to sit down beside me. But she doesn't; instead she stands between my legs like she doesn't want to lose me. I'm a bad mother, I think; I shouldn't be letting her do this audition today. What chance does she have among all these other children? I don't want to say this to her, but I can't imagine she'll get the part and I don't know if I should prepare her for this or let her find out on her own.

I pick up a discarded newspaper and begin to flick through it; it's been ages since I had the concentration to read a newspaper. I turn a page and see a photo of an elderly woman, her eyebrows frowning in concentration, holding up an ornate frame containing a blurred picture of a young woman in a high-necked dress. This is the elderly woman's great-grandmother, a woman who had been missing from family records since 1895 when she ran off with a lover to Canada, leaving a husband and eight children. No one knew what had happened to her, but now she's been found on the online 1901 census, back in England, taking in washing and lodgers.

'Mum,' says Molly urgently.

I look up; I've forgotten where I am. 'This is interesting,' I tell my daughter. 'This woman here,' I tap the picture of the elderly woman, 'has managed to find out what happened to her great-grandmother by looking on this census thing . . .'

'Move,' hisses Molly, and I see there's a short, stocky man hesitating at the table, unable to get past me. I shift over and he takes the chair, the two little girls with him sitting down too. He has a form in his hand – where did he get that from? Am I supposed to have a form? – and he frowns as he starts to fill it in. 'Previous parts?' he says out loud.

'*EastEnders*,' says one of the girls. She has a bob of yellow hair and eyes so blue she might be wearing coloured contact lenses. She waits until the man has written this down. 'And the soap advert. And *Holby City*.'

I put out my arm, give Molly a hug across her tummy, feel how stiff her body is. 'Mum,' she urges, 'we need to fill in a form.'

I'd thought she was nervous, but now I see how shining her eyes are, how happy she is to be here.

At last Molly is taken out of the studio room with a group of other children, all wearing their name stickers like evacuees about to board a train. I stay at the table, unsure what to do. More children are coming in now, new ones, having their photographs taken, their measurements written down. I pick up the newspaper again, but I can't read it; I want to know where the children have gone.

Out in the corridor I see a woman standing very close to a big double door plastered with film posters. The glass at the top of the door has been covered with black paper, but it's coming down at one corner and the woman is straining up, trying to look in. She turns guiltily as she hears me, but when she sees I am just another parent she looks back into the room.

'Are they in there?' I ask.

'Yes,' she whispers, 'but I can't really see them.'

I join her at the door, straining to look in as well.

'I'm sorry,' says a man's voice, and we turn to see the young man in the low-slung jeans. 'We really prefer it if parents and guardians could stay in . . .' and he nods at the studio room, holding out one arm to invite us back in.

'What are they doing in there?' I ask.

'That's the workshop room,' he says, still with his arm out, still expecting us to move. 'It's a lot of fun!'

'There's an awful lot of kids here,' I say. 'How many are you seeing today?'

'Oh,' says the young man, 'a hundred or so.'

'Really?'

'That's every Saturday for the next month.'

'Jesus,' I say. 'Four hundred kids! What's the film about anyway? They haven't told us.'

The young man gives a false cough. 'Ah, the casting director would rather the auditionees didn't know in advance.'

'Yes,' I say, 'but they're already in there now, aren't they?' I can hear I'm being pushy, but I can't help myself. I seem to snap so easily these days, like I've run out of patience, like I just don't have the energy to be agreeable any more.

The man reaches up, trying and failing to fix the black paper that has fallen off the side of the glass. 'It's a horror film,' he says at last.

'They didn't tell us that.' I exchange a look of alarm with the other mother. 'What sort of horror film?'

The man looks like he's trying to decide whether he can say or not. But I can see he thinks it's a good story, that he wants to tell us, that he's excited to be involved in this. 'Well, it's about two families. They go on holiday together and the children come down with a strange bug that turns them into monsters, and then they kill their parents.'

We're walking home along the Holloway Road; it's bitterly cold, and although the sky has turned blue there is still ice on the side of the road. Molly isn't saying much. She hasn't told me what they did at the audition; she doesn't seem to want to talk about it at all. As we left, the man in the low-slung jeans handed her a crumpled photocopy:

Dear Auditionee!
Thank you very much for spending the time coming to see us today! If we decide that you are appropriate casting for this project we will get in touch with you, so as the old saying goes, 'Don't call us, we'll call you!'

'What did you all do in there?' I ask once more. I am consumed with the desire to know.

Molly keeps walking. 'Do you think Jojo will have missed us?'

I watch her walk and wonder if perhaps she's disappointed in herself, if she wasn't as good as she thought she would be, if everyone else was better than her. I speed up and take her hand, feel her slim young fingers in mine, but she's annoyed and shrugs me off.

Molly is tired now, her shoulders sagging like they do when she comes home from school. 'Why haven't we got any decorations?' she complains as we come down the path to our house. 'Mum? When are we going to get some?' On every side, neighbours have set Christmas trees in the windows, lights twinkle, living rooms glow orange from within. But I don't want to decorate yet. It's too painful thinking of last Christmas when we were all still together.

'We'll get some next week,' I tell her.

'And is Granny Rose coming for Christmas?'

'No.'

'Why?'

'I don't know, Molly. I guess she's busy.'

'So why can't we go there then?'

'Next time,' I tell her, because I can't face a Christmas in Edinburgh. Mum's not happy about the separation. It doesn't matter what Ben did, she thinks we should stick together for Molly's sake, and I have a feeling that's why she isn't coming down to see us.

I open our unadorned front door and at once I can smell the sharp acrid smell of dog's wee. 'Shit,' I say.

'Mum!' Molly objects, pushing past me into the hallway.

I hurry after her and open the kitchen door before she reaches it. Jojo has been busy. She's ripped apart the old beanbag she usually sleeps on and the kitchen floor is scattered with millions of white polystyrene balls like a fake snowstorm. The cupboard doors below the cooker and the worktops are all open. There is a small travelling iron on the floor, its lead gnawed to shreds. I walk carefully around into the back room, see how the four-seater sofa has been moved away from the wall, and there is the dog, curled in the corner, snoring, lying with an old computer monitor of Ben's in her paws.

Molly is in the bath, and I'm sitting in my office looking at a temping website. I don't want to continue living on handouts from Ben; I want my own income now.

'Mum!'

'Yes.'

'Where are you?'

'Right here.'

'Oh.' I hear the sounds of splashing and then Molly asks with a fake casualness, 'When are you going downstairs?'

'In a minute.' I make a note of a couple of jobs, wondering

if I can still type as fast as I used to, and try another site. Then I hear a whispering. Molly is talking to someone. I get up and step quietly on to the landing. Through the open bathroom door I can see the smooth wet skin of my daughter's curved back, and from the way she's sitting I can tell she has something in her hands.

'Do you know what, Lizard?' she whispers. 'I went to an audition today . . .'

I freeze where I am, feel tears well up painfully in the back of my eyes. I didn't know she still had this lizard. Ben gave it to her from the inside of his Christmas cracker last year. It's a tiny cheap thing, green and yellow with a rubbery stickiness, but she's kept it all this time and here she is talking to it like it's precious. She won't talk to me about her day, but she will tell a little green lizard.

'Mum!' Molly says suddenly, in her normal voice. 'I know you're there.'

7

It's late. The dog spent half an hour barking at the wall in my office, but now she's gone downstairs. Molly's fast asleep, with her lizard on her pillow beside her. I set up my old laptop, think of what I can do to keep myself from ringing Ben and having another argument about how I don't want to sell the house. I'm about to email my friend Heather in Edinburgh, but then I remember what I saw in the newspaper this morning about the woman who found her ancestor on the online census. Who do I know who would have been alive in 1901? I hunch forward on the bed, lift the laptop towards me and google the census. I click on the first site that comes up and start to type out my grandmother's name, Martha Blackwood, in the search box. It's just possible that Granny Martha had been born by 1901, although I don't know the exact date, and while I know it was in England I'm not even sure where. It's too late to ring Mum and ask, and Mum doesn't like answering questions about family anyway. 'Don't be so nosy,' she always says.

I think of my first day at secondary school, when our history teacher asked us to draw a family tree. I came home so eager to start, telling her, 'Mum, Miss Jessup says we've got to do a family tree.'

'She does, does she?' asked Mum. She was standing in the kitchen, busy spreading butter and jam on toast.

'Yes, I'm going to do it now.' So I made a tree, as our teacher had showed us. I wrote my name and my birthday and my place of birth at the bottom of the page and surrounded it with a big red circle. Then I made circles for my mum and dad and for their mums and dads.

'So,' I asked, my pen poised, desperately keen to do my homework, 'when were you born?'

'What?'

'When were you born, Mum?'

'1945, you know that. In London.'

I wrote it down, excited by the fact my mother had been born in a big city like London. I waited while she put two slices of toast on a plate and licked butter from her fingers. 'And where was Granny Martha born?'

'Oh,' said Mum vaguely, 'that would be somewhere in the south.'

'And your dad?'

'Not known.'

I stared at her, baffled.

'Just put "not known". Do you want some more toast?'

'But what was his name?'

Mum didn't answer.

'He was American, wasn't he?' I knew this because Dad had told me and I thought having an American in the family seemed like something to boast about. 'He was a soldier, wasn't he?'

'He was.'

'And he was black, wasn't he, Mum?'

'He certainly was.'

'So what was his name?'

Mum picked up an apple and then a knife. 'Annie,' she said, waving the knife warningly in the air, 'I never met him.'

Still I looked at her, waiting for more. People were always asking me, 'Where's your mum from?' And whatever I answered they would say, 'No, but where is she really from?'

'So what shall I write down?'

Mum sighed and began peeling the apple. 'Do your father's side, pet.'

'But what about your dad?' And I felt tearful that my mum didn't have a father and furious that she couldn't or wouldn't tell me anything about him.

'Annie,' she said at last, 'will you mind your own interference?'

As I got older I would sometimes think about my unknown grandfather, wondering if I had anything of him in me. What did he look like? What was he good at? But I also learnt not to go there, that Mum would never be anything but maddeningly evasive on the subject of her father and that what she wanted was for the past to be left alone.

I wish Granny Martha were alive so I could ask her now, as an adult, about her American soldier. But she never spoke to me about him, not how she met him and not what happened between them.

I loved Granny Martha and I loved staying with her as a child. In the mornings I fed the finches she kept in large wooden cages at the end of her garden, birds as brightly coloured as if they had been dipped in cans of paint. In the evenings she ran me a bath, but only ever an inch or two of water because that, she said, was how it was during the war. And after my bath she brushed my hair a hundred times. Then she would bring out a packet of snowballs, their chocolate-covered marshmallowness smothered in flakes of coconut. And she stood in her tiny Edinburgh kitchen, eating her snowball with her eyes closed, stopping sometimes to break into her favourite song, 'Lover Come Back to Me'. There was something sad about the way she sang this song, but something hopeful too.

Sometimes, though, I saw another side to her. There were

evenings when she stood in her front room, peering out between the blinds, watching a neighbour, saying, 'What's he bleeding doing then?' Those were the times when she didn't seem like my granny, when she seemed to come from somewhere else.

'What are you *doing*, Granny?' I'd ask.

'I'm just biding my time', she'd say, still peeking out through the blinds. 'Just biding my time.'

I press the search button on the census site and see there are five results under the name Martha Blackwood. But all of these women are in their thirties or older, so they can't be her. I go back to the home page, wondering who else I can look for if I can't find Granny Martha. Then I see there's an address search as well, so you can find out who lived in your house in 1901. Idly I put in 43 Stanley Road, London. And there it is, just like that: there is only one entry and it's my house. I stare at the census roll of everyone who used to live here a hundred years ago in the civil parish of Islington, in the ecclesiastical parish of St Paul, in the urban district of Upper Holloway, in 1901.

I feel a shiver of excitement, as though I've just stumbled across something that I didn't even know I was looking for and, now that I've found it, seems so important. I feel, for a moment or two, happy. I've found my house; I couldn't find my Granny Martha but I put in my address and I found it; I've found some connection between where I am now and who used to be here before me. I think how funny it would be if the old inhabitants were a mother and daughter like Molly and me.

I click the census result, but in order to read it I need to buy credits. So I spend five pounds to look properly at what I've found. First on the census roll is William George. He's the head of the family, back when that's what men were. He's fifty, he was born in Essex and his occupation is police inspector. So a police inspector lived here? I would never have thought of that. I don't know what I had imagined, a clerk perhaps, or a shopkeeper or someone who worked in a bank, not a police inspector. Then comes Fanny George, his wife. She's forty-eight. That's all it says. It doesn't say where she was born. Then comes a son, Arthur, and another, Albert, and a daughter, Violet. These are such starchy, old-fashioned names. And there's a little baby too, because her age last birthday is 'o'.

I come down to the next page, and now the surname changes; now it's the Painters. So there were two families in this house. The father is an omnibus driver born in Dublin and the mother a dressmaker, and they have children as well, two daughters. Ellen is a feather curler. What on earth was a feather curler? And here's the other daughter, Lily. It doesn't say what she does, there's only a squiggle in the occupation column. But Lily Painter, what a lovely name. Lily Painter. I say it out loud sitting here in my bed on this frosty silent night. I smile to myself, feeling silly, but I say it again. Lily Painter. It has a rhythm to it, a rhyme, a sound of the past. Lily Painter, who lived here a hundred years ago, in the civil parish of Islington in 1901. I wonder what she did.

8

Inspector William George

Spring 1901

Monday, 1 April 1901

A return at last to milder weather. I rose early this morning to jot down a few lines concerning the taking of the national census, for I feel it was most significant that last night all our dear children chose both to visit and to stay. Albert came alone, without his wife Dottie or the boys, Arthur came looking rather the worse for wear, and Violet, to my wife's great surprise, came from Clerkenwell with her daughter, born just four weeks past. Fanny was quite furious with Violet for bringing the child out of the home at such an early age, saying such modern attitudes to child-rearing leave much to be desired. However, she was pleased to have a full house for once, especially as she has just last month decorated the back parlour. Aside from the freshly painted walls she has hung two rather handsome mirrors, for she has a fondness for mirrors and the brightening effect they have upon the home. Fanny has also cleverly embroidered a new overmantel, which we all admired, and she intends to commission a drawing of our new granddaughter, for which she has already purchased a rather becoming circular frame.

We enjoyed a most convivial family evening together, despite a number of rather inappropriate discussions between Fanny and Violet concerning, firstly, the pros and cons of wearing a corset so soon after birth, which our daughter says is necessary to restore her figure and which Fanny most vehemently says is not; secondly, the best age at which a baby be weaned; and thirdly, the disadvantages of using baby comforters. At this point our little granddaughter began crying most piteously. This resulted in a heartfelt warning from my dear wife never to dose the child with anything resembling opium or any of these modern patented soothing mixtures which, as I can attest, are the cause of a great many inquests held on children these days.

I do believe my wife and daughter thoroughly enjoy these heated exchanges, though I heartily wish that on the more intimate topics they would wait until the men were out of the room. We then entered into a discussion of plans for the coming Easter weekend. Fanny spoke with quite some passion about the delights of Weymouth, which she assured us is the Naples of England with its genial climate and unrivalled sands, and all within easy reach of London. 'Not that you or I have ever been, nor indeed intend to go, to Naples, Fanny my dear,' I ventured to say, but when this remark was met with much mirth from Arthur I rather wished I hadn't. Fanny then made it clear that if Weymouth was not to be, she would visit Crystal Palace, and if I declined to accompany her then she would enlist her good friend Mrs Edith Hacker of Danbury Street. If this failed, she informed me, she would be just as content to go with our lodgers Mrs Painter and her daughter Lily. Indeed, since Lily made her debut as a chorus girl last month her name is rarely off Fanny's lips.

I confess the evening at the Empire was rather enjoyable, although in my line of work the audience were of as much interest as the performers, an amusing group of acrobats notwithstanding. While not exactly drunk and disorderly, there were a number of young gentlemen in the pit below whom, while washed, brushed and dressed for the occasion, were extremely rowdy and gave the unfortunate lady baritone a severe roasting. Still, that is the world of the music halls. Naturally there were also a number of women quite openly looking for gentleman friends for the night. I did not recognise any of them by sight, and I am quite familiar with the brothels in my area, so I suspect they came from Camden. It was for this reason perhaps that the manager, Mr Vernon H. Ryde, upon seeing our theatre party, gave word that we be admitted at once and without a fee. He clearly felt it would be in his best interest, and that of the hall's reputation, not to mention any extension of its licence, to have an inspector present.

I was pleased to find the general atmosphere of the Empire not as foul smelling as in some of the smaller halls; indeed there are theatres in London where the air is fouler than in a sewer. However, while the various turns were reasonably entertaining, I found the very popular comedian Frankie Monk most unfunny, and in particular his rather drawn-out routine involving a dull-headed police constable, which was met with much ribald mirth from the audience.

But our lodgers' daughter Lily performed with zeal. Her three songs were most delightful and in both language and actions not in the least disreputable. Of all the six girls she was easily the most graceful. Indeed, Lily made such a pretty picture that the scene quite brought tears to Fanny's eyes, for she is a woman for whom music affects not only the senses but also the emotions. My wife is convinced Lily has the makings of a great songstress or actress one day.

However, the evening triggered something of a domestic disagreement between our lodgers, who began a heated quarrel in their bedroom next door. Mrs Painter was rather vocal in her opinion of the dubious morals of the girls of the music hall, saying she never would have gone if Mr Painter had not insisted. I do hope they are not going to make a habit of such exchanges.

Tuesday, 2 April 1901

Today I return my thoughts to the matter of the alleged Finchley baby farmer. Despite Divisional Superintendent Dyball's near complete lack of interest in the matter, I have made a number of discreet enquires as to whether there are any individuals registered to foster or otherwise care for children residing at 12 Arthur Terrace. I have found there are not. However, although the law now requires such carers to notify the local authority if they have taken in more than one child under the age of five, this rarely happens and there is hardly the manpower to check on them.

Wednesday, 3 April 1901

We spent this evening in the front parlour, quietly reading from this morning's papers until I made a dramatic and significant discovery. I had begun with today's reports on the war front, which over recent months have become but a saddening daily litany of those wounded, killed and taken prisoner. I then turned to the classified advertisements, beginning with the lost property and then the miscellaneous column, when my eyes alighted on the following:

> Good Home offered for Baby of gentle birth; a mother's love and care. Small premium required. Doctor's references. Apply Nurse Sach, 12 Arthur Terrace, East Finchley

Hastily I closed the paper and suggested Fanny prepared a little warm milk before bed. But she would have none of this and upon realising I was attempting to divert her attention, she fairly snatched the paper from my hands.

'What were you reading, William?' she asked. It took her but a moment to locate the advertisement that had caused me such alarm. 'Oh!' she cried. 'That's your baby farmer, isn't it? And now she's advertising for a baby!'

'Hardly *my* baby farmer,' I protested. 'Interesting that she does not request just any baby, rather she wishes to adopt a baby of gentle birth.'

'Oh William, it's all about money!' cried Fanny. 'See how she asks for a premium, and why would she want a premium? If she longs to adopt a child why can't she just adopt one? No, the premium is the price the poor mother must pay never to see her child again! How much do you think it would be?'

'Five, perhaps ten pounds,' I told her. 'It could even be as high as fifty pounds.'

'Fifty pounds!' cried Fanny. 'Where is a poor young girl to get such a sum?'

'Well,' I responded, 'from the father of the child, I would assume.'

'Ah, the father,' said my dear wife, rising from her chair, 'and if the *father* took any responsibility then why would a young girl turn to a baby farmer? And what will this Nurse Sach do with a child she has adopted for a premium? Will she really raise it as her own, with a mother's love and care? I don't think so! William, remember Mrs Dyers! Remember Ada Williams! Why don't the police do something?'

'The police do do something, my dear,' I said, 'that is why both were hanged.' However, such is the brazen nature of the advertisement that I resolved to take the bus to East Finchley this very weekend. Entrapment can be a sticky business, but it will do no harm to visit the place and meet Nurse Sach. If things are well, then this will allay Fanny's fears, and if they are not then I shall attempt to discuss the matter once more with Divisional Superintendent Dyball and, at the very least, to pass on the relevant information to our colleagues in S division. Either way, as my dear wife says, it will be good to set the mind at rest.

9

Sunday, 7 April 1901

I had very little sleep last night owing to a raid on a gaming
house on Seven Sisters Road. It was a carefully planned
operation, following an anonymous tip-off received a week ago,
and I am pleased to report it was entirely successful. Constable
Jack, a powerfully built man, concealed himself at the entrance
to the cul-de-sac that led to the suspected gaming house. At
midnight, four of us joined him there and, having no legal right
of entry, we were prepared for a rough house. We waited but
a few minutes for a gambler to arrive whereupon we seized him
and instructed that he give the proper knocks upon the door,
despite his whimpering that he would be killed if he did. Once
inside we found thirty-three men crowded around the faro table.
So intent were they on the game that they did not see us in the
gloom and at once we gathered up the cloth and the money,
nine pounds in total and a tidy sum!

Having had just three hours' sleep, I then set off for East
Finchley to visit the alleged baby farm. I have not been to this
northern suburb for some time and I somewhat misjudged how
long a journey it is from Holloway. Chilly as it was, I would
have preferred to spend the journey on the top deck near the
driver, but as misfortune would have it I was forced to accom-
modate myself in the lower deck. I then settled down for a most
uncomfortable ride. I cannot count how many elbows knocked
into me or how many boots, caught up with dirty straw, trod
upon my toes, and all the while a lady's bag pushed most

furiously into the side of my stomach. When the wretched conductor let still more persons aboard I decided to alight well before my stop, eager to escape the stifling throng.

I then walked briskly along the High Road past the White Lion public house, turning left before the Congregational church and continuing for some ten minutes until the bridge led me over the railroad tracks. The coming of the railway has had a most significant effect on the development of Finchley, but despite the evident rise in population and the increase in both traffic and buildings, it was still a pleasant walk.

As I crossed the bridge, however, I saw a group of children sitting dejectedly in the street. They were badly dressed and undernourished and the scene reminded me of a case during my latter days in Finchley when a woman lodging on East End Road was charged with neglect. There had been several complaints from neighbours and the landlady had obtained a warrant of ejectment, as a consequence of which I called at the premises on several occasions. The first time I did not find anyone home, but on the second occasion, and with the assistance of the landlady, I gained access to the rooms. In the first I saw no bed or bedding, just three children sitting around the fire on some old boxes, on their faces an expression of weary anguish. I could not see a particle of food of any description. I then heard a baby crying most pitifully from a box on the floor and, as gently as I could, I lifted the child and attempted to coax it and tell it its mother would soon be in. A number of people came then to see what the fuss was about, two of whom were fellow lodgers, an elderly fellow and a young girl with a pinched face who watched the proceedings with much interest. The baby's cries softened somewhat as I held it in my arms, and I suggested that the landlady bring a little tea and bread and butter for the older infants, which they ate most ravenously.

'She's at the pub,' said the landlady. 'I've told her that the baby is completely starving and she turned on me and told me to mind my own business! I've heard her say, "You little bastard," to the child, I've heard her say, "I will chop your bastard head off."'

At that point the mother returned and, upon seeing me, declared that she had always done her best by the children but that they were always ailing. I had no option then but to take her into custody, although I was loath to deprive the children of their mother, however unfit she appeared to be. While the case went to court, and received some coverage in the press, the woman was found not guilty. Whether she was reunited with her children and whether conditions then improved, I do not know, for shortly afterwards I was promoted to inspector and left Finchley.

Still thinking of this case, I made my way to Arthur Terrace and to the suspected baby farm. It is a respectable-looking street, populated by rather handsome red-brick houses. I did not approach my intended destination at once; instead I strolled in a carefree manner along the road until I reached a footpath leading to the railroad, and there I stopped to light a cigar. The day, though still exceedingly cold, was now growing sunny and bright. The cigar lit, I went once more down the road and stopped outside number 12, a semi-detached house with a good deal of ill-tended shrubs, largely rhododendron, in the front garden.

I knocked once upon the door and as I did I heard a woman calling out, her voice muffled, and then, very faintly, a baby's cry. There was then a great unbolting and unchaining of the door, until at last it was opened by a woman of medium height, not more than thirty years of age, dressed entirely in black. She wore a high-collared dress, with a clean black kerchief tied quite tightly around the neck, and I have to say she was remarkably handsome, with dark eyes and jet-black hair.

'Nurse Sach?' I enquired, tipping my hat.

The woman on the doorstep tilted up her chin and looked over my shoulders as if seeking who else could be there.

'Nurse Sach,' I said again, 'I, ah, read your advertisement . . .'

'Oh, I see,' she said, her face relaxing into the most beguiling smile. 'Do come in.'

Nurse Sach led me into a narrow and spartan hallway where there was a distinct smell of boiled bread. The carpet upon the stairs was thread worn, although the golden metal runners that held it in place were reasonably new. At the top of the stairway was a long window and through this the April sunshine poured in so profusely that, as Nurse Sach went up before me, her body became a black silhouette outlined in a remarkable yellow glow. As she reached the landing she called up the stairs, 'Mrs Merith! We have a gentleman here to see us.' She then stopped and spent quite a while arranging some knick-knacks on the windowsill before pinching off a number of dead buds from a potted plant. Such was the narrowness of the hallway that as I progressed upwards I nearly bumped my head against a hat rack on the wall, and had to quickly put out my arm to steady the top hat that was perched there rather incongruously.

Nurse Sach remained on the landing, busily adjusting a painting on the wall. Then she led the way up a short flight of stairs and into a kitchen, large and well furnished. In the corner by the fire an elderly woman sat somewhat slumped upon a chair. She was perhaps fifty years or more, attired in an old black silk dress, with a good-natured, homely sort of face and small eyes as black as a berry.

'Mrs Merith!' said my host. 'We have a gentleman . . .'

Mrs Merith shook herself upon the chair and made to stand,

although it clearly pained her to do so. I waved that she shouldn't trouble herself and she sat back quite gratefully on the chair, one hand grasping a well-worn walking stick that leant by her side. Despite her age and apparent frailty, her flushed face indicated she had just completed a household chore of some kind, and a clothes horse set before the fire was hung with damp infant apparel, many with initials neatly embroidered on to the cloth. I glanced about the kitchen and noted upon the sideboard a packet of cornflour, a tin of condensed milk, a row of baby jars and a collection of tin boxes, which I took to contain infants' food. There was also a large jug of cordial, some measuring cups and a bottle or two of some unidentifiable liquid. Some way from the fire stood a sewing machine and in the far corner of the room, thrown carelessly upon a chair, was a large black cloak and, beside that, a large wicker basket such as a farmer's wife might use.

It was only then that I realised there were infants in the room. Both were seated on the kitchen floor, one a flaxen-haired child with very prominent ears whom I took to be a boy around eighteen months. The other was somewhat older, a girl with large, handsome brown eyes and a mild harelip. Both looked reasonably well cared for, with some colour upon their cheeks, although there was a faint whitish stain around the girl's lips.

'Good morning, little fellow,' I said, addressing the flaxen-haired child. I repeated this twice, until I was forced to enquire, 'Does he have trouble with his hearing?'

'Yes,' said Nurse Sach at once, 'indeed he does.'

It was then I noted another infant, just a baby in a small basket upon the floor.

'Well, sir,' Nurse Sach said, smiling agreeably, 'these are the little ones we care for. Johnny here . . .' and she indicated the flaxen-haired child, 'has been with us for quite some time and we are planning to buy one of these new caps for the ears that are most comfortable and hygienic. Eva here,' and she indicated the brown-eyed child, 'has been with us not so long. We've been very busy saving up and it won't be long before she'll have an operation to correct her harelip.'

I took the opportunity then to study Eva further, and as I did I realised that her sweet face reminded me quite painfully of our daughter Mary, lost to this world many years ago and for whom my dear wife and I will for ever mourn.

'Oh, Mrs Merith!' cried Nurse Sach, startling me from my thoughts, 'Will you look at the mess on Eva's face! Such an eater she is! The moment she finishes her mid-morning milk and bread, there she is wanting her lunch of beef tea and milk pudding!'

Mrs Merith looked blankly at my host for a minute before lifting herself up from the chair, taking Eva by the arm and wiping at her face.

'And this is Lottie.' Nurse Sach indicated the infant in the basket. 'Such a dear, sweet baby.'

'But oh Lord, how she has been unwell, the poor little lamb,' said Mrs Merith, sitting down again with a sorry shake of her head.

'Come now,' said Nurse Sach, 'Baby is getting on lovely and we wouldn't part with her for all the world. It's not easy raising a child by hand, is it, sir, without a mother's milk?' She looked at me then, with an expression of great sadness in her eyes. 'And she's such a lovely baby, she coos and smiles and cries very little and she eats well and is always happy, isn't she, Mrs Merith? She sleeps like a top by my bedside, sir, and only has two bottles a night.' Nurse Sach bent then and gently rearranged the blanket over the sleeping baby. 'There is nothing, is there, sir, like having children around the home? I wouldn't ever take a child for the sake of money.'

'Of course not,' I concurred, a little surprised, as I had not suggested that I suspected her of doing any such thing. Nurse Sach ushered me then into a small, tidy parlour next door and, after allowing me to take up position by the fire, asked how she could be of assistance. It was then that I realised I had entered the room as a police officer might, with an air of authority and confidence, and not as a gentleman friend of a lady in difficulty. I had decided that, if questioned, my occupation would be that of banker; in any case, I would be the seducer happy to pay any amount of money in order to rid himself of the burden of a bastard child. 'I wish to make an enquiry about . . .' I began, my voice suitably uncertain.

'About a child,' responded Nurse Sach helpfully.

'Ah yes,' I said, 'about a child.'

'Is it for a . . . friend of yours?'

'Ah yes, a friend of mine.'

'A lady friend? Well, she needn't fret, I'm a trained midwife and able to give the best care to both mother and child.'

'You take in the mothers here?' I asked, unable to hide my surprise.

'We can do,' said Nurse Sach,' if the need arises.'

'So this is a lying-in home?'

'My, sir, how many questions you like to ask!' She laughed quite charmingly. 'Now, as to this child . . .'

'Ah yes,' I said, with some hesitation, 'she is three months old.'

'I see, sir.'

'Yes, and her mother has found a position in Yorkshire.'

'And she cannot take baby with her?' said Nurse Sach, with a sympathetic nod of her head.

'Indeed no, and her sister is no longer able to look after the child. Now, there is the question of the fees . . .'

'That would be five shillings a week, sir, which considering the expense of feeding and laundry I'm sure you'll find very reasonable.'

'Ah yes, and if the child were to be adopted on a permanent basis?'

'That would be thirty pounds, sir.'

'Ah, thirty pounds,' I replied.

'Baby will have everything she needs,' Nurse Sach said with a smile, 'and mother can visit her any time she wants.'

'She can?'

'If she desires to. Some mothers, sir, like to keep in touch and I'm more than happy to provide monthly reports as to how baby is doing.'

I nodded that this was a most agreeable arrangement and Nurse Sach suggested that I return in two weeks' time, with both the premium and the child. I paused at the door to the kitchen then to bid goodbye to Mrs Merith, who did not notice me, so engrossed was she in her task. She was sitting before the fire with the baby lying on her lap. I saw her carefully sponge the baby's eyelids and then, humming a hymn to herself, she wrapped a small strip of linen around her finger and inserted it in the baby's mouth.

'There you go,' she said affectionately, 'you poor little lamb.'

Nurse Sach accompanied me back down to the hallway, and it was then that I heard a muffled baby's cry. I glanced to my left and, through a partially opened door, saw the back of a young woman wearing a blue dress with an apron tied tightly around her waist. She appeared to be busy gathering up a great many sheets of newspaper from the floor. I was about to introduce myself when Nurse Sach stepped in front of me and closed the door.

'Here we go then, sir,' she said, opening the front door.

I tipped my hat and bade her farewell and although I did not turn to look back, I felt her waiting on the doorstep as I made my way down Arthur Terrace.

I returned home feeling utterly exhausted, both from my journey to Finchley and from last night's raid, as a result of which I shall spend a great deal of tomorrow at court.

'Oh William, sit down and tell me what happened,' cried Fanny the moment I came in. 'Did you find the house and were there babies there?'

'Indeed I did,' I said as I removed my hat and unbuttoned my coat.

'So what was it like?'

'Well, it's a large house, my dear, with a good number of rooms, all tidy and clean. In the kitchen there was a healthy fire, freshly washed infants' clothes . . .'

'And what was she like, your Nurse Sach?'

'Genteel, my dear, very genteel indeed.'

'And the children?'

'Well, I saw two infants in the kitchen, as well as a baby.'

'And you're saying they looked well?'

'They looked well enough.'

'And what were the children doing?'

'Doing?' I asked, somewhat irritated by this cross-examination. 'Why, they were simply sitting there.'

'Playing?'

'No, not as such. In fact at first I didn't even notice they were there.'

'And how old were they?'

'I would say both between one and two years.'

'So *why*,' asked my dear wife, 'were they not playing? For goodness' sake, William! Have you not had children of your own! You look as if you've never had little ones running around your feet! What child of that age simply sits upon the floor and does nothing?'

I nodded uncomfortably; this was what I had been thinking during my return journey. For despite the outward appearance that everything was well at 12 Arthur Terrace, and despite Nurse Sach's display of concern for the children in her care, the quietness of the infants in the room was troubling.

10

Sunday, 21 April 1901

Two weeks have passed since my unannounced visit to Nurse Sach of East Finchley and this morning I set off once more, on the pre-appointed time and day. I had resolved to explain that I was quite unavoidably unable to bring my 'child', and to take the opportunity to more closely observe the infants. In particular, I wanted to ascertain whether the reason for their quietness was because they had been drugged. What Divisional Superintendent Dyball would make of this second visit, should he know, I would rather not think.

As I left home I came upon my neighbour, a gentleman who has recently moved into number 41 Stanley Road. He is Mr Gilbert Pickles, a clerk at the Holloway post office and altogether a very dignified individual, dressed each morning in bowler hat and with the high sense of propriety often to be found among postal workers. Fanny, however, says he resembles an onion, seeing as he has a remarkably round and shiny face. We exchanged a few words concerning his arrival in the street, he suggested we meet sometime for a neighbourly drink, and I then caught the bus to Finchley.

Familiar as I was now with the route, I walked briskly to Arthur Terrace and knocked smartly upon the door of number 12. But even as I did I noted the rhododendrons in the front garden were now in an even sorrier state, and a pile of rubbish had been left carelessly, and I would surmise quite hurriedly, near the gate. I waited, however, for Nurse Sach to appear or, failing that, Mrs Merith, for it would take the elderly woman some time to come down the narrow stairs.

At last I had no option but to look in through the letterbox, to see nothing but a deserted hall and a sense that not a soul was within. I attempted to look in the front window, but was unable to because of the drapes, and I then looked up at the house in case I should see any sign of movement upstairs. It was at this point that the front door opened next door and a young servant girl hurried out pushing a large new perambulator, clearly taking baby for an airing.

'Good morning,' I called out in a jovial fashion.

'Sir,' she said, politely enough.

'I'm looking for the ladies here at number 12. Are they at home?'

'What, those two that lived there?' asked the servant girl, and she pulled such a face of dismay that I wondered for a fleeting second if she could be the anonymous letter writer. 'Oh, they've gone, sir,' she said, 'left in the dead of night.'

'Indeed,' I said as mildly as possible, although I confess I was rather shocked. Nurse Sach had appeared comfortably able to afford the premises in which I had found her, and she did not seem the sort of person apt to make a midnight flit. 'So both Nurse Sach and Mrs Merith have gone?'

The servant girl looked confused. 'I don't know Mrs Merith, sir. All I know is Mrs Sach was in charge and often Mrs Walters was there as well.'

'Mrs Walters being elderly and slightly invalid?'

'Yes, sir.'

'I see,' I said, for clearly Mrs Merith is using an assumed name. 'And the infants too, all gone?'

The servant girl nodded and hurried off.

Monday, 29 April 1901

For the past week Fanny has spoken of nothing but the disappearance of Nurse Sach and the infants, and I too am left wondering what has happened to the baby in the basket, the flaxen-haired boy and sweet little Eva with the harelip. I have repeatedly checked the miscellaneous column in the *Islington Gazette*, but the adoption advertisement placed by Nurse Sach has now disappeared.

I have been tempted to bring the matter to the attention of Divisional Superintendent Dyball, but, aside from the anonymous letter and my brief visits to Arthur Terrace, I do not have a lot to go on. However, I have now established that a beat constable did see two women with a cart of belongings in Arthur Terrace on the night of Friday, 19 April. But when he stopped in order to question them, he heard a whistle from an adjoining beat and rushed at once to assist. As a result, it is not clear where the women have gone, and they may have moved just about anywhere in London by now.

11

Lily Painter

It was an early summer's morning when the Empire's manager, Mr Vernon H. Ryde, called me in and told me of his plans. 'Lily, my dear,' he said as we stood in the hallway that led to his private office, 'you're a comely young girl and I'm thinking you would make a very good sister act.' I was about to tell him I had but one sister, Ellen, and that she would rather hang herself than tread the boards, but I was glad I held my tongue. For Mr Ryde had the other two sisters already in mind, my friend Daisy Morris and a Yorkshire girl called Florence Mae. 'You're about the same height and you look enough like sisters. As if the punters would care if you weren't! So that's it then, all done. You're the Sisters May. You'll be fourth on the bill, after Bill Mackie and his canaries and Will Fornby and his rats.'

How excited my sweet landlord's wife had been when I told her the news. 'Oh!' she cried. 'Lily, I can't wait to see you. Will you have a dresser now, do you think?'

I shook my head.

'A dressing room perhaps?'

Again I shook my head.

'Oh well,' sighed Fanny, 'your day will come.'

Two weeks later I arrived for our final rehearsal before opening night. There was a change in the air: summer had truly arrived, the birds were singing and the leaves were new and green upon the trees. The Empire's box office was closed, for it was early morning still, but I could see in through the double glass doors, at the marble stairs and golden railings leading up towards the dress circle and the foyer bar. It was perfectly empty, the doors bolted tightly from inside, and a theatre foyer without people is the strangest of things. A foyer is designed for people; it is waiting for their sudden footsteps and the rustles of their dresses, for their perfume and cigar smoke, for their laughter and anticipation of the evening to come, for their unspoken agreements that domestic quarrels be put aside at least for tonight.

And then, as I looked away from the foyer doors, I saw a young man with paint and brush hurriedly changing one of the playbills, and I stood and watched as he pasted out the name Bill Mackie and pasted in another: Gus Chevalier. I had not seen or heard of him since my debut as a chorus girl when he had appeared for one turn only, but I had thought of him often and wondered where he had gone.

'We're closed, darling,' said the young man painting out the playbill.

I nodded, unable to speak. He didn't recognise me and for a moment I wanted to open my cloak and reveal the costume I had beneath, a jaunty sailor's outfit of white and blue. 'Cat got your tongue?' he asked with a cheeky look as he put away his paint and brush, and I went quickly to the stage door, pushing upon it impatiently for I could not wait to find out if it was true, if Gus Chevalier was really there. Backstage everyone was busy, each with their job to do, checking the lights, the props, the costumes on the rack, and from a gilded cage on a small wooden table came the shrill call of Bill Mackie's canaries.

Everywhere was the sound of muffled footsteps, treading softly, broken only by an occasional clang, the drag of a trolley, a murmured instruction. My feet padded quietly on the carpeted floor that sloped down from the stage to the auditorium where, in the darkness, Mr Ryde sat. Every now and again he leapt from his seat, strode up the steps to the stage and shouted out what changes needed to be made. High above the stage, two spotlights let out a soft, blurred triangle of hazy light so that twinkles of white danced in the air, floating among the black curtains of the wings like snow, dancing and never falling.

There were others sitting out there in the darkness too. I could see two figures on the rose-red velvet auditorium seats and another two standing in the aisle, but I could not see if Gus Chevalier was there. Then I heard Daisy, heard her light, airy laugh as she called out her greetings: 'Morning, my love. Morning, morning, morning, my love! How are you darling, all right?' I could hear her humming one of our songs, 'Well, Did You Ever', stopping only to call out, 'Lily! Is Lily here?'

And then the others arrived and the auditorium became noisy with the chatter of performers. There was touching now, a hand held lightly to a cheek, a tap upon the arm, a hand across the back, a darting kiss upon the lips. And among all of us there was an air of self-importance, for we were what the stage was waiting for; we were the ones the audience were coming to see.

Will Fornby arrived, holding his performing rats aloft in a wooden box, and people stepped away quickly, offended by the smell. The actors in the auditorium became louder still, especially the men among them, and in particular Leo Burns, a serio-comic and a handsome fellow who was more than a little in love with himself. On stage he was well known for delaying his leaving so long that the act after him would run on, anxious for their fifteen-minute turn.

Then the stage manager called up instructions to the fly-men standing high up in the gantry. 'Bring the trees down!' he cried, and the fly-men pulled at the ropes. Slowly, magically, the painted trees came down, the backdrop went up, the lights went on, the orchestra began to tune and we were ready to begin.

The ballet dancers were first; I stood in the wings and watched them gallop on to the stage, enjoying the moment when a dancer crosses the invisible line between backstage and stage, when they leave reality behind and the music hall begins. From where I stood behind them in the wings their movements seemed exaggerated but I knew from the auditorium, from the circles and the gods, they would look natural and perfectly so with their beige fleshings taut against their thighs, their smiling faces, wide eyes and red pouting lips.

'Stop!' called Mr Ryde, and he strode up the steps to the stage, moved one dancer forward, one back, paced them and counted their steps. When then he turned his attention to the conductor the dancers relaxed, and as they stood and chattered in whispers they became smaller, slighter, more like their everyday selves.

'Not here, my love.' An elderly stagehand was pulling gently on my arm, for I had stepped out a little too far and was in the way. I moved back, positioned myself far enough from where the acrobats were changing into their suits and the duettists fixing their dresses. The wardrobe assistant watched, biting her lip. She pulled a small torch from her bosom and flicked it over the duettists, turning down a collar, puffing up a bodice. Next to me in the wings Leo Burns came up close and jigged up and down, humming, shaking his hips, all because he could not wait to get on, for his turn to begin. Then a scratching came from just behind him and I saw him jolt in fear and look around, for Leo Burns was mortally afraid of rats. But it was only Daisy scratching playfully upon a wooden prop and she popped out now, laughing, as Leo Burns scowled and walked away.

'He'll never make a star,' said Daisy, 'as long as he's got a hole in his arse.' Then suddenly she took my arm, 'Have you heard?'

'What?' I asked, my voice a whisper.

'Bill Mackie had a heart attack last night, that's why his canaries are crying like that, and now,' she laughed, 'your fancy man is on the bill.'

I blushed, pretending this meant nothing to me, but Daisy laughed again and began to sing softly, 'The boy I love is looking now at me. There he is. Can't you see?' And she turned me just a fraction so that at last I saw him, saw his sloping shoulders and awkward gait as he stood there waiting backstage.

That evening after rehearsal I stepped out on to the street and found Gus Chevalier standing beneath a lamp, his head bent in concentration as he lit a cigar. 'Aha!' he said when he caught sight of me and he gave a theatrical bow. 'I was wondering when you'd come out.' I must have looked alarmed then, for he smiled and shrugged his shoulders. 'It's Lily, isn't it?'

'Yes,' I said, and I felt helpless then for I could not think what else to say. I wrapped my thin old cloak around me and I wondered at this man who stood so ordinarily upon the pavement when only a few hours before he had been singing with a voice that sent shivers down my arms.

'I enjoyed your act today. Been on the stage long, Lily? You look as if you have.' Gus Chevalier lifted his eyebrows in a quizzical way and blew a plume of smoke from his lips.

'Since I was six,' I said, and I stepped backwards as two gentlemen pushed past me, eager to gain entrance to the Empire.

'Really?' Gus Chevalier moved away from the street lamp and came to stand by my side.

'Yes,' I said, a little flustered. 'My uncle was a performer in Dublin.' And I looked up at him and it was only then that I saw his eyes, saw for the first time how his pupils were black pinpricks in a sea of blue and how they seemed to fix me in one spot and refuse to let me go.

'Ah, so it was your uncle.' Gus Chevalier nodded in a knowing fashion. 'It was my father who put me on the stage, curse him. I made my *debut*,' and he threw his cigar upon the pavement and crushed it with his boot, 'at the age of four. Oh, I didn't do much, a little coster dance, some birdsong, nothing anyone hasn't done before.' Gus Chevalier laughed and his hand moved towards me as if to touch me on the arm, and then quickly he took it back. 'But it's not what I want to do, Lily,' and his voice was low as if he didn't wish anyone else to hear. 'I'd rather act, if only anyone would give me half a chance. I'm sick of this clowning. I'm twenty-four and I've been doing this for twenty years, but do you know what? Still today I have that horrible sensation' – he looked away then and his expression was wistful – 'that horrible sensation that people won't want me. But perhaps you don't know what I'm talking about.'

But I did, I knew exactly what he was talking about, for that was why we all were here, for people to want us. I turned then at the sound of Daisy's laughter, saw her come wobbling up upon her bike.

'Ooh!' she cried when she saw us standing there. 'Am I interrupting?' And she laughed and rang her bell and called, 'Hop on, Lily!'

I shook my head, embarrassed at her teasing, and when I glanced at Gus Chevalier the expression on his face seemed to be one of wounded pride. I wanted to speak, to reassure him and to continue our conversation, but his jaw was firm and he looked away, as if he regretted having revealed himself to me at all.

*   *   *

I did not see him much after that, for once the show had started then we were never on the stage at the same time. But when I could I would hover in the wings to see his turn, watch as he walked out on to the stage, almost hold my breath in anticipation, waiting for that moment of transformation. I was alert, always, to any mention of his name, listened intently if any other performer should talk about him. Some spoke of him in a slighting manner behind his back, said his voice was nothing much, that he saw himself as belonging somewhere better than the music hall. They said they didn't know why the audience seemed to love him so, but I did, I knew that Gus Chevalier had something special about him.

Sometimes, when he came off stage, he found me there and he would bow and hesitate, as if to speak. But then wordlessly he would walk away. Bill Mackie soon recovered from his heart attack and took his place again upon the bill, and Gus Chevalier left the Empire and I heard he took a turn at Collins' and I wondered when I would ever see him again.

12

Two weeks after the season ended, Mr Vernon H. Ryde sent for me again. I was relieved at his summons, for during the days and nights spent away from the stage I had been forced to stay at home and do the chores and listen to my mother's complaints. And what I wanted, more than anything, was to rejoin the music hall and be part of the world I loved.

It was autumn by then, a day so dark and dismal that the Empire shone like a beacon of hope on the Holloway Road. In the hallway that led to Mr Ryde's private office performers were huddled excitedly in little groups, and when Daisy saw me she came over and cried, 'Oh, isn't it something? Don't look at me like that, Lily; it's the panto, silly, why else do you think he's called us here?' Then she scowled as Leo Burns came strolling down the hallway towards us. 'Oh, here's the one with the hole in his arse.'

Leo Burns pretended not to hear. 'Ah, the lovely Lily. What brings you here today?'

'I've been called to see Mr Ryde.'

'Really?' Leo Burns clicked impatiently upon his fingers. 'He called you in, and Daisy too?'

'And why not?' snapped Daisy. 'We had more applause than some.'

Leo Burns scowled and scuffed at the carpet with his foot.

And then Mr Ryde called for us and we crowded into his private room, thick with cigar smoke that curled in clouds of white around his desk. 'Gentlemen,' he said, stroking thoughtfully on his beard. 'Ladies. I have it in mind to do *Dick*

Whittington and His Cat.' He removed the lid of a glass decanter and stopped to sniff its contents before leaning back in his chair. 'It's one of my favourites and the punters' too, good over evil and all that. Now, I'm thinking a real spectacle, three hours or more. I'm talking dance, song, comedy. I'm thinking Morocco harems, sailing boats and hordes of rats, fairies with electrical lights in their hair . . .' He looked around at the people in the room, savouring our sense of expectation, our thrill at being chosen. 'Now, I already have my star turns, and that's what I need to bring the punters in. I've got Frankie Monk as the Captain and he'll bring the house down, I've got our Principal Boy Miss Madge Merry and our Principal Girl as well and' – Mr Ryde paused and poured himself a drink – 'Miss Rose Henderson will play Alice Fitzwarren.'

Leo Burns let out a long low whistle.

'Now,' said Mr Ryde, leaning forward on his chair and slapping his hands so forcefully upon the desk that the amber liquid in his glass trembled, 'that blasted Tommy Fellows has come down sick. So I'm trying Gus Chevalier as King Rat because I know the ladies like him. Where the devil is he anyway?'

At this my heart began to beat fast against my chest, and I looked around the room as if expecting him to be here.

'So!' said Mr Ryde. 'You know me as a man who likes new talent and I'm going to be taking a risk with some of you lot, but . . . Daisy, you're a fairy.'

At this Daisy let out a cry and clapped her hands.

'And I'm warning you, girl, any more of your giggling and you're out. Don't think I don't know what you're up to the minute my back's turned. Lily, you're a fairy as well.'

'So what am I?' asked Leo Burns plaintively.

'A rat.'

'Not Idle Jack?' said Leo Burns as the others in the room began to laugh. 'Not Ship's Captain?'

'Not Ship's Captain, I've told you, boy. Who do you think you are? That's Frankie Monk.'

'How long will the panto run?' asked Leo Burns.

'Well, what do you think?' snapped Mr Ryde. 'Boxing Day until the end of next February. That's it then, all done.'

Leo Burns gave a shrug. 'Two months' work, can't say no to that.'

'Two months, boy,' said Mr Ryde with a final tug on his beard, 'or two days if you don't catch on.'

It was dusk when I left the Empire that night, and the foyer was crowded with theatregoers arriving for the evening's entertainment. By the circle bar I saw Mr Ryde dressed in his evening suit, patrolling the crowds. I saw him tap a man upon the shoulder and snap, 'Would you do that at home?' for the man was just about to stub his cigar out on the beautifully carpeted floor. 'Ah, Dr Crippen!' Mr Ryde exclaimed as he slapped a man in evening dress upon the arm. 'Come and have a drink. Is your wife with you tonight or is she singing?'

I made my way through the crowds, thinking of what costumes Daisy and me might wear, of wings and wands, of sparkles on our dresses and lights in our hair, of how the audience might love us. And there he was beside me, Gus Chevalier.

'Ah Lily, I've been looking for you,' he said, as if we were often in the habit of meeting like this, as if he had not been the one who had walked off the Empire's stage night after night, passing me by without a word. 'Heard the news? I'm King Rat!' And he drew himself up to his full height and gave a furious pantomime frown.

I smiled then and I looked up at him, at the pinpricks of

blackness in his wide blue eyes, and I waited. Then his shoulders sagged. 'It's only panto, Lily, but I've had enough of singing at Collins', and at least I get the chance to act a bit and who knows where that will lead.' Then he thrust his left hand into his pocket and fixed me with his eyes. 'I've been wanting to ask you something, Lily. This Leo Burns, do you know him well?'

'No,' I said quickly, in case he should think I had any interest in Leo Burns.

'Well, just now was the fourth time he's asked me for money and I've told him, I don't carry money, Leo, because I fear being taken advantage of by the less wealthy, like yourself.' Gus Chevalier waited for my smile and then when it came he smiled too. 'It's a fine night for celebrating, isn't it? It's not often I get to play a villain! How about Romano's?'

'Yes,' I said at once, for I had heard of the wonderful Romano's and the people who went there, and I had long dreamt that one day I would go.

Gus Chevalier did a little quick-footed dance upon the pavement and the people crowded around the Empire's door turned to watch. 'Well, did you ever, a girl who knows her own appetite! Turn again, Lily! It's supper at Romano's for us!'

'Oh, but I can't,' I said, for although I longed so much to go I knew it was impossible. Father was waiting for me at home, Mother had chores she wished me to do, and if I was to go to the West End, if I was to follow my heart, then a quarrel would surely follow and our home would be full of bitterness once more.

'Oh,' said Gus Chevalier, and his face tightened and I saw a pulsing at his jaw. 'I'm sorry to have asked,' and I could see the hurt in his eyes as, with a wave of his hand, he walked away.

13
Annie Sweet

January 2009

I'm looking at our Christmas decorations and they seem ridiculous, limp and left over. Maybe I should take them down, the ragged silver star that opens like a concertina, the chain of plastic icicles, the paper cardholder decorated with dancing reindeer. The moment I put them up they felt all wrong, but Molly chose them and I wanted to make this Christmas extra special for her. She's back at school next week and I need to get a job, but I don't what I'm going to do when I get one. I can't afford to pay anyone to look after her, and she doesn't want to go to after-school Play Centre. I still don't have any friends in London, and I don't know anyone well enough to ask them to have my daughter. I need to make more of an effort at Molly's school and to get to know some parents better.

'Mum!' Molly's in her bedroom; she sounds upset. 'My bed's wet.'

'What?'

'I said, my BED'S WET!'

'What have you done?' I come to the doorway.

'I haven't *done* anything. Feel it.' Molly pokes disgustedly at her duvet.

I put my hand palm down, the duvet is wet and warm and smells of wee. 'Where's the dog?'

'I don't know, I kept my door shut.'

As I move back, there's an odd scrabbling noise and one meaty brown foreleg emerges slowly from under the bed.

'Jojo!' Molly shouts.

The dog has quite a struggle getting out; I don't know how she ever managed to cram herself under the bed in the first place. Molly grabs her collar and tries to help by pulling her until I tell her off. Finally the dog gets out and stands and shakes her ears with a loud flapping sound.

'Did you wee on Molly's bed?' I say. Oh God, I'm talking to a dog. 'Did she?' I ask Molly. 'She must have jumped on your bed and bloody weed on it!' Jojo looks guilty and starts backing towards the door. I yank the duvet off the bed, pull off the cover, strip Molly's sheet.

'Are we going to be late, Mum?'

Oh God, the audition is today. Molly didn't get the part in the horror film – at least we never heard from them again, so I assume she didn't get it – but she's been asked to try for another audition and it's this afternoon. I used to be so efficient, what's happening to me? When Ben was still here I was always the organised one. I was the one who paid the bills, who made the doctor's appointments, who went to parents' evenings. Now without him, I seem to have lost the skills I had and life feels permanently out of focus.

We leave the house and head for Archway. This time Molly has a scene to prepare and she has the script in her school bag; she's put the pages in there so they won't get crumpled. I've told her what the agency said, that this is an unpaid student film, that even if she gets the part, she won't get anything for it. It's students from the University of Westminster and the film is called *The First Super Girl*. I like the title, but from what I've read of Molly's scene, the play doesn't make much sense at all. The agency has said it will be entered into 'various festivals' around Europe and South

America, as if that should make up for the unpaid weeks of filming.

'Mum . . .' Molly starts nagging as we get in sight of the Tube station.

'What?'

'When is Granny Rose coming?'

'I have no idea.'

'You said she would come. You said.'

'Yes, Molly, I know. Your granny will come and see us as soon as she can.'

'And you said I could have a new hair clip, because it will make me feel, you know, good about myself.'

I stare at her and grab her hand as a motorbike swings past. I don't remember saying any such thing. 'Where did I say I was going to get a hair clip from?'

'From Woolies.'

'It's shut down, Molly, I told you.' I point down Junction Road to where Woolies used to be. We can still see the red of the shopfront, but all the windows are covered in grill bars. I was oddly sad when it closed down, because although I didn't know this Woolies well, the one back home on Lothian Road was always my favourite place to go as a kid. It's where Mum took me for school supplies: pencil cases decorated with butterflies and shiny covered notebooks and rubbers that smelt of bubblegum. It's where Granny Martha took me for sweeties, and she would make a real expedition of it, taking for ever to get dressed and present-able for the outside world, with her coat and her hat and her handbag. Then once we were there she'd encourage me to fill my paper bag from the pick and mix, loading in handfuls of chocolate eggs coated in delicate pink shells, rubbery green and yellow sugar-sprinkled snakes, chewy mini fried eggs and floppy little cola bottles. 'There you go, love,' she'd say. 'Don't tell your mother.' And the fact Woolies has gone, that it's a casualty of the recession everyone's talking about, makes me feel I've lost something. When I go back to Edinburgh, the Woolies on Lothian Road will have gone as well and I won't be able to go there and remember Granny Martha. I think of winter evenings when she'd let me stay up late to watch the telly, and the cold mornings when we huddled in bed and looked at her scrapbooks, their thick pages heavy with glued pictures of the Royal Family, faded newspaper clippings showing weddings and christenings and funerals. What Granny Martha loved was their relatedness, which member of the Royal Family was married to whom, which children were cousins, nieces and nephews, who would inherit a title or even a crown, and I couldn't understand why Granny Martha was so interested in a family that wasn't even her own.

Molly stands stiffly on the escalator at Archway. She hesitated twice before getting on, with a fear she hasn't had for a long time that the metal steps will eat her up. Two people had to make their way around her, and I'm annoyed she's fussing like this when she's the one who wants to go to the audition.

'Are we going to be late?' Molly is standing on the step in front of me and she turns around to check she has my attention.

'No.'

'I bet we are,' she says, and she sounds just like her father.

We're nearly running by the time we get to Regent Street, and when we reach the University of Westminster we have just ten minutes before Molly's 1 p.m. audition. It's a big pillared building, as grey as a pigeon. It looks like it needs a thorough wash. I rush her through the glass doors, expecting someone to meet us, or a sign to show us where we should go, like there was at the last audition, but there's nothing. I pull Molly one way and then stop and pull her the other. 'Mum!' she yells, 'You're making me nervous.'

I stop and ask a man in uniform and he sends us up stairs and along corridors until we come to a small room with a glass window. Inside all I can see are the white tops of student desks. There's a note taped to the door – *Super Girl Audition! Gone for lunch! Back at 2 p.m.!*

We're in the small, bright room with the director, a young woman with yellow hair knotted high on her head and big golden hoops in her ears. She found us next door and brought us in here – they'd broken early for lunch because they thought Molly wasn't coming. Molly is furious with me, as if I've deliberately made her late. The director sits on a grey plastic chair, another woman is beside her but she hasn't been introduced, and a man with a camera is waiting to begin. I want to leave the room so Molly won't be put off by my being here, but the director smiles and waves that I should sit to one side.

'OK, Molly,' she says, 'shall we begin?'

I expect to see my daughter brace herself, but she looks strangely relaxed.

'From the top,' says the director, like she's some hotshot in Hollywood and not a university student in London. I've no idea how Molly is going to do this. In her scene her character is walking along a street, wearing a big red anorak, pink hat and wellington boots. She is to smile and look around. She has a ball under her arm. Then she approaches a playground and sees an old man sitting on a swing. It's only after all of this that she actually says anything. Her first line is, 'What are you doing on the swing?'

Molly walks over to me and I watch her anxiously, think she's going to ask to leave, but she ignores me; she's just come to this spot so she can begin. She pulls at the collar of an imaginary anorak, adjusts an imaginary hat, puts an imaginary ball under her arm, and then walks across the floor in a flat-footed way as if she has wellies on. How does she do this? Has she practised these exact movements, or is she just making it all up now on the spur of the moment? I don't know which image affects me more, my little girl alone in her bedroom teaching herself how to pretend to wear an anorak and wellies, or my little girl right now acting in front of the director. Why isn't she scared? I would be scared. I would feel sick at the idea of people watching me. I still don't know what's behind all of this. Does Molly long to be noticed, to be applauded, to be loved? Or does she just enjoy the drama of pretending to be someone else?

As she reaches the chair where the director sits, Molly turns and I can see that she's imagining that the rest of the room is the children's playground. She stops, catches sight of someone, frowns. She's a little exaggerated now, but still believable. 'What are you doing on the swing?' she asks in a snappy voice, a voice that sounds just like mine.

When the scene is finished, the director and her companion clap. 'That was great! Well done, Molly.'

Molly shrugs, like it was nothing to her.

'Now let's do it again. This time I want you to imagine you're the old man.'

I look at Molly. How is she going to do that? But she does, and then she does another four run-throughs of the same scene in different ways. Afterwards I take her to a café and buy her a big piece of cake.

'Sorry, Mum, I was a bit scared.'

I look at her eating her cake. Does she think she's doing this for me, that it's me who wants her to get the part and that this would somehow please me? 'I thought you were brilliant. Did you enjoy it?'

'Yeah. I suppose.'

'Well then, if you enjoyed it, that's all that really matters, isn't it?' I say this brightly but I feel silly; I don't feel like these words are mine, because I'm a bad mum and I shouldn't be letting her do this. I don't want her to be rejected, and she will be. 'Just tell me why you want to do this, all these auditions.'

Molly eyes me suspiciously.

'I mean, do you really want to keep going for auditions when, you know, you're not going to . . .' I hesitate.

'You mean when I'm not going to get the part?'

'I didn't say that. I meant there are hundreds of children, maybe thousands, doing this as well and they can only choose one, can't they?'

'But one day, Mum,' says Molly, putting the last of the cake in her mouth, 'they'll choose me.'

'Molly,' I say, and I take her hand across the table, feel how cold her fingers are. 'Are you OK?' I think of the evening I overheard her talking to her lizard in the bath, telling it things she didn't want to tell me, and I wonder what she will tell it about the audition today.

Molly shrugs, pulls her fingers out of mine. 'Do you still love Dad?'

I'm so unprepared for this I don't know what to say. 'Well, that depends on what you mean . . .'

Molly sighs and rolls her eyes. 'But it has nothing to do with me. And you both still love me very much.'

'Yes, Molly, we do and . . .'

'You could have asked him to stay.'

'No, Molly, I could not.' I pick up a spoon, start adding sugar to my tea, and as I look at my daughter I feel a vast chasm between us, like we're not sitting opposite each other at a small café table, but instead we're on either side of a gaping valley with miles in-between. I see that Molly blames me, that whatever Ben has done she wants to blame me.

14

We get home to find the dog's been busy. I open the kitchen door and see a big shit in the middle of the floor, soft and fresh and steaming. All the cupboards have been opened and from somewhere in the kitchen there's an irritating beeping noise. Then I see Jojo's opened the freezer door and left it open, which is why the alarm's ringing, and she's managed to pull out the middle drawer and bite off a big chunk of thick cold plastic. There's an empty sausage packet on the floor and an empty packet of breaded cod. I look around for the sausages and the fish, walk into the back room and look in the dog's bed, but there's no sign of them; she's eaten them all. And they were frozen solid.

'Where's Jojo?' asks Molly, coming in after me.

I look around, completely confused. Where is the dog? Then I see that the double wooden doors that separate the two down-stairs rooms have been battered apart. I left them tied from the other side with a bit of old rope so the dog couldn't get into the front room. But Jojo has been using her body as a battering ram; she's managed to force a gap between the doors and squeeze herself through. She's gnawed at the doors as well; there are marks on the wood where she's scratched them with her nails and large dents where she's bitten them with her teeth. I can't think why she was so desperate to get from one room to the next. Cautiously I go back into the kitchen, down the hall and into the front room and there is the dog, sleeping on the sofa.

'Go upstairs and finish your homework while I clean all this up,' I tell Molly.

'I don't have any homework.'

'Well, go and finish . . .'

'My drawing?'

'Yes, go and finish your drawing.' I swear to myself as I scoop up the shit, bleach and mop the floor, throw away the empty food packets, try to find a way to jam the freezer door shut. When I've finished I go upstairs to find Molly waiting for me on the landing. She's holding a roll of Christmas wrapping paper, silver with little angels on.

'I found this in your office,' Molly says reproachfully.

'What's that?' I ask, although I know at once what it is.

'Why is Father Christmas's wrapping paper in your office?'

'And why were *you* in my office?' I ask. 'What were you doing in there?'

Molly eyes me; she knows she's on to something. 'Did you,' she speaks slowly, like I'm hard of hearing, 'wrap the presents from Father Christmas? That was the paper he used for my CD player.'

'Yes,' I blurt out. 'He was too busy to wrap them himself.'

Molly starts beating the roll of paper hard against the bannister. 'Be honest with me! Is Father Christmas real or not?'

I sit down on the stairs; I can't really bear to look at my daughter. Does she still really believe in Father Christmas – surely she doesn't by now. And why isn't Ben here to deal with this? He was the one who always encouraged her. 'No,' I say, because I have to, because she's asked me to be honest and if I lie about this then she might never believe in anything I say again. 'He doesn't exist. People believe in him, though,' I say weakly, 'lots of children believe in him. He's a nice thing to believe in, isn't he?'

Molly bursts into tears, which run in big swells down her face.

'I'm sorry,' I tell her. She lets me hug her and then she cries into the crook of my neck, and it makes me think of when she was a baby and I would pace around the bedroom at night with her in my arms while Ben snored. In the morning I'd ask, 'Didn't you hear her crying?' because I couldn't believe that he hadn't, that her cries hadn't woken him the way they had me.

'So who ate the mince pie?' Molly pulls away from me.

'How d'you mean?'

'Mum! The mince pie we left out for Father Christmas. If he doesn't *exist* then who ate the mince pie? And the whisky, who drank the whisky? It was *you*, wasn't it?' Molly howls and runs up the rest of the stairs and into her room and slams the door so hard I think the wood is going to shatter.

I can't believe this is the same girl who a few hours ago was so full of confidence, who performed in a room in the University of Westminster without a moment's hesitation, who seemed so sublimely in control. I stay on the stairs, not sure if I should go after her or not, not sure if this fury is really to do with Father Christmas and his wrapping paper or if it's more about her father moving out and she wants a reason to be angry with me, so she can behave as if I've betrayed her. I have to stop myself from saying, *It was your father who always ate the mince pie, your father who always drank the whisky, it was all his idea.* Then Molly flings the door open again. 'So what about the tooth fairies?' she shouts. 'Mum? So what about the fucking tooth fairies?'

It's past midnight and Molly is finally asleep. This will be the day she grew up, when she found out the big lie about Father Christmas, a lie that most of us are involved in, parents and schools and books and newspapers and shops. Even the TV news runs an annual bulletin on Father Christmas. I can't remember when *I* found out, but I'll never forget today, when Molly discovered the truth, because I feel I've let her down and that I haven't handled things the way I should have done. I can hear Ben's voice in my head, *Annie, don't make such a drama out of things*, and I don't want to but I feel like I'm going to cry.

I'm hunched up in bed, my socks still on because it's so cold. I think the heating's broken down again, but I don't want to get out of bed and feel the radiator and find out this is true. Ben usually dealt with things like heating, he just knew how to do these things and it's ridiculous that I don't. It can't be that difficult to work it out, there's no reason why I shouldn't be able to do this, but it's the fact I have no one to discuss it with. I can't ask Molly what she thinks we should do because I'm the only adult here now, the only one in charge. Suddenly I think of a day, not long after we married, when Ben had been on a trip to Glasgow. I met him at Waverley station on his way back and he'd come hurrying off the train, wrapping his arms around me, saying how much he'd missed me and how he never wanted us to be apart again.

This is ridiculous, it's no good going over things like this and yet I can't seem to look ahead, to find anything in the future worth thinking about. And it's cold, it's too cold in this room and the heating must have broken down and I don't know what to do. I look around, at the pile of clothes on the floor that need washing, at the stained cups of tea I haven't taken downstairs. I stare at the boarded-up fireplace and think about the sort of heating this house used to have when it was first built. People would have had coal fires then, in the two fireplaces downstairs and in this one in my bedroom. Coal fires would have been cosy; there would have been a glow in the room.

I've got my laptop on my lap and for a moment I think about looking up how to restore old fireplaces, but I need something else to do, something to distract me, some sort of problem that needs to be solved. And then I remember the census site. I should have saved the pages I found before and printed them out, the list of everyone who lived here in 1901, but I didn't, so now I have to use up more credits finding them again. I like looking at the names: William and Fanny George, Frederick and Elizabeth Painter. It gives me a strange feeling of reassurance that people lived here before me, that I'm part of some continuous chain. Once, long ago, someone sat in this room, just like I'm doing now. What were their lives? Were they happy, or were they angry and bitter like me?

But the names, the ages and the occupations, the information on these census rolls, aren't enough tonight. It's not enough to know that Frederick Painter was an omnibus driver or his daughter Ellen a feather curler. I want to know more about these people. I want to know everything about who my Lily Painter might have been.

Perhaps I need to start at the beginning; perhaps I need to find out about her mother. I see there's a box at the top of the site where you can search through certificates for births, marriages and deaths. So I type in 'Elizabeth Painter' and 900 results come up. How on earth am I going to look through all of these? Then I realise that this wouldn't have been her name anyway. Painter is Elizabeth's married name, and I don't know what she was called before that. I stare at the website, feeling annoyed and frustrated. I don't know what to do. I'm not that interested in where someone was born or when they died anyway, I don't want to know what went wrong; I just want to know what they did when they were alive. Did Lily like living in this house? And where would all these people have slept?

I'd like to think my room would have been Lily's, but it can't have been because she was just the lodgers' daughter; the landlord and his wife must have kept this, the biggest bedroom, for themselves. Perhaps the Georges' children would have slept in the room that is now Molly's, or perhaps it belonged to Mr and Mrs Painter and the children slept downstairs. But I feel certain that Lily and her sister would have been in the room that's now my office. So they got the coldest room, the smallest room, the room with the sloping floor and no fireplace at all.

15

Molly didn't pass the audition; I just got the call. It's 8 a.m. and I'm standing at the front downstairs window, looking out at the falling snow, thinking about how to break the news. Molly will have heard the phone; she'll come running through in a minute and ask who it was. The sky is grim and looks polluted; outside the cars are all covered with snow as thick as sponge. No one's gone to work; London closes down when it snows, like it's never happened here before. The English just give up, the buses stop, even the Tube trains stop. From the window I see a cat leap from one rooftop to another, making black pitted holes in the snow as it skids down the tiles and is gone.

It snowed yesterday as well, and we went to Hampstead Heath. There are days I've been there when I can walk for an hour and barely pass a soul, but yesterday it was full of people with expensive wellington boots and wooden sledges and dogs like huskies churning up the snow. Everywhere were fathers telling their sons how to build a snowman – 'No, it's like this, Oscar! Cyrus, what you do is make the bottom part first. Here, stand there while I do this . . .'

Molly was envious – of the sledges and of the children with the bossy fathers. Or maybe that's just what I thought, because although she sees him once a week, she doesn't often speak about Ben when she's with me. Is this for my sake, does she think it will upset me? Sometimes, during the rest of the week, it's like he never existed, like it's only ever been me and her.

And when she says, 'Dad wants to know if . . .' then some-times, just for a moment, I think, Who is this 'dad'?

I keep on looking out the front window at the falling snow. A year ago, just after our first Christmas at Stanley Road, it was snowing then as well and perhaps that was when it all started. I wanted us to go on the heath together and have a family trip out, to throw snowballs and laugh and go to a café and drink hot chocolate.

'What are you two doing today?' Ben had asked in the morning. It was Sunday; Molly and me were up and ready, but he was still in his dressing gown.

'I thought we were all going to the heath.'

'Not me,' said Ben. 'Work.'

'On a Sunday?'

'It's just for a couple of hours. You go out, enjoy yourselves.'

'Come on, Mum,' said Molly.

And so then we got ready, put on our wellies and our gloves and hats, and I tried to keep a happy face, although I wanted Ben to take part, I thought we couldn't be a proper family without him.

'So when will you be back?' he asked, standing at the doorway. 'This afternoon?'

'Probably. We'll go to the heath, get some lunch . . .'

'Why not go shopping as well?'

'Yeah!' cried Molly. 'I didn't wake you up this morning, and Dad said I could have new leggings if I didn't wake you up . . .'

'OK, OK, we'll see.'

'So,' said Ben, 'you'll be back at what, four or something?'

Then we got to the heath and Molly met a school friend called Jodie. I liked the look of Jodie's mother; I'd seen her in the playground wearing fishnet tights and bright orange lipstick. She always seemed to have a howling baby in a buggy, but she didn't look like the average school mum. They invited Molly to go and play at their house and off she went, and I thought, Ben won't be working all day, he'll have finished soon; we can have the house to ourselves and it's been a long time since we had that. Maybe that's what we need, I thought, some time to ourselves. Because something had shifted between us since we bought the house and he started his new job, things weren't as they had been before. But then maybe that was just how marriage worked.

Everything had slowed down that day: the roads were quiet and the few drivers who had ventured out drove slowly, almost soundlessly, in the snow. When I turned off Holloway Road and into Stanley Terrace I decided to walk in the middle of the road, in the track lines of sludge, and it made me feel like I was doing something different and reckless, like I was a kid again.

I fumbled with my key at the door and shouted 'Hi!' as I went in. There was no answer, the hallway seemed dim and there was an odd unfamiliar smell in the air.

'You're back early.' Ben stood at the top of the stairs, still in his dressing gown.

'Jesus, you gave me a fright!' I stopped on the stairs and then started walking up towards him. 'It was lovely on the heath! Molly's gone to a friend's. I thought we could spend some time together.' As I reached the landing, Ben turned and began walking back up; he was going to the bedroom, perhaps he was leading me there, perhaps he was thinking the same thing as me. I came in after him and the room was warm and quiet and still. 'Why aren't you dressed?'

Ben didn't answer. He took off his dressing gown and quickly pulled on some trousers. So we weren't going to bed together after all.

'And why are the curtains closed?' I sat down on the bed.

'What is this, an inquisition?' Ben laughed as he took a shirt from the wardrobe. 'Oh honestly, Annie, the curtains are closed because I'm getting dressed.'

'But you weren't when I came in.'

'What do you mean?' Ben had his shirt on now and was looking for a jumper.

'Well, you're just getting dressed now, so you didn't need to close the curtains until now.'

Ben put on his jumper and pulled irritably on the sleeves.

'And I thought you were working?'

'Annie,' he said, heading for the door, 'give us a break.'

So was that it, was that the day when it all began?

16
Inspector William George

February 1902

Saturday, 8 February 1902

It is difficult to believe so much time has elapsed since first I began this journal, and such was my disappointment over the disappearance of the East Finchley baby farmers that I quite lost my enthusiasm for writing. Now, with preparations under way for our dear King's Coronation, I feel ready to begin again. Already coachbuilders, robe makers, furriers and silversmiths have been called into service, and I have no doubt that several hundred police pensioners will be recalled for the day. Any earlier doubts, expressed in some quarters, about his capacity to be King have long since faded and I anticipate the event will be one of great jubilation.

Saturday, 22 February 1902

My dear wife has been once again to the Holloway Empire, where our lodgers' daughter Lily continues to perform most successfully in *Dick Whittington and His Cat*. Fanny is now convinced of two things. The first is that our lodger's daughter is heading for great things and soon, such will be her success, she will no longer need to lodge in such a humble abode as ours! The second is that Lily, it seems, has a sweetheart. Fanny says it is something a woman can tell.

Friday, 14 March 1902

This evening I had a most interesting conversation with our neighbour Mr Gilbert Pickles. I had gone to the Crown public house directly after work, partly because I am interested to see the effects of the new licensing act and partly for some quiet time to myself before returning home. The Crown is an interesting site and perhaps worth describing a little. It is such a wedged-shaped building, now lying on the junction of Stanley Road and Stanley Terrace, but standing on what was once but a simple country crossroads when our present busy roads were but fields separating one hamlet from the next. There is, as is usual, both a public bar and a large saloon, but unlike other public houses, which tend to appear warm and inviting from the outside and prove rather stark within, the Crown is a comfortable place in which to spend an hour or so. It is also a very useful setting in which to gather information, seeing as it is here that the working man is most free to speak his mind – as long as he drinks, that is.

Once inside I greeted the proprietor Mr Sam Bonehill, a short, florid-faced man, and then seated myself down in a corner nook near the fire, from where I could have a good view of the comings and goings. Mr Bonehill offered me a complimentary whisky to warm the bones, and we stood and chatted a while. He drew my attention to the new motif above the doorway to the saloon, which reads, 'Haste is slow', and which appears to be a corrupted form of the better-known proverb 'Make Haste Slowly'. He was also keen to show me a new elaborate fire basket, topped with rather alarming-looking little bald goblins, which, he informed me, his wife purchased at the Chapel Market.

It was not long before my neighbour Mr Gilbert Pickles came in, and I saw him look around as if in the need for company this evening. I waved him over and enquired if he would like to join me for a drink, which indeed he said he would.

Mr Pickles proved himself a most lively companion, with an opinion on a great number of current topics. We discussed the recent smallpox outbreak, for which he blamed the mob of anti-vaccinationists, and we then fell to discussing the licensing act and from there the nature of the local public houses. We both then agreed that drunkenness is the curse of today's society. I told him how one of my constables just last week saw a potman at the Archway Tavern putting a drunken woman out on to the gutter. The woman in question, Bessie Sawyer, a familiar figure in these parts, was taken to the station and was later fined. Two days later, however, she was again arrested, charged and fined. In all, this is her fifty-second time!

'Do you know,' said my neighbour Mr Pickles after I had finished relaying the above, 'I had an odd encounter at the Tavern last Friday night.'

'Indeed?'

'Yes, I was about to enter when my way was blocked by an elderly woman. I noticed her, you see,' – and here Mr Pickles put down his glass and leant towards me over the table – 'for she was carrying a remarkably large basket, as if going to market, which naturally,' he laughed, 'she could not be doing so late at night. I asked her politely to step aside, which she did, and it was then I saw what the basket contained: a baby.'

Naturally Mr Pickles now had my full and undivided attention.

'And did you have a good look at the woman?' I enquired.

'Oh yes. I would recognise her at once. A very broad, heavy face.'

'And she was dressed in a large black cloak?'

'Why, yes she was.' Mr Pickles leant back and sipped his whisky thoughtfully.

'And did she walk in a normal fashion, or did she need the aid of a stick?'

'She walked with a limp,' said Mr Pickles. 'How did you know?'

'Just a hunch,' I told him. 'Please go on.'

'Well, I turned to her and remarked, "It is a very cold night for a baby to be out," to which she replied, "Oh, it is that, sir, but the poor little lamb has been ill and I have just taken her from the hospital and now I am handing her to her mother."' At this, Mr Pickles raised his eyebrow to indicate his surprise that a baby be taken from hospital at such an hour.

'How very odd,' I said. 'Please go on.'

'Well, a few moments later, I was still standing there outside the Tavern when I saw another woman alight from a bus and the baby was handed over.'

'And did you see this other woman well? Quite handsome perhaps? Aged around thirty? Dressed all in widow's clothing?'

'Well no,' said Mr Pickles. 'I would say she was far younger. She wore a pale fur coat and . . . well, I'm afraid I can't recall much more than that.'

'Of course not,' I said, regretting that my desire to know if these two individuals could possibly be Nurse Sach and Mrs Walters appeared to be making my neighbour a little uncomfortable. I looked up then, at the motif above the doorway, 'Haste is slow', and I wondered if being hasty could in fact result in slowness because by hurrying mistakes may be made. 'It doesn't matter,' I told Mr Pickles. 'Another drink?'

Sunday, 11 May 1902
I have been unable to write in my journal for quite some time owing to the demands of work, but this evening I was able to join my dear wife in the back parlour. Fanny was much taken with reports that the womenfolk of Australia will soon be awarded the vote.

'Don't you think it's about time women sit in Parliament here?' she asked, in a voice that, from experience, indicated a certain desire for a quarrel.

'I think that would be more comfortable than standing, my dear.' I said this in a joking manner, but Fanny took great offence.

'I don't think it's something to laugh about, William.'

I was loath to get drawn into such a contentious topic, and turned my attention instead to the paper. I was hoping to find mention of our lodgers' daughter Lily, who is now third on the bill at the Empire, having been engaged to sing a number of Parisian songs with another young girl, such was her success in the panto. Just last week Fanny attended a performance with her good friend Mrs Edith Hacker, and the bill, as she described it, was rather eclectic. A newly composed Coronation March received an ovation, a troupe of acrobats performed a revolving cycle trapeze turn in which one of the ladies raised a stationary bike in mid-air, and a set of musical dogs played a remarkable game of football upon the stage. There was also rather a drama, it seems, when the strongman on the bill, a Mr Saxon, challenged anyone to lift his sack of flour weighing 282 lbs, promising them £10 if they could carry it off the stage. Unfortunately for Mr Saxon, one member of the audience had no trouble in doing this and in fact carried it off and back again in twenty seconds and now awaits his £10! But it was Lily, Fanny tells me, who received the most rapturous applause, with a voice that was as clear and as sweet as she has ever heard it. My dear wife is more convinced than ever that Lily has a sweetheart, and she believes Mrs Painter will be most furious when she finds out.

Tuesday, 13 May 1902
We have made a most remarkable find. I had just returned from a lengthy night shift and had settled myself down to read the

morning paper, when my eyes alighted upon the following in the miscellaneous column:

Comfortable Home with accommodation for Ladies before and after Accouchement. Skilled nursing with a qualified Midwife. Baby can remain. Apply Nurse Sach. Claymore House, Hertford Road, East Finchley.

'Aha!' I cried triumphantly, laying the paper on my lap. 'Here she is again!'

Fanny rose at once and within a moment was by my side. I waited until she had read the advertisement and we then looked at each other.

'So, this is your Nurse Sach? And now she's running a lying-in home? Skilled nursing indeed! And do you see this, "Baby can remain." Well, you know what that means, she's at it again, advertising for babies. Oh William, we must go at once.'

'*We?*' I enquired.

'Well, William,' said my dear wife, and her pretty blue eyes were quite piercing this evening, 'don't you want to know if she still has the children?'

'Fanny,' I said, folding up the paper with a heavy heart, 'it has been a very long time and I have to say I think that is most unlikely.' While I am as interested as my wife as to the whereabouts of the infants previously under the care of Nurse Sach, my visit last year may well have been the trigger that set the baby farmers fleeing from the house. If I am to visit this new abode, then I will have to do so without being seen.

17

Lily Painter

A single knock upon a door can change a life for ever, and that is what happened that warm spring night when Gus Chevalier came looking for me. I had not spoken to him since he had asked me to Romano's, and all through the months of panto that followed he had come on and off the stage as if I was not there. Now he was playing the Earl of Derwent at the Camden, and I had seen the reviews and heard how well received he was. I thought his music-hall days were over now, and he was an actor as he wanted to be.

Daisy had already changed and left the dressing room that evening, while I was the straggler, as I so often was, sorely reluctant to leave the Empire and step back into the world outside. I was sitting by the mirror, my face half scrubbed, still in the short red velvet tunic that I wore beneath my gaudy yellow Parisian dress. By the dressing table lay my fine white parasol and my feathered hat, and on the floor my dainty dancing shoes.

'Come in!' I called, because I sensed, without needing to turn from the mirror, that it was him. I watched in the glass as the door opened, and I saw him standing there, his tall stooped figure at the doorway, a smile, a little hesitant, upon his face.

'Lily,' he said, his eyebrows raised in that quizzical way. 'Am I disturbing you?'

I didn't answer and so he took this as an invitation to come in, the thick wooden boards of the dressing-room floor creaking uneasily beneath his boots.

'I saw you this evening, Lily – you and Daisy. You were wonderful.' His voice was rushed and eager, and as he came to where I sat his hands reached out and touched me quickly, lightly, on the shoulders. Still I looked at him in the mirror and I felt my shoulders burn from where he had touched them and I wanted him to touch them again. Ever since that day I'd first seen him when I was but a chorus girl, when I had heard his song and seen him transformed upon the stage, I had wanted him to touch me like this.

Gus Chevalier laughed. 'Well, I'm getting to act at last, Lily, and they seem to like me. Will you come and see the play?' And again he touched me lightly on the shoulders, but this time I took his hands in my own and we stayed like that, looking at ourselves. It is the strangest thing, looking at a lover in the mirror, for you look straight into the other person's eyes before you in the glass, and yet it is only when you turn and see each other in reality that the spark is felt and the flame ignites. Outside in the corridor we heard laughing and light footsteps, a bell rang somewhere, and I thought I heard the low grumble of Mr Ryde's voice.

'Close the door,' I said, and I waited as he closed it and returned to where I sat.

'It's funny, isn't it, Lily?' he asked, and he hesitated then, his face unsure. 'We've known each other for a while, and once or twice I've tried to . . . and I thought perhaps, well . . . and I still don't know if . . .'

And it was then that I stood and faced him, for I was tired of waiting, of hoping what might be. Instead I put my hands upon his cheeks, smooth and freshly shaven and smelling faintly of cologne. I felt the linen of his jacket rough and warm and comforting against me. And as we stood there, there was a sudden, muffled knock upon the door, and a girl's voice shouting out, 'Well then, I'll hurry her up!' and I knew at once it was Daisy. We waited, rigid against each other, ready to fly apart if Daisy chose to come in, but she didn't, for another girl called her and she sped away laughing cheerily, the sound of her footsteps disappearing down the hall.

And then such a hurry there was, as if neither of us had eaten for so long that the taste of our lips made us feel a hunger we had never known. I felt his hair slip under my touch, felt his lips as warm and soft as a pillow left in the sun. His fingers travelled over my face, brushing gently at my hair, scooping it in his hands and holding it up above my neck, kissing me upon my skin.

'Do you want me, Lily?' he breathed, hot into my ear. 'I've always wanted to know. Sometimes I think you do, sometimes I think you don't. Only tell me that you want me.' And still kissing, he lifted me gently up upon the dressing table, and I felt the mirror cold and hard against my back. His fingers began to travel warm and urgent upon my legs until he reached the hem of my tunic, and he slid his hands against the softness of the velvet and found my flesh beneath.

I didn't know what would happen next, I knew nothing about the facts of life, I seemed to only know things that evening once they happened, because I had been waiting for this for so long.

'You want to be careful,' Daisy said as we walked home together the next afternoon, she on her bike and I by foot.

'Careful about what?' I asked. 'You sound just like my mother.'

'You'll get a reputation, darling. People will say you're as common as a barber's chair!'

'But don't you like him?' I asked. 'How can you not like him?'

'That's not what I'm talking about, Lily. I know he was in our room last night.'

'But Daisy, have you never had that sense of, that sense of rapture . . .'

'Oh, you're a fallen woman!' laughed Daisy, but then she stopped and her cheeky face was serious. 'Sometimes, Lily, I think you're as innocent as a newborn child.'

Those months that followed were the happiest of my life. Each night I sang with such love in my heart that the audience, from start to finish, were mine. And afterwards, when the curtain fell at the Camden, Gus would come and seek me out. Some nights we stayed within the dressing room once Daisy had left, lying close in each other's arms; other nights we went outside and strolled along the road, side by side, hand in hand. It didn't matter where we were, only that we were together now and I no longer cared what my parents would say, only that he was mine. We had a future together and we had a future on the stage. Late into the night I lay in the bed I shared with my sister Ellen in our room on Stanley Road and I listened to the wind outside and I hugged myself and thought of Gus. He would be a star, I knew it. And so would I. Then one evening he came to tell me the news: his play would tour the provinces.

'Will you write to me, Lily?' he asked. 'I'll write to you, I'll write to you every day I'm away.'

18

It was Daisy who saw what was happening; it was she who found me one afternoon standing in our dressing room after the matinee with both hands upon my stomach.

'Oh Lily,' she said, 'is it too late to get you right?'

'What will I do?' I whispered, sinking low upon the chair, for I had just then felt the quickening, sensed the first movement inside.

'It's not the worst thing in the world,' said Daisy in her cheerful way. 'Just keep your clothes as loose as you can. It's happened to a lot of girls before you, Lily – My oldest sister Bertha, that's why she left the stage, she was fourteen when she had the baby, and Mother brought it up as if it were her own.'

'My *mother* would never do such a thing!' I cried. 'Oh Daisy, she'll be hysterical with shame, she'll turn Father against me and they'll both throw me out! What will I do with a child? How can I stay on the stage like this?'

Daisy sat down then and she looked at me with concern. 'Have you told him?'

'No.' I thought of the letters Gus had sent from tour, letters from unfamiliar northern towns full of his exciting news. I didn't know yet when he would be back.

'He'll leave you, Lily, they always do.'

'Oh, he can't! He never would!' But what if he did? What if he didn't want me with child? What if he would abandon me to my fate?

We sat together in the dark dressing room, thinking about

this, until all at once Daisy cried, 'Oh, it's so unfair!' and she threw a hairbrush and it slapped hard upon the floor.

After that day I tried so many things, listened feverishly to the others talk, the whispered conversations about the pills that never seemed to work, the chorus girl who ate gunpowder until she fell so ill her secret was discovered. On stage I kicked as high as I could, kicking desperately, hoping that I would get back to the girl I had been. At home I begged to be allowed a hot bath, so hot that when I got out I felt so dizzy I hoped I would collapse. I ran up and down the stairs, several times a day, I lifted heavy tubs until my arms ached. One morning our landlord's sweet wife Fanny found me like this, trying to run down the stairs with the coal tub, and she told me I could harm myself.

'I'm all right,' I told her.

'Are you?' she asked, in that direct way of hers, and I coloured quickly and put the coal tub down and I was sorely tempted, for a second, to tell.

Then one day Daisy brought me a newspaper and she laid it out upon the dressing table. 'You need to get away, darling. You're going to have to think what to do; you can't stay around here much longer. Look at this one, it's in East Finchley. That's not so far away, but no one will know you're there.'

'Finchley?'

'Yes, you can have the baby there, Lily, and then – well then, darling, everything will be all right, won't it? See, it says baby can remain.' Daisy laughed when she saw the look of puzzlement upon my face. 'Don't you know what that means? It means the baby can stay there, they'll get it adopted for you.'

'Adopted?' I said, and inside I felt a movement so strong that I held my breath and clutched my hands hard against the dressing table.

The very next day Daisy and I composed a letter to the advertiser and soon after I set off alone, directly after the matinee show. As I hurried through the streets I felt that everyone who saw me knew my condition and that my blouse left loose over my skirt did nothing to hide the truth at all. I half expected people to walk around me on the street, and I thought that one or two stopped in curious interest to watch as I went by. For several nights I had been plagued by such bad dreams that my sister Ellen complained bitterly she could not sleep for the way I tossed and turned. I tried to lie quietly in our bed, but when I did sleep I dreamt always I was on top of a precipice and about to fall. For what would my future be now? If I did not leave Stanley Road soon, then everyone would know, the quarrels would begin, I would lose my job and then my home.

Eventually I found the street and it was quiet and pleasant in the bright June sunlight, with clean wide pavements and tall grand trees on either side. I stopped before a house halfway down with wide front windows and freshly painted gables, saw the white brick sign upon the wall with its pretty lettering, *Claymore House*. As I stood there, hesitating for a moment, I saw a lady come out of the house and climb daintily into a new carriage and be driven away.

Quickly, before I could change my mind, I walked up the short flight of steps and knocked upon the door. At once it was opened by a pretty woman, her fine black hair pinned fashionably upon her head, around her shoulders a soft blue cloak trimmed with white fur as if she had only just come in.

'I'm Nurse Sach,' she said, and she smiled in such a friendly way that I felt a sudden surge of relief. 'You must be Lily, won't you come in?'

She led me into the front parlour, a large warm room with such lovely pictures upon the wall: a girl with auburn curls, a gentleman and lady dancing in evening dress, an angel sitting upon a golden bough.

'I read your letter, my dear, and I hope you received mine. Sit down, please. So, you're looking for a comfortable home during your confinement?' Nurse Sach spoke in a kind, matter-of-fact way, as if there was nothing shameful or unusual about my circumstances.

'Yes,' I said, 'I should like to know the fees.' I spoke so softly that she hadn't, it seemed, heard me and there was silence in the room, broken only by the sudden sound of horses' hooves outside. 'The fees?' I asked again, looking up.

'Don't fret yourself,' Nurse Sach said, smiling, and she patted me twice upon the arm. 'We can agree on the terms. They don't vary much. A guinea a week and three guineas a week during confinement after the baby comes.'

'Three guineas a week?'

'I'm sure there's someone who can assist with the terms – the father perhaps?'

'Yes, of course,' I said hurriedly, too hurriedly, for Nurse Sach looked a little disapproving now, as if she thought I didn't even know who the father was.

'So, I would say,' she looked at me thoughtfully, 'that you will need to move in about three months from now, the end of September perhaps. Then you can settle in here and make things for baby, for what mother doesn't like to see her baby dressed prettily?'

I nodded, unable to speak.

'And afterwards, have you thought about what you will do?'

'Oh!' I cried, and all my fears came flooding out and I began to sob. 'I've no idea what I'm going to do. It's impossible for me to have a baby with me!'

'There, there.' Nurse Sach patted me again upon the arm

and offered me a handkerchief. 'Why don't you get it adopted? I know plenty of ladies who would adopt if you'd agree.' She left my side then and moved to a small oak table in the middle of the room and began to straighten a pretty white cloth. 'Why,' she said, turning to me, 'I have a lady just now who lives in a flat at Kensington Gore, a titled lady, who would adopt a baby, all for thirty guineas.'

I looked at Nurse Sach and I felt a surge of hope, for if my baby were to be adopted by a titled lady then it would want for nothing more. 'Who is the lady?' I asked.

Nurse Sach took a vase of small blue flowers and she brought it to the centre table and placed it carefully down. 'I cannot say that, Lily,' she said, surveying the vase critically, 'the ladies don't like the mothers to know their names or where they live in case,' and she stopped and looked at the vase as if she didn't quite like its position – 'in case the mothers want to take them from the ladies who adopted them, but you may see your child twice a year if you like. I can tell you that they are well-to-do ladies who have no families of their own and they so desperately want children to adopt.'

'But,' I burst out, 'if they're wealthy ladies then thirty guineas would not be wanted!'

'Ah, the ladies,' and Nurse Sach gave an indulgent smile, 'like to buy presents for the babies in memory of the mother.'

We were interrupted then by sounds at the door and I heard a man's voice and shortly after a little girl came running into the room. 'Mama!' she cried, and she threw herself at Nurse Sach. 'I've been looking for you!'

Nurse Sach lifted the girl onto her lap, smiling warmly, and she removed the girl's bonnet and smoothed her hand upon her hair. 'Now then,' she scolded, 'you're disturbing us. Off you go with your father and I'll be back later.' She kissed the child on the top of her head and placed her back upon the floor, and the gesture was so intimate and loving that I was forced to look away.

The little girl ran back to the door and it was then there came a baby's shrill cry from somewhere in the house. 'That's Betty's,' said Nurse Sach, 'her baby was born just yesterday morning. It's a good little soul and there's a doctor up there attending to her. Now then, Lily, why don't you come and look around? Let's go and meet Mrs Walters. She's like a mother to the girls.' She took me down the hallway to the kitchen, a bright comforting room that smelt of warming milk, and I realised how hungry I was as I looked at a plate of bread and cheese upon the table.

'Mrs Walters,' said Nurse Sach, 'This is Lily.'

'Hello, my love,' said Mrs Walters, and she grasped a stick that leant against the chair. 'Aren't you a fine young girl?' She smiled and looked me up and down and was about to say more when she was overcome with a fearsome bout of coughing. 'Oh, my blessed Lord,' she said when at last she could draw breath, 'I've such a sore throat.'

'A drop of something will see to that,' said Nurse Sach with a kindly nod. 'Now off you go, Lily, and don't worry about a thing. We'll see you when the time comes, won't we, Mrs Walters?'

19

Annie Sweet

March 2009

It might sound ridiculous, but I'm almost hoping Molly will get called for another audition. It gives us something to plan for, to look forward to, and it breaks my heart when she asks, every day when I pick her up from school, 'Any news, Mum?' She never asks about her dad like this, she rarely wants to know what he's up to or whether she can see him more than she does, but when it comes to auditions she just can't wait for another one. It's as if the auditions keep her going. She hasn't had another call since *The First Super Girl*, and I think I was more disappointed than her when she didn't get the part.

I've started work now, only part-time temping in the Archway Tower, a slab of grey that looms over the Tube station, but at least the agency I've signed with have found me a job, and at least it's close to Molly's school and to home. I was happy, when the agency called me in for a typing test, to find I could still type as fast as I could twenty years ago. Only I didn't tell them I've had virtually no experience since then. Dad is pleased; he thinks I'm getting stuck into something. 'Why not do accountancy?' he used to say when I was younger. 'You can always get a job if you're an accountant.' But of course I'd gone to university and studied English, because that's what you do when you don't know what to do.

And then when I hadn't been able to get a job, Dad had insisted I do a twelve-week secretarial course. Now, he says, it's just as well I did.

Archway seems to be in the process of closing down, not just Woolies but other shops too. The new organic food shop and the off-licence both set tables outside with plastic bowls of battered-looking fruit for a pound. No one seems to be buying them. It's even worse on Holloway Road; every week a cheap clothing or shoe shop puts up a final-sale notice and then the next day there's just an empty space with a *To Let* sign. A few weeks ago someone optimistically opened a new estate agents; now they're out of business too. Everything around me seems to be in the process of failing.

I get to Molly's school just as the gates are opening, which is a relief because I still feel a bit awkward standing out there with the other parents, who all seem to know each other so well. I say hello to Jodie's mum, thank her again for having Molly that day of the snow and ask if her daughter would like to come round to ours. I admire her brightly coloured coat and wish I could remember her name. I'm about to ask, when the baby in the buggy starts howling.

Molly's going to be happy today. I've had an email from the agency about a feature film. They say a casting director is coming in and there'll be parts for quite a few children. I leave Jodie's mum and find a good spot in the playground so I can see the door where the kids come out. I like to try and look at Molly as if she isn't my child, as if she was just a child I saw and didn't know. But this never works, because the moment she comes to the top of the steps it's as if I'm the only one she sees, and she waves and beams and starts running, her book bag bouncing against her tummy. I want to leap and fly over the other parents and grab her in my arms, but she looks serious and businesslike as she reaches me.

'Any news?' she asks, with a fake casualness.

'Yes, actually.'

Molly stops. 'An audition?'

'Do you really want to do this, Molly?'

'Like, duh!' She rolls her eyes.

'OK then, it's a film, called *A Christmas Story*.'

'What do you mean, *A Christmas Story*?'

'That's the name of the film, you know – Jesus and everything.'

'Oh.' Molly looks disappointed. 'What's my part?'

'Well, there are lots of parts. It sounds quite interesting in a way. It's about an infant school that puts on a nativity play, a musical one, and all the parents want their kids to have the starring role and it becomes a big sort of battle between everyone. They say you have to choose which part you'd like, then they'll ask you questions and you have to answer in character.'

Molly nods. She gets this idea at once.

'So, if you're a shepherd then I suppose they might ask you, I don't know, what you have for lunch, or how you look after sheep. You also have to prepare a song or a poem or a dance.'

'Let's go, Mum.' Molly grabs my hand and I smile because her enthusiasm is infectious. 'Let's get home.'

As we walk up the hill from her school, several kids shout out 'Molly!' even though Molly has told me she doesn't have any friends any more. She marches ahead and then suddenly stops and turns. 'Why didn't you bring Jojo?'

'Then I couldn't come into the playground, could I?' I ask.

'But don't you think she's missing us, Mum?'

'I'm sure she is,' I say. Some days I think about taking the dog back to Battersea and telling them I just can't cope with the mad barking at a blank wall and the fact that she can't bear being alone. But then I feel guilty. We've taken her in and now we have to keep her; I just hope one day she settles down. I couldn't do that to Molly anyway, take away the dog she loves.

Molly has decided she will be an ox. I've tried to persuade her out of this and have suggested she could be the innkeeper or a wise man or an angel. But she wants to be an ox. She has prepared both a song and a dance as an ox and she can't wait until Thursday when we go to the agency's theatre after school.

'Do you think anyone else will be an ox?'

'I shouldn't think so,' I say carefully.

'You don't seem very excited, Mum.'

'Well, it's just that I'm going to have to sort time off work to come with you, you know.'

'Why can't Granny Rose come with me?'

'Molly!'

'What?'

'How is she going to come when she's in Scotland?'

'OK, I'll sing her my song on the phone instead, and she'll have some ideas to help me.'

Molly is pleased with this plan; she thinks Mum is the font of all knowledge, even if it means knowing how an ox should sing. Twice in the past few weeks Mum has said she's coming down, but I haven't told Molly this and it's just as well because at the last minute Mum has changed her mind. I'm more convinced than ever that she doesn't want to come here because she can't face up to the fact me and Ben have separated for good.

We're standing in the pouring rain waiting for a bus. I picked Molly up from school a little late, and now we need to get to

Barnsbury, which is half an hour away. Her audition is at half past four. We're never going to get there in time. The bus comes and I take Molly's hand, rush for the doors, pretend we're not jumping the queue. I put my Oyster card to the screen and the red light beeps. Molly's already got on the bus and I have to call her back. 'Wait a minute,' I say. But the people behind me don't want to wait. I pushed in and now I'm holding them up. I try to stand to one side to find my purse, but I already know I haven't got any money. I think about begging the bus driver: *My card's empty, please, I don't have money and I have to get my daughter to an audition, please let us on.* But when I look at him he's not looking at me, he's just gesturing with his thumb that I have to get off, like I'm a piece of scum.

It's four o'clock already, I've got no money and I can't use the bus. We're definitely going to be late. I see an empty black cab coming down the road and quickly I put out my hand. Molly looks at me in amazement; she's never been in a black cab before because I've always told her they're too expensive. I open the door, hurry her in, and tell the driver where we want to go and that I'm going to pay by debit card. Then we sit back in the fineness of a black cab and Molly looks out of the window. For a while we're silent and it takes me a moment to realise why this seems odd, and then I know it's because she's growing up. Molly doesn't need me to entertain her any more, to distract her with I-Spy or feed her a snack or offer her a book. She is happy enough just to look out of the window and watch the world go by.

At the theatre the foyer is packed. Behind the desk a young woman looks flustered, like something's gone wrong and she's being blamed and she doesn't think it's her fault. 'The casting director hasn't arrived,' she says. 'She must have got held up.

If you want to take a seat, we'll call you the moment she comes and try to get as many of them in as we can.' She looks at Molly, who is stomping up and down like an ox, and smiles. 'Just be yourself.'

At last Molly gets called in and I wait in the foyer next to three other mothers, all with their blonde hair in ponytails. One is reading a copy of *Stage* magazine; she has a pen in her hand and every now and again she circles something. The woman next to her is showing off some photographs she's had done of her daughter. They are huge and glossy and black and white, almost as big as posters. Her daughter is smiling frantically in all of them. She says they cost her eighty pounds, but she thinks it's worth it. I wonder whether I should get any pictures done and whether I should be scanning ads. Perhaps I'm not helping my daughter enough, perhaps I shouldn't always be warning her she won't get a part or preparing her for failure, instead I should be helping her more. I don't know what Ben thinks about Molly's auditions because we haven't discussed it. I suppose she's told him about them, but she hasn't reported back what he's said. And anyway, I feel like this is something between Molly and me.

An hour later Molly comes out with the other children. She looks very hot.

'How did it go?'

'Fine. I'm hungry.'

'Did you remember your song and everything?'

'I'm hungry.'

'Was anyone else an ox?'

Molly scowls at me like I'm the one who forced her to be an ox. 'The lady said I did it very well,' she says with great dignity as we get outside and find it's started raining again.

20

It's Saturday morning and Molly has gone to her dad's for the whole weekend. We've never done this before. Normally he collects her from school on a Friday, but instead I did that yesterday and then he came in the evening to get her. I called out, 'It's your dad!' and pretended I was far too busy in the kitchen to come to the door. But I could see him; the kitchen door was open and I could see along the hall and to the front door, saw him bend to hug her, saw how she threw herself on to him.

'Hello, Annie,' he called out in a sing-song voice.

'Yes,' was all I could manage, because it's all so strange that I can't really bear it. I don't know how to behave when Ben, who used to be my husband, comes to this house, which used to be ours, and takes our daughter away.

'Have you got everything?' I called out to Molly. 'Toothbrush, nightie, books, and don't forget to do your homework on Sunday . . .' Then once they'd gone I ran like crazy to the front room and looked through the window because I wanted to know who was out there, waiting for them in the car. I watched them, father and daughter. Molly looked very obedient. I wondered how long it takes her to relax with him and whether she's as argumentative with Ben as she is with me.

Now I have the whole morning stretching ahead of me. I've tried to come up with something to do. Yesterday I found a book at a charity shop about how to trace the history of your house, and today I'm going to the library and then the local history centre.

* * *

I never noticed we had a library so near our house and it's so beautiful, the library on Manor Gardens, bright orange brick with clean white pillars. It looks like someone's really been looking after it. The entrance is dark and cool, the stone looks ancient, the archway so low I almost have to stoop. I read on the council website that this was Islington's first public library and at the official opening in 1906 the queues were so long that the police had to be brought in to keep control. There's no chance of that today.

Inside there's an empty stone hallway with leaflets about community things and a small display, only a couple of boards, with photos of the area from a hundred years ago. This is exactly the sort of thing I'm looking for, and I stand and stare at a grainy scene of the Seven Sisters Road. The road looks vast and there's a man, or maybe a boy, right in the middle of it, with a long-handled broom. On either side are large shop awnings, one with an advertisement on the side for Lipton Tea. There's a horse-drawn omnibus on the left, half blurry as it drives off down the road, and in the distance where it's grey and smoky-looking there's another one coming, piled high with people up top. It's such an urban scene, and if you changed the vehicles and the people's clothes, and narrowed the road and removed the awnings, it's still the Seven Sisters Road today; especially the end near the intersection with Holloway Road, where the pavements are always crowded with shoppers and where fruit and veg is still set out on stalls. I look at another picture, of the Archway Tavern and the tram terminus, see the layout of the crazy intersection was just the same as it is today, only where there were tram lines, now there are zebra cross-ings and islands and traffic lights.

I go into the library, look at the single shelf of local history books and pick one out at random. I open it and the hardback covers creak; on the bottom of the inside page there's a brown half-moon stain where someone has rested a teacup. I flick through to a chapter on villas for the middle class and stop at a photo of the Holloway Road *c.*1901. I don't really know what I'm looking for; I just want to know how things used to be around here when Lily Painter lived in my house. Eventually I choose three books, and as I get a bus to the Islington local history centre at last I feel I might have something to go on.

The history centre is inside the Finsbury Library and the building is modern, sloping and grey. The walls are grey, the concrete walkway is grey, the railings all around are grey. I walk through the entrance and turn left into the local history centre. It's a small quiet room that makes me think of school, with a blue-flecked floor and a single Formica-topped table. Along the facing wall are wooden shelves full of red-bound books with golden writing down their spines; to the right is a row of desks where two women sit in front of computers. Just before me is a rack of postcards and leaflets and a list of laminated rules. There is to be no food or drink in here and no mobile phones, and I am not to lick my fingers to turn any pages.

I go up to the desks. 'Yes?' asks one of the women. She has very pink cheeks and a flower-shaped clip in her hair. 'Can I help?'

'Hi. I wanted to . . . well, I wanted to find out about the history of my house.'

'Uh-huh.'

'I know roughly when it was built, and I know who was living there in the 1901 census.' I'm expecting the woman to look impressed with what I've found out so far, but instead she just about stifles a yawn. 'So,' I finish lamely, 'I want to find out more about it.'

'Well, we've got lots of information here,' says the woman.

'You could start with the register of electors. Or the rate books. Or some local directories. I'll get Danny to help.'

A man comes over; a tall, light-skinned black man with long braided hair. He's wearing jeans and a tracksuit top and when he asks, 'Can I help you?' it's in a languid way with his hands thrust deep in his pockets. He looks so casual that it's as if he doesn't really work here, like he's just walked in off the street to help out for the day.

'Yes, I wanted to find out more about my house, in Holloway. I'm interested in the people who lived there in 1901 and I've been told to look at the registers of electors?' I hear how polite I sound, as if I'm engaged on a work project and I'm so efficient that I can only give the bare facts.

'Right you are.' Danny smiles and he seems amused by something. 'If you could put your things in one of those lockers . . .'

'Sorry,' I say because I haven't been obeying the rules, and I put my jacket and bag away. When I turn back, Danny has gone over to the shelf of thick red books.

'These are the registers,' he says. 'They've got everyone who was registered to vote. First you need to find your polling district. Where's your house?'

'Stanley Road. It's just off the Holloway Road.'

'Upper Holloway,' Danny says, and his fingers start travelling along the books. He doesn't seem so languid now; he seems focused on the job at hand. 'I think that's polling district number 6. Here we go. This is 1901.' He lays a book on the table, but just when I think he's going to help me further he walks off.

I open the book. It has a pleasant dusty smell that reminds me of a flower press I had as a child, a little wooden press with four shiny screws that held sheets of thick green blotting paper in place. I remember the excitement of putting in a flower, soft and damp and freshly picked, and returning to it months later to find it so perfectly dried and fragile and preserved.

I begin to turn the pages of the electoral register, almost expecting a flower to fall out. But all I can see is columns of numbers and names and addresses. The pages are so thin that as I start to turn them again the paper tears, just a little sound-less sliver of a tear in the top right-hand corner. I stay like that, my fingers frozen on the page covering the tear, worried that someone has seen what I've just done. Will I be fined for destroying a book? Will they ban me from coming in here again? I look up; Danny is chatting with the women at the desk, no one is taking any notice of me, so carefully I turn the pages again. And here it is: 43 Stanley Road, and here is William George, the inspector who used to live in my house. It's like he's a person I already know and I want to tell someone, 'Look, I found him!' even though I already knew he'd be here. But William George is the only person listed under my address because presumably he was the only person allowed to vote, so how am I going to find out about any of the women, about Lily Painter or her mother or her sister? None of them are mentioned here because they couldn't vote; it's like they never even existed.

I go back to the lockers, take out a pencil and the pad I brought with me, and sit down to copy out what I've found, even though it isn't really anything at all. Carefully I put the book back on the shelf, take down the register for 1899 and quickly find Stanley Road and William George again. But when I take down the book for 1898, he's gone. Now the only person registered to vote is Henry Coy. What a lovely name, Henry Coy. I wonder who he was. I take down an even earlier book, but now polling district number 6 itself has gone. So now I know exactly when the house was built: 1897.

'How's it going?' Danny asks. He's appeared out of nowhere

and he seems to be finishing eating something. 'Sorry, very unprofessional of me.' He smiles and wipes what look like biscuit crumbs from the side of his mouth. 'I never got a tea break today.'

I shrug to show that I don't care that he's eating, and pile up all the books on the table ready to put them back on the shelf. My shoulders feel stiff, I need to stretch, I'm not sure how long I've been here. The clock on the wall says midday, but I can't have been here that long. I look around at the shelf of books; the register for 1901 pokes out because I haven't put it back neatly enough. 'I'm sorry,' I say quietly, 'but that first book I looked at, one of the pages got a bit torn.' I sound like Molly: I haven't said I tore a page, only that a page got torn.

Danny bends his head and whispers in a conspiratorial voice, 'Don't worry, it happens all the time.'

I stand up quickly, feeling silly for even having told him about the torn page. 'What I really wanted was to find out more about the people who lived in my house, you know, how they lived and everything.'

'Oh, well the registers won't be much help with that.' Danny glances over at the women at the desks and he looks a little annoyed. 'Have you checked other earlier censuses, or had a look at birth, marriage or death certificates?'

'I did try a census site, but . . . I got a bit overwhelmed. But I do know there were two families in my house, and it's one of the daughters I'm interested in, Lily Painter.'

I almost expect a flash of recognition to pass over Danny's face, but he just nods. 'Lily Painter . . . is it family research you're after?'

'Yes, I guess so.'

'Do you have any other family records to go on, people in your family who could help?'

I feel foolish now; he doesn't understand me. 'It's not my family, it's just I wanted to find out about her.' I don't know how to explain that I just want to know about Lily Painter because she lived in my house and I like the sound of her name, and because now I've started looking for her I don't want to stop. I want to keep on going because I like having a project and a reason to go places I wouldn't normally go. I feel as eager as if I had a homework assignment, and I want to do it right, even though at the back of my mind I know there is no point to this search at all.

'Well, we've got all sorts of stuff that could help,' says Danny, 'books on the borough's history, vestry minutes, just ask and I'll dig it out for you. To see how people lived you could look up local places of interest, for example in the card index.' He points to my left at a table of sweet little wooden drawers I hadn't noticed before. 'And we have the local paper, the *Islington Gazette*, on microfiche so you could read newspaper reports. Both the machines are booked today, but if you came back another time? Give us a ring and I'll make sure I'm here.'

I walk out of the local history centre and back into a miserable March day. But I'm feeling energetic now because I'm on the hunt for something that has nothing to do with my everyday life and I don't know what I might find.

21

Inspector William George

July 1902

Saturday, 12 July 1902

A dull wet day and altogether rather depressing; but at last I am well enough to write. After these past six weeks confined to what has become a veritable sick room, I thought I should spend my last days prostrate upon my bed, too weak to do more than occasionally pat my dear wife's pretty hand. But now I am considerably stronger, both in body and spirit, and fully intend to resume my duties as soon as possible.

Where to begin? It seems events conspire against me every time I attempt to pick up my pen to write! As I have said to Fanny, if I weren't in the force then I would scarcely get sick leave at all. To which she replied, 'If you weren't in the force, William, you would scarcely have been set upon and hit over the head.'

I have not divulged the full details of the case to my dear wife, although much of it was reported, with reasonable accuracy, in the press. Suffice to say, on the night of 29 May, two of my beat constables were alerted to a robbery on the Holloway Road after a ruffian approached a gentleman and snatched his watch and chain. My constables diligently followed the culprit to a dilapidated warehouse where he joined two others and they quickly bolted themselves in. When the constables called for assistance I was first on the scene, and I endeavoured to gain entrance via a glass roof. Sad to say I am not as fit as I once was and indeed fell clear through the roof and into the premises below, at which point I was thoroughly set upon by the gang.

All three men were duly arrested and sentenced, while I have been confined to bed for these past six weeks. Indeed for two nights I was, Fanny tells me, quite delirious. That, however, is most likely due to the medicine prescribed by Dr Day, and once I had regained my prior state of mind, I quite refused to take any more.

My dear wife has shown herself a most diligent nurse, and for her neat-handedness and quiet manner there is no one who surpasses Fanny. I confess to not being the easiest patient to care for, for it is hard for a man to be laid low in such a manner so that he even relies on his wife to bodily help him from the bed. Indeed, such was my discomfort with this that I requested the assistance of our lodger Mr Painter in order to rig up a rope contraption, tying it from the head to the foot of the bed, and which, upon grasping, I could use to move myself around. Both Mr Painter and I were highly pleased with the results.

Monday, 14 July 1902

For some weeks Fanny has been most concerned about our lodgers' daughter Lily. She says she no longer appears to be the carefree girl she was when she first began to lodge with us, although she continues her most successful run at the Empire. Indeed Lily, when she is at home, does seem far slower in herself and more apt to tears at the most trifling things. Just this morning, as I made my way unsteadily downstairs to collect my newspaper, I came upon her in the hallway in a most distracted state. When I bade her good morning she looked at me quite startled. 'I was expecting a letter,' she said, before wrapping her shawl around her and hurriedly leaving the house. I did not, of course, ask from whom she was expecting a letter, although Fanny most certainly wished I had.

'What is up with the girl?' she asked. 'She isn't looking right at all. And why isn't her mother more concerned?'

Thursday, 24 July 1902
I am pleased to report that plans for our dear King's Coronation are now back on course. I was most upset to think I would miss the original date for the celebrations due to my injury, and while it was a terrible blow that the King should have become so unwell, it means at least I shall be on duty once a new date is set.

Monday, 28 July 1902
I am anxious to resume work. I cannot take the clutter in this room any longer, so many boxes and bottles and nursing items, so many flannels and bowls and saucers, so many items of food prepared so lovingly by my dear wife in the hope of attracting my appetite.

There is another reason for my increasing desire to return to work, and that is the case of the East Finchley baby farmers. For fate struck me a heavy blow just as I was intending to visit Nurse Sach's new premises, and there is nothing as unsatisfactory as unfinished business.

Sunday, 10 August 1902
I am exhausted. Suffice to say, the Coronation procession yesterday was met with feverish interest and the streets of London were thronged with residents and visitors eager to witness every part of the great day. My dear wife Fanny was not only among them, but has acquired a number of memorabilia, including an

overpriced china coronation mug, a considerably garish wall plaque and a rather handsome horse brass, which have fairly taken up every available space in the parlour.

Saturday, 4 October 1902

I have been much taken with work these past few weeks and have been unable to jot even a few lines in my journal. Indeed, today is the first day I have been able to return home at a reasonable hour and when I did I was greeted with some rather astounding news. 'William!' my dear wife cried the moment I opened the door, and she came rushing to the hall to relieve me of my coat. 'You look quite windswept! Take a seat and I'll bring you your tea.' I could see she looked very bright, which is cause for some cheer for she has been quite forlorn since our lodgers' daughter Lily left last week, called away on family business of some urgency in Dublin, which may explain why she has been so urgently checking the post these past few weeks. 'I've got some news, William. Sit, sit, won't you, and I'll tell you all about it.'

Once I had taken my seat and my cup of tea, Fanny began by announcing some less than astounding news. 'Edith has a new lodger.'

'Indeed,' I said.

'William,' said Fanny quite crossly, 'just listen. The lodger's taken Edith's back parlour on Danbury Street for five shillings a week and she's paid in advance —'

'Yes, yes,' I said, blowing impatiently on my tea.

'Well, Edith says her new lodger is an odd one and not quite right in the head. She says she was a nurse at St Thomas's and that all her luggage has been left in Yorkshire and will soon arrive, but there hasn't been a single case yet. Her name is Mrs Walters . . .'

'Mrs *Walters*?' Quickly I put down my tea. 'Are you sure?'

'That's right. She gave Edith her card saying she wants to advertise her services. And listen to this, she told Edith she's expecting a baby and she'll be taking it to a lady in Piccadilly to be adopted. She even asked if Edith would mind its being in the house one night . . .'

'And who,' I enquired sharply, 'was to bring her the baby?'

'Well, that's it!' cried Fanny. 'It's a Nurse Sach. A Nurse Sach of Claymore House, East Finchley.'

'Good God,' I murmured.

'Mrs Walters told Edith the babies of Claymore House are always being taken away to be adopted . . . by *ladies*,' said Fanny in a most sarcastic manner. 'But she says she's very displeased with the work there. She told Edith she wouldn't go back to Claymore House if she could get nursing cases outside, and that's why she wanted to put a monthly nurse card in the window. She said, William,' and Fanny lowered her voice, 'that she has to do all the dirty work and the other one reaps all the benefit.'

'Indeed,' I said, 'the "other one" being Nurse Sach?'

'Who else! And Mrs Walters was in quite a state this morning. She told Edith she's just waiting for the word, she's expecting a telegram and when it comes she will be bringing a baby back. And just think, whose baby will that be? Where's that Nurse Sach getting the baby from, William? And see how she's willing to cast it out like some mangy dog! Titled lady, I don't think so. No, that baby will be abandoned, left to its fate, thrown upon the streets . . .' Fanny was now so agitated that she nearly knocked the sugar bowl from the table. 'What's wrong with us all? There should be a law against it.'

'Fanny, my dear,' I told her as calmly as possible, 'you know very well there is a law against it.'

'Yes, but what good are laws if there is no one willing to

enforce them? And where is the *law*, William, that would force a father to claim his child?'

Friday, 10 October 1902
I return from work to find Fanny once again in a state of great excitement.

'William, you wouldn't believe it!' she cried as soon as I came through the door. 'Mrs Walters has had a telegram! Edith saw her this afternoon setting off in a hurry with her basket saying she was going to fetch the baby!'

At this I turned and left the house, for if we are to establish that Mrs Walters is receiving a baby from Nurse Sach of Claymore House, and if we are to find out what she intends to do with it, then we need to move as quickly as possible.

22

Lily Painter

The day I left my family's lodgings in Stanley Road is one I cannot forget, however much I would like to. It was a winter's day it seemed, although only September still, and it was dark and gloomy out. I left home early, carrying just a small bag packed with my few clothes and some baby garments that I had begun, secretly, to make in the dull quiet hours when I was not upon the stage. Wistfully I looked back at what had been my home, for I had been happy there and I didn't know if or when I would return.

As I reached the Holloway Road I looked around at the people going to work and was overcome with such a sense of dread that for a moment I could not walk. But on I stumbled and, as I did, I felt as if the walls of the houses on the streets would fall on me. And I felt such guilt, for I had lied to my father, told him his brother had written from Dublin, that he needed me there to help him in a show, that he had even sent the money for my fare. I said I would write when I arrived, that I would return as soon as I could, and if they suspected anything, then they did not say. And Gus, I didn't know if I was right not to tell him, but I didn't know what he would do if he knew. However fearful I was of what was to come, I only wanted to have my baby and to see it adopted, and for it to live a better life than I could give.

When I arrived at Claymore House, Nurse Sach was not at home. I was quite relieved, for while I had saved enough money from my turn at the Empire for the first few weeks of my confinement, after that I did not know what I would do. Instead the door was opened by a young girl with sunken cheeks, her limp hair drawn tight behind her ears, a tattered blue and white apron hanging from her waist.

'Yes?' she asked.

'Is Nurse Sach here?'

'No. She expecting you?'

'I'm Lily,' I told her, clutching my small bag in my hands.

'Are you?' she said with an arch of the eyebrows. 'Hester,' she said, opening the door just wide enough so that I could come in. 'How much is she charging you then?'

'A guinea a week,' I murmured.

'So, you're in the attic, with Rosina. Come on then.' Hester set off up the stairs and meekly I went after her. When we reached the first landing I saw a child sitting patiently on the stairs, a catapult in his hands. 'This is Archie. He's mine,' Hester said a little fiercely. 'Wait there,' she told the boy, 'I'm coming back down.'

'He's a lovely boy,' I said.

'Huh,' said Hester, not turning her head. 'Just don't go asking who the father is.'

'No,' I said, for I would not have dreamt of asking any such thing.

'He was a passing fancy and I don't care for him any more,' Hester said with an angry scowl. 'He wouldn't even give me a penny for my boy, because that's how it is, isn't it? We pay for our few moments of pleasure with pain and poverty.' Hester stopped then upon the stairs. 'Still, this house is better than some places I've been. Here we are, this is your room.'

It was an attic room, a bare little space, with two beds, a single chair and a washing stand in the corner with jug and basin both sorely cracked.

'This is Lily,' said Hester, speaking to a young girl with a small, delicate face and wide-set eyes who lay quite motionless upon the bed. 'This is Rosina.'

'Oh, how nice to have company,' said Rosina, attempting to sit up. 'My head really hums today! Perhaps doctor could come again and give me a tonic?' Rosina smiled, and it was a little girl's smile with dimples so deep I fancy I could have lost my finger in them.

'A tonic?' Hester snorted and left the room.

'Doctor was here just Thursday, and when he prodded around inside me,' Rosina told me with a blush, 'he said baby had turned around and now its head is down and due to come, so it's all going to be over soon. Georgie won't half be relieved.' Rosina smiled affectionately so that I knew Georgie was her sweetheart. 'He says this is the only way, and he's right, isn't he?' She moved to the edge of her bed and pulled up her petticoats so that I should see her legs. 'See how swollen they are? And these veins are ready to burst! I can't even get a pair of boots on any more, I'm so swollen – with water I suppose.' Then she laid out her hands and I saw her fingers were sorely swollen too. 'Sometimes,' Rosina said softly, 'I have to hammer them on the wall to take the awful pain out of them.' She sighed and looked around the room. 'It's all right here, you know. We keep ourselves to ourselves and we won't be here long, will we? And it's a luxury being in bed every day, though I wish there was something pretty like a looking glass.'

Rosina was so delicate and so sweet it was no wonder that, despite her swollen legs and hands, she wanted a looking glass, whereas I was happy not to see myself in any glass ever again. Looking glasses belonged to my variety days; they reminded me of when I sat and applied my make-up and felt that trembling excitement of what was to come. Now I didn't want to see myself at all.

'You know, Lily, you look so familiar.'

'Do I?' I kept my face away from her then, busied myself with my belongings, wondering where to store them.

'Yes, I feel I've seen you somewhere before.'

It was then that we heard a dreadful sobbing coming from across the landing, and another girl came to the doorway of our attic room.

'Hullo, Ada,' said Rosina. 'This is Lily.'

'Can I come in here?' asked Ada, and I could see, from her bright face and the way she stood, that she was a girl of determined cheerfulness. 'Maggie won't let up. She's quite hysterical today, she's been crying for I don't know how long. Do you know what she asked me this morning? She asked me where the baby would come from!' Ada laughed, but not in meanness, and oh, Ada had such a laugh, she fair opened her mouth, showing a row of crooked teeth, so that it was impossible not to want to laugh with her as well. 'What do you want, Lily?' she asked, coming into the room.

I thought for a moment that she was asking what I wanted in life, but then she patted her stomach and said, 'I want a girl. I know it's silly, but yes,' she nodded, 'I want a little girl. And I'm going to choose a Bible name. I'm going to call her Catherine and whoever takes her, I'm going to tell them that.'

I looked at Ada then and I thought if I was to have a girl then I would call her Martha, because it was a pretty name, a name for a girl who would belong to a lady.

The days that followed at Claymore House took on a strangeness I had never known before, a waiting, a not knowing what would come. Every morning Rosina and Ada and I made the fire and swept our rooms and then we sat together and sewed and knitted for hour upon hour, making vests and gowns and nighties, bibs and shawls and booties. We embroidered them with the initials we had chosen and then we folded them neatly into the boxes we kept beside our beds. We knew we would not see our babies for long and we wanted to send them away with everything they would need. Nurse Sach encouraged us in this and said the ladies would be most pleased. But as night came we lost our sense of hope and our spirits became low, and very often I lay in bed and heard Rosina hammering her poor swollen fingers upon the wall until I had to cover my ears, unable to listen any more.

Sometimes Nurse Sach appeared in our attic room and I looked forward to this, for she seemed to bring fresh air and a feeling of the outside world with her. I hoped she might bring her little girl one day, the child that had run so lovingly into her arms the first time I came to Claymore House. But she never did.

Some days I went downstairs and sat with Hester and helped her with her work, or tended to her boy, just for something to do, for I was not used to being idle. One morning I began to sing while I cleaned and my voice felt strange and unfamiliar. But the others said it sounded beautiful and begged for me to sing them songs they knew, until I said I was too tired, afraid that one of them would know me from the stage.

On some days Mrs Walters came to Claymore House, always with her basket and her big black cloak, and she too sat in the kitchen, complaining of her health and taking nips from a bottle she kept in a pocket in her dress. 'Ah Lily, my love,' she would say, 'I'm not feeling well today. I'm only longing for the time to be at rest and to join my dear husband, who is ever near. Oh how I long to be at rest!' One morning I sat there, feeling the baby inside me swimming so, and I asked out loud what the future would be and Mrs Waters looked at me and laughed.

'The future, Lily?' she said, and she took a swig from her bottle and her face flushed red and she began to cough. 'That's in God's hands, bless His Holy name.'

In the third week Maggie, the girl who didn't know where babies came from, had her child. The doctor was called and he used the tongs to get the baby out and there was an awful lot of blood and Maggie shouted, 'Oh help me! I know I'm going to die!' It was that evening that I heard Hester have a dreadful row with Nurse Sach. I was about to come downstairs when I heard their voices in the hall, and I hesitated where I was upon the landing.

'Get out,' Nurse Sach said to Hester, and she sounded quite unlike her normal self. 'Get your things and get out at once. Who are you to ask me about my business? I only asked you to do one small thing! All these years, Hester, all these years and I ask you to do one little thing and this is how you repay me!'

'But it's not the first time, is it?' said Hester in a sulky manner. 'All right then, I'm going.' There was a clattering in the hall then as she gathered her things and called for her boy, Archie. Still I looked down from the landing, and I saw Hester holding Archie by the one hand and a small case by the other, and Nurse Sach standing with her back against the wall, watching.

'I'll be glad to go,' said Hester as she moved towards the front door, 'and then there will be nothing on my conscience, will there?'

At this Nurse Sach seemed to have a change of heart, and I saw her reach out quickly and take hold of Hester's arm. 'Wait a minute,' she said, 'don't be so hasty.'

'Let go of me,' Hester said, but she didn't move to take Nurse Sach's hand away.

'Hester,' said Nurse Sach, and her voice grew soft and sweet.

'I was wrong to shout at you like that, yes I was, and I can't very well stand here and see you and your little boy walking into the dead of night with nowhere to stay.'

'I'll go to my sister's,' said Hester, but her voice was muffled and I watched as reluctantly she put her small case down upon the hallway floor.

'Forgive me,' said Nurse Sach, and she patted Hester upon the arm. 'Come back inside where it's warm. Sleep on it, Hester, and if your mind is still made up tomorrow then I shan't try to change it.'

Then Hester agreed, she and Archie retreated to their first-floor room, and I returned to the attic, thinking it odd that all the while they had been quarrelling Maggie's baby had slept so quietly next door and hadn't made a sound.

23

The pain began on a morning in the sixth week and I felt it more or less all day so that by evening I found it hard to keep my voice steady. Rosina sat with me and urged me to squeeze her swollen hand. 'Who will have her baby first, Lily?' she teased. 'You or me?' But when Nurse Sach was called she took one look at me, as she stood there at the door still in her bonnet and shawl, and said, 'Baby's coming early then.' She removed her outdoor clothing and called for Hester. 'Fetch the flannels and hot water,' she told her, 'a skein of sewing thread and lard. Out,' she said to Ada and Rosina, rolling the sleeves of her blouse high upon her arms. 'This isn't the place for a crowd.'

When Hester came walking heavily up the stairs, her little boy Archie trailing behind her, Nurse Sach sent her back down to fetch some old newspapers from the scullery. When the newspapers were brought, Nurse Sach spread them all out across the floor around my bed and I looked at them in a kind of wonder, not knowing why they were there. She moved me from the bed then, laid some sheeting on the mattress, and then she passed a broad bandage around my body. When she was done, I cried a little in fear and could barely drink the tablespoonful of castor oil she insisted I take.

Then I was alone and time passed until I could see, from the tiny attic window, that it was night-time now, and sometimes I floated and dozed and dreamt of I knew not what, to be woken by the pain again. And then I felt a great weight bearing down upon my body and Nurse Sach was there.

'Lie on your left-hand side,' she told me, and her voice was harsh. 'Draw up your knees, Lily, and bend yourself forward.' I did as I was told, although I felt a cramp of such severity it was as if my legs were turned to iron. 'Now push against the bedpost with your feet,' she told me. 'Push now, push.' I reached out with my feet and found the bedpost and I pushed upon it until I thought the bones in my feet would crack.

When daylight came, still I was no nearer to the end and it was then I felt my body begin to tremble and to tremor and then to thrash, so violently and so dreadfully that the very bed shook. Nurse Sach thrust a piece of sweet-smelling flannel before me and told me to inhale. I turned my face away, but she took my head and turned it back. 'If it was good enough for Her Majesty, Lily, then it's good enough for you.' And so I did as I was told and I felt my head begin to melt and I felt a thunder in my ears and then everything went quiet. And then the sounds came – I thought I heard Ada and Rosina laughing, I thought I heard an audience first cheering applause and then suddenly roaring disapproval; and I felt a panic rise inside me and then everything went black.

'You should have called me earlier.' It was a man's voice, a man's voice in the room, and he seemed to be speaking from very far away, as if he were down in the kitchen or out in the street and I somehow able to hear him. I opened my eyes, saw the doctor by my bedside. 'What have you given her?' he demanded of Nurse Sach. 'What? I told you never to administer that yourself, and it's too hot in here, open the window.'

'Oh, it's perfectly safe,' muttered Nurse Sach. 'I'm a trained midwife, for goodness' sake.' But she must have opened the window for I heard a creak and then the cold night air rushed like a demon into the room. The doctor did not look at me as he moved down to the foot of the bed, although indeed it was so dark in the room that I could not see him well. But I could feel him as he lifted the blanket that covered me and as the mattress sank a little under the weight of his hands. 'How long has this been going on? She's very small. There isn't room here for a bird to pass.' Then I felt a swell inside me and again I pushed upon the bedposts and at last it happened, a feeling that I was about to lose something vast that was part of me, and finally my baby came.

'Well, look at that,' said Nurse Sach. 'It's a girl.'

'A girl?' I asked, and desperately I tried to move, to turn on to my back so that I could see my baby; I so wanted to see how my baby looked. But Nurse Sach had taken my baby and she was wrapping her, and I could just see a glimpse of wet black hair peeping out from inside the flannel I had made.

'Please,' I said, holding out my hands, but the doctor shouted suddenly and there was much flooding then, the blood came fast and hard, and I heard him say, 'The afterbirth is grown to her side. What have you got? Give her brandy.'

Nurse Sach held a bottle to my lips and oh, how it burnt, how it felt like fire upon my dry lips. And then I felt the doctor's arm inside me, felt it rough and hard and thick as his fingers tore my flesh from my side. The blood poured so greatly then that it soaked though my clothes and through the mattress and dripped upon the newspapers on the floor until they were as crimson as the tunic I had once worn upon the stage.

When I came to I could feel my underclothes stiff and soiled and I looked around for my baby but she was nowhere to be seen. I could feel the bandaged towel had been buckled tightly around my body, although I couldn't remember this being done or by whom. Hester came and she was gentle then, as she washed my face, my neck and my hands.

'She's a lovely little thing,' she said, rinsing out the cloth.

'Is she? Oh please, Hester, I want to see her so, please bring her to me.'

Hester stopped with the cloth in her hand, her face unsure. Then she left the room quickly and came back with a bundle, and she pulled back the flannel so I could see. I looked at my baby and she was yellow, like a plum without its skin, and I felt this couldn't be right. In the folds of her skin was a white greasy curd and in other parts the skin was red and inflamed, and she shone from the lard that the washing had not removed.

'Her name is Martha,' I told Hester, and as I said her name the soft white skin of her eyelids opened and we looked at each other. And then what joy there was, to look upon my child, to look with a feeling that I had something all of my own. I held her and with all my heart I prayed for a happy ending. Then Nurse Sach came and she scolded Hester and took my baby and said she was to dress it.

'Baby is very weak,' said Nurse Sach the next day when she came and offered me some tepid gruel. 'You do want the best for her, don't you, Lily?'

'Yes,' I said. I could not move much then, for my body hurt and my feet were tender from where they had pressed so hard upon the bedpost.

'So then, have you considered what we discussed before, Lily?'

My eyes filled with tears because I had thought of nothing else and I knew I could not keep my baby and I knew I had to do what was best for her.

'You're lucky,' said Nurse Sach as she sat down upon the edge of my bed, 'because I have a lady waiting on a baby just now in Piccadilly, a titled lady. She is dying for a baby, Lily, a sweet little baby to call her own. She will hire a wet nurse for her, Lily, and feed her till she's plump, and she will get everything that is best in life.'

'She will be kind to my baby, won't she?' I asked.

'Of course she will,' smiled Nurse Sach. 'And only thirty guineas . . .'

'But thirty guineas . . .' I said, my voice faltering. 'I don't know if I can . . .'

'I'll write to the lady,' said Nurse Sach kindly, 'and I'll see if we can get it done for less. She's a lady of a good position, perhaps she won't mind.'

'Can I see my baby?' I asked.

'No, baby is sleeping now.'

The next day Nurse Sach came at teatime and said she had a telegram. 'Lily,' she said, as she sat once more upon my bed, 'the lady has written. She says she's willing to take the baby for twenty-five guineas.'

'I will try . . .'

Nurse Sach smiled and patted me on the arm. 'You can pay half now if you like and the remaining later, and you will have to sign a paper giving up claim to the baby.'

'Please,' I said, 'tell the lady her name is Martha. She will be kind to baby, won't she?'

'She will be very kind,' said Nurse Sach. And then she left and came back with my baby and said, 'Now kiss it goodbye.'

And I did. I closed my eyes and I felt the softness of my baby's cheeks with my lips and I began to kiss her and to sob until Nurse Sach said that was quite enough and wouldn't do at all.

*   *   *

My baby had gone. My flesh began to knot into lumps and milk began to ooze, and each day my bandage was tightened further. Hester covered me in flannels and a poultice and still it did no good. But I tried to console myself: my baby would live with a titled lady, she would be well fed and well loved. And although I had signed away my claim on the piece of paper Nurse Sach had given me, although I did not know the name of the lady nor her address, I knew that one day I would see my baby again, for Nurse Sach had said I would be allowed to see her twice a year. And I knew that just a glimpse of her would be enough, that I would gladly stand cold and ragged and shivering in the street just to catch a glimpse of my baby in a carriage going by and to know that she was well. It was my gift to her, my gift of a better life.

24

'You have a gentleman here to see you,' said Nurse Sach one morning after my baby had gone. I had heard, even before she arrived at my door, the sound of unfamiliar footsteps on the stairs. I had thought it was a new girl whom I had not yet met, although I knew the steps were too heavy for that. And when she said 'gentleman' I could not think who it could be, I could think only of my father and I was terrified that he had found me. And so when I looked up fearfully from my bed, I could not believe my eyes.

'Lily,' said Gus, 'I . . .'

So big he was, standing in the doorway! His arms hung low by his sides and his hands clasped the door frame so fiercely I could see the whiteness of his knuckles. I so wanted Nurse Sach to leave us then – I was dreaming and I did not want her in my dream when Gus Chevalier was there. But in she came and she fussed around the room, adjusting the curtains, picking up a piece of flannel and folding it in her hands. I wanted her to go so I could look at him before my dream broke and I had to wake. Then Nurse Sach bowed her head a little, cast me an odd look from the corner of her eyes and was gone. Then how Gus flew to my bed, how he fell upon his knees and clasped my hand, how he raised his eyebrows and smiled at me in his quizzical way.

'Oh Lily, you should have told me.'

And then I knew it wasn't a dream and I remembered where I was and why, remembered too my soiled underclothes and the stained mattress beneath me. I felt so dirty then that I pulled my hand away. 'How did you find me?'

'I asked Daisy,' he said. 'If only you had told me,' and he looked around the room and I could see that the bare furnishings distressed him. 'You could have written! All those letters I wrote, Lily, and you never said a word.'

I felt angry then, for what good would it have done if I had told him? What would he have done?

'Where is she?' and he smiled playfully then and began to finger at my hands.

'They tell me it's a baby girl. Who does she look like, Lily? Does she look so pretty like her mother?'

And then I saw he didn't know, that he didn't understand at all, and I began to sob.

'What is it? What's wrong?'

I could not speak; I could not bear to hear him talk this way. And then at last I told him, 'She's gone.'

'Gone? Gone where?' And again Gus looked around the room.

'Oh Gus! I didn't know what to do, I had to come here before everyone found out, and think, what could I give her? Nothing! Much better that a lady take her, that she grow up to be a lady's child. And she was so weak, Gus, so very weak when she was born . . .'

'So she's gone?' Gus stood up and I saw a pulsing at his jaw. 'Just like that?'

'And why not! What else could I do?'

There was a light knock upon the door then and Nurse Sach came in. 'Don't mind me. Here's your tea, Lily,' and she handed me a plate, a very clean large plate, and upon it was a freshly cooked mutton chop. She helped me to lift the meat to my mouth and as she did so she turned to Gus and said, 'There is the matter of the rest of the money. That's twelve guineas left for the lady, sir, and then there's the next few weeks while Lily gets herself right.'

Gus looked at me and there was a coldness in his blue eyes, and when I nodded he took his wallet and counted out some banknotes and with his fingers trembling slightly he handed them to Nurse Sach. And I thought, Does he really want her? Does he really want our baby? Perhaps with Gus by my side we could find a way to keep our baby, but as I tried to speak to tell him this, he had already reached the door and I felt a rushing in my ears and the world went dark again.

That evening I woke to find that Gus had gone. I heard more footsteps upon the stairs and the doctor came in. He nodded at me wordlessly and I flinched when I saw him, thought of his arm pulling away at my insides. He instructed me to lie still on my side while he examined me, and I did as I was told but my legs would not stop trembling. At last he put away his instruments and he closed his doctor's bag and left, and then I heard him in the hallway, heard his words quite clearly as he spoke to Nurse Sach. 'Where's her baby?' he asked.

'The baby?' asked Nurse Sach in surprise. 'Her sister has it in Holloway.'

I waited to hear if the doctor would say more, but he only said, 'Good evening' and I heard his footsteps going back down the stairs. Nurse Sach did not return to my room and I lay there thinking, Why didn't she tell the doctor about the lady who has my baby? Why did she say my sister has her? And for a second I almost thought it was true, that my sister Ellen did have my baby with her in our room at Stanley Road. I almost wanted it to be so. But the lady had my baby; surely the lady had my baby by now, for I had kissed her and said goodbye; surely she was being nursed and loved. And now I would find her; as soon as I had my strength again then Gus and I would find her and we would bring her back.

Later I heard noises below, footsteps in the hallway and muffled voices. I thought I heard Mrs Walters and the tap tap of her stick upon the floor. Then the front door closed again. I fell asleep and awoke in the darkness to find Nurse Sach standing over me.

'Did my baby go?' I asked.

'Yes,' she said curtly.

'To the lady in Piccadilly?'

'To the lady in Piccadilly.'

'But you told the doctor –'

'I told the doctor what?' said Nurse Sach sharply. 'She went just this evening, Lily. The lady came and fetched baby just now.'

'Just now?' I asked, struggling to sit upon the bed. 'But I thought –'

'You thought what?' said Nurse Sach, and she stared at me with a hardness in her eyes and then she turned and closed the door.

The following day Rosina had her baby and it was a boy and she called him James. I was the first to see him, and Rosina said if things had been different then I could have been his godmother, and I cried at this. I helped her hold him in her arms, saw he had the most beautiful green eyes, and I watched her wrap him tenderly in the soft blue flannel she had spent so long embroidering with his name. That night a telegram was sent, for Hester told me so, and a lady came and took Rosina's baby, and so now both our babies were gone and only Ada with her determined cheerfulness was left waiting to have her child.

25

Annie Sweet

April 2009

Molly didn't pass the audition, so she won't be having a starring role as an ox after all. They didn't write or email or ring and so I had to call the agency myself. 'She did very well,' said the agency woman, 'they all did very well, but none of them were quite right.' And I think of all the effort Molly put into being an ox and her song and dance, and the cab we took, and it all seems such a colossal waste of time and money.

It's Thursday and we're on our way to school. I'm not temping today, I could have done something fun with Molly later. But instead she's going to Jodie's house and I've booked myself into the local history centre to use the microfiche machine. We've got the dog with us, and she's pulling on the lead like she wants to escape. As we walk down the pavement, people part to let us pass; they don't like the look of Jojo at all. I haven't told Molly this, but two days ago a Staffy mix dog was stolen from a boy on Holloway Road and CCTV cameras found it an hour later, being kicked half to death.

'Why can't you pick me up from school today?' Molly asks as we get to Archway.

'Because you're going to Jodie's.'

'But only because you asked them to have me.'

Molly is good at this; she's an expert at inducing guilt. And she's right in a way, because although I asked Jodie's mother if we could have her daughter to play, when she suggested that Molly go to theirs instead I jumped at the chance.

'I told you, I'm going to the local history place, I'm going to find out more about our house.'

Molly rolls her eyes. 'That's not really important, Mum.'

'Not to you, no, but it is to me.'

I drop Molly off at school and start to walk home. Every time we pass a baby in a buggy Jojo pulls towards them and wants to sniff the baby and I have to say, 'Sorry, she's really friendly' because the mothers look scared. I don't know why I've never thought of this before, but maybe Jojo used to live with a family that had a baby; maybe she's even looking for that baby now, checking everyone who goes by. I wish the people at Battersea had told me more about her past.

I get home and fill up her water bowl, give her a Kong toy stuffed with cheese and dog snacks, hope that will keep her busy while I'm out. But she knows I'm going; she shadows me, her tail slapping unhappily against her legs. I'm just closing the kitchen door when I think I hear a sound upstairs and for a crazy second I think it's Ben. I go cautiously along the hall and look up the stairs, and of course there's no one there, it's just a flashback moment because this was how it finally happened, this is what I've been trying so hard not to think about for so long.

I'd taken Molly to school just like this morning. I was going shopping after that; Ben had given me a list of things that would take me some time to get, like a lead he needed for his phone. But I'd forgotten my card and had to come home and then, because it was such a lovely day, I'd opened the back door and sat outside and drank some coffee. It was secluded in the garden: the ivy covered one whole section of the trellis, and the lilac next door had come into bloom and the honeysuckle was just beginning to put out wet little yellow fingers. I closed my eyes and listened to a woman chatting somewhere on a balcony or at an open window, the clang of scaffolding further down the street. Then I heard another sound, like a yelp. I opened my eyes, put my coffee cup down, half expecting a cat to come leaping over the trellis. Then I got the strangest feeling, and without thinking what I was doing, or why, I walked back into the house and through the kitchen to the bottom of the stairs, when I heard the sound again. I kept going up the stairs and to the landing and up again and to our bedroom, and there they were. It was warm in the room and there was a smell of perfume and sweat. The floor was littered with discarded clothes. And there was Carrie on her back, her head on my pillow, on my sheets, on my bed, with my husband. For a moment I couldn't think who she was, she was too out of place, she didn't belong here. But there she was, Ben's secretary, who'd come round the day we moved in, the woman who'd shaken my hand and told me what a lovely house I'd found. And I looked at them on the bed and I wished I'd had a gun because I would have shot them both.

'Fuck!' Ben said, and he leapt up and grabbed his dressing gown. 'Annie, wait.'

But I'd already left the bedroom and dizzy with fury I rushed back down to the kitchen and out into the garden again. I was like someone who has just been told some dreadful news and can't take it in and instead just resumes what they were doing. So I sat there in the garden by my cup of cold coffee, my fingers shaking. I heard footsteps coming down the stairs and the front door open and close, just as I had heard viewers going up and down the stairs and in and out the front door that first summer's day we viewed the house.

'Annie,' Ben said, coming out into the garden.

'Don't fucking come near me.'

'I'm sorry.'

'Sorry?' That was it?

'That you had to find out like this.'

'Oh, for God's sake.' I turned and looked at him although I almost couldn't bear to; I didn't want to see what he was wearing or what expression he had on his face or how he was standing or what he would say next. 'Then why the fuck did you bring her into our house! Of all the stupid, cruel things to do! You wanted me to find out, didn't you, Ben? Because you're a bloody coward and you couldn't bring yourself to tell me what was going on, could you? All this time, all this time I've been asking if something was wrong and obviously there was. I can't *believe* you would do this.'

'Annie . . .'

'You are such a shit.'

'It goes two ways you know.'

'What the fuck do you mean, it goes two ways?'

'I mean I've been unhappy for a while.'

'*You've* been unhappy?'

'Well, you haven't been the easiest person to live with you know.'

'*I'm* not the easiest person to live with?' I threw my cup on to the garden paving stones, and when it didn't smash I picked it up and threw it again. 'What about you? Ben, you're the one who's done this! How the fuck can it go both ways?'

'Annie, if you calm down we can talk about this.'

'Calm down! Why? What is there to talk about? What on earth could there be to talk about? You brought her here, Ben. You brought her into our house.' I stood up then, feeling sick rise in my throat. 'Have you thought what you're going to tell Molly?'

'No.'

'Funny that, isn't it?' And suddenly the future seemed to stretch ahead of me, the telling Molly, the moving out, the separation, the telling everyone else, the days and the nights alone. I didn't want to talk about it; it was done. Ben had shattered everything and I'd never be able to look at him again. I stormed towards him and shoved him backwards with my hands and screamed loud enough for every neighbour on the street to hear, 'Get out! Get out of my house!'

26

I get to the local history centre, put my things in a locker and tell the woman at the desk my name. She takes me over to two old machines in the corner of the room that look like the sort of computers the teacher used to wheel self-importantly into the classroom when I was sixteen. She points to a wooden cabinet, asks which year of the *Islington Gazette* I would like to read. I tell her 1901 because this was the date of the census, so I feel it's where things might start.

'Here, I'll do that.' Danny appears, a little sleepy-looking, that same languid look on his face. 'How's things?' he asks, and he pulls out a chair for me and I sit down at the microfiche machine.

There's a couple next to me, both elderly. The man has a folder in his lap and lots of photocopied sheets. They're talking in whispers so I whisper to Danny as well: 'I don't know how to do this.'

He laughs, opens a drawer in the wooden cabinet behind me and starts looking. 'You said 1901? What month?'

'April,' I say for no reason, except that it's April now.

He picks out a small white paper box, unties the string that holds it together, and takes out a circular black reel of film. Then he expertly slots it in place on the microfiche machine, pulls out the film quite roughly and binds that in place too. Now I'm looking at the blurry image of a newspaper page.

'There you go,' says Danny, showing me how to use the buttons to scroll up and down and how to adjust the focus. 'I'll leave you to it.'

I press a button and suddenly the words on the screen start whizzing by so fast they become one white blur and there's a dreadful mechanical rattling noise like the whole machine is going to explode. Then, just as suddenly, it stops. I'm looking at the front page of the *Islington Gazette* for April 1901. I press the button, slowly now, read an advert for Beecham's pills that make you look well, feel well and keep well. It just seems to be adverts on the front page, which is odd. So I scroll down and the font is so small, I don't know how anyone used to read it. I have to squint my eyes and focus hard, and although I don't know what I'm looking for, I already feel anxious in case I might miss it.

I come to another set of adverts, which look a little like show bills. There's drama and vaudeville, plays and shows, comedians and comediennes, lady baritones and mimics, dancing dogs and a troupe of jugglers, even a minstrel show. I look over at my elderly neighbours; they're making notes now, frowning hard at their screen. I fiddle around with the buttons on my machine until the words are enlarged, and I see a small headline saying 'Holloway Empire' and I wonder if that's where the Odeon is now. I begin to read.

Every week a fresh programme at this popular palace of varieties, and the bill that was submitted last night was received with enthusiasm by the crowded audience attracted to the two performances. That very talented comedian Frankie Monk is here, and also the Trapnelle Family, the clever acrobatic troupe. Both these turns are admirable in their way and in themselves fully worth the small charge made at the entrance doors; but there are other items which command general approval.

I smile as I read. It's a dull review, but I like the language, the careful choice of words.

Particular mention can be made of the chorus girls, such charming young ladies and, in the case of Lily Painter, most talented and shapely.

'God!' I say out loud. The couple next to me glance over. 'Sorry,' I say, but I can't believe it; I've found her, I've found my Lily Painter just like that. Here she is, here's her name, and here she was performing as a chorus girl at the Holloway Empire. Then I think it could be another Lily Painter; it could just be someone with the same name. But I'm sure it's not, I'm sure it's her. I'm sure this is the Lily who used to live in my house. I put my pad on the desk and start to write things down, the date, the page number, the names of the other performers, but my hands are a little shaky and my handwriting wild.

'Do you know if this prints out?' I ask the couple next to me.

'It's supposed to, but we've been having trouble with it,' says the man. He shows me which button to press on my machine, but when I press it nothing happens.

'I'll go and ask for help,' I say, standing up. I can see the man's papers clearly now, see that he's holding a photocopied death certificate, and on their microfiche screen the couple are reading the *Islington Gazette* as well. I lean a little closer and see from the headline that it's a news report about someone who died falling down the stairs.

'Is it a relative?' I ask, looking from the death certificate to the microfiche machine.

They hesitate, and then at last the woman says, 'Yes.' The couple look away from me then and I feel uncomfortable standing here, unable to ask anything else as they clearly don't want to talk about it. It troubles me that we've all just found what we were looking for, that we've all been looking in the past for something important to us, and that it's made me so happy and them so sad.

I can't believe it's five o'clock already; I'm going to have to go. I haven't eaten and I feel light-headed and hungry. The machine won't print out and Danny says I'll have to come back when it's fixed, but that doesn't matter because I've found my Lily Painter and if she was in the music hall, if she was a chorus girl, then I'll be able to find out more. Maybe she went on to bigger and better things, maybe she became a star; Molly would like that, to think that a music-hall star once lived in our house.

I pick Molly up from Jodie's house. She lives in a flat near the school and the living room is full of baby paraphernalia: nappies and nappy bags and wipes and plastic toys and discarded bottles of milk.

'Sorry about the mess,' says Jodie's mother. I know her name now, it's Lisa. She picks up her baby boy, who is howling as usual.

'I hope Molly was OK.'

'Oh, she was a great help. It's always much easier if Jodie has someone to play with.'

I look around the room, see in the corner an odd wire sculpture of a woman, her hands together as if in prayer. 'That's lovely,' I say, and Lisa smiles and jiggles her howling baby up and down in her arms, and I know it's her who made the sculpture and that it belongs to a life before she had kids.

'Thanks so much for having her,' I say, and I wonder if Lisa has a partner and I have a feeling that if she does then he isn't much help.

*   *   *

We get home and I hurry Molly into her bath because I can't wait to look up the Holloway Empire, to begin building an image of how Lily Painter's life might have been. Molly asks me when I'm going downstairs and I tell her soon, and happy with that she starts whispering to her lizard. I sit in front of my computer, ready to start, when Mum rings.

'Annie,' she says, 'I can't talk for long.'

'Fine,' I say, and I hold the phone under my chin and start googling Holloway Empire.

'Your father wondered if you had any plans for the summer.'

'No, no plans.'

'What are you doing? I can hear a tapping sound.'

'Sorry, I'm just . . . typing something.'

'Oh well, I better get off.'

'No, wait, Mum, I wanted to tell you this anyway. I found a list of people who used to live in my house. They're all on the 1901 census.'

'Oh yes.' Mum couldn't sound less interested if she tried.

'Yes, there were two families here and one of the daughters was called Lily Painter, which I thought was a really lovely name. Well, today I went to the local history centre and I found out she was a music-hall star. Well, not a star maybe, but she was in the music hall.'

'Oh yes.'

'Isn't that interesting?' I ask. I sound like Molly, the way she speaks when she wants me to sound amazed and I'm not.

'I don't know what you want to find out about her for.'

'Because she used to live here! Because I wanted to know what this house would have been like back then.'

'Have you spoken to Ben recently?'

'No,' I say, feeling furious, 'I haven't.'

*   *   *

I wake up suddenly in the night. Something has woken me, but I don't know what. I can just about hear Molly sleeping in her room and there's a faint beeping noise coming from the kitchen because the dog must have opened the freezer door again. She needn't have bothered; I don't use the freezer any more. But I can't hear anything that would have woken me up. I'm not sure what time it is, but I know I fell asleep early. I hear quick, high-heeled footsteps on the street outside. Maybe the pubs have just closed, or maybe it's later than that. It's freezing in here tonight, as if the temperature has suddenly plummeted and a winter storm has rolled in. The curtains shiver and I realise I've left the window open, although it's unlike me to leave it open at night.

The phone rings from my office, frighteningly loud, and I think maybe it rang before and that's what woke me. I stumble a little on the landing, get down to my office, but then the phone stops and I think, *Who would be ringing me at this time?* I stand there looking at the phone, feeling ridiculous. Then I step into the room. It feels strange in here tonight; the air is heavy and unpleasant. I walk towards the window and the floor slopes so suddenly and pulls me with such force that I could almost be drunk. I have to get something done about this room.

I hear a noise from downstairs and then the dog comes padding quickly up the stairs. She gets to the doorway and looks at me nervously. She begins to edge into my office and as she does she gives a growl, a deep broken rumble. 'Shush,' I tell her, afraid she's going to start barking and wake Molly, 'shush!'

Then I remember what I was dreaming just before I woke up. I was watching Molly on a stage, not a stage I've ever seen before, but something very big and grand. I could see she'd forgotten her words and I was trying to shout them out. I must have strained so hard, been so desperate to help her, that I'd shouted them out loud and woken myself. This reassures me, makes me feel I've resolved something, that now I know why I woke. But as I leave my office I see I've left the computer on when I was sure I turned it off hours ago. I sit down at my chair, press a key and the screen comes to life. I see the census role I was looking at earlier and I see the name Lily Painter and my skin begins to prickle. I look at the goosebumps on my arms and think what my Granny Martha would have said: 'Look, love, someone's just walked over your grave.'

27

Inspector William George

November 1902

Tuesday, 11 November 1902

A cold day with a fair chance of snow later. Some weeks have passed since I wrote in my journal, owing partly to my disappointment over the baby farmer Mrs Walters. When she received the telegram from Claymore House I fully assumed that she would soon be back at Danbury Street with a baby, and that police investigations could then have begun in earnest. But to my considerable surprise, Mrs Walters returned home empty-handed. I am baffled as to whether she did intend to collect a baby from Claymore House that night or whether, despite the telegram from Nurse Sach, the entire matter was a false alarm.

Fanny meanwhile remains deeply saddened by the departure of our lodgers' daughter Lily, who is yet to return from Dublin. How odd, says my dear wife, that Lily would have left so suddenly, just when she was doing so well and had such a promising future before her.

Thursday, 13 November 1902

Significant news. Mrs Walters has received another telegram and yesterday afternoon she returned to her lodgings, this time with a baby. The infant is a few days old at most, according to Fanny's friend Edith; it looks healthy, has remarkable green eyes and is wrapped in a pretty blue flannel. Upon hearing this I set off at once to request a meeting with Divisional Superintendent Dyball. I relayed the facts of the case so far, that Nurse Sach, the subject of the anonymous letter, is running a lying-in home called Claymore House and advertising for babies, that Mrs Walters is lodging at Mrs Edith Hacker's house in Danbury Street and has attested that she works for Nurse Sach, and that she has, just yesterday, brought home a baby. There is, I suggested, quite enough evidence to justify surveillance on both Danbury Street and Claymore House, although perhaps not enough to obtain a warrant to enter the lying-in home. Divisional Superintendent Dyball's response was less than enthusiastic. While he agrees there may be something fishy going on, he is most annoyed that I took it upon myself to follow up a case that he had clearly said was a waste of time and resources. He appears to consider this a matter of some insubordination. However, he then announced he would place a detective on watch at Danbury Street and that Detective Wright, a newcomer to the area and said to be a most diligent officer, is just the man for the job. With Mrs Edith Hacker on the inside, as it were, and with Detective Wright observing from the outside, we can at least be assured that Mrs Walters is under close scrutiny and that no harm will come to the baby now in her care.

Friday, 14 November 1902
Fanny barely slept a wink last night fretting about the baby and Mrs Walters and, as we have not heard from Mrs Edith Hacker or Detective Wright this morning, nothing would convince her that things were in hand unless I was to pay a visit myself.

It is quite some time since I have been in the Danbury Street area, and the journey there was frustratingly long, but it is much as I remember it. I alighted from the bus near the police station on Upper Street and walked in a southerly direction down Cross Street until I reached the Duke of Cambridge public house, which surely does one of the largest trades in the area. The residential section of Danbury Street is taken up with squat brown houses, which appear gloomy even in the crisp air of a November day. Indeed, I could not help but feel a sense of foreboding as I crossed the road and made my way to Mrs Edith Hacker's house.

'Inspector,' she said, upon opening the door, 'I was just on my way to you now. Oh, this is terrible, but she's gone.'

'Gone?' I said, aghast. 'And with the baby?'

Mrs Hacker did not reply, but led me into the house and to a downstairs back room where she pushed at the door. It was dim and cold inside and there was an unpleasant lingering smell, which may be due to the back of the house lying so near to the canal.

'Inspector,' she said, 'oh, this is terrible. I never saw Mrs Walters go, but the baby I saw lying on that bed just last night has gone.'

Saturday, 15 November 1902

To my intense frustration, Detective Wright was not on watch at Danbury Street yesterday. I am quite furious at this and can barely bring myself to write the dreadful news that while Mrs Walters eventually returned to her lodgings, the baby did not. Not only that, but Mrs Edith Hacker has now informed us that Mrs Walters received another telegram and, as incredible as it may seem, has returned with another child. It is again a healthy-looking infant and just a few hours old. Mrs Walters has asserted that it is a boy and that it will be going to the wife of a coast-guard who resides at South Kensington.

Sunday, 16 November 1902

Detective Wright is now on watch at Danbury Street. He has been in place for some thirteen hours. As yet, there has been no sign of movement from Mrs Walters, who does not seem disposed to be taking the baby anywhere at present. Mrs Hacker was here but an hour ago to report that Mrs Walters has at least given the infant some bottle and has now lit a fire in the room, both of which allayed our fears somewhat.

Tuesday, 18 November 1902

It is exceedingly late, but I feel it necessary to commit to my journal what has occurred this terrible night. At approximately 4 p.m. this afternoon Detective Wright saw Mrs Walters leave Danbury Street carrying a bundle and, once I heard the news, I found it impossible not to set off myself. Although unsure of Mrs Walters' exact destination, I chose to head for South Kensington station, for if a baby were to be handed over to a would-be adopter then this would be the most likely place. As it turned out, I was right. I arrived at the station to find Detective Wright standing just outside the ladies' lavatory. I alerted him to my presence and we spoke quietly.

'She's in there, sir,' he said, nodding towards the lavatory. 'She was loitering around outside for a while. Now she's been in there for an hour or more.'

'She'll come out,' I told him. 'All we need do is to wait.'

Indeed, some ten minutes later Mrs Walters came hurrying unsteadily out of the ladies' lavatory with a bundle in her arms. She then looked up and down the street several times and made as if to cross.

'Madam! You there!' cried Detective Wright. At this, Mrs Walters looked around and saw the two of us behind her, although she showed no sign of recognising me. 'We are police officers,' said Detective Wright, 'and I want to see what you've got there in your bundle.'

Mrs Walters appeared a little confused at this; indeed, she looked around as if attempting to locate some alarming sound, and still she held the bundle tight in her arms. 'Why?' she asked.

'Because I have reason to believe,' said Detective Wright, 'there is a baby in there and that it is not as it should be. Come with me.'

We led her back into the ladies' lavatory, whereupon Mrs Walters sat down heavily upon a chair. 'I suppose you will take me to the station,' she said as her body began to quiver in a most alarming fashion. I noted how changed she was from the good-natured woman with the homely face I had first met at Arthur Terrace, who had sat before the fire gently sponging a baby on her lap. Her face now was sallow, her bright eyes dim, and as she continued to sit there the quiver became a shake until it seemed she would quite fall from the chair.

'If you don't mind,' said Detective Wright, 'we want to see the baby.'

It was then that Mrs Walters began to unwrap the bundle that lay upon her lap. First she drew back a thin grey shawl, then some equally thin linen, the end of which was clearly marked with a laundry number, and both of which smelt strongly of carbolic acid. Finally she laid the clothes open and revealed what was inside. She sat back quite comfortably on her chair, a strangely contented smile upon her sallow face.

'There he is,' she said, 'the poor little lamb.'

I confess I was totally unprepared for the sight. For there before me was a baby boy in a nightgown, his pitiful body just a few hours old, his jaws and hands tightly clenched, his tiny toes turned completely inwards, his tongue badly swollen and his lips already partly blue.

'He's dead,' said Detective Wright with a tremor in his voice, and he turned to one side and covered his mouth.

I came forward then, to attempt to replace the linen over the pitiful child, but as I did Mrs Walters began to wail and she held the bundle closer and refused to let me near. 'I never murdered the dear, I never did, I just woke and found him there and didn't know what to do! Oh my blessed Lord,' she wailed, 'I never did.'

'Mrs Walters,' said Detective Wright. 'Whose infant is this and where did you get him from?'

Mrs Walters did not answer, but she appeared even more agitated and began to stamp her feet quite violently upon the floor.

'I have to inform you,' continued Detective Wright, 'that anything you say might be used in evidence against you.'

'All right,' shrugged Mrs Walters, and then she stopped stamping her feet and her body ceased quivering, 'all right. I won't say anything and then I can't say wrong.'

28

Lily Painter

I was the one who opened the door that fated evening, for I
had been sitting with Hester in the kitchen and when we
heard a knock she told me to answer it. It had been a week, I
thought, since the lady had taken my baby. And although my
body was still too weak to work, I was so low in spirits I could
not remain alone in my attic room. Now Rosina had left, I would
come downstairs for company whenever I could. Three times
I had written to Gus Chevalier to beg him to visit again, to say
that with him by my side then we could find our baby and take
her back. But the letters had gone unanswered, except for the
last which had been returned unopened, and I did not know
what I should do. And so when we heard the knock upon the
door that night it was I who walked along the darkened hallway,
the floor as cold as ice beneath my stockinged feet, and I opened
the door and saw two policemen upon the step. The wind blew
fierce then and I could see the storm clouds gathered in the sky,
hanging thick and black above the street.

'Nurse Sach?' enquired the taller of the two policemen, a
round-faced man with a stomach that strained against his smart
frock coat.

'No, sir,' I said, my voice uncertain, not knowing what was
the matter or what I should say.

Then I heard Hester's steps in the hall behind me and I drew
to one side as she came to the door, wiping her hands upon her
apron. 'What is it?' she asked, and at that very moment, through

the open door, we saw Nurse Sach come walking briskly down the street. She didn't see the policemen at first, she only realised they were there when she came to the pillar that marked the first step to Claymore House, and when she did I saw her flinch.

'There she is,' said Hester brightly, as if this was something she had been waiting for.

'Gentlemen.' Nurse Sach gave a nod of her head. She walked up the path and to the porch with such confidence that the policemen stood to one side to let her pass. Then they all came into Claymore House and Hester hurried me back into the kitchen, urging me to be quiet and sit, and to leave the door ajar so that we would be able to see and hear everything that was said.

'We are police officers, madam,' said the man who had addressed me earlier, and I looked at Hester and she gave me a wink, for there was nothing they could be if not police officers. 'Do you know a Mrs Walters? A Mrs Annie Walters of 11 Danbury Street, Islington?'

'Walters?' replied Nurse Sach, in surprise. 'Walters?' she said again, as if it was a name she was not familiar with. 'No.'

'Oh!' I cried from where I sat in the kitchen, and Hester shushed me with an urgent gesture to her lips.

'Why,' asked Nurse Sach, 'what has she done?'

'She has been arrested,' said the policeman. 'By two of our officers this very evening, on suspicion of murdering a male baby.'

'You don't say!' cried Nurse Sach.

It was then that my heart started beating fit to burst. I looked at Hester, but she bent her head and refused to meet my eyes. I felt my vision go a little, as if the lights had suddenly dimmed, for I could not believe what I had just heard. Mrs Walters arrested, and for murdering a baby? Mrs Walters with whom I had sat in this very same kitchen only a few days before? It couldn't be true! I leapt from my chair, but Hester caught me roughly by the arm.

'Wait,' she urged me, 'just wait or we shan't hear anything else.'

'She's detained right now at King's Cross police station,' said the policeman. 'She says she works for you and we have reason to believe you have given her the baby.'

'Well!' said Nurse Sach. She was turned away from me in the hallway but I could see the familiar rigidness of her back. 'I don't know any Mrs Walters and I have never given her any babies!'

'Oh!' I hissed to Hester. 'She's lying!'

When neither policeman spoke, I saw Nurse Sach draw herself up in her most haughty manner before declaring, 'I take in ladies to be confined, gentlemen. There's one in my house at present. She was confined last Saturday morning of a baby, a boy, it's with the mother now. Dr Wylie attended her.'

'Ada!' I cried, for Ada had had her baby on Saturday, just as Nurse Sach said, and although it was a boy and not the girl she had dreamt of, she had cried so many tears since the lady had taken it to be adopted.

'I should like to see the baby,' said the policeman.

'That is impossible,' said Nurse Sach at once. 'The mother is too ill.'

This was true. Ada had been so ill since her confinement that she barely had the strength to eat. I watched from the doorway then as the policemen conferred, and a little while later another gentleman arrived and I heard him addressed as Dr Russell. 'We should like him to go into the room where the lady is,' said the policeman, 'and see the mother and if there is a baby there.'

I saw Nurse Sach then, as she made a move to the bottom of the stairs, but the shorter of the two policemen held her back.

'The baby's not there,' she said just as Dr Russell took his first step upon the stair, and she spoke curtly as if the policemen were foolish to ever think such a thing. 'It has been taken away.'

'Taken away?'

'Yes, to be adopted.'

And that was when I began to sob, for if it was Ada's baby that Mrs Walters had taken and so coldly murdered as the policemen said, then what had happened to my baby? What had happened to my baby Martha with her big brown eyes and her apricot skin? My baby all wrapped in the flannel I had made, her initials so lovingly embroidered, each stitch made with such care? Had my baby gone to the lady in Piccadilly as Nurse Sach had said, or had Mrs Walters taken her too? And I tried to remember. I thought desperately of the day Gus Chevalier had come and how angry he had been to discover our baby gone. I thought of the night Nurse Sach told the doctor my sister had my baby, and the evening when I thought I heard the tap tap of Mrs Walters' stick upon the hallway floor.

'Nurse Sach,' the policeman said, and his voice had a finality that was terrible to hear, 'I shall have to take you into custody for being an accessory to murder.'

'Murdering!' cried Nurse Sach. 'Never! Do you really mean to say that these babies are dead, that she has murdered them?'

It was then that Hester could hold me back no longer, and I flew out of the kitchen and into the hall. 'Where is my baby?' I cried. 'Oh, what have you done with my baby? Did the lady take her?' I turned to the policemen who stood there watching, but neither said a word. 'She took my baby!' I cried. 'She said it was going to a lady in Piccadilly. Where is she?' And then I fell upon Nurse Sach and I grasped the bodice of her black dress and I felt the cloth cold and silky between my fingers.

'Let go of me!' said Nurse Sach, and angrily she tried to remove my hands but instead I held her fiercely and would not let her go. I heard the sound of tearing then, felt the cloth split beneath my hands, but still I held her, still I cried, 'What have you done with my baby?'

29

After the policemen took Nurse Sach away I went upstairs to Ada's room and there we sat, the two of us, and held each other tight and cried our bitter tears. Then Hester came and said the policemen would be back, that they would come to question us soon.

'Hester,' I implored her, 'did a lady take my baby?'

'What do you think?'

'Oh, tell me, did a lady take my baby or did Mrs Walters? Hester, please, I beg you. You must know what happened to my baby.'

'I didn't see a thing,' said Hester, and she left the room.

I looked at Ada and then I looked away, for I could not bear to see her ghostly face. 'Ada,' I said as softly as I could. 'Did you *see* a lady take your baby?'

'No,' she sobbed, 'Nurse Sach said the lady had come and then my baby was gone! What will we do?' she asked. 'Oh Lily, what will we do?'

And then I left the attic room and hurried downstairs, and as I entered the kitchen I found Hester crouched upon the floor before a large brown box, her little boy Archie sitting patiently beside her. 'What's that?' I asked, and as Hester caught sight of me she began to push the box hurriedly under the kitchen table. At once I bent down and I pulled at the box and quickly opened the lid. Oh, how many babies' clothes there were inside! All the white work we had spent so many hours on; the vests and gowns, blankets and bibs, shawls and socks. So many there were, so many baby clothes made like I had made my own, some trimmed with lace, others with ribbons, pink and yellow and blue.

'Where did you find these?' I asked Hester.

'Right under there,' and she pointed at the table.

I picked up a flannel, looked at the initials sewn so beautifully on the edge. It was not mine, it was not a flannel I had made, and furiously I began to pull the baby clothes from the box, flinging them on the table, the chair, the floor, searching to see if my baby's clothes were there. For if they were here in the box then my baby didn't have them, they hadn't gone with her at all, a lady hadn't taken my little Martha, she had gone where she had no need of clothes at all. At last I stopped for I could find nothing that was mine, and I looked at the mess I had made and I took the clothes and I began to sob as I folded each one carefully, neatly, and placed it with a kiss back inside in the box.

Then I saw a letter upon the table. 'Is this for *her*?' I asked, picking up the letter, and I held it in my hand, saw it was addressed to Nurse Sach.

'Lily!' Hester protested as I began to open it.

'What?' I asked. 'Why shouldn't I?'

Hester looked fearful. 'She'll find out.'

'But she's not here, is she!' I held the letter in my hand and I stared at Hester long and hard. 'Why are you so afraid of her? What do you know about the babies? Tell me! Did *you* ever take a baby from Nurse Sach?'

Hester bowed her head and began to pick at her apron with feverish fingers.

'Did you?' I grabbed her roughly by the arm until she cried out and pulled away.

'I did take a baby once . . . I took it to a lady in Plaistow.

She told me to. She told me never to mention her business to others. She threatened me, Lily, said she wouldn't give me work any more or a home for me and Archie if I didn't do as she asked.'

'And was there a lady in Plaistow?'

'Yes, there was.'

I sat down then, heard my heart beating loud in my ears. 'And you gave her the baby?'

'Yes,' Hester said, and she hung her head. 'She wanted me to give my baby away too, Lily. When I first went to be confined, Nurse Sach said –'

'You went to be confined with Nurse Sach?'

'Not here, at another place, on Arthur Terrace. I saw her advert and then I went there and Archie was born and she said I should give my baby to be adopted. She said a lady in Balcombe would adopt him for twelve pounds and she'd have a mail cart and a cot waiting for him, Lily, but I didn't have twelve pounds and I didn't want to let my baby go.'

'Oh!' I cried, for why had Hester refused and I and Ada and Rosina agreed?

'Mrs Walters said so as well, she said the baby would always be in my light and I wouldn't be able to work. She said,' and Hester stopped and looked at her boy Archie still sitting quietly upon the floor, 'I was a fool to keep it and for just five shillings she would take him away.'

'But you stayed with Nurse Sach?'

'Yes, I did the housework and she paid me a few shillings a week and then she didn't pay me anything at all, she said I could work in return for my keep and Archie's. She gave me a home, Lily, for me and my boy,' and she looked up at me then and I saw her eyes were full of tears. 'And every time I thought I might leave, every time I tried to find a way –'

'She stopped you,' I said, remembering the day I had heard the quarrel between them in the hall.

'A lot of women do take their babies with them, Lily, they come and go and never give their proper names or their addresses, but sometimes . . .'

'Sometimes?'

'Well, the babies go alone. Mrs White paid twelve pounds, Mrs Harris paid thirty and Mrs Young . . . I never felt right about it, Lily, but what could I do? I kept hoping the police, if someone told them, then they would do something. But then if they did find out, Lily, then maybe they would arrest me as well.'

It was then, with trembling hands, I opened the letter addressed to Nurse Sach and I smoothed it out upon the table and began to read. 'It is from a lady in Woking Village,' I told Hester. 'She wants to know if the ladies at Claymore House have a baby she could adopt . . .' I stopped then, unable for a moment to go on. 'She says she would be glad as she's a young married woman but isn't likely to have any children of her own.' I read the letter again and then again once more, for I thought perhaps a lady like this had my baby after all. But I could not wait to see if this was true, I could not wait until the policemen came again, so I sat down and quickly wrote a letter to Gus Chevalier to tell him what I knew, and I gave it to Hester, asked her to post it and knew that she would. Then I took my bonnet and my shawl.

'Where are you going?' asked Hester.

'I am going to find Mrs Walters,' I told her, 'because if Mrs Walters was the one who took my baby then I shall find her and I shall murder her myself.'

I closed the door of Claymore House behind me, and as I set off into the street the snow began to fall and I shivered and my teeth shook in my mouth. I had no money, I could not catch a 'bus or tram, and so I walked. And as I did I felt the houses were falling down on me just as I had felt that day I left my family in Stanley Road and moved into Claymore House. I had not been outside since my confinement and as I walked I felt my body shudder with every step as if my insides should fall out. I began to see strange specks of blood upon the pavement and I heard a rushing in my ears, so that I almost stepped into the path of an oncoming tram and the conductor shouted and swore at me. Still I walked, stumbling in my urgency, through Finchley and then through Archway, until the night deepened and the hours passed and at last I reached King's Cross.

I stopped then in front of the police station, its windows like black gaping eyes, and I went up the steps and found so many people inside I did not know what to do, which way to turn or who to ask for help. Then I was thrown roughly against a wall by a sudden movement within the crowd.

'There she is!' cried an elderly lady. 'There's the baby farmer!'

I looked to where she was pointing, saw a hunched figure being taken down the stairs by two policemen, and I knew that it was Mrs Walters. I saw her struggle, to try and free herself from the policemen on either side.

'I never murdered the dear!' she cried out. 'I never killed the baby, I only gave it two little drops in its bottle the same as I take myself!'

'Come on you,' said one of the policemen, tugging on Mrs Walters.

But still she struggled to break free. 'I am being made a tool of! I'm not going to take all the blame! I took the other baby back to her!' And at this Mrs Walters pointed up the stairs and I knew at once it was Nurse Sach and I watched in dread as I saw first her boots and then the black hem of her dress appear.

'Back to the cell,' ordered the policeman again, and he pulled Mrs Walters down the stairs, but she turned her head once more, called out to the crowd, 'Nurse Sach knows where the baby is! I took it back to her on Friday. I never murdered this one. I was going to give it back to her. I never killed the baby!'

'But where is my baby?' I screamed, and I tried to fight my way through the crowd. 'Mrs Walters! Where is *my* baby?'

And then the crowd grew rough and I tried with all my strength to break through until a policeman touched me gently upon my arm. 'Miss,' he said, 'Miss . . .' but I threw off his hand and I rushed outside, looking around wildly in the falling snow, and I thought I heard bells ringing then, I thought I heard them calling out for me, *Turn again, Turn again.*

'Are you all right, dearie?' An elderly woman stopped me there upon the steps. 'You can't be running out on a night like this. Where are you going?'

And then I knew what I would do; I would go back to Stanley Road and to my landlord, Inspector George, for he would be able to help me. I would tell him everything and he would help me find my baby.

'To Stanley Road,' I said, and I drew my cloak around me and half blinded by the falling snow I came quickly down the steps towards the road.

30

Annie Sweet

May 2009

The sun is out and Whittington Park is full. Kids are tearing around the football pitch, slamming into its wire walls. We walk down the tarred pathway past women pushing buggies, and each time we do Jojo pulls closer, wanting to sniff at the baby inside.

'You should keep a dog like that on the lead,' says a man jogging past.

'She is on the lead!' I snap, but he's already jogged by.

I let Jojo off in the dog area, but there are no other dogs to play with so she doesn't do much. 'Throw her a ball,' I tell Molly and I watch them play a while and I'm happy watching them, but there's a niggling at the back of my mind, almost a guilty niggling, because I'm wondering when I can snatch some time to find out more about Lily Painter. Now I know she was in the music hall, now I've seen her name in the newspaper review, I can't wait for the chance to find out more. Did she become a star? And if she did, then did she stay in this house on Stanley Road or did she move out, did she get married, did she have kids, where did she go next and what did she do?

It's Saturday and Molly's gone to her dad's for the night, although I don't think she wanted to. She moaned and fussed all the way. We went past where Woolworths used to be; now it's turned into Iceland, a big shopping space of bright soulless light. Carrie's flat is near the Tube, the top floor of a large corner house with grand peaked windows. This is the first time I've seen it, because Ben has always picked Molly up before. I want to leave her at the front door, I don't want to speak to him or to see *her*, I just want to drop Molly off. I pray to myself that it won't be her who opens the door.

'Hello!' says Ben.

'Hi, Dad,' Molly says a little shyly, but then he holds out his arms and she rushes towards him and I grit my teeth because the whole thing makes me want to cry.

'How's things, Annie?' he asks.

'Fine,' I say. 'I'm just off to the local history centre actually.'

'Mum's finding out all about our house,' Molly tells him.

Ben raises his eyebrows. I'm hoping he's smart enough not to bring up the topic of the house and his insistence that we sell it.

'See you then!' I say, and I kiss Molly and get away as fast as I can.

The local history centre feels familiar to me now. I've already booked the microfiche machine and I've asked if the printer's working and I know exactly what to do. I can't see Danny, so I just put my things in a locker, open the wooden cabinet drawer and take out a film of the *Islington Gazette* for 1901. I thread the film into place and find the page I read before, the review of Lily Painter at the Holloway Empire, although I know now the Empire doesn't exist, that it was demolished years ago.

I look through the rest of April 1901 and I can't find Lily Painter mentioned in any of the reviews, but I see her name in the Empire adverts all through May and June. I decide to skip a bit and take out the film for 1902, and the first page that appears is full of playbills. The Grand Theatre has a play called *The Fatal Wedding*; Collins' has Little Tich at the top of the bill and then someone called the Singing Navvy; the Holloway Empire has Vesta Victoria, followed by Miss Katie Iris and a full Coon Chorus. What was a Coon Chorus? I hope my Lily didn't do that. I read about how Miss Vesta Victoria delighted the audience with her robust vocalism and I smile at the language like I did before – it's so formal and careful and somehow soothing – and for a second I want to be there, back in 1902, with bristling programmes and rousing receptions. And then suddenly I find her.

A strong company and full houses are the order of things this week at the Holloway Empire. We must mention with all possible praise the piquant singing of Miss Lily Painter, who made her modest mark at the Empire's most wonderful *Dick Whittington*, a lady whose songs now are as charming as her manner, with youth, beauty and talent to commend her, and who gives the audience a regular whiff of the boulevards.

A whiff of the boulevards? So Lily Painter was in a pantomime and now she's singing French songs? I picture her on a music-hall stage in a white dress perhaps, Edwardian, with a high neck, maybe a hat, a parasol. I wonder why I can picture it so well and then I think of the dream I had when Molly was on the stage and she forgot her lines, and this was the sort of stage I was dreaming about then. I wonder what Lily Painter would have done after her act, when she came home to Stanley Road to her family and her landlord. Were they proud of her? Because I am, I'm really proud of her, this young girl who appears to have made it on the London stage. I feel like she's mine, and with a surge of excitement I get out the next film for the summer of 1902. At first I find Lily Painter still piquantly singing at the Holloway Empire but then, after a few months, her name disappears from the bill. I look at the other adverts, hoping to find her performing at another theatre. Maybe she wasn't singing in Islington any more; maybe she'd moved on somewhere else.

I stretch my arms and my neck; I've been bent in front of this machine for what seems like hours. I look up just as Danny appears. 'I thought I'd find you here,' he says with an easy smile. 'Still looking for your Lily Painter?'

I'm impressed that he remembers her name, but then maybe that's just his job, to remember what people are researching. 'Yes, last time I found her at the Holloway Empire in 1901 and I've just found her these again in 1902, but now I seem to have lost her.'

Danny looks over my shoulder and he's so close I can smell him, a fresh coffee and peppermint smell. He leans back and glances around a little furtively before taking a small white box of Tic Tacs out of his jeans pocket. He flips up the lid to offer me one. 'Very naughty,' he says with a smile. I haven't had a Tic Tac in years; they remind me of my Granny Martha. She always had mints somewhere on her person, in a handbag or a raincoat pocket; sometimes they were large, rough-edged rounds of extra-strong mint, sometimes they were wee little Tic Tacs, and we would pop them in our mouths and see who could suck on them the longest. I put one of Danny's Tic Tacs on my tongue and for a second I'm eight years old again, lost in a sensation of memory and taste.

'All the variety reviews would be on this page,' says Danny as I crunch on my Tic Tac.

'Yeah, I know.' I move the button around a bit, taking in the headlines: 'Recital at Finsbury Park Church', 'Bakers in Council – an advance in the price of bread'. Then at the top right-hand corner I see a big black headline, far bigger and far blacker than any of the others: 'BABY-FARMING AT ISLINGTON, MISSING CHILDREN, REMARKABLE REVELATIONS'.

'What's this about?' I ask, looking round at Danny, feeling a stab of alarm.

He pulls a chair over and sits down. 'This is interesting. Let's see.' He zooms in further on the headline. 'Is this the Sach case? It was quite famous. This has to be Amelia Sach and Annie Walters, the baby farmers.'

'But what was a baby farmer?'

Danny starts scrolling down the page. 'They took in babies, usually from women who weren't married, like taking in laundry really, just to make a bit of money.'

'Like taking in *laundry*?'

'I didn't mean it like that,' Danny laughs, 'I just meant it was a way for poorer women to make a living. They were just like childminders, although there were a few nasty cases where someone pretended they'd look after babies or get them adopted, then abandoned them or sold them on or even, well, killed them. These two, Sach and Walters, were hanged for murder.'

'They were hanged?' I don't think I want to know about this, it all sounds a bit grisly. 'So it was a famous case. Is there a book or something on it?'

'Not that I know of, no. I think they're mentioned in a couple of books on Holloway Prison, but that's about it really.'

'But they were famous at the time?'

'Oh, very. The older one, Annie Walters, lived in Danbury Street, not far from here, just at the back of Upper Street. She was the one who apparently killed the babies, while Sach, who lived in East Finchley, was the one who gave her the babies.'

'How do you know so much about them?'

Danny shrugs, drums his fingers on the metal table. 'I did my thesis on infanticide in Edwardian London.'

'Really? Why did you write about that?'

'Well, I wanted to be a historian,' Danny stops drumming on the table, 'and I thought infanticide was gruesome but interesting. Then I sort of stumbled on to adoption. I couldn't believe there weren't any adoption laws back then, and that led me on to . . . well, I didn't finish it actually.' Danny laughs, but when he turns to look at me the openness of his eyes gives me a shock. They seem naked somehow, like someone who has just taken off their glasses. I see delicate lines in the corner of his eyes, and high on his forehead, where his braids begin, there's a little fuzz of wispy grey hair, and I realise he's older than I'd thought. I want to ask him why he never finished his thesis but he's started scrolling down the screen again, businesslike, intent on finding something. 'I'm sure there must be longer reports here.'

'Stop,' I tell him, 'that one, there.' And this time it's a big article, taking up several columns.

Annie Walters, 54, married, of 11, Danbury Street, Islington, was charged at the Clerkenwell Police-court yesterday with the wilful murder of a male child, name unknown, aged about four days, of an unmarried woman named Ada Galley. Amelia Sach, 29, married, of Claymore House, East Finchley, was charged with conspiring to commit the murder. Both Miss Ada Galley and a Miss Rosina Pardoe were called as witness, but not of course Miss Lily Painter . . .

'What!' My voice is loud, too loud, like I've just shouted in my sleep. 'But that's her, look it's her! What's she doing here?'

I put my finger on the screen and a jolt of ice seems to travel down my arms.

... but not of course Miss Lily Painter, also suspected of being victim of the baby farmers, whose body was discovered on the night of 18 November lying outside King's-cross police station having thrown herself under a tram. The verdict at last week's inquest was suicide while of unsound mind.

'No!' I say, and again my voice is too loud. 'That can't be!'
'Are you all right?' asks Danny.
I just keep pointing my finger at the screen.

Miss Lily Painter had had a brief career as a music-hall artiste. After her death, a letter written to her sweetheart was found outlining her desire to find the baby she had handed over to the callous baby farmers.

'Oh my God,' I whisper. 'This is awful. She gave her baby to the baby farmers, that's why she disappeared, that's why I couldn't find her, because she was pregnant.'
'Are you sure you're all right?'
I just look at the screen, not daring to say anything else because now I think I'm going to cry and this isn't a good place to cry, sitting in front of a microfiche machine in the local history centre, next to a man I don't even know. And if I do cry then maybe I won't be able to stop, maybe I just won't be able to hold myself together any more. And this is crazy, because Lily Painter is nothing to me; she's just a name I found on a census roll. But I was so happy to be looking for her and now I feel such an overwhelming sense of loss. All

this time she's been alive in my mind, a person I've wanted and longed to know about, and now just like that, she's gone. It's like I've come to some terrible dead end. If I hadn't looked up the census and if I hadn't seen that Lily Painter lived in my house in 1901 and if I hadn't had this stupid idea to find out more about her and if I hadn't found the article about the baby farmers then I would never have discovered any of this.

A woman comes over and she says something to Danny, but I don't take it in.

'It's my break,' he says, getting up. 'D'you want a coffee?'

31

We're sitting in a café near the local history centre. There's condensation on the windows and the air smells of bacon and disinfectant. Danny's brought two cups of coffee and I haven't told him I don't drink coffee, ever since last year; it makes me feel sick. But the thick white enamel of the mug feels solid and comforting in my hands.

'So the woman you were looking for, she had a baby,' says Danny.

'Yes.' I look up at him. I'd almost forgotten this, I'd only been thinking about Lily Painter being dead. 'What do you think happened to her baby? Did the baby farmers . . .' I hesitate. 'Did they kill it?'

'I'm not sure,' says Danny. 'I know they were charged with killing Ada Galley's baby, like you've just read, but I think there was another baby. I think Annie Walters got arrested with another baby before that.'

'So was that Lily's baby?'

'I don't know. You'll have to read more newspaper reports. Although . . .'

'What?'

'Well, that's why, when you first came in and said you were looking for someone called Lily Painter, that's why I thought I recognised her name.'

'You didn't look as if you did.'

'Didn't I?'

'No.' I feel a bit awkward now because we're talking about

what we both thought the day I first came to the local history centre, and there's something a little intimate about that. 'So how would I find that out?' I ask. 'How would I find out if Lily's baby was killed by the baby farmers?'

'Well, you could look up the inquest, or the trial.'

'And what if they didn't kill it?'

Danny looks at me with sympathy; he can see how hopeful I am.

'No, really, what if the baby lived? But then again, how would I find out about that when I don't even know the baby's name! I don't even know if *it* was a boy or a girl. Oh God. This is so depressing, I wish I'd never started this.'

Two women come into the café and take the table next to us, and Danny moves his bag to give them more room.

'You know what I don't get?' I say, and I rest my hands on the edge of the table. 'Why would Lily Painter have killed herself? Why on earth would she have thrown herself under a tram? I don't think she did. The paper says there was a letter to her sweetheart' – I pause because sweetheart is such a romantic word – 'and if there was a letter to her sweetheart saying she wanted to find her baby, then that's what she would have done, isn't it? She would have done everything she could to find her baby. Why would she have killed herself?'

'Perhaps because she failed to find her baby.' Danny looks down at the table, starts moving his mug around so it makes circles and then wipes at them with his fingers.

'But it looks like she killed herself before the trial even started, doesn't it? Do you think she blamed herself?'

Danny starts drawing lines of wetness between the circles he's made on the table.

'Have you got children?' I ask, and I don't know where this question comes from because I wasn't thinking about it at all.

'Yes,' says Danny.

'Oh.' I stare at him; I wasn't expecting him to say this. 'Boy or girl?'

'Boy.'

I wait for him to say more about his boy, his name and age, but he starts drawing with his fingers on the tabletop again. I look at him and think, So you're a family man, you have a child, a boy, and probably therefore a wife or a girlfriend, so what are you doing here, why have you invited me here? It's work, Annie, I tell myself, he's just doing his job. He's a historian, a librarian, and this is what he does. There is nothing personal in this at all.

'I don't live with him.'

'Oh.' So that's it, I think, that's why he's not saying much.

Danny looks at his watch and stands up. 'Sorry, but my break's over.'

'Oh, sorry, I've taken up your whole break.'

'I couldn't think of a nicer way to spend it.' Danny looks around and I don't know if he's being funny about this café or if he means it was good to spend it with me. This is ridiculous, I think, getting up as well. I'm too confused with what I've found, I can't make sense of anything today.

'Do you want me to call you if I find out anything else?' Danny asks, and I thank him and give him my number.

I walk all the way home, stopping once at a bus stop on Upper Street but then feeling too impatient to wait. I walk on, thinking about my poor Lily Painter. First she was a music-hall star and then suddenly she's dead. And she was so young, only seventeen or eighteen. She lost her baby and it isn't fair, it's too miserable to think about.

Normally when I turn off Holloway Road my heart sings

when I see Stanley Road, but this time it doesn't, it feels like a dead weight, because I've imagined Lily Painter living here, I've thought about which room would have been hers, I've imagined her coming home from the music hall, I've thought about what her family and landlord were like and whether she got on with them. But that's when she was still alive to me. Now I wonder what her family made of her death. If she turned to two baby farmers, did her parents even know she was pregnant? Had they thrown her out of the house? And afterwards, did they go to the trial of the baby farmers? Did they leave 43 Stanley Road, or did her family stay here in my house?

I reach home and reluctantly open the gate. When I come into the house I smell wee and this makes me so furious I throw my bag on the floor and swear as I march down the hall into the kitchen. The tiles on floor are a bright steaming yellow. 'Jojo!' I shout, as if the dog's going to answer me. I look into the back room and for a second I can't think what's so odd. Then I take in the fact the sofa, the big four-seater sofa, has been moved away from the wall. It's as if a shark has attacked it: the cloth has been ripped, there is stuffing spilling out like frozen white candyfloss and I can see the bare wood of the legs. Jojo hasn't done anything like this for a while; it's been weeks since we had destruction on this scale.

When the phone rings I'm still angry enough to snap when I pick it up: 'Yes?'

'Hello, Annie.'

'Oh, hi Mum.'

'Where have you been?'

'Why?'

'I've been calling you all morning, pet.'

'Well, why didn't you call me on my mobile?'

'Oh, your mobile.' Mum doesn't believe in mobiles, she doesn't seem to think they're real phones.

'How's Dad?'

'He's fine, he's taken up chess, don't ask me why. So where have you been all morning?'

'I've been at a local history centre.'

'Oh. Still trying to find out about your house?'

'Yes.' I don't like the way she says 'still', as if this is something I should have given up on or grown out of long ago. Now I don't even want to tell her what I found out today.

'I've been thinking, Annie. How far are you from Dick Whittington's cat?'

'What?'

'That little cat statue on Highgate Hill. Someone was just talking about it the other day.'

'Mum, if you came down and visited us then you'd see where we are. We've been here how long? Nearly two years and you still haven't come to see us. Molly's always asking when you'll come down. I don't know what to tell her any more.'

'Oh dear,' says Mum, 'someone's at the door, I'm going to have to go.'

I look at the phone and think, Why did she ring me, was she going to ask me something? She can't have rung just to ask me about Dick Whittington's cat.

'Mum, wait, I want to tell you something. You know how a woman lived in this house a hundred years ago, Lily Painter? And you know how I found her in the music hall?'

'Did you?'

'Yes, I told you. Well, today I found out something awful, I found out she was pregnant, that she handed her baby to some baby farmers and then she killed herself.'

'Oh Annie, in your house?'

'No! Don't say things like that, that's creepy. She threw herself under a tram or something. Only I don't think she did.'

'Oh,' says Mum. 'Why's that?'

'I don't know, I just think that, if she was looking for her baby, and I know she was, then she wouldn't have killed herself, she would have waited, to see what the baby farmers had to say, so she would know what happened to her baby. Don't you think?'

I wake in the night and find myself getting out of bed and walking into Molly's room to check on her until I remember she's not here, she's at her father's. I can feel a sense of her, a smell of her, still in the room, and it's like the house is missing something and so am I. A flicker of light runs suddenly across the walls and I look up and see the light bulb glowing, faintly, like it's losing energy. How has the light come on by itself? I press the switch on the wall, but instead of turning off, the light continues to flicker. I press the switch again and now the light seems to grow stronger. Then it fades and the room is black.

I close Molly's bedroom door and come on to the landing. I can hear a beeping noise from downstairs, which means the dog's been at the freezer again. I hurry down the stairs, feeling annoyed, but when I come down to the kitchen the freezer door is shut and Jojo is fast asleep in her basket.

It's spooky being down here all alone at night. The kitchen's totally dark but for a glow coming from the fridge, like an empty control centre waiting for someone to come in and switch everything on. I want to be back in bed asleep.

I go upstairs and into my office and put my hand to the wall to steady myself. It's freezing in here, as if all the warmth of the day has been sucked away. From outside I can hear the sounds of a party, a night-time party after a sunny Saturday. But the music sounds odd, like an old-fashioned organ, and when I open the window to peer out to see who's having the party it's totally silent outside. I look over the dark shapeless gardens below; I can just make out the tops of bushes and trees, the steps of a metal fire escape and the peaked roof of a small wooden hut. No one is outside, not a soul. I put my hand to the latch to close the window and as I do I have the unnerving feeling that someone is there. Someone is looking out of their window, watching me.

I focus on the houses opposite. None of the windows are lit, but I'm sure there's someone there. I think about turning my light off, but I feel frozen, like I can't move. Still I keep looking. I can make out differences in the darkness of the windows now, varieties in net curtains, some patterned, some plain. I look over at a window to the right – it's higher up than mine and the curtains are thick and heavy. Suddenly the curtains move and a gap appears between the folds. I stand and stare but nothing happens, I can't see who's there. Then a light springs to life in a window to the left; it's not a bedroom but a hallway, and I see the shadow of a figure climbing slowly upstairs. I wait until the figure disappears and then I shut my window with a determined bang. I hear breathing now, erratic and slightly wet, and when I swivel round I see Jojo has come quietly up the stairs and is standing there at the doorway. 'God, you gave me a fright,' I laugh, and I'm about to walk towards her, feeling strangely grateful for her company tonight, when she lowers her back and gives a menacing growl. She's not looking at me, her growl's not for me, instead she's looking at something just behind me and I don't want to look round, I don't want to know what I might see if I do.

32

Inspector William George

December 1902

Wednesday, 3 December 1902

A most unsettled day. A misty start followed by torrential rain, and the weather does nothing but further deepen the pervading sense of gloom in our house. While all around us, it seems, neighbours are beginning preparations for Christmas, preparations that begin earlier each year, in our household it is quite another matter. My dear wife Fanny says she has not the strength this year, and shows no interest in purchasing or decorating a pine tree; indeed, she has evinced no interest in anything at all since we learnt the terrible fate of our landlord's daughter. 'Oh, if only we'd known, William,' she has said to me repeatedly, 'If only we'd known about poor Lily before it was too late! All that time, William, all that time and we had no idea! Why didn't she tell us? If she couldn't tell her family, she could have told me. Why didn't we find out until it was too late?' When I suggested that it was quite clearly a sense of shame and disgrace that drove our lodgers' daughter into the arms of the baby farmers, Fanny disagreed. It was, she says, less a question of morals than of financial burden and lack of familial support.

We know now that Lily went in secret to Claymore House sometime at the end of September, telling her family she had been called by her uncle in Dublin, which is the story she seems to have also given to her fellow artistes. On 10 November she gave birth to a healthy girl, according to the two servant girls confined at the same time, and was persuaded by Nurse Sach to give the child up for adoption. When my colleagues arrived at Claymore House on 18 November to arrest Nurse Sach, it was Lily herself who let them in. And that night, quite deranged with grief, she set off to find the prisoners and beseech them to tell her the whereabouts of her baby. Officers at King's Cross assert that a young woman matching Lily's description arrived at the police station in a very distraught state and shouted at the baby farmer Mrs Walters. She then rushed outside and an elderly lady, who was just then attempting to enter the police station, came upon her on the steps. As it was by then snowing, the lady implored her to return to the warmth of the police station. Lily, however, refused, saying she must go at once to Stanley Road.

I must lay down my pen. This distresses me more than I can say. I doubt that Lily had any intention of turning to her family for help; rather I suspect that the person she wanted to see was myself. I now have the most terrible sense of failure, for I was in the ideal position to protect a young woman lodging under my very roof, and in that capacity I let her down most miserably. Despite Divisional Superintendent Dyball's initial lack of interest in the matter of the baby farmers, it is still only me who is to blame. The anonymous letter writer singled me out in the belief I was a caring man, with the hope I would investigate the baby farmers and discover their dreadful business, and I have failed.

The Painters, of course, are gone, having moved out two weeks ago with their elder daughter, and it was a sorry sight to see Mr Painter so badly aged by recent events. He indicated that they were to travel to Dublin, for they desired to escape London as soon as they could, and indeed I believe that if they had remained then this house would hold nothing but painful memories for them. And it holds so very painful memories for my dear wife Fanny and myself, for we welcomed a young woman into our home, I like to think we treated her as parents would treat a daughter, and now we have lost her for ever.

Thursday, 4 December 1902
Fanny is sleeping. I hope tonight she will rest soundly and without the bad dreams that trouble her these days.

I have spent the entire day at the Clerkenwell court, both giving and hearing evidence. I expect the inquest will continue for some time, for there are a number of witnesses from whom we are still to hear and one or two matters that are yet to be fully explained. One of these is the exact cause of the death of the pitiful infant we found with Mrs Walters at South Kensington station. The post-mortem has shown an effusion of blood on the back of the skull, although there was neither fracture nor wound. Medical testimony has established the cause of death as asphyxia, which could have been the result of pressure over the mouth and nostrils. However, it could equally have been the result of overlaying, whether accidental or intentional, and this would not be the first baby to die in this manner. Mrs Walters still insists, as she did that evening of her arrest, that she awoke to find the baby dead beside her and in a panic fled her lodgings at Danbury Street. However, I doubt very much that this will hold up in court. Mrs Walters has quite openly admitted to giving the baby chlorodyne, which she said was to help it sleep. She would not be the first person to administer such an opiate to a restless child, but chlorodyne is so powerful that in a four-day-old infant the effect is almost certainly fatal. While no traces of poison have been found in the infant's body, it would take such a small amount to cause its death that it is unlikely that any would be found.

Nurse Sach, meanwhile, having initially denied any knowledge of Mrs Walters, was then confronted with her at the police station. She then declared that indeed she did know her, that Walters worked for her but that she never gave her any babies. What the prosecution will have to prove, of course, is that she did indeed give her a baby and, with the existence of the telegrams and the servant girls' evidence to date, that should not be difficult.

Moreover, it has now been established that Mrs Walters was indeed seen with another infant just a few days earlier. A tearoom attendant has lately come forward to testify that on the afternoon of 14 November, the dreadful day that Mrs Walters left her lodgings with a baby and then returned without it, Mrs Walters visited Lockhart's tearooms in Whitechapel. The attendant noticed the elderly woman had a bundle and, when the wrap fell off, she saw what looked like a doll, indeed upon seeing the baby she asked if it was a doll, seeing as it was making neither sound nor movement. Where that baby's remains are now, I fear we shall never know, just as we shall never know what happened to the two infants and baby I saw that day in the kitchen of Arthur Terrace.

There are other missing babies as well. During the search conducted at Claymore House on 24 November, my colleagues discovered some 300 articles of baby clothing in various boxes within the lying-in home. Dr Wylie has testified that he attended at least twelve cases at Claymore House over a period of just three months, although he does not seem to have concerned himself much about this. Indeed, when one of the servant girls began to tell him she had paid money to Nurse Sach he simply said it was no affair of his and he didn't wish to hear any more.

Clothing aside, other items were also discovered during the search at Claymore House, all of which suggest Nurse Sach had been running a successful adoption business. These items include a Post Office bank book with a substantial credit of twenty pounds, a memorandum book with the names and address of a dozen women, as well as a number of professionally produced business cards. There was also a letter from a lady at Woking enquiring after a baby to adopt, which my colleagues believe to be genuine and which lends some weight to Nurse Sach's solicitor's argument that she was running a reputable business. She was, he says, quite unaware of the activities of Mrs Walters when she handed her the babies.

As for now, we know that the dead infant found with Mrs Walters at Kensington Station belonged to the servant girl Ada Galley, and it seems likely that the dead infant found with her at the Whitechapel tearooms belonged to the servant girl Rosina Pardoe. As to what happened to Lily's baby, that remains a mystery. But such is the frenzy among the general public that the baby farmers be brought to justice, and such is the widespread belief that they are responsible for the murder of dozens of babies, there is little doubt as to the outcome of this inquest.

33

Friday, 5 December 1902

Amost remarkable thing has occurred. I was lying in bed, feeling rather poorly and concerned that I am once again suffering from the effects of the injuries I received last summer, when I heard a knock upon the door and then my dear wife calling me down quite urgently. And so I made my way rather slowly down the stairs to find a most dishevelled-looking young girl upon the steps, a basket in one hand, shifting anxiously from one foot to the other.

'Yes?' I asked. Something about her struck me as familiar, although I could not recall having seen her before.

'Inspector George?' she asked, and when I nodded that indeed it was I, she looked fearfully around before attempting to thrust the basket into my arms. 'It's not right, sir,' she said urgently, 'this baby has done no one any harm. You take her.'

'What on earth do you mean?' I demanded, aghast at the idea there was a baby in the basket.

'Oh please, sir,' said the girl, again attempting to thrust the basket into my arms, 'Lily would have wanted it, I'm sure she would.'

'Lily?' cried Fanny, grasping the girl by the arm. 'You knew Lily?'

'Yes, ma'am,' and again the girl looked around fearfully. 'My name's Hester. I worked for Nurse Sach at Claymore House.'

'Oh, that dreadful woman,' said Fanny, and quickly she took the basket from the girl and peered within, whereupon her face broke into a most tender and beautiful smile. 'Oh, the poor little mite.'

'Do you mean to say –' I began.

'That this is Lily's child?' asked my wife.

The young girl nodded. 'Look after her if you please,' she said, and then she turned abruptly on the steps and if I had not held her back I fear she would have fled.

'Come in,' I ordered quite harshly, for I was most concerned that at any moment someone would pass and witness this extraordinary exchange. Hester protested that she could not, that she had left her own child unattended and had to return, but she did at last consent and come inside. But once in the front parlour the girl would not even remove her bonnet or shawl, she was so eager to be gone.

'How and where did you find this baby?' I demanded. 'And how do you know it is Lily's?'

'I found it in her bedroom, sir, the day after the police came.'

'In whose bedroom?'

'Why, Nurse Sach's.'

'The baby was there all alone?'

'Yes, sir. I heard a pitiful crying and I couldn't think what it was, I even thought it was a cat got in somehow, but then I looked under the bed and there was the baby in a box! Oh, I was so happy when I found her, sir, and I was going to tell Lily this when she returned, but then' – and here the young girl's voice broke and she struggled to compose herself – 'I left that night, sir, before the police came back, with the baby and my boy, and I went to my sister's in Camden. I thought I could look after her, and she is such a good baby, but I can't any longer. Please will you keep her?'

'Oh, it's a wonder she survived!' said Fanny, and she placed the basket on the parlour floor, took the baby out and began to hold her in her loving arms. 'Hush now,' she whispered as the baby awoke and began, hesitantly, to cry. 'Hush now.'

'But how,' I asked, 'can you be sure it is Lily's?'

'Well sir, Lily had a girl, I was there at her confinement, and the baby I found beneath the bed was a few days old and looked just like her.'

'A few days old!' cried Fanny. 'However did she survive in a box?'

Hester shook her head. 'I don't know, but there was a bottle, ma'am —'

'But,' I interrupted, 'why ever did Nurse Sach keep the baby so long?'

'That I don't know either,' said Hester. 'Perhaps she was waiting on someone to take her and they never came. But I know this was Lily's baby because she was wearing the flannel Lily made for her. See, sir,' and Hester rose and came to stand by my wife, 'see here are the initials she embroidered. It's an "M" and a "P", ma'am. The "M" was to stand for Martha, that's what Lily said. Oh please, you will look after her, won't you?'

'Of course we will,' said my wife, as carefully she began to trace the embroidered initials with her fingers.

'Fanny!' I protested. 'We can't just take in a baby!'

'Oh William, what else can we do? This poor girl doesn't look like she's able to put flesh on her own bones let alone take in a baby, not when she already has a child of her own. Where could she go?' and Fanny looked down at the baby in her arms, sleeping peacefully once more. 'Do you think the Painters would want her? We don't even know where they are. Who is the father?' she demanded.

'I only saw him once, ma'am,' said Hester. 'He came a few days after the birth and paid Nurse Sach some banknotes. He was a good-looking fellow, very tall. He wore no hat.'

'What was his name?'

'I'm sorry, ma'am, I don't know. Oh!' and Hester clasped her hand to her mouth. 'There was a letter. The night Lily left, she gave me a letter to post and I said I would and I never did.'

'Do you know where the letter is?' I asked.

'I'm not sure, sir. I think I put it on the table, but perhaps the police took it.'

'So we shall find the letter and the father,' said Fanny. 'And we'll tell him about his child.'

'And do you think,' I asked rather bluntly, 'that he will take responsibility for her?'

'Well then, what can we do? William, do you want to leave a baby in a workhouse? How long would she survive there? A day perhaps? A week?'

'No, of course not,' I said hurriedly. 'But this is a police matter. We are in the midst of an inquest, Fanny! We cannot simply take the child.'

'Why not!' Fanny burst out, as if forgetting the presence of the girl sitting so anxiously by the fire. 'We are to blame as well, aren't we, William? We *knew* about the baby farmers, ever since that letter we knew something was wrong.'

At this the girl Hester started suddenly in her seat.

'What?' I asked, turning towards her. 'Do you know something about the letter?'

Hester pulled at the shawl around her shoulders with trembling hands. 'I never forgot you, sir.'

'Whatever do you mean?'

'I've seen you before, sir, at a house on East End Road. You were the one who took the mother in because she wasn't caring for her children –'

'East End Road? You were there?'

'Yes, sir. I was a lodger there and I saw you in the room

with the children and I saw how gentle you were with the baby and how you didn't want to take it from its mother. And then when I was living with Nurse Sach, a lady at the laundry said she knew of you, sir, that you were an inspector now –'

'And it was *you* who wrote me the letter?'

Hester nodded and then hung her head.

'Oh,' cried Fanny, 'you see! We are all to blame, William; and this sweet little child,' and here my dear wife began to rock the infant in her arms once more, 'has no blame at all.'

'But she is not our child, Fanny! We can't very well keep her, that is impossible.'

At this the baby woke again and began to cry and Fanny asked where its bottle was and Hester fetched it from the basket and then my dear wife walked out of the room with the baby in her arms, only stopping once to look at me with an expression that I know, from long experience, is better not to question.

34

Thursday, 11 December 1902

Today we returned from Southend-on-Sea. My dear brother Henry was most overjoyed to welcome the new member of his family and his wife Mary Ann quite beside herself with happiness. There is no doubt in my mind that Lily's child will grow up as the apple of my brother's eye and will be given every love and care that he has in his power to give.

The idea only grew upon me gradually. Following the most unexpected visit from the girl Hester, Fanny and I spent the next few days in deep discussion, and while I could see that in some ways the poor child was our responsibility, I could not agree with my dear wife's insistence that we keep her. Fanny spent those days entirely within the home, for fear a neighbour would see the child, and I confess I was most concerned that anyone would hear its cry or, God forbid, Divisional Superintendent Dyball should get wind of things. Our neighbour Mr Gilbert Pickles did give me a rather odd look one morning after the baby had cried most pitifully for over an hour, and I feared he knew something was afoot, but he was, of course, too discreet to mention it.

Fanny spent the time entirely by the baby's side, singing and rocking her, feeding and bathing her, and, as I watched, it was then that I had a sudden thought: let the baby start a new life. Let Lily's child grow up somewhere not in London, overshadowed by her mother's tragic fate, but somewhere with a loving family and good sea air, where she can grow to adulthood and know nothing about the dreadful circumstances of her birth. And where else could this be but with my dear brother, a man who has for so many years longed for a child?

We agreed, after some discussion, that the baby should retain the name her mother gave her, that of Martha, and while she will now take my brother's surname, she will also keep, in fond remembrance, her mother's name Painter as her middle name.

I did, of course, prior to going to Southend, try my best to find any possible alternatives. When a man is about to seriously risk his career, no decision should be made in haste. First I attempted to locate the whereabouts of our former lodgers, placing a series of strongly worded advertisements in the Dublin papers imploring them to contact me as soon as possible on a matter of the greatest possible urgency. These, however, went unanswered. I also located the letter written by Lily to her sweetheart, which was indeed already in the hands of my colleagues, and discovered the father of her child to be an actor named Gus Chevalier. I wrote to him at once, only to find by return of post that the fellow has set sail for America. My dear wife says this is heartless in the extreme. Why would he do this, she asks, when he knew he had a child? I can only assume that he heard of Lily's dreadful death and thought the baby dead as well, and has chosen, much like the Painters, to escape London, and indeed England, for good.

And therefore I had no option but to try and make amends for having failed our lodgers' daughter. I had to do what was best for the child and I truly think the course of action we have taken to be the best.

Shortly before we left Southend this morning, my dear brother took a photograph of the new addition to his family, which Fanny is now keeping beside her at all times.

Friday, 12 December 1902

The baby farmers' inquest has been adjourned. The girl Hester has now, albeit reluctantly, given evidence as to the nature of the business at Claymore House and her employment with Nurse Sach. But she did not, of course, make any mention of the discovery of Lily's baby. I am quite certain that the eventual verdict shall be one of murder and that it won't be long before the case is therefore transferred to the Central Criminal Court. I rather dread my time in the witness box, for obvious reasons.

The gentlemen of the press continue to report on the inquest in a most breathless and excitable manner. It is remarkable how they are eager enough to castigate the baby farmers for putting monetary reward above the sanctity of human life, but are happy enough to continue accepting payment for advertisements of a most dubious nature. On the very day the arrests were announced I noted that the *Islington Gazette*, in its miscellaneous columns, carried four advertisements soliciting for babies, and in today's paper there were six such advertisements, all taken by persons expressing a desire to adopt a baby, and all with a promise of a moderate premium in return for entire surrender of the child.

Monday, 15 December 1902

I have received, in the first post this morning, a letter from my dear brother Henry. He reports that Martha is coming on famously: she eats quite voraciously, sleeps well during the night and has a great love for colourful objects. Fanny is a little cheerier now, and busy making baby garments for the child. She has even agreed that we purchase a pine tree, on which she has placed a number of candles, and she is most concerned as to whether our troops returning from South Africa will be home by Christmas.

Tuesday, 16 December 1902

Fanny has brought little Martha a book for Christmas: Rudyard Kipling's newly published *Just So Stories for Little Children*. When I pointed out that at less than two months old she is unlikely to read the book for quite some time, Fanny was unamused and said an adult can easily read it to her.

Wednesday, 17 December 1902

Rather colder than late and generally overcast. Fanny has been plunged into mental gloom once more. Still she blames herself for Lily's sad fate, and try as I may I cannot dissuade her of this. I have tried to cheer her up in all manner of ways, for I believe it would be in everyone's interest if we could return to some semblance of normal life. It distresses me that I cannot now remember the last time I heard the sound of my dear wife's laughter. I suggested that she distract herself with a visit, perhaps, to a variety show, but she will have none of it. She is not even tempted to attend the Camden, which this year has chosen for its pantomime one of her favourites, *Aladdin and His Wonderful Lamp*. Fanny informs me that until recently Gus Chevalier, the father of Lily's child, appeared at the Camden, and as a result she has declared that she will never go there again.

Thursday, 18 December 1902

The inquest continues. Today a man identifying himself as the husband of Nurse Sach made a sudden appearance in court to protest, unsuccessfully, that he no longer wanted his wife's solicitor to represent her. He is a tall, angry-looking fellow by the name of Jeffrey Sach, a builder originally from Essex, and he resides in East Finchley, not far from Claymore House. The Sachs also have a child together, a four-year-old girl. Fanny is most beside herself at this, and the fact that Nurse Sach, who appeared to so cruelly mistreat the children in her care, is a mother herself. Fanny is also curious to know about the husband, and whether he knew of the baby farming and, if he did, then what role he played in this. But as he is not to be called to give evidence, and as he has not been charged with either aiding or abetting, I suspect we shall never know.

Thursday, 25 December 1902
Christmas Day. I have again received a letter from Henry. He reports that little Martha is well and thriving. She is now able to turn her little head and watch her new dear mother as she goes about her daily tasks, and my brother asserts that she is quite the cleverest baby he has ever seen! She has a full head of hair now, and the most widest, most beautiful brown eyes.

We expect Violet and her family later today, as well as Arthur and Albert. Fanny is at least busy with cooking and general preparation.

In nine days the baby farmers' inquest will resume, and once it does then my entire time shall be spent in court.

35

Thursday, 1 January 1903

A New Year has begun and I can only hope that it is more peaceful than the last. My dear wife and I spent yesterday evening quietly at home, for it was my good fortune not to be on duty until later today, and we retired early to the muted sounds of fireworks in the street. The year that has passed will be memorable on many levels, for the war has ended and our King was crowned. But in our household it will equally be remembered as a year of terrible tragedy and sorrow.

This morning I suggested that we might perhaps, sometime in the near future, consider taking in new lodgers, so as to bring new life to our household, as it were. Fanny says she cannot face it just yet.

Friday, 2 January 1903

The resumed inquest into the baby farmers has, unsurprisingly, returned a verdict of wilful murder. Evidence given by myself, Detective Wright and other officers at previous hearings was read over yesterday, and all that remained was the Deputy Coroner's summing up. He explained to the gentlemen of the jury that they must say whether they were satisfied that the dead baby came from the house of Nurse Sach, whether it was alive when it was handed to Mrs Walters and whether it died from wilful neglect. I am not at all surprised that it took the jury just five minutes to decide. The matter is now one of felony and is bound over to the Central Criminal Court.

Thursday, 15 January 1903

I arrived early at the Old Bailey this morning, for such is the size of the new court that there is a labyrinth of corridors, waiting rooms and chambers to navigate and I was anxious to allow myself plenty of time. Outside a dense crowd had already gathered. There was a sea of black-frocked gentlemen and bonneted ladies and, balanced on the back of a cart, two fellows with cameras aloft, all eager to catch sight of the baby farmers who have now become two of the most infamous women in London. Another dense crowd had gathered by the narrow alleyway that is Warwick Passage, queuing noisily for admittance to the public viewing galleries and evidently eager to gratify their desire for sensation.

I found the appropriate courtroom without delay, one of the largest courts and finely decked out with dark wooden panelling, although conditions were still extremely cramped. As I made my way to my spot at the tables, I looked up at the gallery to see it heavily packed with onlookers and members of the press. And then a respectful hush befell the courtroom as Mr Justice Darling strode in; a most harsh individual and one whom I have encountered a number of times before, forever with his brows deeply furrowed and his lips curled in distaste. It has to be said that not everyone fell silent, however, for there were some murmurings from the gentlemen of the press, among whom Justice Darling is most unpopular largely owing to a case of obscene libel some three years back.

Once Justice Darling had settled himself in his place, with much arrangement and re-arrangement of his robes, the prisoners were then brought in. At once the spectators began jostling furiously in their attempt to see the baby farmers. Both prisoners appeared to regard their surroundings in a most disinterested manner, especially when compared with the throng of excited ladies in the gallery. Mrs Walters sat down at once and remained motionless at first, her hands clasped in her lap. Nurse Sach sat with her head bent, and when she did raise her face she looked a great deal older and thinner than when I had seen her last. Indeed, her time in custody has savaged her once handsome features, and she barely resembled the lady I encountered that day I first paid a visit to East Finchley. Then she had appeared a respectable, if not to say authoritative, figure and it puzzles me still that such an outwardly educated lady should turn to such a business. Much has been made in recent newspaper reports of her appearance and class, and, in terms of her beauty, she has more than once been likened to Charlotte Corday. But while Corday must have been in no doubt that she would be executed for her crime, I do believe that Nurse Sach does not for a moment think she herself will hang. In fact, her attitude in the courtroom appears to be one of stunned disbelief that a woman such as herself should have found herself a prisoner in the dock. And while Corday's motives were clear, and history tells us she believed her assassination of Marat would save the Republic, as of Nurse Sach's motives, they are far more mundane. It is greed, I believe, that rules Nurse Sach.

But to return to events in court today: Mr Charles Mathews, prosecuting on behalf of the Treasury, began by relating the story to date with the view of showing that this was not an isolated case. He conducted himself with characteristic flair, and while his voice is high and thin, this somehow serves only to increase the effectiveness of his speeches.

A number of witnesses then took the stand, beginning with those with whom Mrs Walters had previously taken lodgings, and then the poor girl Ada Galley, who cut a very pitiful figure as she was ushered into the witness box. I confess at this point to feeling some relief, however misplaced, that our poor lodgers' daughter has been saved from undergoing a similar ordeal. I noted how Nurse Sach looked up as the girl reached the witness box and then glanced across the courtroom at her husband with an expression that was impossible to fathom. Mrs Walters, meanwhile, grew agitated and began twitching her shoulders and stamping her feet, much as she had upon her arrest at South Kensington.

Once the poor girl Ada Galley was in position in the witness box, Mr Mathews began by asking if she could confirm her name and place of abode. 'I am Ada Charlotte Galley,' she replied in a most hesitant voice, her face flushing uneasily, her fearful eyes glancing around the courtroom from beneath her simple cloth bonnet. 'I am a servant and live at Stanley Villa, Finchley.'

'And can you explain to us, if you will, how you first came to know the prisoners?'

'Last year I become pregnant.' The poor girl blushed furiously and there was a murmur of sympathy from up in the gallery. 'In August I saw an advertisement in *Daltons* newspaper for a lying-in home. I went there and after I had been there some time Nurse Sach asked me if would like the child I was to bear adopted.' Here the girl's voice dropped so that it was barely audible. 'I said I should and asked her how much.'

Mr Mathews then led the girl through her testimony, before producing an array of infant garments and draping them slowly and most dramatically over the wooden bars of the witness box. 'Ada Galley,' he asked, his voice echoing around the silent courtroom, 'do you recognise these garments?'

'Yes,' said the poor girl, who looked near to collapse, 'those are the things I made for my baby.' When I glanced at the two prisoners it was to see Nurse Sach sitting quite rigidly with her eyes tightly closed and Mrs Walters fumbling desperately upon her person as if looking for something which she evidently could not find. Still the poor girl stood there, surrounded by the pitiful baby clothes, as Mr Leycester for the defence leapt to his feet. 'Did you not, *Miss* Galley,' he demanded quite forcefully, 'tell Nurse Sach that "whatever happens I must get rid of the baby"?'

'No,' said the girl with a sudden force of spirit. 'I never did.'

'You never were anxious to dispose of your child? You never declared upon its birth, "what shall I do with it? I must get rid of it somehow or other"?' Mr Leycester looked around the courtroom, an expression of disbelief on his face. 'Are we to believe, *Miss* Galley, that you had no idea, no *inkling*, as to what transaction was actually taking place? Did you really believe that your child was to be adopted by a titled lady? Rather, I put it to you, *Miss* Galley, that you knew exactly what you were doing when you answered the advertisement and went to Claymore House: you desired above all else to "get rid" of the baby.'

The poor girl simply shook her head and was at last allowed to return to her seat. It was shortly afterwards that I was required to take the stand, and I can only hope I gave my testimony in as clear and forthright a manner as possible. Despite my considerable experience, it is still unsettling to be in the witness box, and there was the added worry, of course, that I should inadvertently divulge more information than was strictly necessary. But I stuck closely to the facts, noting always the day, date, time and place of each event, although at several points I did feel the need to stop and consult my notebook. This appeared to irritate Justice Darling, who at one point asked me quite smartly where my evidence was leading and, at another point, commented that I was going on a bit, which I thought quite unnecessary.

The case has now been adjourned until tomorrow.

36

Friday, 16 January 1903

I have spent the entire day at court. The two gentlemen for the defence attempted, without much success, to accuse the prosecution's case of being nothing but surmises and conjectures. But the onlookers would have none of this and such were their outbursts that Justice Darling more than once threatened to clear the court.

Nurse Sach appeared even more haggard today and listened impassively as her defence counsel argued that she had believed that, by handing over Ada Galley's baby to Mrs Walters, she had obtained a comfortable home for the child. As for Mrs Walters, her defence argued that it had not been proved that she had actually murdered the infant, and that while chlorodyne might be an improper drug to administer to a child, it had not been done with any bad intentions. At this point a lady in the gallery let out a loud cry of 'Shame!'

The evidence and summing up over, the lights of the courtroom were lowered as the gentlemen of the jury left to consider their verdict. They deliberated for just forty minutes before returning to the courtroom, led by the foreman, an elderly bespectacled fellow who appeared overawed by the proceedings. 'We find both the prisoners guilty,' he said, his voice trembling slightly, 'but with a recommendation of mercy.'

'On what ground?' snapped Mr Justice Darling.

'Because, My Lord,' said the foreman with some attempt at dignity, 'they are women.'

Justice Darling looked as if he would like to have disputed this, but instead turned to the prisoners. 'Do you have anything to say as to why the judgement of the law should not be passed upon you?'

'No,' replied Mrs Walters with a strangely indifferent air.

'No,' answered Nurse Sach in a very faint voice, and it seemed as if it was only at this moment that, at last, she realised the nature of her fate.

Justice Darling frowned furiously at both prisoners before declaring, 'Annie Walters and Amelia Sach, the jury found you both guilty of wilful murder of the dead child of Ada Galley. It is plain to me that you, Sach, have been the instigator of the other woman to the actual taking away of life as a part of the business which you carried on.'

'Amen,' cried a woman's voice from the galley.

Justice Darling scowled up at the spectators before returning his gaze to Nurse Sach, whom he then accused of being in the habit of receiving children from their mothers, obtaining money which she kept for her own use, and then handing the children over to be done to death. There was a great hush within the courtroom as slowly Justice Darling donned the black silk cap to pronounce the sentence of death, which was met with great cheers and sobs from the spectators.

The prisoners were then conveyed in separate cabs to Holloway Prison and I very much doubt if the Home Secretary will consider a reprieve.

It is late, the fire in the parlour is nearly burnt out and my dear wife is sleeping. There could not, I believe, have been any other sentence than the one delivered today. But it troubles me still that if I had acted with more force at the beginning when I first received the anonymous letter, if I had insisted that Divisional

Superintendent Dyball take the matter more seriously than he did, if we had kept better watch on Mrs Walters once she took lodgings in Danbury Street, then the outcome may have been very different and the lives of at least two children quite possibly saved. But for now the two women await their doom; the Islington child murder case has nearly come to an end and soon too will my journal.

Saturday, 17 January 1903
I have received another letter from my dear brother Henry. Martha is now able to make the funniest little noises, and she has the habit of twitching her lips whenever her dear mother or father speak to her as if she would like to speak in return. He is quite convinced that this is further evidence of her highly intelligent nature, and I do not wish to disappoint him by pointing out that this is a stage most babies go through! He reports that they have found themselves of late calling her Mo and hopes it will not trouble Fanny or myself if they adopt this as a nickname.

Tuesday, 3 February 1903
The women have been hanged. And so we bear witness to the first execution of women in England in the King's reign. The press has kept us fully updated on the matter, at which the brothers Billington officiated, striving to bring us as much detail as possible. Last night both prisoners were retired to rest at 8 p.m. and were said to have passed a fairly good night, being roused at 6 a.m. when visited by the prison governor, matron and chaplain. However, from the time of their dressing both women exhibited great anxiety and took only a spare breakfast, after which both were offered a glass of brandy by the prison doctor. It appears that while both prisoners saw relatives the day before, still no confession was forthcoming, despite the prison chaplain's repeated efforts.

The scaffold at Holloway Prison is an entirely new one and, while situated only a few yards from the condemned cell, Nurse Sach, we are told, had to be physically carried to the place of execution. Mrs Walters, however, apparently stayed quite calm as the white hood was put over her head and the noose adjusted, calling out 'Goodbye Sach' as the executioner stepped to one side and pulled the lever and she plummeted into the pit below.

They were executed shortly after 8.30 this morning and death was said in both cases to be instantaneous. Walters was given a short drop of 5 ft 10 in, Sach a drop of 6 ft 1 in, owing to a difference in weight and height. After the regulated one hour, their bodies were removed to be buried in unmarked graves within the walls of the prison, and there will remain.

And so I am to close my journal, which I have kept now for two years. When I began, it was with the innocent enough notion of recording the work of an ordinary man doing an extraordinary job. How well I recall the day our lodgers the Painters first arrived for interview, how lively our little household became, and how excited was my dear wife with Lily's successful debut upon the stage. Now our former lodgers have quite disappeared, apparently unaware of the existence of Lily's child and the family with whom she now resides. It is for this reason that having completed my journal I shall place it somewhere safe, for I wish that the secret held within these pages not come to light as long as those affected by it remain alive. I have even considered burning the journal, but Fanny says that will not do. Instead my dear wife suggests that I enclose in its pages a photograph my brother took of little Martha last month, as well as a lock of hair, and deposit it carefully in a place away from the prying eyes of the world and known only to ourselves.

37

Lily Painter

Summer 2009

It is late at night and the mother Annie sits stiffly in front of her computer, her back as straight as that of an attentive school child. Outside the houses are steeped in darkness, hers is the only light. The night is warm but Annie wears her new dressing gown, a luxurious red silk one that she bought two days ago and which falls in graceful lines around her body. She looks up at the noticeboard upon the wall where she has pushed dull brass pins into the soft brown cork, holding letters and bills and newly copied papers. In the middle of the board is a postcard she has bought, a photograph of St Mary's Parish Church from so many years ago, the delicate pointed crest of the church steeple rising high against a beige winter sky, the clock face showing a quarter to four. The street before the church is empty but for a single figure, a woman in black. The hem of the woman's dress grazes the pavement, she has a hat upon her head and her body is sharp against the blurred surface of the road. The woman is standing as if she is about to cross; she has a bundle caught tightly against her chest and she holds it in both arms. Annie looks at the photograph and she wonders who the woman can be and where she is going with the bundle in her arms.

She has been so busy these past few weeks, ever since she first went to the local history centre to find out about her house. There is a determination about her now; she is a woman who will simply not give up. She has found me and my family in this house. She knows about the baby farmers. And she does not believe I killed myself. I have heard her say this to her mother on the telephone, heard her ask how it could be possible that I would kill myself. And she is right; it was the tram, that was all. A split second of a stumble, the flap of my old worn cloak caught in my boot and then the darkness. And then I was there, in Claymore House. But it was empty of people and although I stayed and waited and watched, there was no one there who could help me. And so I found myself back on Stanley Road, and Inspector George was very elderly and his sweet wife Fanny was ailing and bedridden. But I wouldn't go; instead I watched and I listened and I waited.

Annie turns her head; her shoulders are tense as she looks at the window behind her. A light summer rain begins to fall outside and she shivers. She is no longer as comfortable in this house. She is unsettled by the deathly coldness in this room and by the bedroom window left open at night. She does not understand how her computer can be on when she has turned it off, or why the light flickers in her daughter's room. She is a little afraid by the dog, which growls when it enters her office. She is starting to feel me now; she is beginning to truly sense the restlessness that pervades this house.

Annie turns her face back to the computer. Her skin is darker from the weeks of sun and the freckles on the bridge of her nose are a deep autumn brown. 'This is ridiculous,' she mutters. 'I don't even know what I'm looking for.' Her voice is low for she doesn't want to wake her child Molly sleeping in her bedroom upstairs. She sighs and turns off the computer, and then the phone on her desk begins to ring. Quickly she picks it up, her voice a whisper.

'Oh hi,' she says. 'No, I'm awake, you haven't woken me.' She cradles the receiver under her chin, begins absentmindedly to stroke the silky cloth upon her thigh. 'How come you're up this late too? Oh, go on.' She holds the phone tight and listens. 'Thanks, Danny,' she says at last. 'It's really nice of you, I'll look that up now . . .' She hesitates, she wants to say more but then she gives a light laugh. 'No, I won't stay up too late,' and she puts the phone down. I wait for her to turn the computer on again; I want her to keep looking, I have to make her keep looking because I cannot rest and nor can she until she finds out what the baby farmers did with my baby.

'Mum!' Molly shouts from her bedroom.

'What?' Annie is startled.

'Mum!' Molly calls again, her voice urgent.

Annie sighs and walks to the landing.

'Mum!'

Quickly Annie runs up the stairs, propelled by a mother's sudden dread that something is wrong. 'What is it?'

Molly is lying in bed, kicking restlessly at the sheet that covers her. 'I'm hot.'

Annie looks at her daughter. She knows her child is fussing, that it's not the heat that bothers her. 'Do you want the fan on?'

'Yes,' says Molly, satisfied now. 'And I want you to lie down with me.'

Annie lies on the bed and Molly rests her head against her mother's chest. 'You OK?' Annie whispers, and she kisses her daughter upon her forehead.

Molly sighs and they lie together until the child's breathing becomes softer and she falls asleep. And when she does, Annie lies there, very still, without moving. She knows her closeness comforts her daughter, but she seeks a comfort too and she does not know where she will find it.

Outside the rain grows harder. It lashes furiously at the windowpanes and forms a curtain of wetness over the lilac trees in the garden. The wind blows in through the grate beneath the shelf and the framed cross-stitch sample with the daughter's name trembles upon the wall. The stitch is delicate, as delicate as the initials I embroidered into the clothes I made for my baby those days and weeks I spent at Claymore House.

Annie is back in her office. The rain has stopped for now. Outside in the garden is a fox. It has a dirty ginger coat and a ragged, bitten tail, and it is standing still in the deep shadows cast by the lilac trees. The fox looks around, sniffs at something on the ground and then steps forward, its movement triggering a light from an adjoining garden so that it is caught there for a moment, its eyes clear in the night, its white underbelly gleaming. Then it leaps clumsily at the trellis and the jasmine shivers.

Annie senses something has happened, but when she stands and looks outside her gaze is not on the ground but up high above the roofs and chimney pots. She rubs at her arms and draws her red dressing gown around herself.

Molly opens her eyes; she is awake again and she knows her mother is no longer there. She puts out one hand and begins to pat beneath her mattress. She is becoming a secretive child. She hides things from her mother, notes that she has written to herself, packets of sweets from school friends which she places carefully in among the spines of her orderly row of books. And at night sometimes she wakes and checks her hidden goods. Sometimes too she cries, but not loud enough for her mother to hear, for she is frightened by her mother's grief and doesn't wish to make it worse. And on those nights she takes her little lizard and she lays it on the pillow beside her and whispers to it. 'One day, lizard,' she says, 'Dad will come back.' Molly is a sensitive child and she is on the cusp of change. She will sense me too if I force her to.

The mother stands up from her chair. She has not been able to find what she was looking for and now at last she is going to bed. Then she turns, her shoulders flinch, she can hear something upon the stairs. 'Jojo?' she asks, and she waits, but when the dog does not appear she remains there paralysed, her dressing gown pulled tight around her waist. Then she goes up the stairs and the carpeted boards creak beneath her feet. She stops at Molly's bedroom and listens to her daughter's breathing. She does not realise the child is awake again; instead she watches her and smiles because she loves her so. And as she turns to go to her bedroom I am watching her and I think, No, you will not sleep, you will not feel comfortable in this house, not until you have found what happened to my child.

38

Annie Sweet

July 2009

It's supposed to be summer and school's just about to break up and it's been raining on and off most of the night. I don't know how we're going to get through six weeks of holiday if it goes on like this. Molly fusses about getting ready and she yells at the dog when it gets in the way and tries to lick her school bag. But I can cope today because Danny rang last night. Since we sat in the café and talked about the baby farmers, he's been ringing me with updates. First he told me he'd read another newspaper report and did I want to see a copy. Then he said he had to go to the Colindale newspaper library and did I want him to look up anything while he was there, and last night it was to say the entire baby farmers' trial is now online.

I drop Molly off at the school gates. She's laden down with bags containing her costume for the end-of-year play, and in a few hours I'll be coming back to watch her. I take the dog on to Hampstead Heath and we head for the first pond. The water is grey, the small shoreline littered with sticks and chewed-up tennis balls. I sit on the bench by a fallen tree, and just as the sun comes out my phone rings.

'Hi,' I say, getting up, feeling the urge to walk around.

'Am I disturbing you?' Danny asks. I can hear noise in the background, a printer perhaps, so he must be at work.

'No, no, not at all. I'm just on the heath. Thanks for the call last night, but I couldn't find the trial.'

'It's on the Old Bailey site.'

'I know, I saw the site, but it was all these proceedings going back to the 1600s and I couldn't find the right one.'

'Just look up Sach and Walters, it's January 1903,' says Danny. 'I should have just downloaded you a copy and sent it over. I'll do that later.'

I smile as I walk up and down the edge of the pond. I always seem to be saying thank you to Danny.

'You sound tired,' he says.

'Oh,' I laugh, a little thrown by his concern, 'it's just that I'm not sleeping well at the moment, maybe I'm getting a bit spooked with all this baby-farmer stuff. And my house feels weird.'

'Weird?'

I laugh again; I don't want him to think I'm crazy. 'Oh, it's nothing. So did you read the trial?'

'Yeah. Well, I skimmed it. It's a bit dry and wordy and you don't really get a real sense of what went on. Sach and Walters don't say anything.'

'They don't? What, they don't say anything at all and they were on trial for murder?'

'Not a word. I guess they didn't want to give evidence, or the defence thought it better not to get them in the dock. Or then again' – Danny pauses and it sounds like he's crunching on a Tic Tac – 'it could just be a case of selective reporting and they did say something but it never made it into the proceedings.'

'Is there any mention of Lily Painter?'

'No.' Danny sounds apologetic. 'I couldn't see any of the witnesses mentioning her and there's nothing about her baby either, although I didn't read it word for word. But I thought you'd like to see it anyway.'

233

'Oh, I would,' I say quickly, because perhaps I haven't shown how grateful I am.

'But I thought . . .' Danny stops. He's speaking to someone in the background and so I wait, thinking perhaps he's going to suggest we meet again. 'It might be worth following up on this inspector.'

'Oh.' I feel slightly disappointed. 'Which inspector?'

'The one who started the whole thing off. His evidence is throughout the trial – Inspector William George. He's there right from the beginning.'

I pick up a stick soggy with dog slobber and throw it in the pond. I bend to pick up another and then I stop. 'But Danny, he's the one who used to live in my house.'

'Really?'

'Yes. He was the landlord. William George, police inspector. He's right there on the census. Why didn't I realise this before? But that's bizarre, because that means Lily was living with him at the same time he was after the baby farmers.'

'And so,' says Danny, 'he must have known exactly what was going on.'

'Maybe,' I say, although for some reason I feel doubtful.

'Leave it with me,' Danny says. 'It'll be easy enough to look him up. What are you doing today anyway?'

Again I'm thrown; it's been a long time since anyone's asked me what I'm doing today. 'Well, I'm not at work . . .' I stop, about to mention Molly's school play, but I haven't really spoken about Molly to Danny and he hasn't mentioned his child, his boy, again either. It's like this topic is off-limits. And as I throw the stick into the pond for the dog, I wonder if maybe the reason I don't mention Molly to Danny is not because she has nothing to do with my search for Lily Painter but because I don't want him to think of me as a mother, as someone who cooks and cleans and goes to school plays. Maybe I want him to think of me more as a person, an individual, a woman.

I'm walking quickly to get back to school before Molly's show starts. I can't believe there's actually a queue outside the door to the school office; there are thirty parents here already and they're standing excitedly waiting. And then I see him, I see Ben right at the head of the queue. He must have come straight from work: he's wearing a grey suit. I stop on the pavement, take my place at the end of the queue, and stand and stare at the back of his head. I used to know that head, I stroked that head and kissed that head and cried on that head and woke next to that head for night after night for fifteen years. And I thought I always would, I never imagined I'd be without him, I never even considered he wouldn't be around, that I'd be standing alone in a queue outside Molly's school like this.

My friend Heather sent me an email this morning. She wants to know how I am. She says she never thought Ben was good enough for me. And I hold on to this thought as I look at the back of his head; I will continue to remember only the bad things because I don't want to remember when we were in love because that would hurt too much.

And then I see her, I see Carrie in the queue as well. How could he? How could he bring *her* here to a school play with *my* child? Because that's how I think of Molly. She's mine. She is all I have. My feet feel numb and I get a shuddery sensation in my chest. I don't want to look at Carrie, but I do. She's bringing attention to herself anyway, speaking to someone on her mobile, laughing loudly. I don't know if Molly knew her dad and Carrie were coming today; if she did, she never told me. Was that why she couldn't sleep last night and why she wanted me to lie with her? She must have told her dad about the play, they must have had a whole conversation about it, and this makes me feel so shut out of everything I could sit down and cry. But now I need to be a bright happy mother coming to see her daughter in a school show.

The queue moves as the doors open and we hurry inside. It smells warm and spicy in the foyer; the kids must be having curry for lunch. I put my head down and walk as fast as I can along the corridor to the hall, not even taking in all the colourful displays on the noticeboards, only thinking I have to get into the hall as quick as I can and find a seat as far away from Ben and Carrie as possible. I have to act like I just don't care.

The children are all crammed into the hall, most of them sitting on the floor. Teachers try to hush their classes, hissing 'shh!' and putting fingers sternly to their lips. Then the lights lower and it begins. It's a scene from *Oliver Twist* and Molly is Mrs Bumble. She wears an old apron that Mum once gave me, over a patterned shirt that I don't think I've seen before. The children on the small school stage are singing a workhouse song and when they finish Molly looks around at them until she spies one resting, his head on his hands. 'What do you think this is?' she snarls, 'A tea party?'

Some of the parents in the audience laugh in surprise.

'No, missus,' says the boy, who is in the same year as Molly but half her size, 'it's just I'm so hungry.'

Molly draws herself up to her full height. She has a terrible look on her face, and when she speaks her voice is vicious. 'Don't you dare speak to me in that tone, you little gutter rat.'

I feel goosebumps along my arms; Molly is so convincing that I'm a little afraid of her. Two women in the row in front turn around and smile at me. 'Oh, she's good, isn't she?' says one. 'She's a natural.'

I stare at the children on the stage and I see that Molly is the only one who is actually acting. She believes she is Mrs Bumble, she really thinks she's the matron of a workhouse. As the boy playing Oliver begins to speak I see Molly's lips move because she knows his lines as well. 'Right,' she says, 'who wants some lunch then?'

The children on the stage gather around her and she bends her head towards a little yellow-haired boy. 'How about some kippers?' she asks, and she gives a friendly, motherly smile.

The boy pats exaggeratedly on his stomach, looks off the stage and smiles at someone in the audience. 'Yum!' he says.

'Or,' says Molly, turning to another child, 'how about some fresh hot chips? Or what about ice cream and chocolate cake?' She mimes eating cake and licks slowly, longingly, at her fingers. Then she gives a cackle of a laugh. 'No, what you lot are having is gruel!'

The play ends and Molly comes to the front of the stage to loud applause. She bows carefully, but I see her scanning the hall. I know she's seen me and I know now she's looking for her father, and although she's still bowing there's a glint of desperation in her eyes. I look around as well, but to my relief Ben and Carrie have gone.

'That was good, really, really good, Molly,' I tell her after I've made my way through the kids and the teachers and the parents.

'Are you proud of me then?' she says, and her voice is as sharp as Mrs Bumble's.

'Yes,' I say, but proud is not the word – it's more amazement that my child can act like this. I stroke her hair, try to get the feeling of closeness we had last night, the feeling I had when she was little and would slump into my arms. And I'm thinking,

You made sure your dad was here, didn't you, Molly. You wanted us both to be here because you want us back together again. And I'm so depressed at the impossibility of this that I feel my body sag like a bag thrown on the floor.

When I get home the dog is snoring and for once there is no damage at all. I go into my office and the red light on the phone is flashing; there's a message from Mum. I ring her back at once.

'Oh, it's you, pet,' she says as if she's surprised. 'How was Molly's school play?'

'She was brilliant actually, Mum.' I look up at my notice-board and the postcard I bought at the local history centre of a woman on a deserted street before a church. I don't know why, but this image haunts me. I've even convinced myself that what she's holding in her arms is a baby. 'Ben was there,' I say flatly.

'That's good,' says Mum.

No it isn't, I want to say, it isn't *good* at all. 'Actually it was really difficult for me . . .'

'He's her father, Annie. He should be there.'

I'm so irritated and infuriated by this and by her assumption that Ben plays such an important role in our lives that I ask the question I'm not allowed to ask, the question I know she hates. 'Didn't you ever want to know about your father?'

'What?'

I know she's heard me. 'You must have, Mum. You must have wondered who he was, growing up and not knowing anything about your dad. I'm sure you could find out about him now if you wanted. Danny, my friend at the local history centre, he can find out just about anything.'

'Can he now.' Mum sounds suspicious. Any moment now she's going to tell me the kettle's boiling and she has to go.

'Yeah, I'm sure he could. If you gave him the basics he could find out more about your dad. I mean, where was he posted when he came over here? What was he doing exactly? Was he in the air force? What happened to him after he left England? If you had a picture . . .'

'Which I don't,' says Mum, and she's annoyed now, she wants me to stop my interference.

'But if we just had some sort of clue then we could find him. He might even still be alive!'

'Oh, don't be silly, Annie,' says Mum. 'Your grandfather died at Dunkirk.'

I haven't heard from Danny all week and I get so distracted thinking about this that eventually I ring him. When I ask the woman at the local history centre if I can speak to Danny, I think I hear her laugh as she calls for him.

'Hello?' he says. It's a bright, efficient 'hello'. This must be his work voice.

'Hi, it's me, Annie.'

'Oh, hi.' He sounds happy to hear from me. 'Oh shit, I forgot to send the trial stuff over, didn't I? It's been hectic around here.'

'Of course,' I say. Of course he's busy, of course he has other things to do.

'Actually, I've been meaning to ring you because I've found out a bit more about your Inspector George.'

'You have?'

'Yes, I'll tell you when I see you.'

'Oh, tell me now.'

Danny laughs. 'Well, I had a look at the General Register Index and he died in 1937, so he lived to a ripe old age.'

'And his wife Fanny?'

'She died much earlier.'

'Oh.' I feel sad about this.

'They had three children.'

'Yes, I remember, I saw them on the census roll.'

'And,' says Danny, 'I've looked him up in earlier censuses as well. He came from Essex . . .'

'Yes, I think I remember that.'

'And he only had one sibling, which is unusual. A brother who lived in Southend-on-Sea.'

'Southend?'

'Do you know it?'

'No, but it must be nice, by the sea.'

Danny laughs. 'You obviously haven't been to Southend. I used to go there as a kid. Listen, I've got to go to Colindale on Saturday. Could you meet me there and I'll give you what I've got?'

39

Saturday is a bright, sunny day, and Molly is at her father's when I set off to meet Danny. I feel claustrophobic on the Tube, but a few stops before Colindale the train emerges over ground and everything feels better and lighter again. I come out of the Tube station and walk along a small parade of shops until I get to the library. But the building disappoints me. I've read that it holds millions of newspapers going back 200 years so I was expecting something impressive, but it looks like a disused factory. I walk in through the red-topped railings and step inside. On the right is a desk where an elderly man stands in an old-fashioned uniform like a cloakroom attendant. He insists I show some ID and hand in my bag. Then he tells me to sit in the waiting room, which is through a set of double doors. The room is half full even though the library hasn't opened yet, and it's silent but for the hum of a drinks machine and a water cooler.

There are only men in here, and they sit individually on soft, low chairs. Some are reading papers or going through notebooks, others are just sitting quietly waiting. I wonder why they've come today and what it is they're looking for. They could be academics or students doing historical research, or they could be looking for something more personal, trying to track down some missing link or searching for a long-lost relative.

The doors open and Danny comes in. It's like sunshine has just entered the room. He walks slowly, he's smiling, his face ready to nod at anyone and especially at me. I stand up as he gets nearer and then I don't know what to do – shake his hand? But Danny has already moved to kiss me on my cheek.

'So,' I laugh, embarrassed.

Danny hands me a brown envelope. 'So. Here's a copy of the trial, and I've printed out some of the basics about Inspector George. It's a good job we're here, because now there's something else I want you to see.'

We go upstairs and into the reading room, its pale-blue walls and carpet restful after the sun outside. A handful of men have got in before us and are sitting waiting at wooden tables, like a science class without a teacher. A man stands tensely in front of a computer, both arms stretched out, his finger rolling impatiently on the mouse. Then there's a clatter in the corridor and a woman comes in, pushing a wooden trolley of huge red-bound books.

'Have a seat,' says Danny, and I watch him head for the desk, see a young woman beaming as he comes up.

We're sitting in a stall that looks like a Space Invaders booth, in front of a microfiche machine far larger and newer than the one at the local history centre. The screen is lit up, but otherwise we're in a pool of darkness. I can hear, but not see, other people: an occasional cough, the scratch of a badly sharpened pencil on paper.

'I've got something for you here,' says Danny, slotting in the film. 'A friend who works here found it for me in a newspaper index.'

I sit on the single chair and feel him take up position behind me. 'What is it?' I ask. I'm looking at a newspaper page on the screen in front of me, a jumble of adverts and reports. 'Which paper is this?'

'Well, that's the thing,' Danny says, and I can sense, without turning, that he's smiling. 'It's a Dublin paper.'

'Dublin? Why?'

'Look at this.' He leans forward, his hand just grazing my shoulder, and touches the screen.

Urgent Notice. Would Mrs and Mrs Frederick Painter of Dublin contact their former landlord on a matter of utmost urgency. Strictest confidence. Reply at once, 43 Stanley Road, Upper Holloway, London.

'Strange, hey?' asks Danny.

'Oh my God.' I touch my finger to the screen. 'Who put this in, Inspector George?'

'Well, he was their former landlord, like you said.'

'But why's he trying to contact the Painters? What's the matter of utmost urgency?'

'What I think,' says Danny softly, 'is that Inspector George took the baby in.'

My hand falls from the screen and knocks painfully against the sharp metal side of the desk. I hear a cough and a rustle of papers from somewhere in the darkness. 'You think *he* took Lily's baby in? That the baby was still alive?'

'Well, it is possible. If the baby did survive, then he was her landlord, he was a police inspector and he was fully involved in the case. If anyone would know about the baby, it would be him.'

'But how? How could that have happened?'

Danny shrugs. 'I don't know, but he obviously has something he wants to tell her parents. They know their daughter died, so what would he need to tell them? I don't think it's a case of unpaid rent or forwarding post or anything like that. It has to be something important but something he needs to be discreet about. And the baby was illegitimate — that was a big deal back then, that was something someone might have wanted covered up. Some weeks I spend half my time trying to help someone trace an illegitimate relative.'

'Do you think the Painters replied?'

Danny shrugs again and we look at the advert as though if we look at it long enough everything will slot into place.

'And if he did take in Lily's baby, then did he keep it?'

'I haven't found anything yet that says he did. Workhouse records might show something I suppose, but like I said, illegitimate babies are hard to trace. Children could just be passed around from one family to another, from one part of the country to another, and there just aren't the records to trace them.'

'So we've come to another dead end?'

'Not quite. There are still other things to look for – his will perhaps, there might be something in that.'

I pick up Molly from her dad's and she doesn't look like she's had a good time. When Ben opens the door Molly is right there behind him, all ready with her overnight bag. I wave at Ben without looking at him, not because I can't bear to look at him but because I've got other things to think about.

'What did you do today, Mum?' Molly says as we leave, taking my hand and swinging it in hers.

'I had a really good day actually. I went to a newspaper library.'

'Boring.'

'No, it wasn't boring at all. You know how I've been trying to find out about our house and the people who lived there?'

Molly starts humming.

'Anyway, one of them had a baby and I think I may have found it.'

'It?' Molly stops and looks at me.

'Well, I don't know if the baby was a boy or a girl.'

'And did the baby live in our house?' Molly is interested now; she likes the idea of this.

'I don't know, that's what I'm trying to find out.'

'Is it a mystery, Mum?'

'Yes,' I say, smiling, 'it is.'

It's early evening and my office window is open; there's a faint smell of burnt-out barbecue coals from a neighbouring garden. For the past hour I've been at my desk reading over everything we've found so far: the census roll and the newspaper reports, the Old Bailey trial and the advert in the Dublin paper. The dog is in the office with me, but she won't sleep, she won't even lie down; instead she's sitting on the floor, upright like a human, her eyes never wavering from mine.

'What?' I say to her. 'What is it?'

I'm about to pack away for the evening when I hear an odd, muffled shout. 'Molly?' I call, and I get up and walk to the door. I can hear the sound of the TV downstairs; it sounds like a noisy game show. I come to the top of the stairs and look down. 'Molly?' I call again, and then I see her standing in the hallway. She's not watching TV at all. 'You OK?'

She looks up as if surprised I'm here. 'Something just whizzed past me.'

'What?'

Molly doesn't answer, she just looks up and down the hall like she's lost something.

'What do you mean, something whizzed past you – like what?' I say, and my voice is sharper than I'd intended. 'What's going on?'

'I saw,' says Molly, speaking slowly, still standing in the hallway, 'something whiz past me.'

'Yes, but like what? A light? An object? A fly?' I try to laugh but fail.

'No,' says Molly, 'like a person.'

40

Mo George

December 1937

Bleeding hell, will you look at the state of this house? And me like a poor old donkey with all my bags and not a soul to help. I haven't been here for years, not since the last time I saw Uncle William and Auntie Fanny, and it was a lovely little house then. But just look at it now: the gate's hanging by a thread, there's moss as thick as carpet on the cobbles, and the windows look like they haven't had a wash since old King George died. I don't much like the look of next door neither. Why don't they give their front a nice lick of paint and put a pretty plant outside? In the spring or summer it'll be nicer with the trees and all, but on a miserable day like this, number 43 looks like a dilapidated old B&B. Still, it's mine now.

What's he staring at? There's a little lad just come out of number 41, pudding-bowl haircut and ears like the handles of a jug.

'Who are you?' he asks.

'Mo George,' I tell him with a grin. 'And who might you be?' But he's come over all shy now, scuttling away back into his house like he's afraid of his own shadow.

I hunt around for the key, get it in the lock and open the door. Bleeding hell, it's poky in here. Where's the light? There are big wads of paper hanging off the wall and a terrible smell of damp. I wish I hadn't had that egg sarnie on the train; I'm right queasy

246

now. Here we go, into the parlour. Let's open the shutters, let in a bit of light. It's as musty as an old lady's stockings in here.

Auntie Fanny would cry to see this. Looks like someone's gutted the place. Daft old Arthur's long gone of course, drank himself into an early grave, and I never would have expected much trouble from Albert, not with his wife holding the reins, but Violet, I wouldn't put it past her at all. I don't expect she wanted me to have this house and now I'm here I don't much want it neither. I was happy enough where I was; I had my friends and the rooms I rented after I sold Mum and Dad's place. I had my job at Creed & Sons and my Saturday job at the Astoria and I loved that. It's the kids I'll miss the most, the way they come out after the morning pictures rampaging down the streets, shouting everything they can remember. I won't half miss the Astoria, but how often does someone leave you a house in London? What was I going to do when I heard about that, stay in Southend?

As soon as I've got myself settled I'll go along to the Gaumont on the Holloway Road. I don't need to earn much now, but I do love my pictures. They might say I'm past it, but then again they might appreciate a bit of experience, and it looks like that's going to be a smashing place with all the big American films and with any luck some real weepies.

I've half a mind to cry now, the state of this room. There was a sideboard just there and it's left a terrible brown mark on the carpet. Looks like someone's even tried to take the bleeding carpet, the way it's been picked away from the skirting board and rolled up near the window. And that big square patch of white over the fireplace, that's where a mirror ought to be. Where's all Auntie Fanny's knick-knacks then? She used to love her knick-knacks, her coronation mugs and her medals and her dainty pieces of porcelain. The dust on these shelves is thick enough I could write my name, I could write the *Encyclopaedia Britannica* in it. It used to be cosy in here when I came as a kid. Auntie Fanny bringing out her best china and a nice spread: toast and jam, scones and chocolate cake. Uncle William standing there by the fireplace watching, like a right old copper, and Auntie Fanny saying, "Have another slice, Mo. Haven't you grown?" And that doorknob, it's the very one Uncle William tied the cotton to when he wanted to pull my waggling tooth out. Slammed that door till the house shook, and just like he said, it didn't hurt at all. They were good times in this room. Still, no use thinking about that now.

The back parlour's all right, the piano's still here, covered in a grey old dustsheet, but that fireplace will take me a full day to clean. The kitchen's all right too. Black-and-white tiled floor, just like we had at home. But that drape over the back door needs a good wash and the basin a proper old scrub down. And the cooker, it looks like someone's cooked a cat in here; it's that black and covered in hair. Let's see the state of the yard then. Where did all this junk come from? Two broken chairs, a battered old coal scuttle, a bicycle lamp with its light smashed in, two copper jelly moulds full of dirty rainwater. There's not much room to grow any veggies out here.

Here we go, I've got company again. The lad from next door has his face hanging over the wall and now he's got a black cowboy hat on his head like Hopalong Cassidy and a toy gun in his hands.

'Who are you?' he asks.

'I told you,' I say, a little sharpish. 'I'm Mo George.'

'Where's Mr George?' he asks, waving his gun like he's going to do some damage.

'He's gone, love,' I tell him.

'Did he die?'

Cheeky beggar. 'Yes, he did.'

'How?'

'He ran out of breath,' I tell him. 'He *expired*. That's what happens when a person dies.'

That's done it; he's back in his yard as quick as he can.

These stairs creak a bit and it's as cold as a coffin in the room on the landing. I don't think I ever came in here as a kid. Bleeding hell, no wonder it's cold, the window's got a great big hole in it. I wonder who did that. Maybe little Hopalong Cassidy from next door's been throwing a ball. I don't like the smell in here neither; it's like someone's dirty washing. I'm closing the door; I'll clean it later.

This second bedroom's cold as well. I'm not sleeping in here, there's nothing left, not even the carpet. It's a nice view over the yards at the back, but I couldn't feel cosy in here. There are big old sad patches on the wall where pictures used to be, a horrible stain of damp underneath the window and a right nasty crack on the ceiling.

There now, this is a bit better, it's a bit warmer in here. No one's got their hands on this room yet because it was theirs, wasn't it? Uncle William and Auntie Fanny's. There are two separate beds, both covered in a nice butterscotch quilt. Nice walnut bedroom suite too: a dressing chest, fitted wardrobe. What's this then, this pile of rubbish under the bed? Receipts. Well, they're not going to need these now, are they? And a card, a pretty little thing tied with blue cord. There's a countryside picture on the front and inside someone's written all neatly, *Best of happiness, honour and fortune be with you through life.*

That's nice, that's very nice. But you know what? I've got a funny feeling about this place. It's one thing for them to leave it to me, but quite another to live here myself. This house doesn't feel right to me.

41

I've just put my feet up with a nice cup of tea when there's a knock on the door. I've been working my socks off getting this place right the past two weeks and today's Monday and I've just put my washing out.

'Good morning,' she says, standing there on the step, a silly old hat on her head like a giant walnut. She's dressed herself up for this.

'You'd better come in,' I say, and she gives me a right dirty look. I flatten myself against the wall and in she comes, sniffing the air like a ferret.

'It's very damp in here,' I tell her. She nods at me and waltzes straight into the front parlour like she owns the place, which of course she wishes she does. Cousin Violet. She used to be a looker when I was a kid; I thought her very beautiful then, with her long dresses and her hair piled on top of her head. She never liked me much though. I always knew she was right jealous of all the attention her mum and dad gave me.

She called me a bastard once, I won't forget that. One day at the seaside, that's what she said. 'I don't want my kids playing with Mo, she's a bastard.' Only she said it low so that Uncle William and Auntie Fanny didn't hear. But I'd nothing to be ashamed of. Mum and Dad told me right from when I was little about my poor old mum and the terrible accident she had when I was born, and how they took me in and brought me up as their own because they'd always wanted a child. They chose me, they said, and I was the answer to their prayers. I reckon I was luckier than most, the way they loved me.

I point at a chair. 'Won't you sit down?' I ask, because there's no use forgetting my manners. I wait for Cousin Violet to have a good look around, see how I've spruced the place up. The windows are gleaming. I've taken out the rugs and given them a proper beating, and the walls are all washed down. The only thing missing is some bleeding furniture, because she's taken all that, hasn't she, her or her children.

'Well,' she says.

'Well,' I say.

'Settling in nicely?'

'Very nicely, thank you. Can I get you some tea?'

Cousin Violet doesn't answer; she's staring at the fireplace. Then her face twitches all of a sudden and her cheeks go red and she grips the arms of the chair.

'You all right?' I ask. She looks at me like she's just seen a ghost, and I'm almost sorry for her now because maybe she has seen a ghost – this was her home once and maybe she has a right to it still. And I know what it's like to lose someone and to look into a fire and wish they were still here.

'I never asked for it you know,' I say.

Her eyes fly to mine.

'I never. I had as much of a shock as you did when I heard about the will.'

Cousin Violet takes out a handkerchief and dabs at her eyes and she looks just like Auntie Fanny, a woman who could sob at the drop of a hat. 'I never asked for this house,' I tell her again, 'it doesn't seem right, but you've got your place, Violet, and so has Albert, and what would you want with this? It's a lot of work, what with half of the fittings having been ripped out . . .'

'We only wanted some things to remember them by,' Violet sniffs. 'Perhaps I would like that cup of tea.'

I go off to the kitchen, get the kettle on and I'm thinking, What are you doing, Mo? Just give her the place if she wants it so much. Go back to Southend and your friends and the Astoria. What do you think you're doing, setting up home in London? You could go back to your old life just like that. So I take the door keys from where I keep them by the sink and I put them on the tray with the tea and the sugar and the milk and the biscuits and I walk back into the parlour. 'There you go then,' I tell her, putting the tray on a packing case because I haven't got a proper table yet.

Cousin Violet takes her cup in a very dainty manner, looks at the keys and then looks away again.

'Biscuit?' I say.

She shakes her head, sighs and puts down her cup. 'They left it to you,' she says, and she pushes at the keys with her cup like she wants them out of the way. 'That's what they wanted, isn't it?' We look at each other and I know what we're both thinking, but why? 'And you always got what you wanted, didn't you, Mo?'

I'm not answering that. I'm not getting into an argument about that now.

'My mother loved this house,' says Violet, a little softer now.

'Yes, love, I know.'

'And the shops!' Cousin Violet smiles. 'They're having a showboat at Christmas.'

'Who are?'

'Jones Bros. With Uncle Tom and lots of darkies playing banjos.'

'What, from America? Have they got real people from America?'

Cousin Violet just sniffs. 'Well,' she says at last, 'I'd better be off.'

I take her to the front door and I'm about to tell her she can come back any time when she puts out her hand, looks at me long and hard, says, 'I hope you'll be very happy here,' and slams the door in my face. I don't like having a door shut in my face so I open it, but she's gone. Little Hopalong Cassidy is outside though, hanging on to the garden gate going *pow pow pow* with his gun. His mum came by yesterday, just to say hello. Nice lady, Mrs Pickles. I close the door, go back inside and look around the room. I'll get lodgers, that's what I'll do, just as soon as I have the place to rights. I'll get a job at the Gaumont, or anywhere else that'll have me, and I'll take in a lodger or two. I don't want to be alone at Christmas, not in this house.

42

Lily Painter

Summer 2009

Annie is tired this morning. Anxiously she checks upon her daughter still asleep in her bed, and when she comes down the stairs her footsteps are weary. She stops in the hallway and picks up the post, but she does not examine the letters; instead she puts one hand out upon the wall and turns to look back up the stairs.

Here I am, I say, but she does not see me, she does not see a thing.

Annie has not slept well, her eyes are swollen, and she rubs them now and sighs. And as she does I recall another woman standing in this hallway once, sighing in just such a way.

It was a winter's afternoon when the newcomer arrived, a short woman with a soft round face and large brown eyes. Her clothes were smart but frugal, a grey jacket belted tight around the waist, a plain black skirt, a white shirt a little worn around the cuffs. Her stockings were of poor quality and she had patched one leg clumsily with nail varnish where there was a hole. But her hair was well cared for, for she was a woman who prized her hair, and it was lush and black and set in waves.

But oh, how she threw down her bags, how she marched into the parlour and began at once to complain about the dirt and the missing furniture and all the work she would have to do. She poked impatiently around the house, through the kitchen and the bedrooms, and she did not like anything she saw and said everything was old and broken and she would have to throw it out. And when sweet Fanny's daughter Violet came to pay a call, how rude she was and how very quick to take offence, and I wondered then at Inspector George and his decision to leave her his home.

She clattered around her kitchen after that and made herself a supper of sardines, which she ate standing up as if she could not wait to eat but must at once continue putting the house to rights. That night she did not sleep till late; instead she moved restlessly around the bedroom, unpinning her hair from where the curls were secured about her neck. At last she sat before the dressing table, where she had laid out her powder and her rouge and a pretty hand-painted jar of bath crystals. And although there was no mirror then, she sat as if there was and very carefully she began to brush her hair, using slow long strokes that seemed to soothe her.

Then she stopped abruptly, cleaned her brush, drew back the curtains and looked out on to Stanley Road. 'Bleeding dump,' she said. 'What are you doing here, Mo?' The night was black and wet, and a single figure stood beneath the light of the street lamp, his silhouette reflected on the sodden pavement. She tutted to herself, drew the curtains closed, got into her bed and huddled under the blanket. She tossed and turned all night, and once I heard her mutter to herself that she could never be happy in this house.

But in the days that followed, Mo George threw herself into getting her new home to rights. She scoured the kitchen and polished all the surfaces. Upon the parlour windows she fixed new net curtains with a dainty frill, and in the bedroom she put up tailored curtains, pleated at the top and secured with a wide plain belt. She bought a three-piece suite as well, a large settee and two chairs patterned brightly with circles like giant eyeballs, which she seemed to find cheerful. One afternoon she came home with a budgerigar with a lime-green coat and a shiny blue beak, and she placed it in a golden cage in the parlour where it tweeted mournfully in the dark winter mornings. She sang to the bird sometimes, and for a woman who spoke so harshly her voice was soft and seductive and strangely beautiful to hear.

One day her neighbour Mrs Pickles paid a call, knocking upon the door in a hesitant fashion.

'Hullo,' said Mo George, her hair wet for it was Friday and she had been washing it.

'I'm not disturbing you, am I?' asked Mrs Pickles. Behind her stood her little boy, a clutch of broken toffee in his hands.

'Well, I was just setting off for vermouth at the Ritz,' said Mo George, 'but do come in.'

Mrs Pickles looked surprised, but then she laughed and her neat round glasses slipped down upon her nose.

'Come in, Hopalong Cassidy,' said Mo George to the boy. 'Not got your cowboy hat today?'

'Oh, he loves his pictures,' said Mrs Pickles.

'And so do I,' said Mo George, and she led them into the front parlour.

'You've made it very nice in here,' Mrs Pickles said, although her expression suggested otherwise. 'Very modern. If you don't mind me saying.'

Mo George nodded and offered her guest a seat on the chair patterned with eyeballs.

'I was very sad to hear about Mr George,' said Mrs Pickles, folding her hands upon her lap. 'There was a nice turnout at the funeral for your . . .' and Mrs Pickles paused then, wanting to see what Mo George would say and how she would explain herself.

'My uncle,' said Mo George.

'Oh yes, he was your uncle,' said Mrs Pickles, 'yes, I thought I'd seen you here before,' and she waited in case there should be more. 'Well,' she said at last, 'he was a lovely man. My father-in-law Gilbert knew him well, and his wife Fanny. I've been here for ten years or so and I'm on very good terms with everyone. You'll find this is a neighbourly little street, for the most part.'

'For the most part?' asked Mo George.

'Well, the lady at number 60 opposite . . .' said Mrs Pickles, and she stopped as if reluctant to continue. 'Mrs Frith is her name, or was her name I ought to say. An elderly woman who didn't enjoy good health.'

Mo George tutted in sympathy.

'Last week she went out shopping and was taken ill. Came over all funny outside Beale's and had to be helped home. Said she'd swallowed some disinfectant . . .'

'Why would she do that?'

'I'm getting to that,' said Mrs Pickles, in a manner that suggested she was not used to being interrupted. 'She thought it might do her some good.'

'And why would she think that?' laughed Mo George, and she winked at the little boy sitting on the carpet.

'She had taken it in mistake for whisky, which, if you don't mind me saying, she was in the habit of drinking,' Mrs Pickles coughed, 'medicinally.'

'Poor old soul.'

'Yes,' said Mrs Pickles. 'Heart failure and shock.' She sat back in her chair and when the boy looked up, Mo George put out her hand as if to touch him, but then thought better and drew it back. 'And as for the poor girl at number 62. She was working as a maid up on Highgate Hill. Found a month ago drowned in a pond on Hampstead Heath. Her employer was as surprised as the rest of us. As far as everyone knew, she had no worries at all.'

Mo George frowned as if she did not want to know this.

'It was the park keeper who found her,' continued Mrs Pickles. 'He'd seen a woman's coat and watch on the bank of the pond. The water wasn't that deep and she wasn't far from the side, so she could have swum. If only both her hands had not been tied with cloth.' Mrs Pickles removed her glasses and wiped them with a handkerchief as the little boy upon the floor crunched on the last of his broken toffee. 'They say it was a lovers' tiff.'

Mo George stood up at this and went to the kitchen, where she banged around making tea and opening a tin of peaches for the boy. 'She's a nosy one,' she muttered to herself. Then she served the tea and said how lovely it was to meet her neighbour.

By the following year, Mo George had got herself employment. At first she tried the Gaumont and came home very unhappy, telling her budgerigar that they hadn't even given her the time of day and how all the other usherettes were half her age. But then she got a position at the Electric and she set off for work each day in her smart black dress with its tight shiny belt, stopping always to check her reflection in the hallway mirror before putting on her hat. And Mo George seemed to grow happier then and to lose her impatience a little, and she placed an advertisement for lodgers and she bought a radio and set it in the parlour and sang along of an evening and the budgerigar did too. Sometimes she complained to the bird about how her shoulders ached from holding the ice-cream container and how silly Mr Sawyer looked in his dickie bow and carnation, but otherwise she was happy in her work.

Three lodgers came and went, a mournful bookkeeper and two flighty young waitresses, and it was then that everything changed. When Mo George spoke to her neighbour now it was in hushed tones about the war. Mrs Pickles was most concerned as it was not possible to wear her glasses over her gas mask, and she said she would be as blind as a bat.

In the middle of the long hot summer the blackout trials began, and Mo George sadly took down her pleated curtains and her net with frills and put up heavy black curtains instead. Then one Sunday morning she rose early and stood for a long while in the back garden with her mug of tea, looking up at the clear blue sky and listening to the ringing of the church bells. She seemed to be waiting for Mrs Pickles' boy to appear, for several times she looked over the wall in a friendly manner. She poked around a while, inspecting the small row of cabbages and lettuce she had grown, and then she went upstairs and looked out over the gardens and at the bomb shelters erected amid the broken children's swings. A little later she went out, opening the front door just as the coalman passed by, and she looked up again at the sky and saw the barrage balloons floating high as if for a party. Then a butcher's boy came running down the centre of the street, shouting 'War! War!' at the top of his lungs.

43

Annie Sweet

Summer 2009

This is ridiculous. Molly said she wanted to go to the seaside; she was as excited as I was about going out for the day, and now she's making a fuss. We've got twenty minutes before we're supposed to be at the station to meet Danny and she hasn't even put her shoes on.

'Why can't Jojo come too?' she demands, sitting down on the stairs, holding her sandals in her hands.

'You know why.'

'Why?'

'Because I'm not taking the dog on a train! And she wouldn't be allowed on the beach anyway, so what would we do with her?'

Molly pushes her feet angrily into her sandals.

'It'll be fun,' I say. 'It's going to be a lovely day, we can go on the rides and splash in the sea. And you know I want to find out about the man who used to live here, because his brother lived in Southend.'

'Boring.'

'Molly,' I snap as I put my camera into my bag, 'I asked you if you wanted to come and you said yes. What's your problem?'

'I don't want to go with *him*,' she mutters, her head down, fiddling with her sandals.

I feel a tinge of unease. 'You mean Danny?'

'Yes.'

'But he's only a friend, Molly, he's just helping me out. Anyway, you'll like him.'

'No I won't.'

'Fine, you won't, but let's go.'

'Dad thinks you're mad.' Molly stands up, her sandals on, and she stares at me. She wants me to get angry over her father thinking I'm mad, to ask her what she means by this and what else he's said, but I'm not going to.

'Come on,' I say as the dog comes hurrying into the hallway. 'I told you I've got someone to come and walk Jojo, she'll be fine.'

'But why do we have to go with *him*?'

'Because it was Danny's idea, and that was the plan. Because he knows Southend and I don't. Come on, Molly, you haven't even met him yet.'

Molly mutters, just loud enough for me to hear, 'I don't want people to think he's my father.'

I stop with my hand on the dog's collar. I hadn't thought of this. Is that really what she's worried about, that people will think another man is her father? I wish she'd told me earlier so I could have reassured her that no one's going to possibly think Danny's her dad. But as I watch her doing up her sandals I wonder what other worries she has in her head that I don't even know about. And what was all that nonsense the other night about seeing a person whizzing past?

'Mum,' she says, 'I haven't got my bag.'

'Well, get it then.'

'*You* get it.'

I give in because otherwise we're going to be late, and I go upstairs to get her bag. I fling open the door to her room and stop. It's a tip in here, an absolute tip. The door of her wardrobe is open, so are all the drawers, and every single piece of clothing has been taken out; all that remains are coat hangers. I can't think where everything has gone until I see Molly has pulled out a box she usually keeps under her bed and has tried to stuff all the clothes in there. But there isn't room for all of them; the box is overflowing with dresses and skirts and T-shirts and cardigans. 'Molly!' I yell. When she doesn't answer, I go to the top of the stairs. 'Molly!'

'What?'

'Come up here.'

'What?'

'Just come up here.' I go back into her room and wait as she reluctantly comes up the stairs. 'This is a total state. Why have you thrown your clothes all over the place?'

'I didn't do it,' Molly says.

'Oh, don't be ridiculous! Do you think I came in here and did this? Don't tell me,' I say, 'the dog did it?'

Molly sits down on the floor and lays her head on the clothes spilling out of the box.

'What are you doing?'

'They're all messed up,' Molly wails, and when she looks up I realise she's about to cry.

'Well then . . .' I hesitate, my anger ebbing away. 'You shouldn't have flung them in there. What's got into you?'

'Fine, I'll put them all back.' Furiously Molly grabs dresses and tops and cardigans and starts trying to hang them up.

'There's no time for that now. Come on, we've got to go.'

Molly ignores me and speeds up her tidying; she's frantic now, like a girl possessed, her hands shaking as she tries to put her clothes back on the hangers. But she's in too much of a state to do this, so she starts stuffing them into the drawers.

'Molly!' I shout, and I grab her. 'Stop, just stop, OK?'

* * *

I can see Danny waiting outside Holloway station from the opposite side of the road. We stand to cross outside a new café that opened two weeks ago. Before that there was another new café selling cupcakes. The owners decked it out with pictures of bright pink cupcakes on the windows, but after a few weeks it closed down. Now the new owners have renamed it Station Café and there's a logo of a train on the overhead panel. They've repainted it, set out different tables and chairs inside, but still when Molly and I walk past it on the way to school we haven't seen a single person go in or out. The recession is supposed to be lifting, but it isn't on the Holloway Road and I wonder how things are back home in Edinburgh.

The lights change and we cross the road. Danny sees us and waves. There's a boy standing just behind him in jeans and a red T-shirt, and part of my mind is wondering who the boy is with, where his parents are, when I realise he's with Danny, this has to be his kid. He's brought his son with him. The boy looks about Molly's age, maybe a little younger. As we get closer I see he's very slight with a long, dark, serious face and large boyish ears. His eyebrows are thick above his eyes but then fade out into nothing, and I think it's this that gives him a worried air. On his back he has a small rucksack and it seems to be weighing him down.

'Morning,' says Danny, and he's smiling at Molly, not at me. He puts out his hand to shake hers. 'This is Leo,' he says, his hand resting for a second on the boy's head. 'He wanted to come along too, that all right with you?'

Molly nods.

'So which rides are we going on?' asks Danny as he hauls his own rucksack on to his back and sets off down the metal station steps. He's barely looked at me at all, and as I follow him I'm feeling disappointed until I realise he's going to make

263

this a day out for Molly; he's going to concentrate on the kids. I walk down the station steps, thinking of the mess in Molly's room and how it isn't like her because normally she likes things to be very orderly.

Molly and Leo are silent on the train; both behave as if the other isn't there. 'I wish I had my Nintendo,' says Molly, with a bored, grown-up sigh. There's a flicker of interest on Leo's face, but then he turns and stares out the window. I can't work out how things are between Danny and him; they seem comfortable with each other, but I don't know how often he sees his son or if the mother lives close by. I wonder if Danny left her or if she left him and why. But I can't ask any questions like this today.

The train pulls off and Danny brings out snacks, packets of crisps and a bag of tangerines. Then he brings out a small, soft-sided cool box and takes out two little tubs of ice cream. He places each one carefully in front of Leo and Molly, and gives them a wink. Molly can't believe her luck; greedily she takes the ice cream and begins to lick the small wooden spoon.

'Mmm,' says Leo with his eyes closed, and as Molly looks at me and laughs, the mess with her clothes is forgotten and I'm just happy to be out of the house.

The sun is hot by the time we get to Southend, and next to the seafront there's a row of giant coaches as shiny as beetles, full of kids who can't wait to get on to the beach. We walk between the coaches, come down on to the crunchy stones, and before us the sky is a pale blue with bubbles of clouds. Everywhere people are busy: children trying to dig holes; a shirtless man with red, sunburnt tattooed arms carrying a small pink plastic spade; boys with rolled-up jeans jumping shivering out of the sea and clambering up the pier.

We walk down the esplanade to Adventure Island, which is packed with kids and food sellers and funfair rides. Molly aims a fishing hook at a group of bobbing plastic yellow ducks with surprised faces. She catches one and wins a stuffed penguin. Normally she doesn't like stuffed toys, but she holds this one determinedly under one arm. Leo admires the penguin and Molly lets him hold it for a while. They are deciding to be friends.

'I always used to come here as a kid,' says Danny. 'My foster mum loved it down here.'

I feel a jolt of surprise. I didn't know he was fostered; he's never mentioned that before. But then there's no reason why he would have told me about his life when I haven't told him anything of mine. I wonder how old he was when he was fostered and what happened to his other mother. But Danny's walked away now; he's stopped in front of a dragon roundabout and is beckoning us over. Molly and me squeeze into one of the wagons, a smiling attendant flips forward a metal safety bar and we grip it as the dragon goes thundering and clattering up and down the wooden planks, and we start to scream because it feels like we're flying through the air.

'Right,' says Danny, 'what's next?' He looks at me and smiles, and I smile back because of the way he throws himself into things, and I realise it's something Ben never would have done. Ben would have been critical of this place, he wouldn't have wanted to pay money to go on some crappy fairground ride, he wouldn't have liked the crowds or the tacky prizes. But Danny has a sense of fun; he knows how to make the most of things.

Molly chooses the Jolly Roger boat ride. Danny and Leo get into a boat and an attendant comes up and tries to get Molly to join them.

'Don't you want to ride with your dad?' asks the attendant.

Molly looks at me with an expression of panic.

'I'm not her dad,' says Danny with an easy smile, and Molly looks grateful and pulls me into the boat behind. I think she's going to sulk now, but the ride begins and the boats swing in and out and she holds up her penguin and she's laughing again. It's a long time since I've really seen her laughing like this.

Then Molly wants to go up in a metal cage attached to a small Ferris wheel and I tell her I've had enough, but Danny and Leo climb in with her. I stand and shield my eyes, looking up as the cage climbs higher into the blue sky. It's hot now, and my eyes sting from staring at the mass of white spokes, which seem like a crazy metal spider's web. I get my camera out and take some pictures, wonder how long all these rides have been here, whether they were here a hundred years ago when Inspector George's brother lived here and whether people brought their children to Adventure Island for the day. Then they are down and the cage opens and the kids jump out.

'So,' says Danny, 'd'you want to go and look for the house?'

'Aren't we all going together?'

'Well, they're having fun . . .' Danny calls at Leo to wait – he's run off after Molly and they're about to get swallowed in the crowd.

I hesitate. I'd like to do this alone, to find Inspector George's brother's house, but I don't know if I want to leave Molly with Danny because suddenly I don't feel I know him well enough. What do I really know about him, except that he works at a local history centre, that he wanted to be a historian, that he has a child? I don't know anything else about him; I don't even know where he lives. And anyway, Molly wouldn't want to be left with him.

'It's only along the seafront, isn't it?' Danny asks. 'Why don't

I get them fish and chips when they've finished and then meet you on the beach?'

Again I hesitate. It would be best to go alone, I want to go alone, but I don't know if I can.

'Mum!' Molly shouts. 'I want to go on this one!'

I look up at the ride; it's too high for me. 'Not with me you're not.'

'You are such a baby!' Molly shouts.

'Hold on,' Danny tells her. 'Do you want to stay with me and Leo while your mum . . .'

Molly doesn't even wait until he's finished. She's got her penguin under her arm, she gives me a dismissive wave and all at once she's lining up for the ride with Leo.

44

It takes me half an hour to walk back along the esplanade, past a park, and then left into the road where Inspector George's brother used to live. I feel anxious in case the house I want doesn't exist any more, but it's here, right at the end, number 62, a two-storey house painted the colour of dry sand. It juts out on the right with two large, cream-rimmed windows, while up on the second floor there's a little balcony with bright white railings. The small front garden has been paved over, except for a border of yellow flowers on one side. There's no car parked here, and it feels like no one's at home.

I walk up to the front door; it's painted black and has a round circle of glass in the middle like a porthole. I knock, stand back and wait. No one answers. What would I say if anyone was home? I'm looking for the Georges; they lived here a hundred years ago. But why would anyone care, and why would I think I could find anyone who even knew them? I'm about to knock again, even to peek in through the window, when I hear the yapping sound of a dog. I turn to see an elderly woman walking a scruffy terrier, which is straining desperately at the lead. It's only a small dog, with a red collar and sticky-up ears, but the woman doesn't seem to have the strength to hold it back. Suddenly the dog has managed to get off the lead and it's running across the paving stones towards me. I stand perfectly still and it circles my feet, sniffing dementedly at my legs.

'Barney!' yells the old woman. 'Barney!' and she comes hurrying after the dog.

'It's OK,' I say. 'It can probably smell my dog.' I smile at her, feel pleased to have a dog as well.

'You little rascal,' says the woman. She has fine grey hair brushed severely away from her face, which is creamy white and soft with powder. 'They're not in,' she says, gesturing at the house behind me.

'No, I just knocked and no one answered.'

The woman fixes the lead back on to her dog's collar. 'Come on, you rascal. It's home with you.'

'Sorry,' I say quickly, because the woman is turning to leave, 'this is going to sound silly, but I was looking for the people who used to live here a really long time ago.'

The woman nods. 'The Maudsleys?'

'No, the Georges.'

'Oh yes, the Georges.'

'Did you *know* them?'

The woman tugs at the dog's lead again and she seems to be considering something. 'They died when I was a kid, that's all I can say. But they were a lovely couple; my mum was good friends with the Georges, and their daughter Mo.'

'They had a daughter?'

The woman laughs. 'Oh yes.'

'Did they have any other children?'

'No, just Mo. She was a funny one.'

'Funny?'

The woman smiles. 'Lovely sense of humour. She was always giving us ice cream and making us laugh. She left not long after her parents died, went off to London just before the war.'

'Why?'

'Why?' the woman looks surprised. 'She inherited a house, I think. Yes, that was it, she inherited a house.'

'Do you know where?'

The woman looks a little worried now, like she's given away too much information and she's beginning to wonder who I am. But I can't help myself; I know I'm jumping to conclusions but I can't lose this opportunity to question her. I take a deep breath and try to slow myself down.

'The house Mo George inherited – do you know where it was in London?'

'Come on, Barney.' The woman tugs at the dog. 'Time to go in.'

'Would you know if it was in north London?' I'm desperate now; I'm aching to know if this Mo George in Southend could possibly have moved into my house, the house that used to belong to her uncle, Inspector George. 'Do you remember if it was in north London?'

'It might have been north London.'

'Could it have been Holloway?'

'It could have been.'

I smile encouragingly, but I'm getting the feeling that the woman has just decided to agree with everything I say.

'We never saw her again, I don't think. Although . . .'

'Although?'

The woman looks at me; her eyes seem blank for a second, like she can't remember what she just said.

'Although?'

'Yes.' The woman nods. 'Went to London and we never saw her again. Come on Barney, you little rascal.' She walks back across the paving stones and I watch her as she struggles to open the gate to the house next door.

'What were they like?' I call after her. 'The Georges?' But her dog is yapping again and the woman's reached her house and she's opening the door and doesn't reply. 'Thank you,' I shout, 'thanks very much.'

* * *

I walk quickly back to the seafront. The beach is less crowded but I feel a little worried in case I can't find Molly. The sea is out now; the sand stretches into the distance, wet and soft where the water was just a few hours ago, and the pier ends suddenly in nothingness when earlier it was surrounded by waves. There are pieces of rubbish here and there, left over from the day: ice-cream wrappers and crisp packets and a forgotten plastic bucket.

'Mum!' Molly yells. She's far out on the sand with Leo and Danny, her trousers rolled up.

I wave to her and take a picture so we can remember this day, and then sit down on the sand. I take off my sandals, stretch out my naked toes and enjoy the peace. On the train home, when the kids are sleepy from the sea air, I'll tell Danny about what I found, that Inspector George's brother had a daughter and she just may have inherited my house. And why would that be? Why would Inspector George leave his house to his brother's daughter when he had three children of his own? And I think of what Danny said, his hunch that Inspector George took in Lily Painter's child, that the baby farmers didn't kill the baby, that he or she survived. And I wonder if it could be possible that I might have found her baby.

I begin to play with the sand in my fingers, look up at the sky. It's still hot and there are no clouds at all, nothing to interrupt the blueness above. The kids are out on the shoreline, and I can see Danny turn and start walking towards me. I can tell he's smiling.

'They found this,' he says, and he kneels down and opens up his hands to show me a delicate little crab.

I hold out my hand and, gently, he tips it into my palm. I feel the crab tickle my skin and I laugh as it scuttles quickly over my fingers. For a second I think it's going to fall, but then Danny puts his hands out and cups mine in his and we smile at each other, like children.

45
Mo George

Summer 1940

Bleeding hell, will you look at this? There's a huge crowd milling about outside the Archway Underground, mothers and grandmothers and who knows who else, all watching the kiddies come marching along the streets from school. There they are, clutching their cases and their bags of clothing and their gas masks wrapped in cardboard boxes and tied with string like a poor man's Christmas present. Around their necks they have brown paper labels, like goods in a grocery shop. It's a hot, sultry morning, but a sight like this, it gives you a sense of doom. They don't know what's happening, do they? No idea at all. They probably think they're all going to a farm for the day.

Mothers fuss over the kiddies like worried birds. 'I'll visit you as soon as I know where you are,' a woman in a blue mackintosh tells her two girls. *As soon as she knows where they are?* She kisses them and then turns away so they can't see her ball up the ends of her headscarf and wipe at her eyes. Another little girl begins to wail. Her thin white socks have fallen down to her shoes and she hasn't got a case at all, just a tin of spam.

But most of the kiddies look happy enough; they get into line obediently outside the station when the teachers tell them. Some are in high spirits, waving to everyone who's stopped to look. 'Miss Lillie! Miss Lillie!' a girl calls out, and a tired-looking teacher comes over to help. It's the faces of the mothers I can't stand: numb and worried, hoping they're doing their best for the little ones and getting them to safety. Little Hopalong Cassidy from next door went away in the first evacuation last year, but then not much happened so he came back. He said he'd had a lovely time in the country, but his eyes didn't tell me that. When he came to the Electric on a Saturday after that I made sure he had ice cream whether he had any pennies on him or not.

They're off now, the kiddies, into the Underground. The teachers are probably taking them to King's Cross. But the mothers are still standing there in a lonely group, some with tears running down their faces, as if they're expecting the children to come back.

I get to the Electric a little late. You can see the Electric from a mile off, it's like a bleeding ocean liner stuck on dry land. That's what it's supposed to make you feel when you walk in through those doors, like you just got on a ship. It's quiet and soft inside, with a carpet as gentle as feathers, and everything's so shiny, the walnut panels and the pillars and the golden stairway rail. I let Mr Sawyer know I'm here and expect a right telling-off that I'm ten minutes late. He's a stern one, Mr Sawyer; with enough Brylcreem in his hair you could fry an egg on his head. But I like the girls, especially Mavis and Babs, and the projectionist, old man Norman, who's a proper gent. The night I started here the film got jammed and caught fire and everyone started chanting 'Why are we waiting'. But old man Norman just ripped the film from the shutter and, cool as a cucumber, lobbed the blazing reel out of the window.

Here we are then. Home after work. It's late and the house is cold. I'd rather be back at the cinema, in the warmth, having a weep over *Gone with the Wind*. I haven't any lodgers at the minute, so there's no company for me here. Some nights this house feels as sad as when I moved in. It's black as soot in the front room, and if I was foolish enough to put a light on there'd soon be a knock at the door. There's no point in my lovely settee when I can't even see the bleeding thing half the time. And my pictures, all my lovely pictures, they look a right state covered with newspaper. I put the wireless on, ask the budgie how he's feeling, make myself a nice cup of cocoa, think of all the kiddies I saw this morning. What would I do if I had a kid? Would I do as they say and send him away? Or would I keep him close? But I haven't got a little one of my own and there's no use thinking about that now.

There are footsteps outside and shouting. I peek through a chink in the curtain. It's the poor old boy from opposite. He's come running into the street, waving his torch around, hunting for the enemy. Poor old beggar.

I'm on the way back from work when the siren goes off and I have to nip into the church for shelter. There's a big crowd outside the Archway church most nights now, waiting to come in. This has been going on for twenty-five nights on the trot. And there's a bomber's moon tonight. The Reverend is doing his best. He stands at the door and shakes people's hands, says what we all need is a little bit of mental sunshine. 'Isn't it lovely,' he says, ever so posh, 'to see how we're all marvellously cheerful?' There's a sea of blankets and bedding on the floor, a huddle of people from the East End tonight, homeless after the last raid. The women are knitting; the older children squabbling. In the corner near the shower bath a mother tries to get a gas mask on her baby and the little one screams its head off. 'Are we downhearted?' the Reverend calls out. 'No!' the women shout back.

The Reverend begins to pray as the rumble starts overhead and the bench I'm on shakes and trembles. We can hear our lads giving it back tonight and whenever there's a pause we all expect more. The guns are crashing now like waves in the sea, booming and pounding, above us and around us and everywhere at once. It makes me think of when I was a little girl and I got sucked right into the sea one day, dragged in by a giant wave and thrown around like a fish and all I could hear was the water crashing in my ears. When Dad dragged me out I didn't know which way was up and which way was down, that's how confused I was.

It's morning and everything's quiet. Any minute we'll have the all clear and I can get myself home. Sure enough the siren goes off, loud and piercing. And this is the worst bit, coming out after all the hours of waiting and seeing what damage Jerry has done. You sit in the dark and you listen to that and you don't know what you'll find when you get out, which houses are rubble now, whose home has been turned into a bleeding crater, what the crooks have been up to in the dead of night. I step out of the church shelter and head down the Holloway Road. There's an eerie calm on the streets and the sky's as red as blood.

I come down Kingsdown Road, past the shelters they've put in the road, and I pass the sweetie shop. And I can't believe it; there's a box of chocolates in the window. My mouth starts watering. I can't wait to get my hand on that box. I'll pay whatever it costs just to be able to take that box of chocolates to the Electric and treat all the girls. 'Oh Mo!' they'll say, 'wherever did you get that?'

I open the door of the sweetie shop, the bell gives a happy tinkle and I dash over to the window. 'I'll have that,' I tell the man at the counter.

He just laughs. 'You and a hundred others, love.'

I have the box in my hand now, its shiny purple cover so new and full of promise. I can smell the lovely chocolate smell, all powdery and sweet. My mouth is getting ready for the taste of it; my tongue can hardly wait for the thick, sticky sugariness of it all. But something's not right, the box is too light. I don't even have to open it to know there's nothing inside but dust. All night I've sat in the shelter and I've kept my patience and I've listened to the guns, and now it's a silly dummy box of chocolates that makes me cry. 'You all right, love?' the shop-keeper asks. I can't answer him. I hear the bell tinkle as I close the door and I can't bear the disappointment of it all.

Mrs Pickles is on her way to work. She hasn't seen Hopalong Cassidy for three months now, not since he was evacuated again. She hasn't heard a word from her husband either, and her father-in-law is very poorly. But at least she's kept busy at the factory. She says there's only one other lady there, in a roomful of men, and she doesn't like that at all, that and all the explosive. But with her husband away fighting and her boy gone, she'd rather be out of the house anyway.

'Morning, Mo,' she calls. She's got her turban on and her face is caked with all the make-up they give them at the factory. I can see her knitting needles poking out the end of her bag.

'Morning,' I call back. 'Any word?'

Mrs Pickles shakes her head and I wish I hadn't asked. 'What I worry about,' she says, and her words come tumbling out like this is something that's been preying on her mind, 'is that he'll come home and I won't know it and he'll find the place all cold and untidy.'

'I'm sure he wouldn't find it untidy,' I say.

She smiles a little at this. 'Where are you off to, Mo?'

'To see about doing my bit.'

'Where?' she asks.

'The buses,' I tell her. Get yourself a job as a clippie and it's a job for life, that's what they're saying. And if I'm lucky, I can keep my job at the Electric as well.

The recruiting officer is a rough-looking fella with a cauliflower ear, and he wants to know all about my education and previous jobs. I tell him what he needs to know, nothing else. He wants to see my birth certificate so he knows I'm a Brit, and I tell him I'll show him next time. Then he asks how tall I am. 'Well, you can see that,' I want to say as he shunts me over to the measuring chart. There's a girl behind me with peroxide hair and she's looking worried, she must be five foot nine at least. That's too tall. They've told us they don't want a clippie stooping when they have to get the fares on the top deck. On the other hand, you've got to be tall enough to ring the bell.

The girl bends her knees as she stands up against the wall, gives me a cheeky grin. She's got a pretty face and when she's not smiling her lips come together all in a pout. Her name's Jean, she says, and the recruiting officer takes a shine to her. Even if she is a bit tall, he passes her anyway. 'Ladies!' he shouts, and we're herded into the medical room. 'I'm a bit short-sighted,' Jean confesses as we go in. But she needn't worry because the medical man takes a shine to her as well.

They get rid of the ones who aren't up to standard and call the rest of us into the canteen. Then they tell us there's no vacancies on the buses but we can work on the trams if we like. If we like? We haven't got much choice, have we?

I'm off to the depot and it's no joke getting there at four in the morning in a bleeding blackout. I'm on my bike and one minute

I'm going along in the dark, the next I'm flat on my face. The only people who can get around London at a time like this are the cabbies; they get around as easily as cats in the night. It's no joke standing in the cold at the back of a tram going up and down stairs all day, and there's barely any air to breathe on the top deck with all the men smoking away. But still, I love these noisy old trams. I love the look of them when I get to the depot in the morning, all lined up like kiddies' toys. The air is soft in the depot at that time and it's like the trams are sleeping, just waiting for daylight. I love the size of them too as they come down the road, towering over the cars and the taxis, and there's me, Mo, in charge and ringing my bell.

The tram is full of soldiers today, returning from leave. They're heading to the station and they're in a jolly mood, singing and laughing. Only they sing and laugh a bit too loud and clutch their kit bags a bit too tightly, and after a while it brings a lump to my throat. When a little boy gets on with his mother, it's all I can do not to cry, thinking of all the kiddies who've been sent away and how they're motherless and father-less now. And it breaks my heart to think I won't ever have someone I can call my own, and every day I go home and there's no one else there.

46
Annie Sweet

Summer 2009

I've just put my photos from Southend up on my noticeboard, and Molly is smiling in nearly all of them. She's not posing as she normally does when someone points a camera in her direction; instead she's too busy having fun. There is a moodier picture though, and it's the one I took when she and Danny's boy Leo were far out on the shore. They look tiny and alone on a vast expanse of wrinkly sand, and the picture has an odd, dreamy quality about it. The surface of the sand glows a strange watery blue from the light of the sky, and the children are simply stick figures with no features, no identity, no clue as to what they really look like or who they really are.

I've also put up a picture of the house where Inspector George's brother lived, and I'm staring at it, wondering what sort of family lived there, when the phone rings.

'Hi, Annie. How's things?'

'Fine, Danny,' I say, smiling into the phone.

'Are you sitting down?'

'Yup.'

'Good,' he laughs, 'because I've found her.'

'Who?'

'Check your in-box, I've just sent you something.'

I open my email and click on Danny's message.

'It's the Inspector's will, can you read it?'

I download the attachment and peer at what looks like a yellowing sheet of paper bordered with red lines. The writing is beautiful and cursive, but even when I zoom in I can't make out the words. 'What does it say? I can't read a thing.'

'It says . . .' Danny pauses and his voice seems so close in my ear it's as if he's in the room with me. 'It says that Inspector George left his house to his brother Henry . . . as long as Henry then left it to his daughter Mo.'

'Mo?' I sit upright in my chair and grab the edge of the desk. 'It says that?'

'Yes, and this is the clincher: it actually says Mo Painter George. The brother died before the inspector, but he obviously never made a new will and he clearly wanted Mo to have the house.'

'So this is it, then. We've found her. This has to be Lily's daughter.' The hairs on my arms begin to prickle and I feel a sudden blast of cold air from behind. I put my hand to the back of my neck and while my skin is hot, my fingers are so cold it's as if I've plunged them into a bucket of ice. I turn to see if the window is open, but it's closed. My hand is still against the back of my neck and now it feels like someone is bearing down on me, squeezing my head, pushing hard on my shoulders. I look around again, as if expecting someone to be behind me, someone who is making me feel like this. I have to use all my strength to take my hand away from my neck, to lay it on my desk and flex my fingers. I look down at them and they feel warm now, as warm as if someone has just reached out and touched me. Danny's saying something, but I can't hear him properly. 'Sorry, what?'

'I was saying I've checked the electoral rolls as well. Mo's at 43 Stanley Road in 1938 and 1939, then there's a gap because there weren't any registers during the war, and while she's still there in 1945, after that she's gone.'

'Gone where?'

'Sorry, Annie, hang on a minute.' There's a click as Danny puts his phone down, and I hear voices in the background. I flex my fingers again; I can feel heat travelling up my arm and across my chest as if my insides are on fire. But then the sensation fades and I feel peaceful and calm. I look up at the photos of Molly on the noticeboard and I stare at the picture of her standing with Leo on the shore. I think of the last conversation I had with Mum and I wonder how it is that I've found out so much about Lily's family, how at last I've found her daughter, yet I still know so little about mine.

'Sorry about that,' says Danny. 'Where were we?'

'Can I ask you something?'

'Go ahead.'

'Do you know anything about looking for GIs, American GIs who came over here and had kids during the war?'

'Yes, why?'

'It's my mum.' I feel my shoulders sag. I'm not sure if I want to go into this, and Mum would be furious with me if she knew. 'She doesn't know anything about her dad, except he was a GI. An African American. She acts like she's never minded about this, says that she's never wanted to know, but ever since we started this Lily Painter thing, in the back of my mind I've been wondering about him.'

'What was his name?'

'That's what's so ridiculous, I don't know. In fact I don't know anything, not even where he was from.'

'Do you have any pictures? If you had one of him in uniform you could tell a lot from that. And there are plenty of new ways to trace GIs. Some children have even tracked down their fathers and found they're still alive.'

'Nope, not a thing. And anyway, he died at Dunkirk.'

'Well, that can't be true.'

'Why not?' I ask, and feel a little offended that he's telling me that what my mum says can't be true.

I go downstairs; I need to get away from my computer. I need somewhere else to sit and think. I go into the kitchen because it's the warmest place in the house, and I sit with my back to the garden door. I put a clean piece of paper on the table and begin to draw a family tree. In the next room I can hear the dog snoring away in her basket and upstairs the creak of the floor-boards from Molly's room. She's practising for an audition. It's been a long time since we heard from the agency, ever since the *Christmas Story* audition, but yesterday we had a call. They want Molly to try out for another feature film in a couple of months' time; it's about a girl who goes on a caravan holiday with warring parents. That shouldn't be too hard for her, although the agency's warned me that there will be thousands of children up for the part. The idea of the audition seems to have calmed her: she hasn't mentioned people whizzing past and she hasn't gone crazy with her clothes again. Her room is as neat as it always was, and when I asked her what happened that day we went to Southend, she looked like she had no idea what I was talking about.

I draw a series of boxes on the family tree and then I write 'Lily Painter' near the top, with her sister Ellen beside her and her parents just above, Elizabeth the dressmaker and Frederick the omnibus driver, and all their dates of birth. Then I draw a big red line down from Lily, and I write 'Mo'. I look at the chart for ages, as if another branch of the family will suddenly spring out at me. I wonder, idly, what happened to Mo after she left my house. 'What do you think, Jojo?' I ask as the dog wakes up and comes sidling towards the kitchen table. 'What do you reckon happened to Mo?'

When the phone in the living room rings I think it's going to be Ben and I don't want to speak to him. He sent me an email this morning saying he wants to send someone round to value the house. He's still stubbornly saying we have to sell it, even though I've told him he'll do this over my dead body. But when the phone keeps on ringing, I get up to answer it.

'Hello, Annie.'

'Hi, Mum.'

'Molly says you had a lovely time at the seaside.'

'When did she tell you that?'

'What?' Mum is yelling at someone; it must be Dad. 'I'm on the phone!' she shouts. 'So anyway . . .'

'Yes?'

'It was a nice day out, was it?'

'Yes.' Mum is fishing for something and I think I know what.

'Molly said you went with a friend.'

'Yes,' I say, smiling, 'we went with Danny.' I don't say anything else; I'm enjoying not telling her. 'We had a great day out actually, and I found the house where my inspector's brother used to live, the inspector who lived here, and I even bumped into this old woman who knew the family.'

'Really,' says Mum. 'I'm coming!' she yells at Dad.

'Mum . . .' I hold the phone close, feel the hard plastic against my ear. 'Are you sure you don't have any pictures of your dad?'

'Of who?'

'Your dad.'

'Pictures?'

'Yes, any pictures of him?'

'No,' says Mum quickly. 'You know that.'

'Because if there *was* a picture, especially of him in uniform, then it could have quite a lot of clues.'

'Is that right.'

'Yes, Danny says you can pick up a lot of info just from a serviceman's pic. I suppose he means like buttons and medals and so on.'

'Oh, he does, does he?'

'What does that mean?'

'So you've been telling him, have you?'

'Oh come on, Mum, it's not a big secret, is it? Lots of people are searching for someone in their family.'

'Only not me.'

'Only not you.'

'Your grandmother really loved him though, you know.' Mum pauses and her voice is quiet and soft now. 'He was always the only one for her.'

'Oh, for God's sake! So why the hell didn't she tell you more about him then? Why didn't she even tell you his name, where he was from? You had the right to know your own parentage!'

'The *right?*' Mum is angry now.

'Well, anyway.' I don't know what to say, I've hit a brick wall, just as I always do when I bring up the topic of my grandfather. Whatever I ask, whatever approach I take, I haven't learnt much more than I did that day I came home from school and said we had to do a family tree. And all Mum would say about her dad was 'not known'. Only now I don't feel like treading so carefully any more. 'I just told Danny that you never knew your dad, that's all; I just said that all you knew was he was a black GI from America.'

'And he was killed in Dunkirk.'

'Yes,' I say, 'that's what you've always said. Only he couldn't have been, could he?'

'Why's that?'

'Because, Mum, Dunkirk happened before the Americans even entered the war.'

There is absolute silence at the other end of the phone. I'm expecting something, that either Mum will see this as a great revelation, or that she knew this all along. And I can't believe, in all the years I spent at school, in all the years I did history, I never realised something so obvious about a great family lie.

47
Mo George

June 1944

I'm on the tram, ringing the bleeding bell till my hand hurts because the old fella at the wheel today is a little hard of hearing. Twice he's driven off before he ought to, and now he won't stop. I don't want to mess about today; I want this shift over and me back to the depot. It's boiling hot and I can't wait to get this cap off my head. Soon as I get home I'll wash my hair. And then I'm off, because Jean has asked me out to meet her fancy man. She met him last month and yesterday he arrived in town on a five-day pass and he's got a friend with him, she says. We're going dancing at Frisco's off Piccadilly, and Jean says make sure to wear a nice frock. 'You don't want to be seen out with an old bird like me,' I told her, but Jean just laughed.

Here I am at Oxford Circus, all dolled up in my red dancing frock. I haven't worn this for years, not since a Christmas do at the Astoria. Oxford Circus is swarming tonight; there's not a man here who isn't in uniform. It's crawling with Americans and they're all saluting each other every five seconds. There are two GIs behind me who've been following me down the road, jangling coins in their pockets, like that's going to make me turn around and jump in their trousers. They like to taunt you, the GIs. I've seen them outside the Electric, holding up a nylon to a girl, asking if she wants the other one. Well, not me, mister.

I turn and scowl at the GIs and they laugh and start following another girl. They're so young some of them, I could nearly be their mother. Every doorway I pass there's a couple smooching away in the dark. Blacked out or not, London's a magnet tonight.

Jean's outside the Tube, right on the dot of eight. She's all dolled up in a sweet, baby-blue frock that makes her look eighteen.

'This is Joe,' she says all bashful, pulling on the hand of the tall fella beside her. 'And this is Louis.'

I give them both a smile. Jean never said they were coloured fellas.

'Pleased to meet you,' says Louis. He's standing with his arms folded and suddenly he opens them and shakes my hand. 'You look swell,' he says with a grin that is shy and beautiful. Is he having me on? He talks like they do in the movies! I look at Jean, to see if she's in on the joke, but she just gives me a grin too and we all walk off towards Piccadilly. It's easy walking with Louis. Some men are too tall or too short, others walk too fast or too slow, but we fall into step right away. Every time we pass a little bit of light I take a peek at him. He's older than the average GI, with a thin moustache like a movie star, neatly trimmed over lovely lips. There's a small scar just beside his nose and I wonder where he got that from.

We stop at a pub and me and Jean look around for a seat. Louis finds us two near the window and he pulls out the chair for me, waits till I sit down. I grin at Jean; they're awfully polite, these two. We look around; there's plenty of GIs in here tonight, and none of them are coloured. They're a lively bunch, standing at the bar throwing their money around as if they no longer need it. Which perhaps they don't. Jean and me hold our heads high, because that's what we're going to have to do with looks like the ones we're getting.

'So,' says Louis, back from the bar with a drink for me and Jean. 'You ladies from around here?'

'I'm from Southend,' I tell him. 'That's by the sea. What d'you think of England then? Glad you came?' I laugh, because how would anyone want to come here? Five years of war and blackouts and it's a miserable place.

Louis gives his shy and beautiful grin. 'You English, you've got a funny sense of humour. People back home said the Brits aren't a friendly bunch and they're too reserved. But that hasn't been the case at all.'

'Really?' I say, and I'm pleased to hear this.

'Yes, you're awfully helpful at giving directions.'

I laugh and look at him. He wears his hat to one side, like they all do, only he does it with style and his hair peeps out, soft and tight, on one side. It could almost be a party hat, if it wasn't for the fact it's khaki. I don't like the smell of khaki, you smell it on the trams when the soldiers are on, or in the cafés where the soldiers take their tea. It's a sour smell, a war smell. Around his neck is the little metal label with his name on. Blackwood, Louis. I've heard you always want to make sure the name a GI gives you is the same as the name on his label. 'Anyway,' I say, 'it'll all be over soon.'

Louis takes a polite sip of his beer, pulls a face as it goes down. Then he looks at me. He's got a dreamy expression on his face and for a moment it feels like he's looking right through me.

'So,' I say, 'you haven't said what you think of this place.'

Louis shrugs. 'We're just strangers in a strange land, honey.' Then he laughs. 'I love the sights, but I can't say I like the climate, or the warm beer.' He sips his drink again, making a face. 'Your beer's an acquired taste, and somehow,' Louis licks his lips, 'I can't get around to acquiring it.'

'What sights have you seen then?'

'Well, when we got here yesterday the first thing we wanted to do was have a look around town, but we couldn't see a thing, hey

Joe? The only way we could get around was to ask one of your bobbies.'

'You should have taken the taxi tour, I told you,' says Jean, shifting closer to Joe. 'It's only a few shillings and it takes you all over.'

Joe squeezes her arm, stares at her with longing. He's a quiet fella, not like Louis.

'So,' says Louis, 'we went for supper at a restaurant, paid fifty cents for beans on toast.' He laughs. 'In the morning we went to see Downing Street, Scotland Yards and the House of Parliament. Next leave I'm going to Edinburgh, there's a lot of buddies who've been there.'

I keep my head down because I'm smiling at the way he says Scotland Yards, like there's a lot of them, and House of Parliament like there's just the one little house. I feel a bit envious though, because I've never gone to see the sights. 'Then what did you do?' I ask.

'We saw where Dickens lived and where he wrote his books.'

'That's nice,' I say, because I don't know much about Dickens and I don't want him to think I'm stupid.

After the pub we go to a restaurant. It's a lovely place with candles on the table and big heavy cutlery all shined up and a floor so clean you could eat your dinner off it. A sour-faced waiter shows us a table, tucked right away in the corner, and people stop talking as we walk through. Me and Jean ignore them. We're supposed to be allies, I want to say. Louis and Joe are over here fighting our war, and they'll hurt and bleed just like the rest of them.

Louis pulls out a chair and I sit down, have a read of the menu. This is off-ration; there's a choice of two starters, seven mains and four puddings. This is style. This is fine dining. I've only ever had food at a café before. Joe orders rabbit, Louis orders liver and so do me and Jean. The fellas ask for a bottle of wine and the sour-faced waiter brings it with a nice clean napkin folded over it, then he brings a nice little bowl of salad. Louis tucks into his liver. 'You enjoying that?' I ask.

Louis smiles. 'Every last bite, honey.'

'What do they give you to eat where you're based?'

'Mutton.' Louis nods his head. 'A hell of a lot of mutton, excuse my language, you can smell it a mile away. And the eggs, it's enough to make a buzzard gag.'

Jean starts laughing and so do I. Neither of us knows what a buzzard is.

'What's so funny?' asks Louis.

'It's the way you speak.'

'What d'you mean, the way we speak? We speak English.'

'No you don't!' I nudge him with my elbow and he looks surprised. 'What's it like where you come from then?' I ask. Joe is looking at Jean; he hasn't even tasted his food.

'Where I come from?' asks Louis.

'Yes.'

'That would be Boston.' He smiles.

'I'd like to go there,' I say.

'I don't think you would.'

'Why?' I ask. 'Why wouldn't I like to go there?'

We're standing close, me and Louis, on the dance floor, and it's like I'm the starring lady in a film. He has his hand resting on the small of my back and I've got my hand on his shoulders and we're swaying to the music 'Lover, Come Back to Me' and I don't want this evening to ever stop. My stomach feels calm tonight; it's not knotted and tender from fear like it is most nights when the raids are on. When Louis tips his face down towards me and gives his shy and beautiful smile, I close my eyes and wait for the kiss because why not, why not be happy while you've got the chance, why not be cherished for once?

48

Bleeding hell, he's gone and written me a letter. I find it on the doormat when I come back from the depot, and I pick it up quick and take it into the kitchen. Then I slice open the envelope and unfold it. The paper is thin, there's a smudge of mud on the bottom corner and between the sheets is a photograph.

July 1st

My dear Mo,

I don't have a hellova time to write tonight and I hope you don't mind me writing, but ever since that dance I think of you often. How are you? I'm well and feeling fine. The sun was out again today and that was nice because it seems like the sun is rationed over here. I got ten letters from home today – whooee! I would like to see you again, Mo, if I may. I have two days off this month and have it in mind to come to London again. Will you be there?

Your friend

Louis Blackwood

I hold the letter close and tears come to my eyes because he's thinking of me, he really is, and ever since that night I've been wondering if I'd see him again. I put the photograph down on the table and look at it. He's one hell of a handsome fella. I'm going to tell him to come just as soon as he can because

I'm thinking of him too. I'm glad I'm all alone in this house now, that I haven't any lodgers at the minute, because now I can ask him here.

'Morning, Mo,' says Mrs Pickles when I come out my door. 'You look lovely.' I smile fit to burst because Louis is coming tomorrow. I've been working hard to make the house all nice for him. I bet he hasn't had a home-cooked meal for a long time. I wonder what he eats back home. I wonder what his family is like. Why hasn't a handsome fella like him got a sweetheart waiting for him? Or maybe he has. Come on, Mo, I tell myself, don't think things like that.

'Did you hear?' asks Mrs Pickles.

'Hear what?'

'About her at number 35. You know the tall lady who always wears navy blue?'

'Yes,' I say, although I don't.

'Well,' sniffs Mrs Pickles, 'she's been fined for *acquiring* a lady's coat without coupons. She said she was just trying to take the coat home to see if it fitted when the shop man stopped her.'

'Cheeky thing.' I'm about to go when Mrs Pickles waves me closer.

'And you know the old dear who lives on the corner of Cornwallis? The one whose son was killed at Arnhem? She went out with a jug to fetch some beer on Saturday, fell over that low wall that runs at the corner, caught her neck on the broken jug.'

'That's awful,' I say.

'Severed her jugular vein,' nods Mrs Pickles, 'and bled to death.'

'Well, I must be off,' I say, before she tells me anything

else I don't want to hear. Sometimes it would be nice if Mrs Pickles just kept things to herself.

I look out the window, see Louis come walking down the street, his kit bag thrown over one shoulder. I can tell he's whistling. I take a last look around the room; I wish I could check myself in a mirror. Still, when he walks in he'll smell the pot roast and maybe it will feel a little bit like home to him. If he's still here in the morning I'm going to show him how to cook with dried eggs so he doesn't gag like a buzzard. The trick is in the mixing, I'll tell him, you only add a little water, then you beat the lumps out and then you add some more, and as long as it's creamy you can work with it.

I keep looking out the window. He's coming nearer and curtains are twitching all along Stanley Road now. Have a good look, I say, because here's my man. I open the door and there he is, leaning against the wall, smiling. The GIs have this way of standing, they like to lean.

'Good morning,' he says in a terrible English accent.

'Well, good morning to you,' I say.

And here comes Mrs Pickles just back from the shops. She gets to the gate and she stops. She sees us and her mouth hangs open.

'Come in,' I say to Louis, and he does and then he sighs like a man stepping into a hot bath, and he drops his kit bag with a clatter on the floor. He takes me in his arms like we're dancing and his hand feels right and warm against my waist, and when he smoothes my hair and looks at me it's like he needs to remember something.

'That's enough of that,' I laugh, and I pat my hair back into place.

'I brought you this, Mo,' he says. He hands me a lovely tin

of salmon and then brings out something else. It's chocolate, a Cadbury's bar.

I could swoon. 'Thank you,' I say, and I put it to my nose and smell it and close my eyes, and Louis reaches for me and we dance in the hallway again.

'I'd like to have met you in another place, Mo,' he says softly in my ear, 'in another time.'

'Why's that then?' I ask, trying to be cheerful.

'Tell me again where you come from,' I say as we settle ourselves in the kitchen. I make some tea and toast, spread the slices with the jam I've been saving, set out my best china tea set. Louis takes his hat off and runs his hands over his head. He stops, then he does it again. 'That all feels very far away to me right now.'

I bite at my toast. I can hear the kitchen clock ticking. Louis's not saying a word. 'How did you get that scar then?' I lean over and touch his face.

He flinches. Then he smiles and covers my fingers with his. 'That's no war wound, Mo. That's where I fell off my bike.' He laughs, but he keeps on holding my fingers like he won't ever, ever let them go.

I have never seen a man so at home. He's propped up in my bed, one arm behind the pillow, and he's listening to me and I'm telling him all sorts of things. I don't know why, but I am. I tell him about the mother I never had, and the mother and father who brought me up. I tell him about the sweetheart I lost when I was eighteen and how I thought my heart was broken for ever. I tell him about working at the Electric and working on the trams. Then I look at Louis, because it's his turn now to tell me about himself. He tells me about the battle with the mud, about the mud in the tents and the huts and the food. He tells me he's tired, that it's a dirty and pretty rough life. But he doesn't tell me much of home. 'Tell me about your Cadillac,' I say.

Louis laughs. 'I don't have a Cadillac, honey.'

'Well, what do you miss most from home?'

Louis takes a while to reply. 'You know what I miss? Real honest-to-goodness coffee.'

'Be serious,' I say, giving him a poke. 'There must be people you miss.'

'My folks? Of course I miss them.'

'Anyone else?'

'No, Mo, there's no one else.'

'Well, that's good then, isn't it?' and I roll myself on top of him.

When he leaves in the morning, I don't want to watch him go but I do. I peek out through the curtains and see him walking off down Stanley Road. He's moving in a jaunty way, full of life. He gets halfway and I think that's it, he's going to be gone. But then he turns and puts his kit bag on the pavement and he waves with both hands because he knows I'm watching him. Then he picks up his kit and sets off down the road and now he is gone. At first I feel happy but then I feel so sad; I put on the wireless, ask the budgie how he's doing, and set about cleaning the kitchen because I don't know what to do. But when I walk into my bedroom to change the sheets, I can't. I lie down and I smell Louis on the pillow and I breathe in deep and wonder where he is now.

'Morning!' I call to Mrs Pickles. She's got her bag, she's off to the shops and so am I. But she hasn't heard me; she must have her mind on something else. I hope nothing's happened to her husband or her little boy. 'Lovely morning,' I say. Still she doesn't answer. Something's up, because I know she's heard me this time. Then she stops halfway down the path and she looks at me, only her eyes don't meet mine. She looks away and gives a sniff like there's a bad smell and a tut like someone's done something they shouldn't have. 'What?' I say, and I look around. My front pathway's nice and clean, there's nothing out on the road.

Mrs Pickles sniffs again. 'You're going to end up like your mother.'

'Excuse me?' I stop where I am, like I just got slapped.

'I saw him you know, your Negro Yank. You should have more self-respect.'

'Self-respect! What are you on about?'

'Like I said, you're going to end up just like your mother.'

I laugh in her face. 'What do you know about my mother!'

'Oh, everyone knows about your mother,' says Mrs Pickles. 'Ask anyone on Stanley Road.'

I look over at the houses opposite. What is it that everyone knows?

'Well, she lived there, didn't she?' Mrs Pickles jerks her thumb at my house.

'You what?'

'She lived in your house, didn't she? Don't look at me like you didn't know.'

'She did not,' I say. How could she? My mother died just after I was born. She had her terrible accident, and Mum and Dad took me on and brought me up like I was their own, which I was in the end.

Mrs Pickles looks at me with eyes as cold as pebbles. She's been my neighbour for six years, we've had our chats, shared our news, borrowed our cups of sugar, and now she's looking at me like I'm a piece of dirt. 'But not before she'd disgraced the family.'

'Disgraced the family? Whatever are you on about?'

'Well, she got herself in the family way, didn't she? That's why she topped herself, everyone knows that.' Mrs Pickles nods as if she's satisfied now, she's got things all cleared up. It's a good job she isn't standing any nearer or I'd spit in her face.

'My mother never killed herself!' I say. 'You stupid bitch.'

Mrs Pickles shrugs like she couldn't care less and marches off towards her gate.

I'm too shaken to go to the shops now, so I go back inside and shut the door and stand in the doorway like I'm going to be sick. That's why this house never felt right to me. From the very beginning I had a funny feeling about it, and now I know why.

49

Mrs Pickles doesn't talk to me any more, and that's a relief. But I've seen her gossiping with neighbours on the road, seen the way she pretends to drop her voice when I come by. Still, I hold my head up high. There's no one I can ask, no one who will tell me the truth about what she said about my mum. Because they're all dead and buried now, aren't they? My mother, Uncle William and Auntie Fanny, my mum and dad. And they never told me. Why did my mother kill herself? Because she got herself in the family way like Mrs Pickles said? It doesn't do to think about. I could ask Cousin Violet. I could ask her what she knows. I'm sure she'd be delighted to tell me. So I'm not going to give her the pleasure.

All my life I thought my mum came from Southend or somewhere nearby. No one ever said she was living here in London. Now what am I supposed to do? What was my mother doing in this house with Uncle William and Auntie Fanny? Was that why I was their favourite and they always spoiled me rotten, because she lived with them and she killed herself? So that's why they left me the house.

I've got another letter from Louis. It's here when I come back from the depot. I pick it up off the floor, stop myself from opening it until I'm settled in the kitchen with my cocoa. It's been three months since I saw him, when he came to London for just two days. But he writes to me every week. I've written to him plenty of times too, but then I've ripped the letters up because what can I say? I've missed my monthlies and don't know what to do. I thought it couldn't be possible at first, not after all this time, not now. But I don't need a doctor to tell me what's going on. I'm not going to work on the trams much longer, I don't like to think what would happen if I fell down the stairs.

I make my cocoa and sit at the table and open the letter. *My dearest Mo.* I sip my drink, try to take my time, but the cocoa tastes like mud. Everything tastes strange to me now. I put down my mug and look at the letter. Louis says he's coming to London next month. He says it might be the last time and I want him to be here so I can tell him. Louis, I'll tell him, you're going to be a daddy. And what will he say? Will he say, *Whooee.* And then we can go to America, when the war is over, and be a family. Or won't he be pleased at all?

I'm at the Electric and there's nothing like walking into this place and feeling you're in another world, especially now with all the raids again. I'm glad I'm not on the trams any more. The shelters are filling up and there's a good number of people down in the Tube stations most nights. Anyone caught out on the street is treated to a right old firework display. It would be pretty if we didn't know better.

I let Mr Sawyer know I'm here. Then I stand with the other usherettes to parade before the 4 p.m. show. It's *Dive Bomber* with Errol Flynn and I've seen it more times than I care to remember; Sunday films are always a repeat. But the boys love this film, and their fathers too.

'Mo,' says Mr Sawyer, 'you need to get those buttons seen to.' He's about to fiddle with his hair when he remembers all the Brylcreem. I look down at my uniform; I'm straining at the seams. One button has already popped off, and there's two more waiting to fly. I try to hold my tummy in but it's no use, I can't make a bump like this disappear.

'Too many pies,' I tell Mr Sawyer with a grin.

'Well, lay off them then,' he grunts, and moves down the line to inspect Mavis's lipstick.

I try to stand patiently, but I can't keep still. I'm moody and I've got bubbles in my stomach. Louis hasn't written, ever since he was supposed to tell me when he was coming to London; he hasn't written at all. I haven't heard a word in six weeks now. He's been sent away, he must have. He must be fighting over there by now. He'll be fighting over there and then he'll come back for me.

I feel heavy this afternoon and out of sorts. I've got terrible heartburn. But at least I can stretch my legs, not like poor old Rusty, the old girl in the ticket kiosk who can barely move in there it's so small. I reach the auditorium, turn on my torch, feel a little touch of power because no one is going to find their way about without my torch. Two fellas make a lot of noise coming in and they're cheeky to Mavis, so I'll find them a place where they can't see very well, like behind one of these pillars. The stalls fill up quickly, especially with the kiddies. There are two boys slap in the middle of the front row, bouncing up and down on their seats. One has a look of little Hopalong Cassidy. Boys like this know the name of every single fighter pilot. Boys like this come running out after the film, bombing and flying all their way home.

When the lights go off, the kiddies start whistling and shouting. But then the film starts and they shut up quick enough. I watch the two young boys at the front. They feel safe in here; everyone feels safe at the pictures.

I move to the back to keep an eye on things. I'm so tired I could fall asleep standing up. I'd do anything to sit down.

Perhaps I've dozed off, because before I know it there's a group of people coming in and I have to put on my torch and show them where to sit. I walk back down the auditorium, shine my light over a courting couple in the back row. 'Cut it out, you two,' I say. When I get back to my position Mavis is there with a cheeky grin.

'Oh Mo,' she whispers, 'you're just jealous.'

Jealous? I'm no such thing. But I don't smile back and I pat my tummy in the darkness. Why hasn't Louis written? If he was injured he would have written, unless it was bad. But if he was a prisoner, no one would know to tell me. If he was dead, no one would know to tell me that neither. I pat my tummy again, wonder what my mum thought when she had me inside.

It's interval time and I make my way to the front and stand there with my tray. The straps are biting into my shoulders. There's twenty tubs of ice cream left and I can't wait until they're sold. An old boy buys two and then he holds his change in the light of my torch to check I've given him the right money. Cheeky beggar, this is just like being on the trams.

The film's nearly over when there's a massive thump. A couple leap from their seats. Dust floats down from the ceiling and into the orchestra pit. I turn to take a look at the projectionist, old man Norman; I can just see him at the end of the beam in his little room.

'That was close,' says Mavis, hurrying up next to me. One of the boys at the front laughs. Then everyone turns their attention back to the screen.

Errol Flynn is just getting ready to dive-bomb when Babs comes up and takes me to one side. 'Mr Sawyer wants us to find two boys. There's a girl outside saying she's looking for her brothers. They're about seven and ten. She's in an awful state, says their home's been hit.'

I know just who the two boys are so off I go, flashing my torch down the front row where they're sitting. 'There they are,' I tell Babs. 'Come on, boys, you're wanted in the foyer.' They pretend not to hear me, they're mad keen to see the aeroplanes, but after a bit of a struggle they leave their seats and come with me.

I'm just going back to the auditorium when we hear it, the familiar hum of a flying bomb. Rusty comes running out of her kiosk and looks around in panic. A woman throws her child down on the carpet and throws herself on top. I can hear the chant of people praying. 'Keep going, keep going,' an old girl starts saying. She's on the floor too, with her hands over her ears. 'Please God' – I hear my voice, and it seems very far away, like I'm under the sea – 'please God, save my baby. Please God, save Louis.'

I keep saying this, as the hum grows louder. It whirrs and growls until my ears vibrate. Then it stops. The silence is thick. None of us knows where the bomb's going to land. And here it comes, a whoosh of air. A woman screams, then another. There's pandemonium in the foyer. People running like headless chickens. The floor trembles. I hold my tummy and make a grab for the bannister just as the windows buckle like balloons.

50

Annie Sweet

Winter 2009

I'm clearing out my office, ready for the builders who are coming tomorrow to take up the floor. I'm finally getting round to doing something about the way it slopes. In the afternoon Molly has her audition and I'm taking her out of school early, which is silly really because she'll never get the part. It's not that she's not capable of playing the child of warring parents; it's just that so are thousands of others. I haven't told her yet, but I think this is the last time she's going to go for an audition, because I don't want to keep getting her hopes up only for her to be disappointed again.

It's amazing how much junk I've managed to collect in here. It's a small room anyway, but with my desk and some shelving and a filing cabinet there's only room for one person, and one dog. Jojo seems to quite like it in here now; she often comes in and snoozes on the floor and I can't remember the last time she barked at the wall.

I'm going to leave the noticeboard up when the builders come, and perhaps just cover it with a sheet. So I take down all the things that aren't needed any more: out-of-date bills and invoices and letters from Molly's school. But I leave the family tree because I want that to stay where it is. I'm still curious to know what happened to Mo. Maybe she moved to a different place in London after she left my house, maybe she went back to Southend, maybe she moved somewhere else altogether. She could have done just about anything with her life, and I've got no clues at all. I'm just thinking about this when Danny rings.

'Hi, Annie. It's me.'

I smile. Danny always says this now. 'Hi, you.'

'Can you make it in here sometime, do you think? I've got something to show you.'

'What is it?'

'Come here,' he says, 'and you'll see.'

'Who is it?' Molly's standing at my office door. I wave her away; she can see I'm talking. 'Who is it?' she shouts, coming into the room.

'Danny.'

She huffs and walks out. Ever since our day in Southend I thought Molly wouldn't be so suspicious of Danny, but she is, perhaps even more so. I think it's because she believes something is going on between us, and a part of me hopes that she's right, that what holds us together is not just our search for Lily Painter's child, but something else. And the first time I really realised this was the day on the beach at Southend when he cupped my hand in his.

I put down the phone and call out, 'Your grandma's coming tomorrow.'

Molly comes running back. 'Granny Rose!'

'Yes, so you're going to have to clean up your room tonight.'

'Where will she sleep?'

'She can sleep in my room, and I'll put a camp bed up in yours.'

'Mum, she's never seen this house, has she? Or Jojo.'

'No,' I say, 'she's never seen it.' I smile at Molly, give her a hug. Why Mum rang this morning and said she's coming down to London all of a sudden I have no idea.

*   *   *

I get the bus to the local history centre. I was going to bring Molly today but she refused, so she's at her dad's. I walk through the library and straight away I see Danny standing at one of the microfiche machines. He's wearing a fresh white T-shirt and a pair of baggy army trousers, and I think with something like nostalgia about the day I first came here looking for Lily Painter. How excited I was to find her in the music hall, how disappointed when I lost track of her, and then how depressing it was when we found out about the baby farmers and her death. I don't know if I'm glad I started this. But if I hadn't come here, I never would have met Danny, and today I'm going to try to tell him this.

He waves when he sees me and waits until I walk over. I think he wants to give me a kiss hello and I want to do the same, but this is where he works, it wouldn't seem right. Danny looks around furtively, takes a box of Tic Tacs out of his trouser pocket, flips up the lid and offers me one. Then quickly he puts it away again.

'What are we looking at?' I ask, sitting down.

'This is the *Gazette* for 1944.'

'Right.' It takes me a while to get comfortable; I'd forgotten how awkward it is sitting in front of a microfiche machine. The chair is a bit low, the screen is at an odd angle, and I can't remember how to scroll down the pages and move left to right. Then I find a front page. It's 11 August 1944. A man is reported missing, believed taken prisoner. The end of the war in Europe is rapidly approaching. Churchill has announced that the downfall of the Japanese may come sooner than expected. There are two reports on people being sentenced for stealing things from bombed buildings. A woman, a Jehovah's Witness, has been sent to prison because she hasn't taken up factory work. Another woman has been fined ten shillings for leaving a light on in an office.

I scroll down to the next page. There's a long column of advice on how to deal with flying bombs. If you're in the street you're to find shelter, and if there isn't any then you're to lie flat on the ground near, but not against, a wall. In the home you're to take down all mirrors and to keep windows open day and night.

'That's odd,' I say to Danny, 'why would you keep your windows open during a war?'

'Because,' he says, 'if a bomb came the main danger was flying glass.'

I nod as if I've already thought of this, although I feel a bit foolish that I hadn't. Still, I don't mind Danny making me feel foolish; it's not deliberate, it's not the way Ben would have made me feel. And then I realise that for the last few years we were together, that was how Ben always made me feel – silly and over-dramatic and foolish – and all of a sudden I feel a strong sense of relief. For the first time I might actually be glad about what happened and that we're not together any more. I no longer have to wonder what Ben is thinking or what he means. I don't have to be anxious about what might be going on. I no longer have to worry about or resent the fact that he never seemed to love our house the way I did.

'You OK?' Danny asks, and I nod and smile and keep on scrolling down the page. Gary Cooper is starring in *For Whom the Bell Tolls*, which seems to be showing at every cinema. I keep going, waiting for Danny to tell me to stop, waiting to see what he's found. I'm on November now, then December, and there's still a few people being taken to court because they've refused to register to take up employment. Biscuit rations have gone up; jam has gone down.

'Why aren't there any bomb reports?' I ask. 'Wasn't London still being bombed then? I haven't seen a single mention of anything being hit.' Ever since I discovered the big lie about my grandfather dying in Dunkirk, I've been reading about the war, drawing up timelines, finding out what happened and when.

'No,' says Danny, 'it was bad for morale.'

'So they just didn't report it?'

'That and spies. They wouldn't want to mention the location of anything that had been hit.'

'But here's one!' I say, a little triumphantly. 'Look,' I say,

Cinema hit by flying bomb. The Electric cinema had a direct hit on the central foyer staircase.

'Go on,' says Danny, and now I know this is what he wanted me to find; this is why he brought me here. 'Keep reading.'

So I do.

Five people were killed, including Miss Rusty Marsden in the ticket office. Nine people were injured, including two usherettes who were admitted to St Mary's Hospital, Miss Mavis Peacock and Miss Mo George.

I turn around to look at Danny. 'Is this her, my Mo George?'

He puts his hands on the back of my chair. 'Well, it's her name.'

'It doesn't say Painter though.'

'No, I don't think they'd put in middle names as well.'

'I thought you said they didn't report bombs.'

Danny nods. 'And that's why this is so unusual.'

I look back at the screen. It must have taken him ages to find this; he must have gone through so many newspaper reports to find it. 'So she was an usherette and the cinema she was working at was bombed. Do you think she was OK? If she was taken to hospital then she was probably OK, right?'

Danny shrugs. 'Perhaps.'

'Or do you think she was badly injured? Oh God, I hope she wasn't. I hope she was OK. But maybe she died? Maybe she was killed and that's why she disappears from my house?'

'I can try hospital records.'

'Thanks,' I say, but I feel worried now, because maybe I don't want to know what happened to Mo after all, maybe I don't want to discover another life cut short or another horrible death. I turn and look at Danny again. 'Why do you help me so much?'

Danny doesn't answer; he just keeps looking over my shoulder at the screen.

I shift uncomfortably on my chair because I might have got this wrong, I might have got everything completely wrong and there is nothing between us at all. 'You've spent so much time on this, on helping me, and I just wondered why.'

Danny leans back and he looks at me at last. 'Because I want to help you, Annie.' He says the words simply, like this is all there is to say.

51
Mo George

March 1945

Here we are then, here come the babies. They pack them like pilchards on the trolley and wheel it into the ward. The nurse reads the tags around their little feet and then she hands the babies out. And I wait for mine. My pride and joy. My baby Rose. Nurse hands her over and I feel the warm weight of her in my arms. She starts to feed, to suck and to swallow, and I stroke her cheek, look into her eyes. How sweet she is. How perfect. She's getting darker, more beautiful by the day. I could kiss the skin off her face.

'Isn't the wee one feeding well?' asks Nurse Evelyn, stopping by my bed. She's my favourite, this young Scottish nurse who never stops running around.

'Where are you from?' I asked the first time she came on the ward.

'Edinburgh,' she said, and she straightened up when she said that, as if it gave her an authority.

This morning she's been in the little room for the premature babies, where my baby Rose used to be, seeing as she came early. When they pulled me from the rubble in December all I could ask was how my baby was and if I would lose her. And they rushed me straight to St Mary's and I've been here ever since. Then she came, my baby Rose, and they put her in that room. It's like a hothouse in there. I'm glad I don't have to look

309

at her and the other babies through the glass window any more, because it's a dreadful sight. But Nurse Evelyn likes to go in there and cuddle them. She has a lot of love in her, unlike some of the other nurses, unlike Sister Jordan.

And here she comes, the nosy parker. She has delusions of grandeur does Sister Jordan, and she's rough with the girls as well. Last night the air-raid siren went off and all the women, or those that could, started staggering around in a blind panic. 'Get *in* your beds,' Sister Jordan shouted like a bleeding sergeant major, 'pull your meal trolley over your head and get under the bedclothes.' So we did and we didn't half look silly. Only three went into labour last night, which, said Nurse Evelyn, surprised the doctors.

Sister Jordan takes any excuse to come over and have a look at my baby. You'd have thought she had come out green. Yes, I want to say as I see her eyeing me, you never seen a baby before? Isn't she beautiful and brown?

Baby Rose keeps on feeding. I move her to the other side, turn my back so I don't have to look at Sister Jordan. I listen to the visitors who have come to see the woman in the bed next to mine, chatting behind the screen, explaining they couldn't manage to bring any butter today. The ward maid is washing basins at the sink, and I can hear the clang of the lift outside.

Sister Jordan stops by my bed. 'Baby needs to go back to the nursery now.'

'Can't I keep her with me?' I ask. 'Can't you fetch a cot so that I can keep her beside me?'

'No,' says Sister Jordan, 'we can't, *Mrs* George.' She's sneering at me now; she's the sort who thinks only married women have babies. 'What do you think you're doing?' She turns her head, so suddenly her cap nearly falls off. The youngest girl on the ward has taken it into her head she wants a natural birth, and now she's crawling around on all fours. 'I'm getting doctor,' warns Sister Jordan. 'You're going to kill yourself and the baby doing that. Come on then,' she says to me, and she wipes her hands on her navy-blue uniform.

So I hand over Baby Rose and give her some kisses and tell her I'll see her in another few hours when they bring her back again. Sister Jordan wraps Baby Rose up and puts her on the trolley, tells Nurse Evelyn to push it back to the nursery. She's about to walk away when she stops. 'What are you going to do with it then?' she asks.

'Do?' I say.

'Well,' says Sister Jordan, and she puts her hands on her hips. 'You're not going to keep it, are you? What's *Mr* George going to make of it when he comes home?'

I look away, refuse to answer.

'Still,' says Sister Jordan, 'it wouldn't be the first. Will your mother take it?'

Nosy cow, it's none of her business.

'You could always get it fostered.'

'She,' I say.

'Or adopted,' says Sister Jordan. 'I suppose someone might take a half-caste. If the council won't.'

I sit up on the bed and give her a glare. 'I don't want to get her adopted! Why would I want to get her adopted? She's mine and I love her!'

Sister Jordan steps back, scowling. 'I was only asking.'

No you weren't, I think, you weren't only asking. Sister Jordan marches off and I lie back on the bed. Why can't they come and put the screen around me too? I want to be alone. Where is Louis now? Can he feel what's happened, can he feel that he's a daddy? I lean over, fetch the photo he gave me and put it under my pillow. I've told him about the baby, I've told him in letter after letter, I've told him I've called her Rose and does he think it's a pretty name? And he hasn't replied. I turn on my side, push my face into the pillow and choke away my tears. There's no use thinking about that now.

It's night-time and Nurse Evelyn's fallen asleep on the settee. It would be a shame to wake her. I'm waiting for them to bring the babies again. I'm aching for Baby Rose. When I'm not with her it feels as if part of me is missing. I can't know she's safe unless she's with me. They're going to discharge us soon, because she weighs over five pounds now. But I'd do anything not to go home. I don't want to go back to that house, that house that never felt right, that house where my mother lived, my mother who killed herself. And I won't be able to sleep in my bed without seeing Louis there, making himself at home, propped up with one hand behind the pillow, laughing at me when I asked him if he had a Cadillac. And I can't expect much help with neighbours like Mrs Pickles.

But where else will we go if we don't go back to Stanley Road? I can sell it, I suppose. It's mine, and even with a war on I could sell it and move away and just get on with life. But if I move, then where will Louis go when he comes looking for me?

52

Lily Painter

Winter 2009

It is a dismal day and the wind blows restlessly through the letterbox of the house on Stanley Road, bringing in dead winter leaves and dust and debris from the street. In the darkened hallway the dog lies sleeping; at times she gives a soft low whine and once or twice she wakes, raises her head and smells the air. The dog is waiting for the mother to return. She has gone to the local history centre to see her friend Danny. For he has found my baby. The baby farmers Nurse Sach and Mrs Walters never killed my little Martha with her deep brown eyes and apricot skin; instead Inspector George and his sweet wife Fanny took my child to his brother in Southend. And all those years, all those years that followed when I found myself in this house, they never said a word about this; instead they kept the secret between themselves. And all the time the newcomer was here, I did not recognise her, I never knew her for what she was to me.

That spring day Mo George came back from hospital with her baby, how downcast she was then, and I felt a pity for her all alone with a little one who was fretful and who did not sleep through the night nor in the day but cried in a pitiful way. And each day, how she would wait expectantly for the post, waiting for a letter from her sweetheart that never came, even when the war was over. 'Where's your daddy now?' she would say to her baby. 'Where do you think your daddy is now?' and she would rock her fretful infant in her arms and dance slowly around the room and sing to her in her strangely seductive voice.

And all those years I never knew. How could I have known, that this was my child? For I saw nothing of myself in her, I did not think to look for that; I thought her an impatient woman who did not like her house, who was ever quick to take offence. Was this Gus; was this his impatience, his quickness to take offence? And her voice, was that a gift from me or from her father? She felt me though, Mo George; she felt the unhappiness in this house, from the first day she moved into Stanley Road.

As the months went by and still she received no word, it was then she decided there was nothing for her to do but to sell her home. And the day came, a warm summer's day, when she packed away her things and put her baby in her baby carriage and left. She did not bid goodbye to her house, not even turning around for a last, regretful look as she stood in her hallway adjusting her hat before the mirror. She told her baby they would go to Scotland, for she had set her mind on Edinburgh, she said, and without a backward glance she left to make a new life with her child.

The house stood empty for a while until the Fletchers moved in. Mrs Fletcher was a young, eager woman with a husband who did not speak much, even to her. The house when they arrived was musty inside and the stairway boards had begun to rot. They could not at first afford to do things to the house, although Mrs Fletcher sorely wanted to. She cleaned up as best she could, placed wedding photographs upon the mantelpiece above the fireplace in the parlour, next to a softly ticking clock. In that first winter the snowdrifts fell and the coal ran out and they went to bed early and huddled for warmth beneath the blankets.

They could not sense me though, not even when I tried. When a chair was moved and they did not know why, they simply moved it back again, and when they were woken by a sudden noise in the night they stirred and shifted and fell peacefully to sleep once more.

Then Mr Fletcher received a promotion at his job in the City and they were so very pleased about this, and his wife kissed him earnestly as he left each day for work with his suit and bowler hat and his umbrella under one arm. Mrs Fletcher began to consult wallpaper samples, and one day a new settee arrived and had to be lifted in through the parlour window for it would not fit through the door. They put a dining table in the back room and a cocktail cabinet in the corner, and glass decanters upon its lid. They laid new carpet on the stairway and bought a new bathroom suite and had electricity installed, and eagerly purchased all the goods that would use it. In the evenings Mrs Fletcher sometimes wore her favourite polka-dot dress and danced unsteadily to the record player, and Mr Fletcher drank his sherry and read his newspaper and was quiet.

But although they enjoyed their home, they were not a reflective couple, they never looked behind them, they never wondered who had lived on Stanley Road before they had arrived, or what would happen once they were gone. They lived only in the present, and I could not wait until they were gone.

In time, after many years of trying, they had a little boy whom they named Olly after Mr Fletcher's father, and they decorated his room with a wallpaper of orange flowers on deep-brown stalks. And Olly grew and went to school and then away to university, and years later when his parents died, he came back to London and he took over the house. And he did not sense me either; he was too busy making his home modern and bright. He put in new windows in the bedroom and took up the carpet downstairs and laid down a wooden floor, and he built an extension for a bigger kitchen and surrounded the garden with trellis. Olly married then and he had a baby boy and again the years went by until he decided the time was right to sell the house and to move away to France. And then the mother Annie arrived.

And what is taking her so long, this rainy afternoon? What has she found today? Has she found where Mo George went, has she found what happened to my daughter after she left for Scotland? The dog stirs again in her sleep. Her eyes flicker open and she lifts her head, sniffs at the wind that howls so restlessly outside. She is waiting for the mother to return and so am I.

53
Annie Sweet

Winter 2009

We're outside the Finsbury Library and we're going to walk to Upper Street to find somewhere to eat. There's a strange feeling between me and Danny; a feeling of suppression. I was certain he was going to say something earlier when I asked him why he's helping me so much, and I'm hoping that outside, away from his work, he might be able to say it. The pavement is crowded; office workers and university students walk along clutching umbrellas, eating sandwiches, drinking takeaway coffees. We stop behind a line of bedraggled school-children wearing anoraks, waiting to cross the road.

'When were you fostered?' I ask.

'What?' Danny's looking right and left, waiting for a break in the traffic. Only there is a break in the traffic now and still he isn't looking at me. Maybe I shouldn't have asked him; maybe he doesn't want to talk about it.

'Were you little?'

'I was about eighteen months,' he says, and suddenly he takes my hand and I feel the smooth hard edges of his nails against my skin. His fingers move and I think he's going to take his hand away and I don't want him to so I press my palm into his and he looks at me at last and smiles.

'Did you have a nice family?' It's a silly thing to ask, but I want to know that when he was a little baby, a little boy, someone looked after him, and loved him, and they must have, or he wouldn't be the way he is now.

'Some of them were fine,' he says as we cross the road. 'Others not so good. I wasn't adopted until I was ten.'

'Do you remember your parents?'

'No.'

'Did anyone ever tell you about them?'

Danny sighs and drops my hand as a woman comes down the pavement with a buggy, letting her pass between us. 'Not really. It wasn't until I was in my twenties that I thought about trying to find them.'

'And did you?'

'No. Both of them were dead. That's why I never finished my thesis. I got a bit obsessed with everything about adoption and then I just couldn't handle it all any more.'

'Do you think that's why you're so interested in ancestry?'

Danny stops and looks at me. 'That's a bit obvious, isn't it?'

I think I've offended him, but he turns and takes my hand again and the air seems to deepen, like a cloud has just blown over the sky. My eyes must be closed because I can't see anything; I'm just sinking into Danny. The traffic is muted like a window has just been closed, and I feel the warmth of his lips and my body is flooded with desire. We could be anywhere in the world and there seems to be no one who exists but us.

The builders are here, there are three of them, and they're big and loud and smell of stale cigarettes. When I open the door I feel overwhelmed; the hallway is too small for all these men. One of them looks past me, sees the dog sitting on the landing at the top of the stairs. I turn around as Jojo gets up; she puts her head down low and gives a throaty growl. 'She's fine,' I tell the builders. 'Just ignore her and she'll be fine.' Only I'm not sure if she will be fine, because I haven't heard her growl like this for a long time, and never when someone else is here. Perhaps it's the fact there are men in the house, when usually it's just Molly and me.

'Oh, I'm used to dogs, love,' says the tallest man. He comes confidently into the hallway, his legs as sturdy as a boxer's. But Jojo doesn't like this; she growls again, a low, angry grumble.

'Just totally ignore her and she'll be fine,' I say.

But the builder doesn't want to be told what to do. 'Here, girl,' he says, holding out his hand, making clucking noises as he walks towards the stairs.

Jojo lumbers halfway down. I can see a patch of hair on her back standing up, and her tail is low between her legs.

'If you just ignore her,' I say, 'and let her come to you . . .'

But the builder is still calling out for the dog, and now she gives a sudden bark that makes her body shudder.

'Stop it,' I say, and I catch her by the collar as she hurls herself down the stairs.

The builders look worried now; they step backwards to the open front door.

'Maybe you should put her out of the way,' says the tallest man who's used to dogs.

I take Jojo by the collar, drag her still growling into the kitchen. 'Good girl,' I say, smiling and patting her, and I close the door.

It takes the builders several hours. They bring in strips of wood and lay them against the landing wall. They're up and down. There are deep male voices, banging, trips in and out to their van. Then at last the tallest one calls out for me to come and have a look. The room is dusty, and I cough when I get to the doorway. Then I look down. Most of the floor has been taken away and there's a shocking, gaping hole where it used to be. I feel unnerved that this is what my office looks like underneath, as if all this time I've been sitting on my chair or standing on the floor on top of something so precarious. The room looks naked, exposed. There's nothing in here that belongs to me any more, except my noticeboard, which I've covered with an old white sheet. I look down into the pit, at the dusty, unpainted bricks and the thick wooden joists.

'It's pretty bad,' says the builder, deadly serious. 'See that one . . .' He squats down and taps a joist with his hammer.

I look at the joist, a thick plank of wood split in the middle like a tree felled by a violent bolt of lightning.

'And there was a lot of junk down there,' says the builder, and he gestures dismissively to a pile of things he's put to one side and left balanced on a remaining strip of wood that runs along the bottom of the window where the floor used to be. There's a small cloth and a dusty collection of papers and leaflets. I can see what looks like an ostrich feather, long and whispery and black, and a red-bound book as large as an electoral roll.

'We'll put in a new joist,' says the builder. 'And raise the level to make it flat and then put the laminate on.'

'Great,' I say, but I'm not interested in this any more, I'm just looking at the pile of things below the window. I can't wait to tell Danny. I want to step over the gaping hole and reach them because they must have been here for years and I don't know if they are just bits of rubbish that somehow got under the floor, or if someone put them here deliberately, if someone took the time to hide them here.

54

The moment the builders are finished and gone I have to rush to pick Molly up and get her to the audition or we're going to be late. I wait in the school office while someone sends for her, and she appears flushed with self-importance at leaving school a little early today. We run for the bus and then clamber on to the top deck, where Molly takes a seat at the front. "I've got to get changed," she says, wrestling her rucksack off her back.

'You're fine as you are.'

'No I'm not.' She unzips the rucksack, pulls out a T-shirt.

'But that looks filthy,' I tell her. 'You don't want to wear that.' I can see a tear under one arm and a stain of something on the front.

Molly doesn't answer; she ruffles her hair until it's messy and then she bends forward, struggling to take off her jumper and put the T-shirt on over the one she's already wearing.

'What are you doing?'

Molly sits back in her seat. 'I thought I'd wear this, Mum, because if my parents are arguing all the time then they wouldn't have time to care for me, would they?' She nods at me, raises her eyebrows. 'Would they?'

My mobile rings and I'm not sure whether to answer it; I don't like talking when I'm on the bus, especially when Molly is confronting me like this. But then I see it's Danny. 'Hi,' I say, keeping my voice low.

'Who is it?' Molly demands.

I ignore her. 'Go on,' I tell Danny. 'Yes, I can hear you. You've seen the hospital records already? And the birth certificate? Go on, I'm listening.'

The studio in Tottenham Court Road is plush, much plusher than I'd been expecting. There's a woman with a clipboard and a name tag waiting at the door. She lets us in and I see a line of parents sitting on grey plastic chairs. Each has a child with them, and all the girls look nice and clean and dressed up; some even look like they have make-up on. There's a faint sound of music, perhaps a radio playing, then a door closes and footsteps come clattering on the shiny floor. Three girls about Molly's age walk self-consciously into the room, heading for their respective parents. Molly looks at them defiantly and I can feel her next to me, tense, ready for a challenge. I try to focus on her and this audition, and not on what Danny's just told me on the phone. I think of our kiss and I hug the moment to myself, although I know Molly has sensed something has happened.

She starts tapping me on the shoulder. 'Mum, Mum, when's my turn?'

On the way home Molly is subdued. I ask her about the audition and all she will say is that it was odd. 'Odd in what way?' I ask, but she just shrugs. 'What did they get you to do?'

'Act,' she says.

'Yes, but what did you have to act?'

'We just did what we were told, Mum. But he said I looked just right for the part.'

'Who did?'

Molly rolls her eyes. 'The director.'

'Well, that's good then.'

'So are you proud of me?'

'Molly . . .' I stop outside our house and put my arms around her. 'I'm always proud of you.' Then I look at my phone and see the time. 'Oh God, Mum's going to be here any minute.'

Molly frowns. 'You say that like you don't want her to come.'

'Don't be silly.' I put my key in the door. I told Mum we'd come and meet her from Euston, but she stubbornly insisted she'd find her own way here, even though she's not used to London. 'Quick,' I tell Molly, 'take that horrible T-shirt off and brush your hair.'

Molly runs up the stairs just as the dog comes bounding down. I can't believe I forgot to lock Jojo in the kitchen, that she's been free to roam the house the whole time we've been gone. I walk up the stairs slowly, sniffing the air. I can't smell any wee. I get to the landing; there's still no sight of anything having gone wrong. In Molly's room I can see a large sag in her new beanbag and some stray hairs where Jojo must have been sleeping, but otherwise nothing's been touched.

'You clever dog,' I tell her when she comes up to see where I've gone.

Then there's a sharp knock on the door and Molly shouts, 'It's Granny!' and she goes running down the stairs and I hear her rush down the hallway and wrench open the door. 'Granny!' she shouts. 'Who are they for?'

'For your mother,' says Mum, and I look down the stairs and see just the top of her head and a flash of red. She's brought me flowers. Molly takes the flowers, busily helps Mum off with her coat, reaches up to try and hang it on the hook on the wall. 'Come on, Granny,' she says.

'Leave her be,' I say, laughing, and Mum looks up at the sound of my voice. I come down the stairs to hug her. She's brought the winter air in with her; there's a halo of chill around her body and her hair escapes a little wildly from underneath a green beret that looks new. 'Very nice,' I tell her, touching the beret.

She flaps my hand away; she's never liked anyone touching her hair.

'Come on, Granny,' says Molly, 'I'm going to show you everywhere. No, Jojo!'

The dog comes crashing down the stairs to see what all the fuss is about and smashes her tail against the wall. Mum ignores her.

'This is Jojo,' says Molly, bending to cuddle the dog.

'Well, pet,' says Mum. 'He's a big ugly one, isn't he?'

'She,' says Molly. 'Jojo is a she.'

Mum turns and hangs up her bag, runs her hands down her copper-coloured cardigan, which she's wearing over a flouncy leopard-print blouse. Jojo can't bear the lack of attention; she nuzzles up against Mum, still thumping her tail.

'Granny,' say Molly, as excited as the dog, 'come on, I'm going to show you all round the house and my room and something I've made for you if you're good and . . .'

'In a minute, pet,' says Mum. 'Let me get my bearings first.' Mum puts her head to one side as if she's heard something and she doesn't know what it is. Then she gives a shiver. 'It's awful cold in here, Annie.'

'Come in then,' I tell her. 'The kitchen's the warmest.' I turn to warn her to mind the step in the hallway to see she's standing oddly still, one hand on the wall, and she's smoothing the wallpaper with her fingers, not looking at it but softly stroking the faded flowers. 'Mum?'

'What?' she says, like I'm interrupting.

She follows me into the kitchen and I expect her to say how nice it is in here, but she just sits down at the table, so I fuss around making tea. I still don't know why she's come to visit us after all this time.

'Dad says hello,' says Mum. 'He had a tournament or he would have come.'

'What sort of tournament?'

'Chess. Oh, he's in the major league now, he won 250 pounds last week.' Mum laughs, but there's a touch of pride in her voice. 'Come here, skinny malinky, and give your old granny a cuddle.'

Molly throws her arms around her, kisses her cheeks. 'But don't you want to look around our house?'

'Of course I do.' Mum picks up her cup of tea like she's no intention of going anywhere.

'So how was your journey?' I ask. 'How did you work out how to get here? Did you get the bus or the Tube?'

Mum frowns at me like I'm insulting her intelligence.

'Come on, Granny,' says Molly, tugging on her hand.

Mum sighs. 'Who died and made you boss of the world? All right then, give us the grand tour.'

'I've just had the office floor redone,' I say, but the two of them are already halfway down the hall. I start wiping the surfaces in the kitchen, listen to them chattering. Molly has Mum in the front room now, which is still full of all the things I moved from my office. I can hear her showing Mum how the shutters close against the window and then open up again. Now they're going upstairs. 'Wait,' I call out, 'Molly, you haven't seen the new floor either.' I get up the stairs before them, fling open the door and there it is, an empty room all shining with its new wooden floor. I can't believe how good it is. I walk to one side of the room and then the other and there's no slope at all; it's perfect and stable and flat. 'They found these, the builders,' I say, pointing at the pile of things left on the floor under the window.

'Oh yes,' says Mum. She comes over to the window too, stands and looks outside, traces her fingers along the sill as if checking for dust.

'Look, Molly,' I say, picking up the things from the floor. 'These could be over a hundred years old.'

'Granny!' Molly shouts from the doorway. 'Come and see my room now.'

I feel annoyed that neither of them are interested. 'You know what I think,' I say, 'I think these things might have belonged to Lily Painter. You remember what I told you about her?' I look at Mum, but she's still standing at the window with her back to me. 'She's the one I found in the census, who got pregnant and gave her baby to the baby farmers and . . .' I stop, because Molly has stepped into the room.

'And what?' she demands.

Mum turns from the window and gives a tut-tut that says, See, you shouldn't talk about these things in front of a wee girl.

'Anyway,' I say, and I start going through the pile. The faded white piece of cloth is just a rag so I put it to one side, along with the whispery black feather, and I look at the papers instead. One piece has been folded and refolded tightly many times, but when I open it up there's nothing but a half-illegible tally of numbers. Then there's an invoice from an ironmongers, a thin sheet of lined paper addressed to a Mr Able. I feel disappointed; these things don't have anything to do with Lily Painter. I pick up a map, again tightly folded. The faded green cover is torn, and when I open it up it's a jumble of streets with no indication of where they are, what country or city or town. I pick up the red-bound book and it's heavier than I'd expected. I wipe the dust off its soft leather cover and I'm about to open it when a postcard falls out. It's brown and faded, a pencil drawing of two donkeys standing on a beach, and the handwriting on it reads, *When shall we four meet again?* I wonder who sent it and who it was for, but when I turn it over it's blank. It's a post-card that was bought and never sent.

'See?' I say to Mum. 'Isn't this lovely? This might have been Lily's. She only lived here two years. And even though she died' – I glance at the doorway, but Molly's gone – 'she had a daughter too, called Mo George, and the daughter lived here in the war. She worked as an usherette and the cinema was bombed. But *now*,' I say because this is what Danny has told me, 'we've found out that *she* had a daughter too. She was born at St Mary's Hospital.'

'Is that right?' Mum turns from the window, and I'm glad to have got her attention at last.

'Yes, there's no father named on the birth certificate so Danny thinks maybe he was a soldier, a GI perhaps. And, Mum, this is really funny, this child was called Rose and she was born on March 2nd 1945.'

Mum looks at me for a moment and then she walks out. I can't believe how rude she's being, not even waiting for me to finish. 'What is it?' I ask, putting the red-bound book on my desk and following her.

'What's what?' says Mum, and she stops on the stairs.

'You just walked out the room!'

'Well, it gave me a surprise, that's all.'

'What did?'

'You saying that.'

'What? You mean that that's your birthday, March 2nd? It's funny, isn't it? Your name and your birth year and your birthday.'

'I mean,' says Mum sharply, 'that I was born at that hospital, wasn't I? St Mary's became the Whittington. You know that, Annie.'

'What do you mean, I know that?' I laugh. 'How on earth

would I know that? How do *you* know that? Are you telling me you were born at a hospital just up the road from here?' I stop on the landing, amazed she's just thrown out this piece of information and that she's acting like I should have known it. 'Mum, I knew you were born in London, of course I knew that, but I didn't know *where*. You never said when we moved in that we'd gone and bought a house near where you were born! For God's sake, Mum, Whittington Hospital is just up the road. Why didn't you tell me? Oh . . .' I put my hand on the bannister, look up at her. 'So that's why you asked me about the cat.'

'What cat?'

'Mum! Dick Whittington's cat. You rang and asked me if that cat statue was anywhere near us.'

'I was interested, that's all. It's not like I remember anything about being down here, Annie. I was a tiny wee baby when we left London.'

'Yes, but if you were born around here then that means your *mum* lived around here. Granny Martha could even have been living in Holloway, couldn't she, when you were born? Wouldn't it be funny if she was somewhere close by? Where did Granny Martha live?'

'Oh, I wouldn't know that.' Mum begins to walk up the stairs to Molly's room. I follow her.

'So you're saying that your mother never talked about where she lived in London?'

'No.' Mum goes into Molly's room. 'This is nice,' she says.

'Mum, did your mother ever talk about when she lived in London?'

'She certainly did not.'

'What, never?'

'Oh, Annie. You know very well she didn't talk about a lot of things.'

'Like your dad?'

Mum looks around like she's trying to find a way out of the room. 'Like my dad.'

And then it hits me with such a sudden force that my legs buckle and I sit down on the bed. I look at Molly and then at Mum. The air in the room seems to be swirling around me and there's a tingling sensation in my toes.

'Mum,' I say softly. 'Is Mo short for Martha? Do you think Mo is short for Martha?'

'Probably.'

'Well, that's that then!'

Mum tuts in annoyance. 'What are you on about?'

I clutch the side of Molly's bed and hold on tight, try to keep my voice steady. I don't know why my mother is so stubborn and why she won't see what I'm telling her. 'Look, I know you're not interested, but I told you about Lily Painter and that she had a daughter. The daughter was called Mo. Mo had a baby, born the same date and place as you, and there was no father, just like you, and . . .'

Mum laughs but then quickly sits down on Molly's chair. 'Don't be silly.'

'I'm not being *silly*!' I look at Molly; I don't want her to be here if we're going to have a row. But she's sitting on the carpet with paper and pen and she's got her head down, drawing with great concentration, keeping herself quiet. 'Think about it, Mum. Think about how everything fits. What do you know about your father? Nothing. Except he was a GI. What do you know about your mother? Not a lot. But you know you were born around here, and she could have called herself Mo, couldn't she? Granny Martha could have called herself Mo when she was younger. And she had a baby called Rose! See? That's what really does it! That's you!'

'Me?' Mum swivels on the chair. She catches sight of herself in Molly's mirror and she puts one hand to her head to adjust her beret. Then she stares at her reflection, like she has no idea who the woman in the mirror can be.

'That baby born at St Mary's, that was you.'

'Oh, it can't have been.' Mum takes off her beret and smoothes down her hair.

'But why not? Everything fits, the dates, the places, the names.'

'Well, my mother wasn't called George, was she? She was called Blackwood.'

'So she changed her name! That would have been easy enough. For some reason she changed her surname.'

'And why would she have done that?'

'I don't know! But then I don't know why she didn't put your father's name down on your birth certificate.' I get up from the bed and stand behind my mother, who's still sitting on Molly's chair. 'And that's why, that's why the house spoke to me the first time I saw it, that's why it spoke to me like it was mine, because in a way it was. I felt I'd been here before somehow, only it wasn't me who'd been here before, it was you, you and your mother . . .'

Mum sighs. 'There is something about this house.'

'Like what?'

'I did feel something funny when I came in . . .'

'You mean you felt like you'd been here before?'

'How would I remember that?'

'Mum!' I say, because she still doesn't get it, she just refuses to see what I'm saying, that I've found her mother and her grandmother and they were here in this house. 'That's why her name leapt out at me the first time I saw it. Lily Painter. Because she wasn't just someone who lived here, she was your *grandmother*. And so in a way this house is ours, don't you see?'

'You're jumping to an awful lot of conclusions, Annie.' She says it mildly, but when she smoothes her hair again I see her hands are trembling.

'No I'm not. We can prove it. We have birth certificates and hospital records and everything. I can ask Danny, and if Mo George moved to Edinburgh once she left here, and if she changed her name to Blackwood, then we've got it, that really has to be it. Granny Martha was Mo George, Lily's daughter. Where are you going?'

Mum has got up from the chair and she pushes past me, heading for the door. 'Mum!'

'Calm down, calm down, keep your hair on,' she mutters as she makes her way down the stairs. I peer down through the bannisters, see her unhook her bag and then carry it with her back up the stairs. She puts the handbag on Molly's table, unclips the old-fashioned brass clasp. 'There you go,' she says, and she hands me a photograph.

I take it carefully from my mother's hands. It's been badly torn and then clumsily patched together again with Sellotape that is soft and sticky and yellow with age. The corners of the photograph are rubbed and worn, and the whole image is covered in a network of tiny lines. But I can see it's a picture of a handsome young black man, wearing a small peaked hat on one side of his head. He has a shirt buttoned tightly around his neck and a very neat tie and a military jacket with buttons on the side. He's not looking at the person taking the picture, he's not even looking to one side, his eyes are focused on something far away and there is a turn on his lips that could be the beginning of a smile.

'That was him,' says Mum quietly, and she stands back, pulls her cardigan around herself. 'That was my daddy.'

There is silence in the room. Outside I can hear a police

siren. Then a truck comes down Stanley Road and the floor of Molly's room trembles. I have never heard Mum say this word before, I've never heard her say 'my daddy'. I feel weak and tearful. I want to talk about this house and Lily Painter and everything I've found, and now she's showing me this. 'But you said you didn't have a photo of him. How many times have I asked you if you had a photo?'

'Oh, Annie.' Mum waves away my question with an impatient hand. 'I found this picture when I was younger than Molly is now. I stole it, I found it in her linen drawer and I took it,' she looks guilty now and worried like a little child. 'I actually took it, and she went wild looking for it, she upended the entire house. And I was just too young to appreciate what I'd found. It was me who tore it, and I couldn't give it back to her like that. Not when I'd torn it.' Mum puts out her hand as if to take the picture back, but I put out my own hand and stop her.

'No,' I say, so loudly that Molly gets up from the carpet. 'This,' I say to her, putting the photo on the table, 'was your great-grandfather.'

'Really?' Molly comes over to look. 'He's got a nose just like mine.'

'I did ask, you know,' says Mum, and she walks over to the window and looks outside. 'That's a pretty wee garden.'

'You did ask what?'

'When I was little, Annie. I asked her and I asked her. Why don't I have a father like the other children? Because don't you think I wanted to know?' She turns from the window and her voice is bitter. 'Do you not think I wanted to know why I was the way I was? Do you not think I noticed my father was black and everyone else was white! Of course I wanted to know who my daddy was. He was American; I wanted to know all about him. But you know what? I never, ever got a straight answer.'

Mum looks at me and she blinks rapidly as if she's close to tears. I stop myself from saying, Well, that runs in the family then, doesn't it? Asking questions and never getting a straight answer. Isn't this what I've been doing for years and hasn't she been the one who has always told me to mind my own interference?

Mum comes away from the window, pats Molly on the head and then looks at herself in the mirror again. 'I would beg her for the slightest piece of information. What was his name?' She throws open her hands. 'Where was my daddy born, where did he come from? Oh, we had the most terrible rows. But she wouldn't tell me. So I just had to get on with it, didn't I?' Mum sighs. 'I thought he might get in touch with me one day, I thought he might look for me and find me, but he never did.'

'So you told me he died at Dunkirk.'

Mum shrugs as if she hasn't the energy to argue with this. 'It was a silly thing to say, but once I'd said it to you I couldn't take it back.'

'But did he know,' I ask, 'did your father even *know* about you?'

'You know what, Annie? I would like to think he didn't. Because if he did, well then, he wasn't interested in knowing me, was he? And if that's the case, I could hate him for that.'

'Don't worry,' says Molly, and she throws herself into her grandmother's arms.

'Mum,' I say softly, and I touch her on the shoulder and her body feels strangely fragile. 'You don't know if he ever knew he had a child. Maybe he never knew.'

'He probably did die in the war.' Mum pats my hand as if to comfort me.

'But maybe,' I say, 'he didn't.'

55
Lily Painter

Christmas 2009

The little girl Molly is very excited today. She cannot keep herself still but is forever bursting into her mother's room where her grandmother lies in bed, a cup of tea waiting on the table beside her. The room is tidy and welcoming and the curtains have been drawn back to let in the bright lemon light of a crisp winter's morning.

'I told you, didn't I?' Molly demands, and she dances around the room. 'Didn't I?' she cries, running out again.

'Yes, you did,' Annie says, as she climbs smiling up the stairs. She still cannot believe that her daughter has got the part in the film. But Molly knew what they were looking for; she knew they wanted a child with messy hair and a stained T-shirt, a child who wants to act with all her heart. Annie cannot believe the payment either; she has told her friend Danny this several times on the telephone. 'So much money,' she has said, 'I can't believe they can pay a child that much and they'll even pay me to chaperone her.'

Danny came round once she had rung, for she said she had something to show him. This morning he is downstairs in the kitchen, where he is making Christmas baubles for the tree. He has a row of soft white balls on the table before him, and he is bent over them sticking in shiny pins tipped with sequins the colour of the rainbow. He has finished one ball and it hangs now against the back door, where it catches the light in a wonder of orange and gold and green. Molly was helping him, but she has little patience today; she is so happy that there are so many people in her house that she must check on all of them one by one, and she is happy too because later she has a friend coming to play.

Annie comes downstairs with a book in her hand and she stands behind Danny at the kitchen table. She is no longer hunched as once she was; instead her womanish body carries with it an ease and a confidence. She wears a new jumper the colour of young ivy, against which her skin glows. Gently she lays the book upon the table and then she puts her face against Danny's neck and breathes in softly. He leans back towards her and they are still for a moment.

'How are you feeling?' Danny asks.

'Fine,' she says, and she smiles, for her heart is settled now. 'Are you going to see Leo later? Will you take a Christmas present from us?'

'Yes,' says Danny. 'I'll be off in a bit. Are we still on for Boxing Day?'

Annie nods and then she stands back from the embrace and picks up the book from the table. She looks at Danny but she does not say a word.

'What's this?' he asks.

'This,' she says, 'is what I found in my office. The builders found it under the floor.'

'A diary?' Danny asks, and he runs a finger around the edge of the book.

'A journal. It begins in January 1901 with Queen Victoria's death.'

'Really?'

'Yes. And it was his, Danny, this was Inspector George's.'

'Are you kidding?'

Annie smiles and she opens the book. 'The handwriting is beautiful, isn't it?' she asks as carefully she turns a page. 'I only just started reading it this morning. I didn't even realise what it was at first, but it's his, it has to be. There's a lot about the weather and his job as a policeman, but then, then he writes about how he and his wife Fanny are about to take in lodgers.'

'And that would be your Lily Painter?' Danny looks up at Annie in wonder; he cannot believe what she has found.

'And that would be my Lily Painter. He must have hidden it, don't you think? He started writing the journal when she moved in, and when he finished it he hid it under the floor. For me to find!' Annie laughs. 'I almost can't bear to read it, Danny, but listen to this:

Monday, 28 January 1901
A cool, damp day. My dear wife Fanny has bought me a journal for Christmas and I have resolved, at last, to write some few lines a day. It is a way to record day-to-day events, in what I trust will be a manner much interesting for posterity . . .'

It is silent in the kitchen but for Annie's voice as she reads aloud from the journal, and Danny is so captivated by the words he cannot move, he can only listen. And I listen too as Annie reads, for it is only now that my story will be told and that there is someone here to tell it.

'And look what else I found,' says Annie, resting the journal on the table for a moment. She takes a small packet from her pocket and she opens it and hands Danny a delicate lock of brown hair and a faded photograph. 'I found this inside the journal. This has to be Mo; this is my grandmother as a baby.'

* * *

Molly is in her room with her friend Jodie. She sits upon her bed, an array of pens and crayons and paper spread out before her. She is making a Christmas card for the dog. Carefully she writes Jojo's name on the card and then she draws a picture and she is lost in thought, only following where her pen will lead. Jodie sits in front of the new doll's house that Molly's grandmother bought for her two days ago. She reaches up and lifts off the roof of the pink-fronted house, rests it on its golden hinges and peers into an attic room. On the floor of the room lies a small doll in a gingham dress and a straw hat, a white plastic horse and a gilded mirror on a stand. Jodie opens the front of the house and there are so many things inside: wooden bannisters and squares of patterned carpet, a dog in a basket and a sleeping cat. She peers into the bottom room, where there is a violin, a frosted birthday cake with candles, a bowl of apples and two teacups on a tray. 'Have you got a dad?' asks Jodie, not turning from where she sits, but cradling the toy birthday cake in her hands.

Molly looks up from the bed. 'Of course I've got a dad.' She says it easily, but her back is stiff at what her friend might ask next. 'I see him every week.'

'My dad lives with me,' says the girl, and she speaks as if it were something to be proud of and yet I sense a sadness about her, a sadness that comes from living in a quarrelsome house. 'So was that your mum's boyfriend downstairs?' Jodie giggles.

'Don't touch that!' Molly jumps up from the bed and she snatches at the little rubbery lizard that her friend has just picked up from inside the doll's house.

'Sorry,' says Jodie, and she moves back upon the carpet, her face a little afraid.

Molly scowls and takes the lizard. Then she hesitates. She looks around at her shelf of neatly ordered books, as if considering where to put it. But then she laughs, a light happy laugh, and she tells her friend she can play with it if she likes. For Molly is happier than once she was; she sleeps soundly through the night and does not wake to check for hidden goods beneath the mattress. She is not afraid of that day she saw me in the hall. Nor does she wonder about the morning I threw her clothes upon the floor and searched so frantically among them, thinking myself back at Claymore House, looking for my baby's things. With a youthful impatience, Molly is only eager for what is to come. She is like a member of an audience, waiting for the curtain to rise and the future to begin.

It is late afternoon and Annie is in her office, sitting before her desk. It is very warm in here; now it is the warmest room in the house. She has even left the window open a little, although it is beginning to snow outside and flakes of white fall silently through the frosty air. She is comfortable here now, she no longer senses she is being watched or rubs her arms against the cold. She feels at home in this room where I slept with my sister Ellen beside me, where I lay and dreamt of Gus Chevalier, where I tossed and turned that fateful night before I left for Claymore House.

Annie has kept the room very sparse and clean, with only her desk, her books and noticeboard, and a basket for the dog. The dog sleeps in this basket hour upon hour after her walk, and she wakes only if she hears the squeak of the gate outside and then she lifts her head and listens attentively. If she does not know the visitor then sometimes she will growl, for she is very protective of the inhabitants in this house on Stanley Road.

Annie is looking at her family tree, which she is very pleased about. At the top of the tree I am there, with my father and my stepmother and my sister, and underneath is my child Martha and below this her daughter Rose, and on it goes this tree of women until it reaches the little girl Molly. Annie looks at it in a satisfied way. She is no longer worried that her former husband Ben will force her to sell this house, for she knows that he knows it is part of her now, it is her family home, and he has agreed not to discuss the matter further until Molly is eighteen. Ben is not a happy man any more. The woman Carrie has left him for a younger man, and Annie is very amused by this.

She looks away from her family tree and turns on her computer, stares intently at the screen. Beside her on the desk she has Inspector George's journal, a bookmark placed carefully within its pages. Next to the journal is a pile of books and newspaper articles about the war and about the babies the GIs left behind. Annie has found pictures of ranks and medals, and a list of all the places the African-American GIs were stationed in the UK. She has called the American Embassy in London and she has written to a records centre in the States because she is searching again, and because she is a woman who will not give up. She has restored the photograph of her grandfather and she has enlarged it and put it upon the noticeboard. She stares at it often with a restless, curious look. 'Come on, Granddad,' she says. 'What happened to you? Did you go back to America, did you know you had a child?'

It is evening and in the front room the grandmother is busy putting tinsel on the Christmas tree. It is pretty this tree, as pretty as the pine tree my landlord Inspector George used to buy and which his sweet wife Fanny decorated so lovingly. Every now and again the grandmother stops and sips from a small glass and licks her lips. She will leave tomorrow to return to her husband in Scotland, but for now she is here in this house on Stanley Road. On the carpet in the middle of the room the dog lies flat on its back, its white belly in the air, soft and vulnerable.

'Look at Jojo!' laughs Molly. 'D'you know what, Grandma?'

'No pet, what?'

'Jojo saw a ghost once.'

'Did she?'

'Yes,' says Molly, 'and so did I. Didn't I?' she asks as her mother comes into the room. 'Didn't I see a ghost once?'

'Maybe,' says Annie. 'Maybe.'

In the new mirror above the fireplace the grandmother can be seen clearing a space on the table, for she wants to make paper chains. Molly sits at the table and she licks a thin strip of the palest sea blue. She curls the strip into a circle, then she chooses a strip of deep blood red and she licks that and links it with a brown chain until it makes a circle too. And she works hard, with concentration, because she has told her grandmother she wants to decorate the whole room. And I look at them, these people in the house, this grandmother and mother and child, and it seems to me that they are fading. They are not as clear as once they were, and their voices are muffled now and far away. But that does not matter, because I have found them and they are mine. Outside the window that looks out upon Stanley Road there is a warm soft light that tells me I am free to go. And I want to know who is out there waiting for me; my father perhaps or Gus Chevalier, my lover whose voice sent shivers down my arm. And if he is there then I can tell him what I know, that after all these years of waiting I have found our baby.

AFTERWORD

This novel is based in part on the arrest, trial and execution of Amelia Sach and Annie Walters. They were the first women to be hanged at London's Holloway Prison after its conversion to a women-only prison in 1902.

I had never heard of Sach and Walters until I moved into a small terraced house in Holloway in the summer of 2007. I wondered when the house had been built, who had lived there before me, how the rooms would have been used. Then one day I found a list of all the old inhabitants on the 1901 online census. Two families had lived in the house; the landlord was a bus driver and he and his wife had a seventeen-year-old dressmaker daughter called Martha Painter. I wondered who she might have been and how she might have lived.

I began to research the area as it had been a hundred years ago, looking up workhouses and music halls. And then I looked up Holloway Prison, where I had briefly worked twenty-years earlier and which was only half a mile away. When I read a list of all the women executed at the prison, it was then I came across the two baby farmers.

The actual phrase 'baby farmer' was first used in the *British Medical Journal* in 1867 when an editorial accused nursemaids and foster mothers of serial infanticide. Sensational trials like that of Amelia Dyer led the public to believe in a secretive network of murderous working-class foster mothers. But in reality, few baby farmers killed the infants in their care.

Very little is known about Annie Walters, and even less about

Amelia Sach. The bare facts of their case can be found in the transcripts of the Old Bailey trial and in newspaper reports. But their voices are rarely heard: they did not take the stand during either the inquest or the trial, and they were hanged without making any confession.

Amelia Sach was a 29-year-old midwife who in 1902 was running a lying-in home in East Finchley where pregnant women came to spend their confinement. (This was on Stanley Road; in the novel it is fictionalised as Arthur Terrace.) By the summer of that year she had moved to new premises, Claymore House on Hertford Road. She appears to have been running a successful and reasonably legitimate lying-in home and adoption service. She found her customers by placing adverts in the miscellaneous columns of local newspapers, carefully worded adverts that promised 'Skilled nursing. Home comforts. Baby can remain.' Sach was married to a builder called Jeffrey who lived nearby, and together they had a four-year-old daughter, but whether he was involved in the business isn't known.

Annie Walters was a 54-year-old midwife. She had been married, but was living apart from her husband. She moved lodgings frequently, under a variety of assumed names, and she worked with — or for — Sach for several months. In October 1902 she moved into Danbury Street, Islington, where her land-lady was married to a police constable. Walters received two telegrams from Claymore House which read, 'To-night, five o'clock', and brought back two babies whom she said she was taking to be adopted. But her landlady grew suspicious; the police placed a watch on Danbury Street, and on 18 November 1902, when Walters left home carrying a bundle, a Detective George Wright was watching her, under the instructions of Inspector Andrew Kyd.

The detective followed Walters to South Kensington station

where he found her with a dead four-day-old boy. She said she had never meant to kill the child, but admitted having given him a narcotic called chlorodyne. This was a lethal mixture, originally invented as a treatment for cholera, and which included laudanum, cannabis and chloroform. Walters may well have been addicted to it herself.

Sach initially denied knowing Walters, or giving her any babies, but she was charged as an accessory to murder. Both women pleaded innocent, even as they were led to the gallows. Although they were convicted of murdering one child, they were suspected of killing many more. After the women's arrest, a tea-room attendant came forward to say she had also seen Walters with a dead baby, and during the search of Claymore House police found 300 items of baby clothes. However, they also found an unopened letter from a woman at Woking Village enquiring if the ladies of Claymore House had a baby that could be adopted. The police decided the letter was genuine.

Sach and Walters were executed on a newly built scaffold in the yard of Holloway Prison and their bodies buried in unmarked graves within the prison walls, although their remains were later moved to Brookwood cemetery in Surrey.

At the time the women were infamous, but they were soon forgotten. Five years after their execution, however, the 1908 Children's Act was passed and as a result of this Act by the 1920s baby farming had almost disappeared.

For a year after I first stumbled across the baby farmers Sach and Walters I became obsessed with trying to find out more about them, retracing their steps and visiting local archives. Then I wondered what would have happened if a young music-hall singer had lodged in a house like mine. What if she became pregnant and one day she saw an advertisement for a lying-in home promising 'Baby can remain.' What would have happened then? And I changed the name of Martha Painter and I called her Lily, after my mother's mother, my grandmother.

Inspector William George is entirely fictitious, as is Lily Painter, although the women she meets at Claymore House are based on real people. Hester Edwards is based on Theresa Edwards, a former barmaid who worked for Sach and who gave evidence at the trial. Two other women also gave evidence, both servants who had given birth at Claymore House: Rosina Pardoe, who never saw her baby again, and Ada Charlotte Galley, whose son Sach and Walters were convicted of killing.

ACKNOWLEDGEMENTS

Heartfelt thanks to the Society of Authors for a grant towards researching this novel and to the Arts Council, and especially Gemma Seltzer, for a grant in order to write it.

Thanks enormously to the following people:
Joan Lock for sharing her knowledge on baby farming and 19th-century policing. Clive Emsley for advice on crime and punishment in Edwardian London and for providing me with the unpublished memoirs of John Monk, Chief Inspector Metropolitan Police 1859 to 1946.

Ruth Ellen Homrighaus and Daniel Grey for access to their excellent PhD research on baby farming, and Dr Ann Featherstone for answering queries on the music hall.

The teachers and students at Islington Arts & Media School and Highbury Fields School who took part in a history detectives workshop on baby farming, and who brought the past to life. The project was funded by Cambridge Education@Islington.

Andrew Gardner, chair of the Islington Archaeology and History Society for his enthusiasm, the staff at the Islington Local History Centre and the British Library Newspaper Library at Colindale, and Alison Lister, curator at the Islington Museum.

My sister-in-law Rosa Maggiora, the management of the Hackney Empire, and Talawa Theatre Company for allowing me to watch a rehearsal.

Emma Jolly, genealogist and author of *Family History for Kids*, for advice, tips and crucial comments on the manuscript.

Petra Fried from Clerkenwell Films for providing me with a copy of *Diary of a Nobody*. My agent Clare Alexander and my editor Stephanie Sweeney, for seriously knocking things into shape.

Finally, to everyone I drove crazy while doing this book, especially Nigel and Ruby. And thanks to Jojo Pink for snoring all the way through.

I am grateful to the authors of the following books and articles:

Amelia Dyer: Angel Maker: The Woman Who Murdered Babies for Money, Alison Rattle and Allison Vale

Bye Bye Baby: The Story of the Children the GIs Left Behind, Pamela Winfield

Dickens's Dictionary of London 1888: An Unconventional Handbook, Charles Dickens Jr.

Marie Lloyd: The One and Only, Midge Gillies

Over Here: GIs in Britain During the Second World War, Juliet Gardiner

A Work-Life History of Policemen in Victorian and Edwardian England, Haia Shpayer-Makov